The Man in the Mirror

THE
MAN
IN THE
MIRROR

A NOVEL BY

MARK TIME

JACKALOPE HILL

Mark Time can be contacted via Telegram (@Mark_Time_Author) or followed on his channel: t.me/MarkTimeAuthor

Cover art by Swifty
Edited by Margaret Bauer
Layout by Margaret Bauer

Published by Jackalope Hill
The fiction imprint of Antelope Hill Publishing
antelopehillpublishing.com

Paperback ISBN-13: 978-1-956887-82-2
EPUB ISBN-13: 978-1-956887-83-9

But if any provide not for his own, and specially for those of his own house, he hath denied the faith, and is worse than an infidel.

1 Timothy 5:8 KJV

PART I

THE THRESHOLD OF ACTION

I

THE ROOTLESS URBAN PILGRIM

He was an average Joe. An average is gained by dividing the total value of a body of data by the number of data points. Joseph Arthur Blaine was a data point, ever being divided and aggregated against the body. His ancestors grew up in times of immense prosperity. In those days, men competed for jobs against other men in their own town. In Joe's day, he competed against the mighty throng of all humanity. The data field was much larger for Mr. Blaine.

Generally speaking, Joe avoided returning to his hometown in the heartland. Every time he did, it seemed a little more hollow, a little less friendly, a little more. . . . Joe couldn't quite articulate it. All animals have a certain sense for impending doom. The decline was more easily observable after a period of absence. The longer Joe was away, the worse his hometown seemed to get. Despite his best attempts at denialism, the rot scintillated abject terror into his unspoken thoughts.

On his last visit home, he decided to visit the old mall. Most of the shops were shuttered. A few urban, streetwear clothiers plied their trade among those perennial last survivors of brick and mortar's death: the supplement and soap shops. Everyone in the mall was a stranger to Joe. Not that he ever was acquainted with the regular attendees at the consumer temple, but this new crop seemed particularly . . . that same feeling Joe couldn't articulate. The tender caress of the smooth jazz emulsified with the inhuman yelps of brawling youths next to the cinnamon roll bakery. Joe fled the mall to drive through the neighborhoods where his high school friends used to live. Many of the houses were now vacant. The town was hemorrhaging people due to flight and Naloxone doses that came just a little bit too late.

Where do they all go? Joe mused as he reflected that most towns in the heartland were like his own.

He now lived in MLK Jr. Country, a sort of amalgamation of several cities in southern California, which merged together as they expanded rapidly due to both foreign and domestic immigration. City-counties like these exerted greater administrative control over the area than the previous layout of cities filled in with suburbs, ensuring a more equitable distribution of resources.

A reluctant surfer of Big Tech's flowing tide, Joe's own life was at slack water. The rent for "his" 850 square foot home occupied the lion's share of his expenses. Joe was married to a gal he uprooted from the same hometown. Both made their hajj to the big city after they got married. The funny thing about pilgrimages is that one usually returns home afterwards. That gutted husk didn't exist for Joe and his wife Jill anymore. The pickings in the big city seemed better than the assortment of minimum-wage distractions and asbestos-riddled huts in their hometown. If opportunity hadn't already moved overseas, it was crammed among millions of teeming souls on the coast. The reality of their newly-acquired surroundings hit them just as they realized they could not afford to move again. Joe and Jill were in for the duration.

In their new location, their only sense of community consisted of going to a faceless megachurch and connecting virtually with the same friends they had back in college. The paradox of being lonely among millions crushed them. They both grew up as Christians and still went to church on occasion even in their new locale. A church Sunday was as follows: at 7:30 a.m. he'd jolt awake at his usual weekday wakeup time. By 7:31, he'd breathe a sigh of relief and return to sleep. A few hours later, Joe would wake up his wife and skip breakfast. Fighting traffic for thirty minutes on a nineteen-mile section of freeway eventually delivered them to Love Today Assembly. Upon entering the auditorium with thousands of nameless others, Joe would wince at the drums. At the conclusion of precisely three songs that sometimes mentioned Jesus, a thirty-something-year-old man wearing a flannel, skinny jeans, and a beanie hat entered the stage.

"Hey guys," he would say into his slim ear mic, "who's feeling God's love this morning?!"

This exhortation was usually followed by cheers and affirmative drumming. After drifting into vague platitudes about being "a good person," the pastor would exit stage left and drive away in a Mercedes S-Class while his minions collected tithe. Calling it church was perhaps an exaggeration, though Joe and Jill didn't know any better.

Joe's bungalow was rented from a national property acquisition company. His landlord did not have a name but rather went by Sun Street Homes. Sun Street owned half of the rental market, while Golden State Housing owned the other half. When searching for a home, his rent choices consisted of a majority of his income or a slightly smaller majority of his income in the "urban" part of town with the "bad school district." Owning a home was out of the question when Sun Street and Golden State started bidding. His wife worked as a secretary in one of the skyscrapers downtown to make up the rest of the bills. Kids were on hold for the time being as their twenties ticked away. The years seemed to rack up faster than they could shovel away their collective mountain of debt.

"Just until we're a little more settled," they reassured themselves without any true definition of "settled."

Joe was rootless. His city was interchangeable with a dozen others. On the one occasion he traveled abroad, he was filled with a deep sense of despair to learn that the "authentic" shops were selling the same Chinese goods as the stores back home. The skyline of his city was only recognizable by its slightly different arrangement of productivity prisms. Joe was much like his city. When he looked in the mirror, he had no discernible description besides what his overlords dictated to him. His height, weight, hair color, and eye color jumbled together in the stew of the unknown. His indistinguishable degree had been awarded to thousands before and after him. His resume more resembled excuses to hire him rather than reasons. Joe's conditions were the result of carefully planned algorithms and think tanks. The sanitized life appointed to him bounced his shell along the guard rails toward the gutter at the end of the lane only to be recycled and bowled again.

Yet latent within him was something else he couldn't articulate: shackled, tamed, castrated, domesticated, this force toiled within Joseph Blaine and tore at the fleshy walls of its prison to escape, attempting to make contact at every turn, but the wax of social acceptability hardened into an exoskeleton around his soul. Joe avoided eye contact, kept his head down, and hoped he could slip through the cracks long enough to retire in four decades, but soon there would be an immolation of his personhood. The forbidden instincts within him would lay roots in the same way a great tree tunnels beneath a foundation and cracks it asunder.

2

BROTHER TO HIM WHO DESTROYS

"Number 243, now calling number 243."

Joe checked his ticket and glared at the number 389. By now the ticket had been folded, unfolded, twisted, rolled, and crumpled. He had been waiting for nearly two hours for his housing voucher. This endorsement was needed for his demographic to live in advantaged areas and required annual recertification. Joe reflected for a brief moment on the cliche of being "just a number" but ultimately thought little of the metaphor.

When, at any time, has the commoner not been a number? he joked in his head.

He had no pretensions of tearing this fact down or waxing intellectual about class relations. Joe's self-awareness of his cog-dom was free of the usual side effect of a desire to change it.

All of history is hierarchical. Can't have too many chiefs. He paused for a moment to wonder if the latter expression was in poor taste even though he left off the descriptor for the chiefs' underlings.

"Number 345, now calling number 345."

Another hour and a half passed. It neared eleven in the morning. The second hand of the clock danced in circles on the wall. It was illiterate yet wrote of profound dread in the minds of those who waited and watched. Joe watched in horror as the employees at the counter began to shutter the windows and go to lunch. His eyes drifted to the pasted brochure on the counter: "SUICIDE PREVENTION AND AWARENESS. You are not alone, there are resources to help you. We care about. . . ."

The lump at the counter pulled a magnetic sign from under the desk and slapped it over the brochure with an inarticulate grunt. It was upside down, but Joe knew what it said: "Lunch hours from 11:00 a.m. to 1:00 p.m. Your request is very important to us, and we will be with you shortly."

Joe's boss agreed only to give him the morning off. Under constant threat of being outsourced, his job security teetered. He needed the housing recertification by next week or he would be evicted. The Office of Inclusive Housing Opportunities (OIHO) only held customer service hours in July for three weeks prior to the recertification deadline. However, given that the paperwork takes a week to process, nearly all applications in the third week would be denied. It was Friday of week two. He carefully weighed his options.

Okay, I can wait here, get my paperwork signed, pay the fee, and get my application in a week before the deadline. I don't think Mr. Raab would actually fire me. I'd probably get a slap on the wrist and then move on, Joe mused as he contemplated the anxious scuff marks on the faded linoleum floor beneath his chair.

His phone buzzed. It was a text from his co-worker, Tyler.

"Hey man, Raab wants everybody back at the office asap. I've seen a lot of corporate dudes. Seems pretty important. Where are you at?"

Joe replied, "No way. I'm at the OIHO office getting my recert. I have to do this today or it'll be too late."

"He seems to be in a firing mood, bro. Up to you. There's a big meeting at 11:30."

Joe swore to himself under his breath.

"Can't have a house if I don't have a job," he grumbled aloud.

He rose from the chair and gathered his things. The others in the waiting room looked at him with two emotions. One was of sympathy for his plight. The other was of relief for his removal from the queue.

3

THE BEIGE HOLE

"Hey, team, gather 'round."

Joe always rolled his eyes when Mr. Raab called them a team. The gray cubicles sat anchored around the sullen assembly in a sea of stain-concealing carpet.

"I want to open up by saying that it's been a real privilege working with y'all." Raab always waxed folksy when he delivered bad news. He was a taller man who played up being from Texas, but he knew nothing of the place outside of Austin. His carefully preened brown hair sat over a constant expression of contempt.

Raab continued, "We've seen great numbers . . . great numbers." He was well-versed in the compliment sandwich technique wherein bad news is flanked on either side by positive reinforcement, though he seldom excelled in making the bread and usually just skipped to the meat. "Look, numbers are great, but corporate is having some issues with this branch's size. The economy is struggling, and competition is stiff out there. I'm just going to break it to y'all. Corporate has decided to move most of our location's workload to our Mumbai office."

"Outsourcing!" Tyler whispered to Joe.

The gathering let out a few gasps and groans. One woman started to sob.

"If it were up to me"—it wasn't—"I would keep every one of you employed"—he wouldn't. "I've posted a list on the corkboard in the break room of the retained and laid-off staff."

Most of the employees began murmuring and shuffling toward

knowledge of their fate.

"Oh, uh, one more thing. . . ." All stopped just for a moment and gave dour stares. "I'm very proud of the work you guys have put in." He nearly forgot the second slice of bread.

"Great, he's proud of me. Let's see if he's going to keep paying me," muttered another drone next to Joe.

As he walked toward the break room, he peaked at the memo in Raab's hand. It was dated for the previous Tuesday. In lockstep with corporate policy, layoffs were always implemented on Fridays.

The break room was a beige hole in the wall where employees would come to huff the fumes of stale coffee and that indescribable smell all office microwaves gain after years of ramen, spaghetti, and dry chicken imparting their foulest qualities. Those at the front of the pack began checking for their names on the bulletin. The first one, a lady from accounting, breathed a sigh of relief and exited the room hoping to not look too joyful. Joe was about in the middle of the despondent procession. The line of employees shuffled one by one past the list in the same manner and pace funeral goers pay their respects, tears and all. As he neared the front, his pulse pounded. Joe feared the worst. His performance was middling among his coworkers at best. Economically speaking, there was no reason to pay him this much for his productivity when Mumbai was far cheaper.

Tyler stood several spaces ahead. He made it to the front and ran his finger down the list of names until it rested on his. "Canned!" he jolted. "Couldn't even tell me himself."

Tyler was among the top performers in the office but, alas, demanded too much money. He stormed out of the breakroom. As he brushed past Joe without a word, the other less successful employees darkened. Next in line was Courtney. Her son had a mental disorder, and she devoted much of her paycheck to his childcare and medication. The company's health insurance was cut last month to reduce costs. She had no reaction. Not a soul in the room could discern her face. Courtney simply walked up, stood for a second, and walked out stoically.

Joe was now only a few spaces away. He strained his eyes to get a preview of his judgment. At last, he made it to the front. His status was no surprise to him, but the wretchedness overtook him nonetheless. On autopilot, Joe drifted to his cubicle to gather his things. He stood behind his chair and took in the scene. The blank computer monitor sat impassively among a few knickknacks meant to evince a modicum of personality. Joe peered above the cubicle's ramparts at the other severed wretches. The mixture of tears and frustrated sighs swelled into a despairing requiem. As Joe collected the items on his desk, he thought about the countless hours he spent bound to this felt cage. If any of his ancestors could see the way he clacked endlessly at the keyboard among tight, enclosing walls, they would have assumed he was imprisoned or enslaved.

Joe floated out of the office building in a daze to his car. A million things rushed through his mind as he sat in the ripped leather cradle of yesteryear's luxury sedan. Emotions began swelling like magma beneath the crust of his shell. Closing the door, he punched the steering wheel and broke the logo. The horn let out a pathetic whimper. Next on the kill list was the sun visor. Overcome with violent rage, he awoke the ancient engine and sped from the parking spot he had spent twenty minutes finding after returning from the OIHO. A hapless pigeon was his next casualty. Joe let out a tortured scream, resonant with the groaning V6.

Sweat pouring out of him in the summer heat without functioning air conditioning, Joe rolled the windows down as he drove to nowhere. He checked his phone at the next stoplight. With anxiety, he realized that he had broadcast his breakdown to his wife's voicemail via butt dial. Panicked, Joe ended the call without clarification.

"Oh perfect!" Joe swore again.

He wondered how she would take such a blow. Joe lamented how much she had gone through since their move from home. They both lost friends, community, family connections, and the knowledge of how they fit into the grand scheme. He couldn't return with only bad news.

Maybe I can still catch the OIHO before they close, get a new job next week, and everything will be just like before.

He paused to wonder if being just like before was anything to strive for.

4

LA GUERRE BUREAUCRATIQUE

Wheeling the rusted hulk around, Joe sped toward the long line that awaited him. Arriving at 12:45 p.m., horror filled his heart when he saw the slinking centipede of humanity stretching out the door and around the block. They would close the doors at three. Halting service was the only thing the OIHO did precisely. He made eye contact with one of the men in line who widened his eyes and shook his head at Joe as if to say, "You're totally screwed."

As Joe searched for a place to park, he caught a glimpse of the Inclusion Banner flying atop the OIHO building. It was a grotesque piece of cloth gesticulating high in the breeze. Colors of the rainbow and a myriad of melanated skin tones intermingled in an unrecognizable desecration. One skin color was conspicuously missing from the banner just as American flags were notably absent from the building. The brutalist architecture of the OIHO signaled its domination and spiteful character to the serfs it consumed through its mandible-like doors. The building was first constructed as a public library several decades ago, evolved to an impromptu druggie camp during a period of urban decline, and finally ended up as a reliable producer of homelessness in its role as the OIHO. The surrounding buildings in the downtown area all followed similar arcs of usefulness, disuse, then malicious use. Any name placards from the original constructions were invariably scuffed, painted over, or crudely replaced along with any statuary. These modifications occurred in the repeated waves of iconoclasm that had become the national pastime.

He circled the block looking for a parking spot and wasted an additional fifteen minutes. The clock on his dashboard, always three minutes behind, blinked unsympathetically at him the same way a forest animal observes some stranded traveler starving to death in the wilderness. Greasy with sweat, Joe leapt from the car and ran toward the line. Breathing heavily, he slowed to a walk as he joined the throng. Three more filed in behind him minutes later. The wind rustled the palm tree next to him but refused to stoop to his level and cool his sweating body.

An OIHO employee sullenly patrolled the queue with a clipboard and the precious orange card that read, "Line Cutoff." She was counting the number of people out loud in an inhuman mumble.

"Seventy-eight, seventy-nine, eighty, eighty-one. . . ."

A homeless man sauntered on the sidewalk across the intersection from the OIHO building. He unfolded his chair and pulled a plastic bag from his satchel. It was popcorn.

"Ninety-four, ninety-five, ninety-six." She paused to look at her clipboard.

Struggling to make the wires in her brain connect, her pen made furious calculations. The employee gave a dead stare at the paper for a minute then pulled the orange card and handed it to number ninety-six.

"OK, listen up!" her voice leaked with false legitimacy. "This card is the line cutoff. They're prolly not gonna see you before closing after that. You can still try and wait in line, but prolly not gonna happen."

The man she handed the card to looked up at the sky and breathed deeply. Joe was four spaces behind him. No one budged.

"I can make it," the woman behind him reassured herself.

Joe concurred and decided that there was nothing to lose at this point. An hour passed in the smothering heat. The brewing magma of his scream in the car subsided as he settled into a dim acceptance. Looking up at the cruel sun, he felt another heat source to his right. Fear coursed through his frazzled nerves. Something pulled his eyes toward his reflection in the glass window. Joe resisted this urge out of terror but ultimately succumbed to the magnetic draw. With a shudder, he realized a profound change in the familiar face he was used to seeing in the mirror.

Joe gazed into the darkened, distorted form, and it gazed back into him. A deep stillness enveloped the pair: a man and his reflection. The world around them faded, and the noisy street quieted to a profound, supernatural silence. For a moment, there was nothing at all besides the transfixing tendrils of shocked disquiet. It was the first time Joe had an inkling of the supernatural. He had looked in the mirror numerous times before but had only seen the tamed, supine image of himself. Now, on this baking city sidewalk, a coup occurred on the other side of the glass. Through the crack in his exterior pioneered by the frustrated screams of rebellion, a new impression appeared before his eyes, ravenously pursuing him into the deepest recesses of his heart with accusations and judgments. Joe always knew these condemnations were there but smothered them to keep the peace. They maintained their standoff until inexplicable dread wrested Joe's eyes from the terrible and damning gaze.

Joe shivered for a moment after his encounter. His heart pounded in his chest as if someone was trying to kill him. He closed his eyes and put his hands on his knees.

It's fine, Joe, he thought to himself, *it's just your reflection.*

He took a peek at the window to confirm this assessment only to quickly avert his eyes. Straightening up, Joe could see the door inside now and held on to hope.

More time passed, and it was now only twenty minutes from closing. He at least was getting clouds of conditioned air sortieing from the door. The temporary comfort of the cool air failed to assuage the anxiety he felt over what he saw in the window's reflection. Resolving to forget the encounter, Joe decided that it was merely an episode of fatigue. The same employee who bestowed the orange card waited at the entrance with keys and a watch. As the previous cardholder crossed the threshold, she grabbed it from him and walked along the line. Making her assessment, she gave the card to Joe.

"Okay, they've been moving pretty quick, but no promises getting in. I lock the door at three o'clock," she bellowed to the assembly.

A sailor whose ship is sunk clings to any wreckage that passes by. Joe clung to the card adrift in the sea of his own thoughts. Turning behind him, he saw at least fifty more desperate souls. Joe looked at the fateful pane of glass further down the line. It was at an oblique angle, and the reflection was no longer visible. A few despondent individuals slunk away from the end of the line. The homeless man chuckled and heckled them as they abandoned hope.

"Hey, I'll save a spot on the sidewalk for ya! Oh, and you! Oh boy, you just wait until you hit the streets. You can work at the corner of 8th Street with the other denials! I'll be your first customer."

Joe finally entered the building and took ticket number 612. Two more made it in behind him before the doors were locked shut. He couldn't bear to look back at those who were turned away.

"We open back up on Monday at 9:30."

Joe knew that coming back on Monday would be useless.

After a sustained period of waiting, a voice called out, "Number 612, now calling number 612."

He leapt up from his chair to engage in the necessary charade. "Hi, I need to–"

The employee angrily interrupted, "Stand behind the red line."

"Okay. . . ." Joe had no choice but to kowtow.

"How can I help you?" The lump was satisfied with Joe's obligatory gesture of submission.

He took a deep breath. "Yes, I need to renew my housing certification."

The dead-eyed troglodyte pursed her lips. "Kay, give me your paperwork."

Joe looked on with furrowed brow as she shuffled through the papers.

"Looks good; now I just need to see your interview sheet."

His soul crumpled like a grounded submarine. "Interview sheet?"

"Did you check in with Mr. Smith before coming in today?" The employee kept her eyes glued on the papers.

"No?" Joe's toes pressed firmly against the red line.

She collected the papers and handed them back. "You need an interview checklist from Mr. Smith before I can help you."

Undeterred, he fired back at the risk of eliciting the employee's "fight or obstinance" response. "I didn't have to do that last year."

The employee perceived the resistance and opted to both fight and be obstinate. "Well, you should have. Who did your paperwork?"

Joe crumpled one of the papers slightly in his hand. "I have no idea."

"Did you read the information packet on how to submit your package?" She directed the crushing weight of the administrative state against him.

Pivoting on his feet, he prepared his parry. "Yes, I checked online before I came in, and it didn't say anything about an interview sheet."

The employee settled in for the killing blow: "I have the instructions right here. Look at this. You see this? Right there. *In-ter-view sheet*. You see it?"

"Yes, I see it, but the packet I read didn't. . . ." Thoroughly pinned, all Joe could do was watch the disaster unfold.

"Where'd you find it?" she prodded him again.

Unsure of the angle, Joe countered, "It was right on your website."

"Which website?"

His pulse rose with disgust. "The OIHO website."

She rolled her eyes. "Which one?"

"Is there more than one?" Joe asked incredulously.

The employee continued, "IT services made a new website for us two months ago."

Digging his hole further, he objected: "What's the URL? I just searched 'Office for Inclusive Housing Opportunities' and I clicked on the first one that came up."

One of the other "inequitables" in the stall next to him gave him a look as if to say, "Shut up or it'll get worse for you."

In a droning monotone, the employee laid out Joe's critical errors: "You're going to get the old one that way. You should have used the new one. You're like the hundredth person I've had to tell."

Joe's anger got the best of him. "Why wasn't it posted somewhere that the website was obsolete?"

"Because we don't use it anymore," she said with narrowed eyes.

He raised his voice: "Then how are we supposed to know?!"

The employee decided she had enough. "Stop arguing with me. You need the interview sheet from Mr. Smith."

"Fine, where is he?" Joe put his hands in his pockets and clawed at his legs in frustration.

In a self-righteous declaration of victory, the lump replied, "His office hours are from 12 p.m. to 3 p.m., Monday through Friday."

"Is his office in this building?"

"Yes." Her tone indicated she was finished with him.

Joe clung to this new hope. "Where?"

"He probably left already," the employee swatted him down.

Undeterred, he fought on: "Well I can still give it a shot."

Reluctantly, she directed him down the hall to the second door on the right. After grinding his teeth on the walk over, Joe knocked on the door that bore Mr. Smith's name placard.

"Come on in." A smooth, Louisiana drawl seeped through the door frame.

Joe entered the office with trepidation but relief that he was still in his office. A dark-complexioned man with gold-rimmed glasses sat clacking away on his keyboard.

"Hey, Mr. Smith, sorry to bother you. The lady at the counter said I need to do an interview sheet before I can get my housing voucher." Joe wiped away the sweat from his forehead.

"Absolutely," Mr. Smith replied as he pulled a form from his cabinet. "Okay, you'll need to get these signatures, and then you can contact me to set up your interview. It's just run-of-the-mill stuff about your background."

Joe looked in dismay at the list of five names with various titles and the diverse demographic qualities he would need to gain their signatures. He saw a thin stack of completed signature sheets on the corner of Mr. Smith's desk. The signatures were mostly unintelligible scribbles apart from a rather distinctive set of loops under the name "Laura Berg" in deep purple ink.

"Are they all in this building?" he quivered.

"Perez and Greene are. Jiminez is at city hall, and so is Darron. You'll need to make an appointment with Berg. She teleworks most of the time and usually only comes in Wednesday afternoons."

Joe stood there dumbfounded. It would take at least a week to track down all of the signatures, not to mention the interview itself. All he could do was let out a pathetic, "Okay."

He slowly made his way out of the building, empty handed except for the sweat-stained signature sheet. The sun beat cruelly on him as he returned to his car. Sweat and tears mixed freely on Joe's face.

The homeless man yelled after him, "Everybody gets screwed, buddy! Everybody!"

5

FORGING AHEAD

Joe sat in his car and relinquished his eyes to the rearview mirror with a tilt of his head. He saw haggard, green eyes set against a prematurely furrowed brow. The imprecatory stare accosted Joe's helplessness. On the other side of that mirror were desires free from restraint, an unabashed, white-hot metal untainted with the base ore of meek compliance. But after all, it was just a reflection. There was no OIHO on that side. There was no outsourcing or Mumbai. There was no alienation, atomization, or rotted heartland.

Joe broke the stare and checked his phone. He had a single text from his wife.

"Babe?? What was that call? Are you okay? You have me super worried."

He could only muster the text, "I'm on my way home."

The drive home was a blur for Joe. Whether he had close calls or ran red lights, he had no idea. He pulled into the cracked, weed-strewn driveway in front of his little bungalow. The drainage ditch in the driveway's entrance jiggled the car's sinewy suspension. Set-tling into his spot, Joe turned the engine off and sat dead-eyed. There was a light on, and he could just make out the ghostly outline of Jill's shadow on the window shade. Her slender, feminine figure sat with great concern in the recliner. Joe received one more caustic glance from the mirror, then entered the small brickwork house.

"Babe, what is going on? Why are you drenched in sweat?" In a suppressed tone she asked, "Were you mugged?"

"No, I wasn't mugged."

"Well, what happened?"

Joe collapsed like a used tissue on the leatherette couch. "What didn't happen today. . . ."

"I'm sorry, baby. Bad day at work?"

"You could say that." Joe put his head in his hands and stared at the faux Persian rug.

"That Mr. Raab is such a joke. I hate that he–"

Joe interrupted Jill's obligatory invocations against Mr. Raab. "I got let go today. Outsourcing. They put up a list in the breakroom of who was and wasn't keeping their job. They even laid off Tyler. Most of the office's work is going to Mumbai."

Jill's face turned from sympathy to dread. "Oh my gosh . . . Joe! How are we going to pay rent? I can't support us on my salary. We'll barely have enough for groceries!" Tears started forming in her eyes.

"Don't worry about the rent." Joe let out a depressed chuckle.

"What? Did something happen with the OIHO?" Jill quivered like a sapling in a strong wind.

Joe remained silent.

Her voice trembled as she repeated her question in a low whisper: "Did something happen with the OIHO?"

Her husband began slowly, "It's not denied per se. Just basically impossible to get done. They changed the rules this year and didn't tell anyone." He let the frustration flow freely. "I have to get five signatures from all over town and then schedule an interview. I'd basically be wasting my time at this point. All applications after Friday usually get denied anyway."

"Oh, Joe. . . ." Jill began sobbing uncontrollably. She feared living in the government housing that would remain their only option without a housing endorsement. "Tessa texts me every day with the horror stories. They found their daughter playing with a dirty needle, and they got in trouble for even reporting it!"

Joe reflected for a moment on Tessa and Jake. They were loose acquaintances who used to live one neighborhood over and go to the same church. They got denied last year due to their neighborhood reaching "equity capacity." Joe remembered feelings of bleak detachment toward their plight.

"I mean, I can still do all the stuff and send it in and maybe there's a chance," Joe lied.

Jill interjected, "I can't live over there. I can't. I can't! How am I supposed to live over there when Whit—" she censored herself, "women who look like me can't even leave the apartment alone even in the middle of the day?"

"It's not over yet," he injected some false optimism.

"No, it's over. It's so over. Joe. . . ." she looked up at Joe with crystalline blue eyes adrift in the welling puddle of tears.

He returned the gaze and stared into her dark pupil.

"I'll leave you if you don't get our house back!" She lashed out, taking Joe by surprise.

"I could—" Joe barely mustered the next words. This wasn't the first time she made this threat. "I could still do the appointments and get my paperwork in." He made air quotes over the appointments.

"What do you mean?"

"I'll have them signed off." The words tumbled from his mouth as if he were regurgitating poison.

"You won't have time?"

Joe lowered his tone. "I'll have them signed."

Jill gave a tortured whisper. "Are you going to fake the signatures?"

Her husband clenched his jaw. "All they'll see is that I got it signed off."

"Oh, and you're just going to waltz in on Monday morning pretending you got all of that done over the weekend?" Jill chided.

"Look, it's the only option we've got!"

"I can't deal with this!" She pushed past him, grabbed her car keys, and slammed the door behind her.

Most of their frequent arguments ended this way. At this point, Joe was numb to the day's cavalcade of disasters. Alone in his transient quarters in the setting sun, his eyes drifted around the cramped living room. On the mantle sat several certificates of meaningless achievement and appeasement. A vast television commanded the visual space of the room. It stood domineering and vacant as if a portal to incomprehensible horror. The couch faced this portal with its back neglecting the views from the window. Just as Joe spent countless hours of imprisonment to the screen in his cubicle, his evenings were spent in voluntary submission to the television. The muddled reflection in the opaque surface stirred existential dread. Joe's sweaty hand drifted to the remote but his finger trembled on the power button.

Casting it aside, he left the house and walked a few miles to the nearest convenience store. Joe hadn't smoked since college but felt compelled to buy a pack of his old favorites. Rushing outside, he drew a cigarette from its sheath and placed it in his mouth. The lighter's flint made a brief flash in the darkness and gave way to a mellow flame. Joe took a long, cool drag. A warm breeze caused the palm trees to sway sympathetically.

The effect of the nicotine was instantaneous. After years of abstinence, his tolerance had returned to zero. The headrush heightened Joe's senses and accelerated his thoughts to cruising speed. He exhaled the cloud into the light of an amber streetlamp. It took on a sallow complexion as it dissipated into the atmosphere, leaving no trace except Joe's buzz. Looking up at the night sky, Joe spied the lights of a passenger plane flying high in the heavens. He wondered for a moment if anyone at all was looking back down at him.

"Anyone at all," he repeated his thoughts aloud.

Looking across the street, the Windview Motel flashed its neon vacancy signs. The building's paint was a sickly and faded blue with two decks of rooms. In decades past, it hosted the throngs of prospective hopefuls traveling west to forage a new dream from the sunny sands of the Pacific. Now its parking lot bore multiple tents, marking the presence of a homeless camp. A single figure, the manager of the motel, stood as a black silhouette on the balcony in front of the main office. He lorded on his podium looking down grimly at his petty fiefdom. The urchins subsisting on his land paid him in food, drugs, sex, or whatever else he deemed a good price for not calling the police to evict them from the lot. With the OIHO denying more and more vouchers, business was booming for these extortion farms.

Even in the night, he sensed the manager's hungry eyes drift toward him like the searchlight of a prison camp. Joe used to drive by Windview on his way to work. As the pool of societal refuse piled up in the parking lot, he changed his route to avoid the negative stimuli. Nevertheless, Windview haunted him like a specter, shadowing his every move and promising to swallow him whole if he slipped. Its mouth hung agape as the manager's silhouette burned itself into Joe's eyes. Unsettled, he finished the cigarette in a few minutes and threw the butt into his reflection in a stagnant puddle. He gave the remainder of the pack to a homeless man on his way home.

Joe awoke the next morning shortly before noon. He was alone in his bed, but he could see Jill's car in the driveway. Sloughing off the covers like a scab, Joe checked the living room. She was on the couch cuddling a bottle of tequila. The housing paperwork still sat on the dining table. He gingerly took them over to the couch and sat on the floor next to her. Racking his frazzled memory to recall the signatures he saw on Mr. Smith's desk, Joe practiced the signatures for about an hour. He took special care to replicate Berg's with a purple pen he fortuitously found in Jill's purse.

Was it two loops or three? Joe rubbed his face in trepidation.

He took the signature sheet in trembling hands and set it on the table. Moving the pens in succession as carefully as two aircrafts engage in aerial refueling, Joe forged five signatures.

6

MONDAY

After a silent and despondent weekend, Joe snuck out of the house to submit his felonious paperwork after Jill left for work. He kept Mr. Smith's signature line blank with the hopes of getting at least some form of legitimacy for his papers. He wore an old baseball cap and a surgical mask so that his interviewer wouldn't recognize him as the desperate, sweaty, and nameless individual he turned away last Friday. Arriving at the OIHO office, Joe breezed past the line. When the employee at the entrance questioned him, he merely notified them of his appointment with Mr. Smith. To his surprise, they didn't ask for any verification. Joe was immediately suspicious of his ease of entry but mused that perhaps his luck was turning. He knocked on the door.

"Come in."

"Good morning, Mr. Smith. I have my interview sheet signed off," Joe lied through his mask.

The bureaucrat nodded and turned toward him. "What's your name?"

"Joseph Blaine."

Despite his disguise, he had to have his real name on the paperwork, lest his efforts be for nothing.

"Hmm, I don't see you listed for an appointment. Well, I do have a no-show, so we can do this real quick." Mr. Smith seemed to not recognize him at all.

"Great." Joe was far more thankful and relieved than he let on.

"Let's take a look at your sheet. Okay, so Ms. Berg explained what to expect in the interview?" The bureaucrat peered over his golden glasses.

"Yeah." Joe wondered what critical information he would be lacking.

"I'm honestly surprised she signed you off. She has a pretty strict adherence to equity quotas and usually won't send . . . guys like you . . . to the interview at this stage in the game," Mr. Smith questioned.

Bemused, Joe confirmed to himself that the process was designed to be essentially impossible. He replied, "I'm not sure, but I'm happy to be here."

"Okay, I'm going to ask you a series of questions about your background after you sign this waiver."

The waiver sat arrogantly on the desk. It proclaimed a series of demands to release his demographic information, consent to periodic home searches, and consent to be electronically recorded. Rounding out the form was a list of executive orders shoring up its wobbly legitimacy along with the Equity and Inclusion Act. Joe signed the paper and quietly resented the tyranny of forced consent. He signed the same form last year.

"Thank you very much. Alright, let's get started with the interview." Mr. Smith pulled up the questionnaire on his computer.

Preparing to do battle with the administrative state once more, Joe settled into the chair in front of the desk. At this point, he noticed that it was considerably shorter than his opponent's.

Mr. Smith began the first volley, "State your name for the record and your current address."

"Joseph Arthur Blaine, 642 Floyd Avenue."

Keeping his eyes on the computer screen, his interrogator asked, "Are you applying for the same address?"

Joe replied meekly, "Yes, that's correct."

"Alright, I'll skip to question 12. Have you been approved for a housing endorsement before?" Smith's dark eyes scrambled across the questionnaire.

Knowing previous approval had a large impact on future applications, Joe felt relief that he could positively confirm.

Turning to face the applicant after the opening skirmish, the real battle began. "Okay, let's get to the important stuff. Age, height, and weight?"

His adrenaline-soaked mind swirled to keep up. "Twenty-five, five foot eleven, 170 lbs."

Making some entries into his sheet, Mr. Smith asked the next questions with a wince as if he knew Joe had all the wrong answers.

"Race?"

"White," the applicant said sheepishly with a twinge of conditioned shame.

"Ethnicity?"

While Joe's ethnic makeup was a mix of various European countries, he knew the question was only asking if he was Hispanic or not, to which he answered, "No."

"None," the bureaucrat corrected Joe's answer and shifted in his chair. "I'm really surprised Ms. Berg approved you to be honest. Well, let's keep going. What about your gender? Are you non-binary? Sexual orientation? Marital status? Anything that might help you out."

The applicant's heart sank with his very inequitable answer: "I'm a married, straight male."

Smith shook his head imperceptibly. "Are you an immigrant or a refugee?"

Joe couldn't bring himself to lie and denied these labels.

"You're up to date on your marriage education at least, right? A lot of applications get denied 'cuz of that," Smith deviated from the script.

"Yeah, we're good through next year." He was thankful he finished his last week.

The bureaucrat scrolled on his computer for a moment. "What was your income last year?"

Joe perked up at the chance to claim an advantageous victimhood. "Actually, I'm unemployed as of last Friday."

Mr. Smith nodded with a conciliatory look in his eyes. "I'm sorry to hear that. But what was your yearly salary before you were let go?"

"$41,000, but I really should be considered under an unemployed status," the applicant attempted to argue.

"Look, I get what you're trying to do, but unfortunately the OIHO does it on a fiscal year basis," his interviewer sighed, "so if you were employed at any point during the year, your status is still considered employed."

Joe's disposition tumbled into a saggy resignation. "Fine."

Smith continued, "Do you have all the most recent immunizations? That's another hit that a lot of people forget about."

The applicant nodded.

The bureaucrat stopped typing and narrowed his eyes. "Why the mask?"

Joe managed a believable lie about his face-concealing disguise, "I just like to be safe."

Smith appeared satisfied with this answer. "Any family history of conviction of a Hate Crime or other violations of the Equity and Inclusion Act? Any family members registered Hate Offenders? That's another big hit."

Knowing it would come up in their investigation, the applicant reluctantly told the truth. "Well, my mom had a misdemeanor Hate Charge a few years ago, but the charges got reduced to just a regular misdemeanor, not a Hate Crime."

"What was the charge?" His interviewer leaned forward in concern.

"Frivolous police call." Joe smothered a disgusted tone.

Smith nodded and leaned back in his chair. "Okay, shouldn't be a problem. She did her reform class afterwards, right?"

"Yes," he replied with pursed lips, "and she did the mandatory counseling with the family."

The bureaucrat stroked his chin. "Okay, yeah, that shouldn't hold you up. Alright, that's pretty much everything. If that's all you have for me, I'll submit your paperwork and you should hear back in a few weeks." He paused and leaned forward in his chair. "But can I level with you for a second?"

Joe assented.

Smith continued with a low voice and concerned look, "Your answers are not great for your application, especially this late. Your application is pretty much going straight to the bottom."

This news failed to surprise the inequitable applicant. "I'm kind of at the end of my rope. I've got to take any chance I have left."

Smith shrugged, then continued typing on the computer. "I get it, but I'd start arranging other accommodations if I were you. Usually, Ms. Berg filters you guys out earlier so that you can start getting your new living situation sorted."

"Well, there's still a chance," Joe said with numb detachment.

The bureaucrat smiled and finished up the form. "Optimism, I like it. Alright, you're good to go."

After thanking his interrogator for no perceptible reason, Joe exited his office. While the chances were bleak, he still maintained hope. Joe had outwitted the administrative behemoth and was at least permitted to roll the dice. He walked briskly from the scene of the crime and rounded the corner in the hallway to the waiting room.

"Excuse me." A sullen mass slithered by him.

Joe noticed the name on her OIHO nametag: Laura Berg. He realized in horror who she was and attempted to nonchalantly check if she would enter Mr. Smith's office. To his immense dismay, Berg entered the office and closed the door behind her. Joe could only assume that Mr. Smith would ask why he was forwarded for an interview.

7

KNOCK, KNOCK, JOE

Joe jolted awake to rude knocking on his door. It was late morning on the following Thursday. Making a few haphazard attempts at job hunting, he spent his idle time in anguish in anticipation of being caught. Jill was at work and taking on extra duties to negotiate a raise. The knocking became more insistent as time went on. Joe put on a day-old shirt and tripped over the curled edge of the living room carpet on his way to the door. This only contributed to his shooting adrenaline. Joe opened the door.

"Good afternoon, my name is Officer Omar with the MLK Jr. County Sheriff's Office," the policeman aggressively introduced himself. He wore a cartoonish skull patch on his vest and the Inclusion Banner on his Kevlar helmet. A rifle hung on a sling from his shoulder. His rotund partner stood eagerly behind him, rifle at a low carry.

"Hi, how can I help you?" Joe successfully repressed a tremor in his voice.

"Are you Joseph A. Blaine?"

"Yes."

"Do you mind if I ask you a few questions?" Omar narrowed his eyes.

"What is this concerning?" Joe stalled to gather his thoughts and strategize.

His adversary brushed past the delay. "Do you have any firearms or weapons of any kind in the house?"

"No, I do not."

The officer checked his notepad. "Before coming here, I checked the database, and it shows you as having some history of gun ownership in your family. Do you now or have you ever possessed any firearms?"

Knowing that the policeman already knew the answer, Joe replied, "I turned in a pistol several years ago," he begrudgingly admitted. "I never even fired it."

Officer Omar raised his eyebrow, awaiting more information.

Joe continued, "And my grandpa left me a gun when he died two months ago, but I didn't pick it up. I notified the police department where he used to live, and they disposed of it."

The officer's demeanor lightened slightly. "Just wanted to check up on that. I was doing an audit of the out of state wills checking for firearm ownership, and your grandpa's came up. I'll verify with the Orange Grove Police Department that it was properly disposed of. But because you didn't tell us that you refused to take it, I'm going to have to search your house just to be sure."

Joe bristled. "Don't you have to have a warrant?"

"This is an OIHO property, isn't it? You signed a waiver saying that you consent to periodic police checkups. We're doing your checkup. If you obstruct us, we'll make sure your housing endorsement gets denied this year," Omar's partner chimed in.

Joe meekly acquiesced and stepped aside from the doorway. The two officers proceeded to leave no stone unturned, no drawer left in its slot. Piles of clothes, keepsakes, and picture frames all gained intimacy with the floor. The glass display cases holding his college diploma and marriage certificate shattered on impact. The policemen tipped over tables and chairs but didn't even bother to check underneath. Joe could only look on in veiled disgust as Omar lingered in his wife's underwear drawer. Making his way from room to room, the officers left a trail of punitive destruction.

Once satisfied with their work, they made crunching strides across the broken glass and debris to the door and Officer Omar said, "Next time, you won't forget to notify us."

Joe closed the door behind them. He wanted to slam it, but he figured it would draw the ire of the thugs. Turning from the entryway, Joe collapsed with his back against the wall. A brewing cauldron of relief and anger filled his mind. He prayed that this visit meant that his deception had gone unnoticed. Joe remained supine on the floor until Jill returned from work two hours later.

"What on earth happened here?!" she asked in a panicked tone amid the mayhem.

"The police showed up—"

"I knew you shouldn't have done that!"

"Keep your voice down! They may have left behind a recording device. And no, it wasn't about that. He came to check on that gun my grandpa left me," Joe defended himself.

"But I thought you gave that up?"

Joe mournfully recounted, "I did, but I didn't notify our county sheriff's office, so they trashed the place."

"Oh Joe, look at our wedding certificate. . . ." Jill tearfully sat on the floor.

Joe paused for a moment and took in her appearance. Her shimmering golden locks fell like fresh snow on her soft shoulders. The tears rolled down her ivory cheeks in a steady stream. Joe made his way over to his wife, warmly embraced her, and said, "Be careful of the broken glass."

They sat silently for a long time amid the wreckage as Jill sobbed. Her husband caressed and held her trembling form softly in his arms. At first cagey toward the gesture, Jill rested her head on Joe's shoulder and gripped tightly at his back. He kissed the top of her head tenderly.

"At least it wasn't the other thing," she censored herself.

The hostilities of the previous few days melted away with the reciprocating warmth of that embrace. Joe and Jill shared a passionate kiss with all the tenderness and latent desire of their first time. They stared intently into each other's eyes and became lost in the comfort of shared affection. Something that had been dead and buried for years leapt up and sent sparks flying in their hearts. Among the debris of their crumbling life, Joe and Jill loved once again. He lifted his wife from the ground and carried her to the bedroom in the same way he first brought her across the threshold of their new home.

8

FIGHT OR FLIGHT

The following two weeks passed quickly for Joe. He spent his time looking for employment on various job hiring sites. The pickings were slim and the wages slimmer. Invariably, the listings consisted of neurotic demands that applicants have years of experience for an entry level job followed by lengthy diatribes about being an "open and inclusive workspace." Comically, the section describing their adherence to inclusion initiatives was often longer than the job listing itself. While the need for money chided him at every turn, his subconscious made no great fuss over the lack of income.

An indescribable amber finality colored those days: perhaps in retrospect, perhaps in reality. Twilight rays bathed his heart in sweet leisure as he forgot about Mr. Raab and the stress of the OIHO. For a transient, evaporating time, Joe could deceive himself into not needing to participate in society's race.

Jill and Joe experienced a rekindling of young love, free from the realism of cold, matrimonial endurance. In soft touches and subtle looks, their affection deepened beyond what they thought possible in their surroundings. Only when Joe was removed from the system's slavery could he be the husband he always wanted to be. His mind drifted to childish fantasies of uprooting from MLK Jr. County and settling in the middle of nowhere with his wife, but this thought was quashed as quickly as he realized there wasn't enough money for even gas or a plane ticket. Joe listlessly held out for a new job to come up in their current locale. Even still, Joe thought of these weeks as the happiest of his life. All the while, the ticking clock of their dwindling savings tolled with the rollover of each digit. The debtors demanded their pound of flesh.

One Thursday night, Joe took Jill to their favorite park to watch the sunset by the sea. They shared some Chinese takeout while sitting on a soft blanket. The crashing waves pounded the surf in an endless attempt to consume the land. The palms, stoic and virile, stretched their fronds in the full glory of the warm glow of twilight. As the sublime evening sun slipped beneath the waves, Jill's anxiety grew.

"Babe, what's going to happen to us?"

"It'll be fine. I'm sure the right job will pop up." Joe reclined on the grass and slowly adjusted his eyes to the darkness.

"No, babe. What's going to happen to us?" Jill spoke with dread.

"What do you mean? With your raise, we have enough in savings at least for a few more weeks. I've got a pretty good lead at Aaronson Consulting. I don't have the masters or Spanish language skills, but my previous experience should make up for it," Joe fibbed.

"No, not that. I don't know. I just feel really worried about the future."

The last rosy splotches dripped from the graying clouds above them. Joe felt as though their honeymoon period was slipping through his fingers like the wet, sinking sand on the shore. He gripped tightly to her.

Joe attempted to find the root issue. "But why? Yeah, I know the job search isn't over yet, but we'll be okay. I'll make up the slack. And don't worry about the housing thing. We would have heard back by now if it were getting denied."

"Something really bad is coming. I just know it." Jill stared blankly at the wine dark sea as night overtook them.

Joe struggled to trust her intuition on many occasions despite its frequent accuracy. He had deadened his own out of years of compliance with the narrative. They sat without a word for a few minutes as the last traces of the day sank into the sea like a doomed trans-Pacific voyager. Joe's own instinct for doom began to stir. The pounding of the waves seemed to intensify to an unbearable volume until he abruptly decided it was time to leave.

They returned to the car in grave silence. The happy colors that permeated the hours preceding gave way to a dark, chthonic hue. The dim lights of the interior cast a hazy reflection on the windshield.

To Joe's horror, his reflection took on the same other-worldly character it did in the window of the OIHO building. Having been obscured by a leave of absence, he again appeared dim and obfuscated. Nevertheless, Joe could still see the eyes: searching, immolating, reaching, eviscerating. The shining, green eyes reflected in the windshield gripped him by the throat. Joe covered his face, but his soul's searchlight remained. Struggling to breathe, Joe turned on the car and snuffed out the reflection. He sighed with relief. After taking a plodding route home, Jill was the first to notice some flashing blue and red lights down their street.

"What is that about?" Joe said to no one in particular.

After a few seconds, he looked over at Jill. She was already staring back at him with the most horrified look. The police were parked in front of the bungalow. They could see a flashlight furiously sweeping inside their house.

"Joe, they know! They found us out!" his wife shrieked.

"Relax! It's probably just more harassment for the gun thing."

Joe had no confidence in this. His heart raced as he pulled up. He parked on the street several houses from his own.

"Stay in the car and lock the doors. I'll talk to the cops." He attempted to project confidence.

"Wait, Joe," she whimpered.

He stopped and rested on the door frame.

"I love you," Jill said tearfully like the tolling of a bell.

"I love you too," Joe nodded as she sobbed quietly.

He closed the door behind him. Joe thought about stopping to kiss her before talking to the cops but decided against it. The strobing police lights caused a disorienting effect as it reflected on the faded surface of their car. Joe looked back briefly to see his wife cowering in the passenger seat. Wheeling about, Joe broke into an inexplicable jog toward an uncertain fate.

"Don't move!" a policeman snarled with his weapon drawn.

Joe instinctively put his hands up. He could only see the silhouette of two heavily armed law enforcement officers in front of a mine-resistant personnel transport against the pulsing lights. A third officer exited the house.

"Get on your knees and interlock your hands behind your head."

He complied as they rushed in.

"Joseph Blaine?"

"Yes."

"You're under arrest for falsifying documentation for your OIHO housing application. You are being arrested as a Hate Criminal."

The officers thrust Joe to the ground and roughly cuffed him. He struggled to breath as an officer's weight ground into his back.

"Where's your wife? Where's your car?"

"She's not here."

"Her car's here," one of the officers retorted.

"She took my car. We had a fight. I don't know where she went." Joe struggled to talk with the weight of the officer on his back.

Suddenly a scream pierced the night air from the direction of the car. Joe managed to turn his head only to see several men armed with pipes and crowbars breaking into his car. It was a common occurrence for opportunistic bands to break into cars wherever the distracted police were making arrests. Law enforcement would radio it in for reporting purposes, but they seldom intervened.

"Hey, do something!" Joe panicked and attempted to get the police to stop the danger to his wife. The officers looked at each other for a moment.

"Do you know her?"

The Hate Criminal's voice revealed his panic. "Why does that matter? Isn't it your job to stop that?!"

"Is that your wife?" one of the officers asked with an apathetic tone.

The female cop scoffed impatiently.

Joe's mind raced as he tried to think of the best thing to say. If he admitted it was his wife, they'd arrest her too. The police were notorious for their treatment of female Hate Criminals. On the other hand, this band of thugs was liable to do worse to her. Joe could hear Jill struggling and thrashing as they pulled her from the car.

"Please, just stop them! They're going to hurt her—"

A gunshot rang out from the direction of the car. The policeman's hold on Joe loosened in that moment enough for him to fully turn his head. A crimson spatter painted the vehicle. Jill lay slumped on the hood with brain matter hanging from her skull. The horrific scene callously slammed the door shut on their story together. Dark, inhuman figures danced, hollered, and looted like scavenging vultures around Jill's lifeless form.

Joe cried out in desperation. Every bone in his body strained as his muscles contracted and rippled. Jill's fair and beautiful face burned itself into his vision as if he were staring at the sun. He would give anything in that moment even to caress her dead body. Joe wished he had held her just a little while longer that night as they watched the sun go down. All time stopped. He experienced eternity in an instant as Jill's porcelain form lingered before his eyes. The leaden weight of years of missed opportunities, affections dropped, love not made, hands not held, kisses not savored, and sunsets not shared rent the withering fibers of his pounding heart. He could almost feel her soul departing and the distance between them increasing into the eternity of cold, dark space. The chill of this distance gave way to a fire rising within him. Joe's mind succumbed to grief and rage.

He awoke. The shock of the gunshot was enough for Joe to gain the element of surprise. He bucked his head backward and managed to throw his captor to the ground. Joe no longer cared if he lived or died. Despite his physical restraints, he was unchained and untethered. Making a rapid movement, he bit at the neck of the first officer. The policeman screamed and clutched with panic at his rifle. Five shots pierced the night air as Joe's mouth filled with a sanguine rush. Grinding his teeth like a rabid dog, he felt the policeman clutch at his neck. One of the other officers grabbed Joe on his shoulder and ripped him from his comrade. The blood sprayed the policeman's eyes for a moment, allowing Joe to roll over. He made a fierce kick at the man's groin. Adrenaline took all semblance of faculty from the Hate Criminal. Like a gazelle pursued into the bush, he managed to scramble up and flee into the darkness of the night. As he made his escape, Joe saw the third officer on the ground with her hands on her stomach, screaming in pain. Two of the bullets from the first officer's panicked burst had found their mark. The last officer fired wildly as he tried to wipe the blood from his eyes.

9

MOLTING OF THE BUGMAN

"ATTENTION: The following is a statement from The Martin Luther King Jr. County Sheriff's Office: Public Safety Lockdown (PSL): A lockdown is in effect as of 9 p.m. and will continue for the next twenty-four hours. Citizens are not to leave their homes for any reason except for medical emergencies. An armed and dangerous Hate fugitive escaped from police custody in the vicinity of Floyd Street. He is wounded and desperate. Do not approach. The suspect is a White male with blond hair and green eyes named Joseph Arthur Blaine, five foot eleven, 170 lbs., and wearing jeans with a blue sweatshirt. Inform the MLK Jr. County Sheriff's Office of any details. Under the Equity and Inclusion Act, rendering assistance to a Hate fugitive is a Hate Crime and will be prosecuted to the fullest extent of the law."

Joe realized his phone was still with him and broadcasting his location as the warning played. He stopped momentarily behind a house a few streets down from his own. Cradling his head in his hands, Joe noticed a burning pain in his scalp as the adrenaline abated. A bullet had grazed the side of his head, and the wound was bleeding profusely. Another round tore a hole in the armpit of his sweatshirt. Joe sat for a moment trying to compose himself. He was thankful at least the third officer stayed back to tend to his wounded comrades. His heart was awash with sadness, fear, and dread. Paralyzed from further action, Joe vomited the contents of his stomach until there was nothing left. Still handcuffed, he slipped his hands under his legs so they could be in front. Mustering just enough strength to throw his phone as far as he could, the fugitive once again slumped to the ground. Joe began babbling incoherently.

"What have I done? I got Jill killed! What have I done? They're coming for me!"

He swore repeatedly as he shook violently from fear. Joe's small, urbanite soul pierced through its insectoid shell. He began to molt. The emerging creature was vulnerable and weak as its new skin adjusted to its harsh environment. The churlish chiding of the whirlwind of recent events beat mercilessly on this supine jelly. The comfort of the shell had been shattered irreparably—at last the bugman could grow.

A light turned on inside the house.

"Who's out there?" a gruff voice called out.

Joe leapt up from his stupor and continued his flight. There was no time to hesitate or grieve.

There's going to be a helicopter and a thousand drones in the air any minute! Joe's internal voice chastised him as if it were his conscience.

He knew he had to find shelter and get rid of his cuffs. Any White caught outside during the lockdown would immediately be hauled in. The only Whites somewhat permitted to be outside during a lockdown were the homeless, but even they would be subject to scrutiny. In MLK Jr. County, one never had to travel far to find an encampment. He settled on the fiefdom at the Windview Motel he observed weeks earlier. The lords of these plots typically resisted any police interference in their little kingdoms. As much as the motel scared him, it was the only option for survival.

Passing a homeless man lying on a street corner, he forked over his credit card in exchange for the man's beanie hat, blanket, and hooded coat after a brief period of haggling. Joe knew full well that his credit card and bank account were already frozen. Street deals like this became cumbersome after the phasing out of paper currency. Joe took out the picture of Jill from his wallet and disposed of everything else. He wrapped the blanket around his back and hid his handcuffs under the coat. Donning his new hat, he set out on the short run to the motel as sirens made their mournful call across the city. Taking pause to smear his face and clothes with gutter grime, he spotted flashing lights in his peripheral vision.

Ducking in an alley, Joe discovered that there were no dumpsters or palettes to hide behind. He got on the ground with his back against the wall and pretended to be out cold from intoxication. Joe shivered uncontrollably from the grief and fear. After taking one last look at Jill's photograph, he attempted to cover as much of the blood on his clothes with the blanket and coat as he could. The squad car lurked, and its spotlight found his crumpled form. The car stopped, and an officer got out.

"Let me see some ID. Are you aware there's a Public Safety Lockdown right now?" the policeman called out as he approached.

"A code wha? I don hav no ID." He slurred his words and imitated drunkenness.

"No ID, huh? Let me see your face." The officer shined his flashlight.

Joe prayed his shoddy disguise was enough.

"Stay right here."

The officer went back to the car to retrieve a face scanner. Joe knew even the grime wouldn't fool the recognition software. He scrambled to think of a way out.

Out of his peripheral vision, he spotted a man walking on the sidewalk. He was a teenaged, White male with blond hair and roughly Joe's height.

"Hey, you!" the officer called out.

"Yes?" the boy replied.

"What are you doing out? There's a PSL."

The teen swore. "My phone died. I'm walking home from work."

"I've had it with White people's excuses tonight!" the officer bellowed.

"I'm sorry, sir, I just didn't have any way of knowing."

The officer cursed him and yelled, "No way. We broadcast the advisory out of everything with a speaker. I know you heard it."

The boy became more desperate. "I promise, I didn't know! I'll go home right now, I promise! I'm sorry!"

The officer turned off his body camera and drew his billy club. The policeman started to beat him savagely. He first struck the boy on the head, which knocked him to the ground. The teen convulsed as the officer struck his torso. His partner exited the vehicle and pulled him off his victim.

"C'mon man, that's enough. He's just a kid."

"Nah bro, he's not a kid. He's old enough to know better. Stay outta my way!" The officer shoved his partner away and continued his violence.

Joe grimly used this distraction to slip down the alley and turn the corner. He could hear the grunts and strikes of the policeman for an uncomfortable distance as he sprinted away.

At this point, the urban troglodytes crept from their lairs to start looting the stores they knew would be empty of staff due to the lockdown. The police only accosted those who were the true targets of the lockdown. As long as your skin tone was reflected on the Inclusion Banner, you were permitted to roam free and pilfer as you pleased. The Public Safety Lockdowns were an extreme deterrent for resisting arrest for a Hate Offense. Any suspected violation would mean open season on White property and lives for a night.

He passed several scenes of Whites being dragged from their homes and beaten by the roving mobs of de facto exempt individuals. He felt guilt that his escape caused their demise. Joe recalled his own feelings of resentment toward escaping Hate Criminals when his own neighborhood came under threat as a result. Dodging a few more police patrols, Joe made it to the motel's homeless camp to hunker down until the night's lockdown was over.

10

A NIGHT AMONG THE DAMNED

The fugitive spent the first few hours of the night alternating between sobbing and dry heaving under a large garbage bag he used for shelter. The other campers paid him little mind except when he got too loud. While normally the camps were hubs of raving addicts, the Windview Motel camp enforced an oppressive silence. It was a bulwark of quiet as the city around them erupted with malice, though it was not the pleasant hush of a forest garden or a church pew. The inaudibility of the camp sprang from the roots of a thousand smothered screams, always only a hair's trigger away from the wailing cries of the damned and the forgotten.

When Joe's mourning became too loud, those near him rose and kicked his shapeless form into compliance. At last, he remained silent. Peeking under the edge of his plastic shell, Joe caught a glimpse of the manager on the balcony. He wondered if this tyrant ever slept or was instead sustained solely by the misery he farmed below. Joe knew his entrance to the camp had not gone unnoticed and he would soon be hauled before the manager.

A woman shuffled over to sit next to him. Though young, she was frail from malnutrition. She had sunken, gray eyes hidden under a horizontal line of self-trimmed, auburn bangs. Most of her teeth were rotted. Huddling by a small campfire, she clutched a stuffed animal, which at one point must have resembled a dog.

"H—Hi," she quivered.

Joe lifted the edge of his garbage bag and fearfully greeted her.

"Who are you?" the woman asked. "You shouldn't have snuck in here. He saw it." She repeated the last phrase in a whisper several times.

"Nobody." The fugitive could barely speak.

"My name's Erica. Not telling you my last name." She introduced herself.

Joe gave a polite nod in hopes of keeping her quiet.

Erica widened her eyes and stared off into space. "I got here about a year ago. But I've been on the streets for much longer. I used to be in LA. My parents lost their jobs because of that law and couldn't afford a home."

"The Equity and Inclusion Act?" He settled into the conversation in a hushed tone.

The girl squinted and clutched her head. "I think so. I don't remember." Erica lifted up her stuffed animal. "Have you met Timmy?"

Joe looked at the misshapen form with despair. "Where are your parents?" He figured she couldn't be more than eighteen years old.

"Prison." Erica retracted her stuffed animal and chewed on her finger. "April 19th. Everyone was there. My parents made me stay home. That was when we still had a home."

The April 19th Incident was the culmination of a series of demonstrations several years prior in response to a crackdown in OIHO enforcement around the country. These policies were implemented most strictly in Los Angeles. Goaded on by Max Martinez, the Republican presidential candidate at the time, thousands of activists gathered in the city to protest OIHO's policies. The Los Angeles Police Department, in concert with the California National Guard, declared the assembly unlawful and dispersed the crowd with tear gas and clubs. After the protesters retreated, counterprotest groups went into various privileged neighborhoods to burn, loot, and kill in full view of the complicit police. Afterwards, the newly formed Federal Consolidated Investigation Authority pursued anyone involved with the April 19th protest for even the most minor of offenses. Posting a vaguely positive endorsement on social media or donating to the wrong fundraiser was enough to get a knock on the door or a frozen bank account. Martinez consequently renounced any ties to the protestors and condemned their actions.

The girl continued, "They made it home that night. But they came into our neighborhood, and my dad shot one. Dad's in for life. Mom's doing twenty. I'm doing a life sentence too." Erica's red eyes welled.

"Little, fourteen-year-old girl with Hate Criminal parents. Just a little girl. The police put me in foster care, but I ran away."

Joe's heart would have ached for her plight if he could feel anything at all besides the grief of losing Jill. "Were you treated badly?"

The girl clawed at her neck. "The one guy was nice enough but his partner. . . . I can't get his face out of my head. I still have nightmares about him! He would do things with me and the other foster kids . . . and make us do things with each other."

Shocked, the fugitive asked, "Could you report him?!"

Erica yelped, "Oh they knew all about him. He had a special arrangement with Child Protective Services. I don't know what he offered them, but the state gave us in return. Some of them even visited and did things too. They called it the party house. I escaped from that hellhole! I escaped. I escaped! I escaped!"

She continued to scream "I escaped!" incessantly. Joe waited anxiously for her to stop, but to no avail. The others in the camp became agitated with this disturbance, but before he could be beaten again, the hour of his audience with the petty lord arrived suddenly. Erica scurried away as quickly as she had come. Two enforcers came down the stairs. Joe peered intently at the procession as they descended to the damned below. They were large men wearing decorative silver chains. The men gorged the silence of the camp with staccato percussion in the manager's hideous orchestra. Only the manager could permit such noise.

"Stand up," one of the men said, "and meet your new god."

Joe stood and faced the men. He could see they were twins in the sickly amber light of the parking lot. Both men bore signs of repeated physical abuse, both dealt and received. He had no choice but to follow the twins upstairs to the manager's office. The noisy movement of the twins' jewelry dictated their marching tempo up to the throne room.

"Wait here." The men went inside the office.

Joe strained his eyes to see inside the shuttered blinds. He could make out the silhouettes of the twins and two figures seated at a desk. Muffled conversation leaked through the cracks in the door as his thoughts drifted to Jill. He couldn't believe it was only hours ago that they were watching a placid sunset by the sea. He again became racked with grief.

"Come in," the manager beckoned and broke his contemplation.

Joe was surprised that he wasn't being restrained or dragged in.

"Sit down." The manager's eyes drifted to Joe's handcuffs.

He sat in a metal frame chair with worn, orange, herringbone upholstery. The room was a sickly yellow and smelled strongly of urine. A fluorescent light buzzed above them, and a large mirror hung on the wall opposite the door.

At last, he saw the manager in the light. He was in his mid-sixties with wispy, gray hair. Circular spectacles sat astride a protruding, aquiline nose. The manager's beady eyes resembled shriveled raisins against his pale skin, which hung on his facial bones like a soiled bed sheet. The manager stared intently at Joe and narrowed his eyes. A boy of about fourteen sat on a stool beside the desk with a pen and paper. He was wearing makeup and a short, revealing skirt.

"I've seen you before," the manager squeaked in a Brooklyn accent. "Yes, yes, I have."

Joe remained silent.

"You were here only a few weeks ago at the gas station across the street. Smoking a cigarette."

The manager remained deathly quiet for what seemed like several minutes, all the while staring into Joe's haggard eyes. He suddenly pointed to a frame on the wall and cried, "You see that? Read it out loud."

Joe lifted his eyes to a diploma that bore the name David Rosenblatt. He read, "Wharton School of Business—"

"Wharton! You see that? Wharton School of Business. The best! I don't miss anything. You think I do this motel stuff because I have to?" He paused long enough for Joe to think the question was not rhetorical.

"I—"

"No! I was the best on Wall Street. I made millions, but I got bored of just shifting numbers around." Rosenblatt paused. "I don't miss anything. I had my eye on you the second I saw you looking over at me all those days ago"—his tone accelerated—"and you had the chutzpah to trespass on my turf during a Public Safety Lockdown—*your* PSL—and expected me to not know who you are? You thought you could just crawl in and spend the night like I wouldn't notice?" What started as an acidic rebuke crescendoed into a screaming tirade. "I don't miss anything! I know exactly who you are, Mr. Blaine!" Rosenblatt slammed his fist on the desk.

Joe's soul sank with dread at the revelation that Rosenblatt knew his full plight. The manager would expect more of him in order to grant asylum in his camp.

"You'll be punished for your trespass"—the manager leaned back and lowered his voice—"but you made the right decision. You came to me instead of the police. They don't mess with me; I don't mess with them. Some of them even partake."

Rosenblatt's verbosity wore Joe thin. He shuddered to think of what "partake" meant. The manager made a small tent with his fingers as he rested his elbows on the desk.

"So, what to do with you? What to do?" Rosenblatt laughed and shifted in his chair. "What do you have to offer me?"

Joe paused for a moment and struggled to piece together words due to the stress of the night.

"I—I don't have much money."

"Let me see your wallet."

"I don't have it anymore—"

"Pat him down," Rosenblatt interrupted.

The twins stood on either side and picked Joe up by the underarms. They proceeded to search his pockets and found the picture of Jill. They handed it to the manager.

"She's pretty. Is this your wife?"

Joe could only nod his head as he held back tears.

"This might just be enough for you to stay here for a bit. She's a little old for me, but she'll do for Oleg. Alex, make a note for the sheriff to pick up the girl from Mr. Blaine's house. And tell them no sampling!" Rosenblatt stroked the side of his face while letting a small grin encroach on his protruding lower lip.

The teenage boy began to write, but Joe burst out, "She's dead!" and began to weep bitterly.

The manager frowned. "This complicates your situation. I was really looking forward to her. And I had a client who wanted one just like her. Does she have a younger sister?" He sighed and placed the photo in his desk drawer. "Never mind, we need to figure out your predicament first. We'll get your bank account, that's a given. How much is in there?"

Joe spoke between sobs, "I lost my job a few weeks ago. Just a grand or so. I have debt."

If he had known he would need to sell his soul to Rosenblatt, Joe may have just surrendered to the police. But he grasped that the Hate prisons were a veritable hell on earth despite the limited information leaked to the public. Joe had hoped to covertly wait out the lockdown at the motel and then continue his flight.

"Compose yourself! This is a business meeting," Rosenblatt chastised. "Just a grand? Not enough, not enough. Don't worry about the debt. You owe me now. What else do you have to offer?"

Joe racked his brain for something he could give. He didn't own his house, and his car was presumably stolen. Jill's car was probably being vandalized or broken into at that very moment due to the PSL.

"I could put you on the market, but I don't know who would want you. You look too old to pass as anything marketable." He briefly smirked at the teen and groped his knee. The boy remained stone-faced. Rosenblatt continued, "And not really the fighting type."

"I can work." Joe knew he would suffer unspeakably if he could not prove himself useful. He could feel the twins breathing heavily on his head as they loomed behind him.

"He can work. He can work, he says!" The tyrant chuckled. "I'm smarter than you, my twins are stronger than you, and I already have dozens of little urchins in the parking lot to do my daily chores. What can you offer?"

Joe launched into a word salad of excuses for skills, the unfortunate muscle memory from dozens of interviews for underpaid positions. Rosenblatt's eyes imperceptibly narrowed over the course of Joe's feeble attempt to save his life. Joe's own eyes began to lose the ability to focus on his captor the longer he talked. As his reflection captured more of his gaze, Joe found his words trailing off.

The manager clapped his hands to halt the speech. "I have an idea. Alex, get Mr. Baron on the phone."

The feminized boy grabbed the phone on the desk and dialed a number from memory. Putting the call on speaker, he sat back in his stool as quietly as possible. Joe made fleeting eye contact with Alex. He gave Joe a fearful and empathizing look from his wretched, mascara adorned eyes. The call toned on the desk as Joe's heart rate rose. He could feel the manager's eyes drilling holes in his fear-stricken body as the room awaited Mr. Baron.

"Why are you calling me at this hour?" Mr. Baron cursed Rosenblatt.

"Shut up, you like my calls. You still picked up," he bantered.

The pair took time to catch up and exchange friendly insults as only old pals could.

"So, is this a booty call, or do you actually have anything to say?" Baron joked.

"You still doing your films?"

"Am I still doing my films? What do you think? Business is booming"—an audible buzz on his phone distracted Baron—"Hey, isn't there a PSL in your area? My security guys just sent me a quick rundown. Some White boy forged his paperwork and then ripped out the jugular of a cop with his teeth!"

"You'll never guess who I have at my motel," Rosenblatt cackled.

Baron swore incredulously. "No way! You're lying. You're lying, you little rat. Don't get my hopes up like that."

The manager took the phone, snapped a picture of Joe's decrepit form, and sent it. The sound of a notification on Baron's end broke a brief lull in the conversation.

He cried, "You're not joking! Do you know how long I've wanted to get a Hate Criminal for one of my films? When can you send him over?"

Rosenblatt clicked his tongue disapprovingly. "Not so fast. Not so fast. There's a price. And I'm charging you more for not believing me."

"Don't jerk me off, Rosenblatt!"

Joe sat back in horror as he wondered what kind of "films" Mr. Baron produced. The two men haggled over his body like jackals scuffling over yesterday's kill. Zeroes and dollar signs flew back and forth with each barrage of offers and counteroffers.

"$10,000. Final offer," Baron contested.

"$19,000. Take it, or I'm calling Aaron Ricketts."

Joe recognized that name after raking his memory. Ricketts was a well-known magnate of the adult film industry. By association, he surmised what Baron's industry must be. Joe's mind was molting as much as his soul through the crucible of that night. Comfortable lies and assumptions fed to him since birth quivered under the weight of new observations.

How did it come to this?! Joe screamed in his mind, wide-eyed in the mirror.

An encroaching tide of accusations flooded in from the impassive reflection behind his captor. His memory tersely answered his question and laid out the charges: Joe bore the mundane horror of the OIHO because it was more convenient than resistance. He let his former neighbors get hauled away in the night because interference meant a break of comfortability. He policed his own mind against hateful thoughts lest he be ostracized. He surrendered his guns because he could not afford to lose his job. He did not oppose the feminization of his church because it was easier to cynically endure it. He accepted the medical products farmed from sacrificed infants because his convictions cowered meekly under the boot of compliance. He did not speak out against the sodomite youth pastor who lured young boys to his home because culture had superseded God in his feeble mind. He let his friends fall into vice and slavery to the flesh because he was scared to lose relationships over confrontation. He let his people be demonized because he still worshiped the individual. Joe's whole life to this point was a series of increasingly ghastly concessions for the transient, volatile, and evaporating prize of being allowed to exist without interference.

But that's not my fault! It's stuff outside of my control! Joe pleaded with his reflection.

The interference would pursue him nonetheless to his next hideout. It would hunt him concession to concession until there was nothing left to feed the beast system. Its lust to devour him would not be satiated with anything less than his immortal soul. Joe's inaction was simply the act of borrowing from his future. He could stave off the negative consequences, if only he stooped lower—and lower he would stoop until the system would bury his suffocating face in the mud.

God, help me please! Joe screamed in his mind.

Blue and red lights flashed in the mirror. They did not pass on as they had done all night but lingered in the parking lot.

"What are they doing?" Rosenblatt flooded with profanities and interrupted Joe's wrestling. "Let me call you back, Mr. Baron. Some idiot cop just pulled up on my land."

Baron sputtered, "Pretty bold guy. Just wait 'til the sheriff hears about this guy interfering with your turf. Call me back, and we'll hash out a better price."

The two shared a hearty laugh and hung up.

Joe sweat profusely as Rosenblatt angrily waited for the policeman to come up to the office. The manager tapped impatiently on the desk until there were three hesitant knocks on the door.

"Mr. Rosenblatt, this is Officer Wallace."

"Oh, it's this square." The manager rolled his eyes. "Come in."

The policeman sheepishly entered the room and quietly shut the door behind him. He was a short man, no more than five foot six, but had sharp and muscular features. He was one of the few White members of law enforcement Joe had ever seen. He got the sense that Wallace had been a worshiper of rules and authority all his life.

"Good evening, sir, my apologies for bursting in."

"Spit it out, Wallace! I had to hang up on Mr. Baron for this little interruption."

"Sir, if you please, this man right here is a wanted Hate Criminal. He killed a police officer," Wallace groveled.

Joe shuddered at the news that he had taken a life. All he knew before this point was that he bit the man's neck.

"So what?" Rosenblatt upturned a palm and contorted his face.

The officer replied, "We need him back at the station to answer a few questions."

"Nope, I got him first. You know the rules. And if it's revenge you want, don't worry. I'll give you a free autographed copy of Mr. Blaine's film debut." Rosenblatt let out a wheezing laugh.

"I know, sir, but we need to find out if anyone helped him forge his documents. Please, let us interrogate him for tonight and then he's all yours."

Rosenblatt leaned back in his chair and considered the proposition.

"Come closer," he said quietly.

Wallace meekly complied and approached the despot. Rosenblatt beckoned him to lean in as if he were about to whisper. With a sudden lurch of his spindly hand, the manager gripped the policeman's neck and hissed, "Just for tonight. He's back here before eight-thirty, sharp. If he doesn't show up, I'll make sure you take his place!" The manager pointed a grubby finger at Wallace's chest after releasing the death grip.

After catching his breath, the policeman stumbled back. "Thank you very much, sir. We really appreciate it."

The cooperation between cop and criminal worked its way through Joe's understanding of the world like an earthquake. He always assumed that the motels and society at large were separate systems, each with their spheres of non-interference. He believed that these local tyrants were nothing more than opportunistic businessmen taking advantage of people down on their luck and nothing more. Rosenblatt's office was the world behind the curtain. This room and millions like it across the country were the engine rooms of erosion. Surface level society, the Equity and Inclusion Act, the motels, the government, the police, the media, and more were all tentacles of the same abomination. These elements appeared separate because the appendages slithered from behind the curtain while belying the common source beyond the veil. The Windview Motel was not separate from the system; it was a mere magnification of it.

The policeman grabbed Joe by the arm and brushed past the twins. The prisoner briefly looked back into the office. The manager smiled while peering under his sloping brow. The whites of his eyes showed under his pupils in a devilish glare. The teen cowered on his stool and seemed sad to see Joe leave. The twins stood blankly, their labored breathing providing the only sound besides the low hum of the fluorescent light. As the door shut behind them, Joe felt the same sensation as when a furnace door blocks the heat from the hellish fires within.

PART II

THE INTERSECTION OF AGONY

II

SELF-HATRED

After Joe was loaded into the back of the squad car, the pair sat without a word as they drove away. The looting had mostly died down, and ambulances played a dirge with their sirens. A few stores stood burning as dark figures danced by the flames. Joe stared at the back of Wallace's head with loathing.

Joe shuddered when he remembered that his father, Robert Blaine, flew a Thin Blue Line flag in the front yard. In truth, he felt a deep sense of detachment from and vague loathing toward his father. He had been a largely useless and weak man. Robert was the dreadful sort to endlessly "wow, just wow" after watching conservative cable news then forget anything that might lead to meaningful action. He was a man of outward cloaks, ever changing with the winds of what was deemed sensible conservatism. In his younger days, Robert bought all the merchandise commensurate with the fandom of center-right media. Any attempt at raising Joe to be a man usually fizzled out in frustration and a retreat to his "man cave." He owned a modest collection of guns but dutifully gave them up because he valued a comfortable retirement. At the very moment his son was being hauled off by the state, Gadsden and Thin Blue Line flags flew side by side in his front yard with the irony being totally lost on him.

As the drive dragged on, Joe noticed they were heading away from the police station downtown. At first, he thought they were headed to a small field office, but Wallace kept going and got on the highway.

He's going to pull off into a field and execute me, Joe impassively thought to himself, *good.*

He welcomed death. The few things that gave him joy were stripped away in one night. Joe hoped for a swift coup de grâce by a vengeful bullet. It would be a merciful end compared to his prospective star role in Mr. Baron's film.

The ride continued for two hours until Wallace stopped the car after pulling off a country road. They sat in silence at the foot of the mountain ranges overlooking MLK Jr. County. Joe's desire for death only grew as his heart fell into a black depression. He prayed that God would forgive him for his lukewarm and insignificant life and reunite him with Jill.

The thought of the man he killed disturbed him, yet Joe was more troubled by something else. No matter how hard he tried, he simply could not feel guilty for it. After years of being guilt-tripped for myriad grievances he had nothing to do with, that part of his brain failed in the same manner an over-torqued bolt shears its head.

Various radio calls squawked in decreasing frequency over the course of the journey until at last there was silence under the mountain. Joe saw that the car's GPS and computer had no signal. They were in one of those ever-vanishing spaces where the acrid, permeating reach of the communication leviathan had not yet trod. They were in a dead zone. The policeman killed the engine, sat for a moment, then put his head in his hands.

"Are you going to kill me?" Joe asked in an apathetic tone after an interminable period of silence.

Wallace stared at the starry night sky through the windshield for several minutes before saying, "No."

The Hate Criminal narrowed his eyes in suspicion.

"I can't do this anymore." The officer sunk in his seat and rolled down the window.

A cool breeze seeped into the squad car from the silent desert night outside. The dry air seemed to constrict around the policeman's neck like a freshly awoken snake.

Wallace rested his head on the steering wheel. "We were listening in on Rosenblatt's phone call for fun," he stumbled through his confession. "The guys at the station were making bets on who he would sell you to!"

Joe was completely taken aback.

The officer continued after a lengthy period of silence, "For what? Just wanting to live in your own house? Is that why you deserve this?

This has been the second PSL I've seen on the force." Memories flashed before his mind. "That officer you killed was a total scumbag! He hated my guts and ratted me out for stopping a woman from getting assaulted yesterday. I was already going to get kicked off the force anyway. I've had it with this!" He tore the inclusion banner patch from his uniform and threw it in the passenger footwell.

Joe wondered how many times the officer debased his conscience before getting to this point. After letting him stew for a minute, he asked, "Why did you ever join? Didn't you know this is what it would be? Didn't you see the other Public Safety Lockdowns?"

"I transferred in from a rural precinct. I did four years over in a small town called Catalina, not far from here. I heard stories about the big cities. . . ."

"But you still went, didn't you? How long have you been with the county sheriff?" Joe interrogated.

He shouted, "It wasn't my choice! I never wanted to transfer, but we got a new mayor in Catalina who started shaking things up. She replaced the chief with a big-city cop and transferred everybody else out to 'gain experience.' I've only been here a year and a half."

"Why didn't you just quit?!" Joe would not relent.

"You don't get it, man. You just don't get it. Cops who leave the force"—Wallace lowered his tone—"cops who look like you and me who leave the force don't last twenty minutes after they turn in their badge."

Joe knew this was the truth.

"My wife left me. She couldn't take life in the city. She took the kids and went to live with her ma. Left a note on the door." Wallace swore. "I've had it with this!"

Neither man spoke for a long time. The squad car's ghostly headlights illuminated the dusty ground under an impressive array of stars. The tension in the vehicle rose to palpable levels. Wallace leaned back in his seat again as he shut off the lights with a deep breath. He put his head in his hands and concealed some tortured sobs.

Joe broke the standoff. "So, what now? You just helped a Hate Criminal. You're a Hate Criminal too now."

"I know, I know." Wallace sat dejectedly. "The number of people I've had to just watch get ripped apart because they were 'privileged'. . . . Something snapped when the other guys were laughing during Rosenblatt's phone call. That woman I saved looked a lot like my sister. And I get boned for it!" He cursed the snitching police officer. "Getting kicked out means getting killed for a guy like me."

Joe wondered what he truly meant by "like me."

Wallace continued, "Look, I'm not racist or anything"—this caused Joe to wince inexplicably—"but people are people. It doesn't matter if they're White or not. I have African-American friends, Hispanic friends, gay friends. I'm not a racist. My wife's Latina. I would've helped that woman whatever color she was. At the end of the day, you've got to look in the mirror and live with yourself," Wallace lamented.

Joe felt a numinous fear. "It mattered what color we were, didn't it?" he asked the officer as much as himself. The sleep deprivation, adrenal fatigue, and grief made Joe's inhibitions porous. He never would have dared to ask such a question the day before.

Wallace became agitated. "And that's the problem, right? The left is so obsessed with race. It literally doesn't matter."

Joe could only half-heartedly agree with Wallace, though just a few hours ago, he would have fully assented. The course of that night destroyed most of what he used to believe. He entered the furnace weighed down by decades of propaganda's slag. Joe had very little in the way of new convictions to replace the gaping holes where societal morality used to be.

"We're wasting time. The dispatcher is probably wondering where I am and why I'm not answering my radio," Wallace cut their discussion short.

"What are you going to do?"

"I'm a dead man if I go back. . . ." He wrestled for several minutes. The full weight of his decisions came crashing down on any stability he had left.

Joe got the sense that Wallace didn't even know what his plan was.

After a considerable amount of teeth grinding, the officer vomited his plan: "I was already going to get killed once they kicked me out." He paused. "I've got a couple changes of clothes in the back. I'm going to try riding rail to where my wife and kid are."

"Riding rail? Is that still possible these days?" Joe never even considered that the watchful state had vulnerabilities.

"You'd be surprised how lax the security is. These trains are ancient, and there's been almost no investment in surveillance for the rail system. Budget cuts and personnel shortages make the trains even more vulnerable. They don't even do a walkaround before they go anymore. When I was still in Catalina, I caught a couple guys riding rail, but I know I didn't find 90 percent of them. It's one of the few ways you can get around the country for free," Wallace relayed with a resigned, distant stare out of the windshield. He closed his eyes and inhaled deeply through his nose. "It's risky, but we're already Hate Criminals after all. Not much to lose."

Joe gathered the courage to ask about his own fate. "What are you going to do with me?"

"I'll set you free, but that's about all I can do. I barely have enough to help myself. I'll give you one of my shirts to replace that mess you've got on."

Joe looked down at the blood stains on his sweatshirt. "Let me come with you, just until we find some trains."

"No, it's risky to travel in groups, and I don't really know you," Wallace stated his objections matter-of-factly.

The prisoner pleaded, "Just until the trains, then we go our separate ways."

Wallace turned fully around to face him. "It's over these mountains here. As the crow flies, maybe five to ten miles, but it's more by foot, of course." He gestured to the looming ramparts beside them. "I've been hiking these mountains since I was little, so I move pretty quick. You won't be able to keep up."

"This is my only chance. I can do it." Joe's voice leapt from his mouth like a fledgling bird plunging from the nest.

The policeman pondered this for a moment. "If you slow me down, I'm leaving you behind."

Joe's animal instinct to survive stated, "Deal."

Wallace exited first, then retrieved his prisoner. After undoing Joe's cuffs, he opened the trunk to retrieve his civilian clothes, a backpack, and a first aid kit. He poured some rubbing alcohol on Joe's throbbing head wound, bandaged it, and gave him a clean shirt. After the pair changed clothes, Wallace used his utility knife to cut off the patch on his backpack that read, "Martin Luther King Jr. County Sheriff's Office / Equity, Justice, Peace / Jerry T. Wallace." He placed it inside the bag along with his uniform. Joe recalled when bands of protestors would chant, "No justice, no peace." Now it was abundantly clear that they desired neither justice nor peace.

"I'm going to shoot my gun inside the car to make it look like we struggled for it," Wallace declared.

Joe objected, "What's the point of that? And how would I make it up there to even reach for it? I don't want any more charges on my head."

"I don't want retribution for my family, and you're a dead man walking anyway if they catch you. An extra charge isn't going to make a difference. It doesn't have to be believable; it just has to take the blame off of me. You're already a wanted cop killer, so it's not implausible that you'd be crafty enough to somehow get my gun and force me to drive out here"—Wallace made firm eye contact—"and I'm the one with the gun, so I make the decisions."

Even in his fugitive status, the officer clung to authority and co-ercion. Joe greatly resented this. The policeman opened the car door and fired two shots toward where the driver would sit. Satisfied with the results, Wallace disturbed the dirt around the vehicle to indicate further struggle. With a brief wince, he cut the palm of his hand and rubbed it on the steering wheel, door handle, driver's seat, and sprinkled some on the ground. Wallace finished the ruse and bandaged his hand.

"Well, you're a real outlaw now. Two cops in one night," he said with a bleak chuckle.

"Aren't they going to notice when the blood trail stops just a few steps from the car?" Joe contested.

"Look, they want your head. The District Attorney and FCIA will jump on this to rack up more charges against you. I have to look out for my family. If they level Hate Charges against me, my family's in big trouble." Wallace rationalized.

Joe relented as he realized his fellow fugitive was overtaken by fear for his family. Wallace was likely to be charged with a Hate Crime anyway for interfering with Rosenblatt.

"Come on, let's get going before sunup," Wallace commanded.

The pair set out toward the mountains. An icy wind swept down from the slopes and retarded their progress in the dark hours before dawn. Joe struggled to keep pace but clung to Wallace's trail like a lifeline. After a period of desperate hiking, Wallace stopped at a small brook to fill his bottle and drink. Joe lagged behind by several minutes but caught up just as the sun began to peak over the mountaintops to the east.

"You've got to keep up, man. We don't have time to lose," Wallace chastised.

"I'm here"—Joe gulped for air—"just keep going."

After taking a swift drink with his hands, Joe caught his breath and looked back at the plains below. He could faintly make out the glint of the police car's windshield. On the western horizon, the city shimmered in the early morning sun, obfuscated by an ethereal layer of mist and smog. A helicopter drummed a swift marching cadence in the distance. Apart from a few columns of billowing smoke, the city appeared peaceful and serene. Joe pondered his former life, which lay as a rotting corpse in the metropolis.

Beyond the glittering skyscrapers, he could see the ocean's mournful horizon melding with the last vestiges of nighttime. Joe stretched his arms in a futile attempt to grasp that night and pull it back. It was Jill's last night on earth, and he could only watch as they both expired. The night before, the sun beat its retreat watching over Joe and Jill in blissful ignorance. As it now rose behind him, only Joe felt its warming rays. He mourned his beautiful Jill, his crushed, flaxen flower left among the refuse of the gutter.

Joe knelt on the mountainside and bowed his head. "Lord, please, just let me go back to the way it was! Work a miracle!" His eyes remained shut for a moment. The sleep deprivation caused him to become dizzy. Breaking the darkness, he lifted his eyes toward heaven and beat with his fists. "Let me do it over. Please, just give me Jill back!" he prayed as Wallace advised him to keep moving.

Joe waited for a minute in feeble anticipation of a divine reset. The clouds sailed above him at a steady, inexorable pace. Billowing and swelling, these aerial glaciers sealed Joe from the heavens as they intercepted crimson rays from the east. A solitary eagle passed over his gaze as his meager faith faltered away.

Joe rose to his feet and wiped the tears from his eyes. The night was a heavy burden on his fatigued, shaking legs. With a shout, Joe picked up a stone and threw it down the slope. The rock gained speed, chipping away at the mountainside in puffs of dust and sand. Gravity commanded the little boulder onward to its uncertain landing below. It made three successively larger leaps then tumbled out of sight forever.

Joe took one final glance at the city. After pointlessly trying to spy his former home, he turned away from Sodom and Gomorrah for the last time. He wondered if he too would be punished for looking back.

12

SWEET ARE THE USES OF ADVERSITY

The subsequent hike passed quickly. The numbness that overtook Joe's soul proliferated to his taxed muscles. The pain of the hike took on a detached character as if he were observing it from above. Wallace pushed ahead at a determined pace, only making brief stops to stretch and catch his breath. It was late morning, and the temperature began to collect its tariff of sweat from the travelers. They surmounted the second rise and walked along a grassy saddle nestled before their next obstacle.

"They've probably found the vehicle by now. There's going to be a helicopter in the air any minute," Wallace relayed grimly.

"Should we try to hide?"

Surveying the surrounding area with his hands on his hips, Wallace lamented, "I haven't found a good spot with some cover. We may have to just huddle in with some of these big boulders and hope they pass over. We should still have some time."

"How much longer until we get to the tracks?" Joe rested his eyes on the next foothill they would have to cross.

"Just over that ridge and then down the slope. Not far at all." Wallace wiped the sweat from his brow.

"Okay, let's keep going."

The fugitives followed the saddle to a dip in the final mountain's profile. A short climb over a steep, twenty-foot slope of loose stones was all that stood between Joe and a glimpse of his ride out of danger. Taking a pause before attacking the treacherous climb, Wallace led the way on all fours over the shifting surface. Several times his feet slid, sending a rain of small rocks on Joe. After a brief apology, Wallace fully extended his arm to reach a handhold above his head. After testing its stability, he began pulling himself upward. He fumbled with his right boot for a complementary foothold. From the underside, Joe could see that the rock Wallace found with his foot was held in place only by a rotted stump.

"Wait!" was all Joe could call out before the rock gave way under Wallace's weight.

Swiftly rolling over, Joe avoided the combined avalanche of rocks and the falling body. Wallace tumbled several more feet and settled next to a dry bush below. After lying motionless for a few seconds, he attempted to sit up. He swore fiercely as a sharp pain shot through his ankle.

"You okay?" Joe could see various cuts and abrasions beginning to bleed.

"Yeah, just a little shaken. My ankle is hurt pretty bad though. I'm going to try to stand up."

After a laborious attempt to stand, Wallace's ankle crumpled underneath him.

He cursed again, then called, "I don't think I can walk."

Carefully picking his way over the slippery rock face, Joe descended the slope to render aid. He considered for a moment whether Wallace would have stopped for him.

"Get the boot off and get the first aid kit out of my backpack."

Joe complied and was further instructed to raise the ankle to prevent swelling and wrap the injury.

"Okay, now go back into the kit and—"

Both men froze. A repetitive, booming sound reverberated through the mountains. Focusing on the injury distracted them from the initial stages of the noise's crescendo. A helicopter's blade shook the peaceful silence of the saddle into a blurry terror.

"Helicopter!" Joe swore and looked frantically for the pursuing bird of prey. "Where is it?!"

"We need to find cover! Over there!" Wallace winced and pointed at a truck-sized boulder with a small overhang about fifty yards from their location. "Don't leave me!" he cried.

In the adrenaline-fueled fear of the moment, Joe could only rely on instinct. Grabbing him under the arms, Joe breathlessly dragged him over to the rock. The fifty yards seemed like a thousand miles under his stress and fatigue. Growing faint, his vision began to cloud and his head bandage began to sag over his eyes. He had neither eaten nor slept for some time now and his strength faded. All the while, the helicopter's advancing beat dictated the tempo of his racing heart.

Wheezing wildly, he collapsed a few feet short of the boulder. Wallace called out in pain with the fall, but realized that they were still exposed. Mustering a burst of fortitude, Wallace lugged Joe along as he slithered on the ground under the rock's slim overhang. Positioning the pair between the boulder and the ridge, they would at least be out of sight in the east-west direction. Joe breathed loudly as he regained control of his body. Wallace instructed him to try to scoop as much dirt and rocks on top of them as possible.

"Now freeze, and don't move!"

The buzzing locust arrived in the saddle between the two foothills. The racket became unbearably loud as it approached close to their position.

"They're going to find us!" Joe panicked and shifted to get up to run.

Wallace slammed his fist into Joe's chest and shouted, "Don't move!"

Luckily, the rock concealed Joe's ill-conceived movement. The fugitives waited in existential dread as the chopper slowed its path to a crawl, its beating blades kicking up clouds of dust. Every time Joe thought the noise couldn't get any louder, the rotor cut through the air like a drumroll for a firing squad at an even greater volume. At last, the two saw it pass overhead. Joe's eyes widened with anxiety as the helicopter began a starboard bank.

"Did they see us?!" Joe bleated in a tortured whisper.

Wallace made no reply and fixed his eyes on the sky above in trepidation. Joe began to pray fervently. His badly battered faith was all that he could cling to.

The helicopter made three turbulent circles over the saddle, then continued south. The searching eyes of the system passed over the fugitives like a demonic glaze, leaving a coating of utter terror. Its clamor followed over the next mountain and declined after an interminable period of waiting. As they lay motionless, Joe noticed the unmistakable smell of urine from Wallace's direction. Neither man spoke for over ten minutes as the threat subsided. The helicopter passed them by for now.

"Thank you, Lord!" Joe breathed aloud.

"Shut up! We're not in the clear yet. They could just be calling in a ground team."

Joe made no reply. Bad news made very little impression on his exhausted mind. Both men lay quietly for a quarter of an hour. As the sun meandered slowly in the sky, their heavy breathing slowed and their hearts calmed. The two were enveloped in the shaky throws of declining adrenaline. It was nearly noon. The temperature rose steadily, but Joe continued to shiver from the fight or flight response.

"So, what now?" Joe asked no one in particular after getting his shaking under control.

"We should stay put at least for the rest of the day. Minimize chances of being spotted. I'm exhausted. We should probably try to get some sleep while we can. Maybe spend the night depending on the moonlight. If it's bright enough, we'll go down this slope at night. I have a flashlight in my pack. I've got to rest this ankle." Wallace winced as he tried to move his foot.

He realized his soiled garments with noticeable embarrassment.

"No judgments here," Joe remarked. "If I had anything in my stomach, it would've been a bad day for both of us."

Wallace let out a hearty chuckle. "If you had done that, I would have just given you up! Put this guy in jail, he crapped on a police officer!"

The unlikely teammates shared a deep, stress releasing laugh. Joe's last smile was with Jill. This thought broke into his mind like a thief, but he smothered it in the name of comfort.

Wallace opened his backpack and pulled out two granola bars.

"Here, eat this. I suppose I owe you one for not leaving me behind."

Joe took the bar ravenously and barely took time to unwrap it. This was the first food he had eaten since early the previous night. The two men shared a paltry meal together under the shade of their protective rock. Their limbs still trembling from the pursuit, a bond formed that can only come about through shared adversity.

"So, do you have a family?" Wallace asked cautiously.

Joe's heart sank again. "I had a wife. She died last night."

His accomplice swore. "I'm sorry to hear that, man. Was it a law enforcement officer?"

"No, some thugs attacked her in the car while they were arresting me. They shot her. Right in front of the cops. They did nothing to stop it."

Wallace waited a respectful amount of time before making his consolatory reply: "I know you probably hate me because I used to wear the badge. But for what it's worth, I think you did the right thing—defending yourself."

"I wasn't even thinking. I was just blinded with animal rage. Compelled by some inner instinct to survive"—Joe made eye contact—"and yeah, I suppose I should hate you. But we're both refuse of the system now."

Wallace curled one side of his mouth in a bleak smile. "Yeah, refuse of the system. Sounds like a trashy metal band you find two-dollar cassettes for at the thrift shop."

"You may have something there. After all of this is over, maybe we can start that up." Joe grinned. "I'll play the triangle."

As the hours passed on and the memory of the helicopter distanced, the conversation ping-ponged between dark humor and the state of the world.

"How did it get to this point?" Wallace lamented.

"I don't claim to know. I honestly feel like a completely different person from the man I was while getting arrested. I think then I would have given a stupid answer like 'Things were always this bad. We just idealize the past.' Now I don't know what to think. It couldn't have always been like this." Joe took brief glimpses at the sun to estimate the time. His lack of sleep started to catch up with him.

"It wasn't. It still isn't in some parts of the country. Catalina was never like that," Wallace declared fervently as if defending his legacy.

"No, I think the rot is everywhere. Just at different stages. MLK Jr. County is a crystal ball for the rest of the country. What happens there is coming everywhere." Joe took a small pebble and tossed it.

Wallace contested, "But there's still the Constitution. Even in DC they have to abide by that. We still have liberties that are respected in the red states."

"The Constitution!" Joe smirked. "Where was that last night?"

"Real America is out there, I know it. One day we'll flip the elections and set the clock back. They've just got to appeal to the new immigrants and their families. They're true conservatives, you know," the former police officer wistfully remarked.

Joe's soul wrinkled under the weight of Wallace's denialism. Even without the full force of knowledge, he knew this was a self-pleasuring fantasy.

Joe charged, "How can you even believe that?"

"Which part?"

"Any of it!" Joe shook his head. "Set the clock back to what?"

Wallace pondered this for a moment. "Conservative values could—"

"Conservative values! What does that even mean?" the Hate Criminal gripped the dirt beneath him.

"I don't know, man. You've got to have hope in something. Things can get better." Wallace retreated.

"I'm not sure how. It got this bad, it can get way worse."

Wallace prodded, "You'll end up as a ceiling ornament with that kind of outlook."

His comrade made a grim reply: "Then I'll dangle without pretense."

The conversation quenched rather quickly after Joe's depressing rhetoric. Wallace suggested they take turns sleeping to prepare for the next leg of the journey. Helios' chariot raced along its path, dropping fiery rays on the men's reddening skin. Their throats ran dry as Wallace's water bottle did the same. Joe's thoughts spiraled into bleak depression in the temporary absence of a threat. It was the first lull in the raging tumult of the previous twenty-hour hours. Without new trauma to smother the old, all Joe could do was meditate on his excruciating loss.

Why even continue? Joe thought to himself. *Why keep running? Where am I running to? I'll just be pursued like an animal for the rest of my nasty, brutish, and short life.*

A grasshopper noisily made its bounding path across the saddle toward the rock. When it came near to the pair, they flinched at the sound because of its vague resemblance to the pursuing blades of the helicopter. The insect landed, leapt, and flew in a methodical tempo until it rested on Joe's hand. The antennae oscillated impatiently over investigating compound eyes.

"Hey, little dude," Joe said softly.

In Joe's mind, the ambivalence of the grasshopper was at least preferable to the abject malevolence of all who pursued him. The impassivity of his insect companion comforted his tormented soul. Joe noticed the serrated tines on the grasshopper's jumping legs.

I wonder if you would try to kill me too? Do you spare me because you are unable to kill me or because you are unwilling? Joe contemplated silently.

The spindly legs of its thorax made small quivers on the sensitive skin on the back of his hand. Making a plodding turn within its own length like a tracked vehicle, the grasshopper directly faced Joe. Spreading its wings, it leapt toward his head and narrowly missed his ear. The insect continued its sojourn across the saddle, onward to a simple life governed by nature's law and its invariable instinct. Joe envied the grasshopper.

"Go on, little dude," he called after it. "I'd fly away too. I am unable, not unwilling."

Struggling to fight the fatigue, Joe plunged into a dark sleep harassed by nightmares and hellish visions.

13

ON THIS SIDE

Night came suddenly in the saddle. The sun sat atop the mountain behind them like a precariously balanced keepsake on a mantle before tumbling down the opposite slope. As it passed behind the rocky crag, a shadow swept the saddle into the darkness of ebbing twilight. The full moon assumed its rulership over the night unfettered by clouds. Joe awoke suddenly to Wallace's shuffling. For a brief, ecstatic moment, the memories of the previous day eluded him. This placid state came crashing down as the fog cleared from his mind.

"How's your ankle?" Joe asked with a parched voice.

"It's pretty sore, but we've got to get moving. That moon is providing a lot of light."

"Won't the outcropping be extra dangerous at night? You took your tumble in broad daylight."

"I was being hasty. We just need to test every hand and foothold before we put our weight on it. The backside of it is pretty gentle and just a bunch of dry bushes," Wallace recalled from his many hiking trips.

"Can you walk?" Joe inquired.

Wallace used the rock to hoist himself up, keeping his injured foot in the air. Cautiously, he let the foot sink to the ground and applied progressive pressure. Grimacing, he limped a few steps.

He declared, "It'll have to do. We don't have any more water and there isn't any until we get to the rail hub."

The men left the safety of the rock and once again made their assault on the outcropping. This time, their attack would be methodical and metered. Wallace again led the way but wiggled each hold before trusting it with his full weight. He avoided using the twisted ankle and largely let it drag behind. Joe crept up the slope in the peculiar, silver light of the moon at a steady pace. After a period of struggle, they reached the crest. Joe contemplatively drew his attention to the moon's radiant surface.

This same moon rose, fell, waxed, and waned throughout all history. Many great and weak men alike had gazed upon this same celestial body and slunk across the same earth. Each man was placed in the same world but bore wildly diverse tribulations with disparate levels of success.

"Keep moving," Wallace chastised his moonstruck companion.

Joe glanced once more at the moon then started the descent down the other side. Weaving their way through a winding path between dry brush and large rocks, the pair alternated between walking and sliding on the loose gravel. Joe could faintly make out the flickering amber lights of a small town.

"Just a mile or two after we get to the bottom, then we'll ride some rail!" Wallace declared joyfully.

"How far do you have to go?" Joe asked as the ground beneath them began to level off.

Wallace's voice took a hopeful ride through the country. "Well, this railhead has three options for the lines that come through here: east, south, and north. Going west would just bring you back to MLK Jr. County. South would spit you out in the desert, or Mexico if you rode it long enough. My family is up on a farm in rural Oregon with her ma, so I'm bound north." He relished the thought for a moment then continued, "Where are you headed?"

Joe paused and contemplated his options. He never thought he would get this far and failed to fully formulate his plan.

"I don't know yet. Maybe I'll just spin a bottle and go where it takes me. My parents are in the Midwest, but I don't want to bring them into this. My dad wouldn't understand why I don't just give myself up," Joe grumbled. "He'd tell me to just trust the justice system."

The plateau stretched before them like a fleece blanket of dry, shrubby grass and gnarled trees. Beyond the plateau, another row of mountains loomed to the east, blocking any chance of an early sunrise.

"I didn't tell you before because I didn't trust you, but the town here with the railhead is my hometown," Wallace intimated, "Catalina."

The name crossed his lips like a gust of wind catching his sails.

"I suspected as much."

Wallace's voice constricted with bitter nostalgia. "My old precinct. More than that—I was born here. I grew up here. The rails are right next to my old high school. My friends and I used to get into a lot of trouble sneaking in there."

After surmounting a small ridge, the pair looked down on a pristine road, laid parallel to the mountains behind them like an asphalt ribbon. The moon continued to provide stark illumination of their surroundings to their adjusted eyes.

"That's State Highway 82. We'll hop across, and then it'll just be a short trip through some soybean fields to the railway."

A lonely sedan passed on the road, oblivious of the wanted fugitives observing its mundane glide through the darkness.

Wallace swore. "I probably know who's driving that car. I wish I could just pop in and see some folks. I haven't been back since I got reassigned. I bet this town hasn't changed a bit."

Wallace's ankle barely hampered his eager progress across Highway 82 and into the fields beyond. Taking swift steps across the pavement, Joe noticed a large billboard next to the road. It read in decorative type, "Visit Beautiful Catalina / Strength and Diversity" set against a scene of the mountains and a smiling, colored spokeswoman. The sky in the picture was replaced with the colors of the Inclusion Banner.

Wallace spied the billboard out of the corner of his eye. At first, his gaze passed on without a second thought, but incongruity with his memory forced him to look again.

"They changed the billboard, I guess," he stated in the same manner as condensed dew falls from a flat surface.

"Probably that new mayor, I imagine," Joe replied.

"It used to be a picture of the founding family of Catalina, the Burds. There was an actual wagon wheel from their wagon hung up there on the board." Wallace lowered his voice into a subdued tone. "I helped hang it on the 150-year anniversary."

"Nothing stays the same when you return to your hometown." Joe recalled the measurable decline of his parent's locale.

Wallace trudged along in silence for several minutes, then uttered fearfully, "I wonder what else is different."

The rail hub sat on the outskirts of Catalina like a cyst. It was connected by a single road, which indicated that many trains came through but few passengers stopped in the small town. It was a liminal space where cargo came to be reloaded and fired in another direction. The pair made a circuitous path just far enough away from the outermost buildings to avoid detection. The moon sank behind a distant mountaintop, and the night blackened considerably. It was a few hours before sunrise, and the sky was at its darkest. Wallace made a dour comment about where his house used to be then led Joe to a small shed outside the fence of the rail station.

"This shed marks the blind spot in the cameras. There's my initials carved in the post."

In the faint glow of a light post, Joe could see several sets of initials scratched into the shed along with crude, carved drawings, presumably of disliked school teachers.

The men clambered over the fence with some minor difficulty. Wallace landed on his ankle and returned to limping after a hushed yelp.

"You alright?"

"Yeah, yeah. Keep quiet. We're almost to my train. The northbound rail is right here." He pointed to a faded, red boxcar twenty yards away. All the train cars invariably had graffiti. This particular compartment read, "Killaz / We On You / ACAB," along with an exaggerated depiction of a phallus.

Joe assisted his stricken companion to the car and hoisted him up.

"You decide where you're going yet?" Wallace grunted breathlessly.

The railyard was completely silent besides the sounds of breathing and fading exertion.

Joe inhaled deeply as if drawing from a cigarette. "I'll head inland—to the east. There's nothing but death for me back in MLK Jr. County. And I don't speak a word of Spanish—and I don't care to."

Wallace gestured over to a dark, natural gas, freight car across the yard. "You see that black one about a hundred yards off? That's on the eastbound track. It goes east for a few dozen miles until it gets around the mountains, then it cuts up north through Nevada, the northwest corner of Utah, and then eastward from there. No telling how long it'll be on this line beyond that."

Its graffiti read, "8th Street Kings / Big Bubba / Sinners in the hands of an angry God / Piss Earth 2025" next to a decorative cross motif followed by a pentagram.

"Utah, huh?" Joe recalled his Uncle Karl who lived an isolated life with his family in the mountains in the northwestern part of the state. "I've got an uncle out there."

Joe had visited once before on his way out to college. He humorously recalled being regaled with wild conspiracy theories about the anti-White agenda, vaccines, globalism, and the elite. Karl was rarely invited to family functions. Joe's skepticism of his claims dwindled rapidly.

The fugitive declared with a sigh, "That's where I'll go."

The men shared a moment of awkward silence where a goodbye ought to have been. Wallace gave some last-minute tips to remain undetected while riding the rail.

"Well, I suppose this is where we part ways." Joe put his hands in his pockets.

"Hey, before you go . . . thanks for not leaving me on that mountainside."

"Just returning the favor. Not every day you jailbreak a Hate Criminal," Joe quipped.

Wallace began to reply but was interrupted by the ear-splitting sound of an electric train horn. His car lurched forward and crept along the tracks like a vast, armored worm. Joe backed away quickly to avoid being caught in the tracks.

As he pulled away, Wallace's state-issued conscience pounced from his inner core and gripped his speech. "May God forgive us both for everything we've done."

The wheels made a tremendous racket in the early morning blackness. The locomotive gradually took in the slack of its line of cars, and the whole apparatus chugged away.

"Forgive us for what?" he called after his comrade defiantly. "Do you really think we're the ones in the wrong here?"

Wallace's face dropped, but he pursed his lips and nodded. "I guess that's between you and the Big Man. Don't get caught! Good luck! I just—"

The last part of Wallace's epilogue drowned out under the grinding of metal on the tracks. The train picked up speed and left the rail hub with the fugitive ex-policeman in tow. Joe watched with mixed emotions as the man faded away and gave a curt wave in the darkness. On the one hand, he was grateful for his rescue; on the other hand, he detested the fact that Wallace had helped the system this long.

Joe was alone for the first time since his series of disasters unfolded. He took a deep breath of the fresh air in through his nose and out his mouth. His eyes drifted skyward to the star-scattered canopy above him. Orion's imposing form looked down upon Joe in stern guidance. The great celestial warrior's stance commanded him to be strong or die.

Sauntering to the eastbound train, his shoes crunched over broken glass under a hanging light next to his train car. As he looked down at the shards, the reflection demanded Joe's attention. Menacing and convicted, his face took on distorted shapes in the array of reflections. Joe's eyes fled between each iteration in the spread of glass, seeking refuge. His counterpart matched each glance and redeployed with furious speed to stay in Joe's view. Finally, Joe surrendered his awareness to a triangular fragment resting at an oblique angle on the supporting post of the light. Disregarding the need to get out of sight quickly, Joe squatted to gain a full audience.

Shadows and the cloudiness of the glass marred his face. He appeared troubled, yet assured of his purpose and guiding principle. This starkly contrasted the listless fugitive staring at the glass. He widened his eyes slightly as if to communicate a matter of dire importance. As Joe turned somewhat to look at the gash in his scalp, the reflection turned to show his wound as well. The bandage Wallace gave him had long fallen away under the commotion of their flight. His hair was matted and greasy with dried blood, dirt, and sweat. Nearly luminescent, green eyes peered under an entrancing frown. Joe resented him. He wished his counterpart could just tell him what to do next. While he seemed to have all the answers and guidance needed for the road ahead, Joe knew all he could receive was a damning look in the event of a wrong decision.

"It isn't so easy on this side." Joe took the shard and impudently tossed it away.

He surrendered himself to the slings and arrows of outrageous fortune, climbed into the freight car, and fell limp. Joe contemplated whether indeed there were men created to be vessels of wrath. All he could do was close his eyes and acquiesce to the providence that forced him onward. Burning, aching, parching, twisting, freezing, thawing, he floated down the current of life's raging river northeast to the mountains of Utah.

14

SEAN McDOWELL

"McDowell!" a shrill, angry voice ripped through the Federal Consolidated Investigation Authority (FCIA) headquarters in Northern
Virginia. "Get in here!"

Sean McDowell flinched at the sound of his supervisor's abrasive
castigation. Pulling his ID card from his computer, the investigator
made his way to the corner office. Danny Chen gave him a sly smirk
as he passed.

Sean was a man of immense ambition. A seven-year veteran of
the alphabet agencies, he was the first in line to join the newly-
formed FCIA after the merging of all the major federal law enforcement entities. Standing at about six foot one with sable hair looming
over deep, blue eyes, Investigator McDowell made a striking impression whenever he entered the room. He was the first of his family to
go to a college that anyone's heard of and break into the prestigious
federal services.

Sean's father, William McDowell II, was a lowly administrator
deep in the bowels of the Illinois Capitol Building in Springfield. His
grandfather, William McDowell I, made Pontiacs on a Detroit assembly line. Sean was the oldest of three children. His sister followed
their father into the Illinois state bureaucracy. His younger brother,
the middle child, was swept away by the flooding tsunami of opioids
gutting the American interior. Sean deeply resented his younger
brother for inheriting the family name William. He held onto this ill
will all the way until William III's untimely death by overdose at the
ripe age of twenty-one, only a few months ago. Sean envied his

brother for his name and felt that he had always been passed over in attention and favor. He mourned his lost sibling but concealed a sense of relief at no longer having the shame of a druggie brother.

After years of slaving away and kissing the right fannies, Sean McDowell finally escaped his provincial origins. He married a silver-spooned daughter of a beltway aristocrat to cement his upward rise. The fact that she refused to take his last name miffed him at first, but he ultimately understood not wanting to adopt such a plebeian moniker. Her stated reason was not wanting to lose name recognition for her legal practice, but Sean knew the real motivation. As with all things in his life, this was a measure of pragmatism. Everything was calculated for the benefit of his career. Sean's marriage and four-year-old daughter were on the utter periphery of his daily considerations. One of the few White investigators on the force, he overcame dozens of cullings and purges by toeing the party line, venerating the necessary figures, and being utterly outstanding at his job—in that order.

Abigail Feldman, his supervisor, impatiently awaited Sean's entrance to the office.

"Close the door and sit down," Feldman instructed roughly.

Sean complied and settled into the plush, leather bench in front of the desk.

"If this is about that Blaine guy, don't worry, I'm already on it. I'm on a flight to MLK Jr. tonight at seven." The investigator attempted to anticipate his boss's demands.

Feldman waited for him to finish. "You're behind on your DTTF reports."

Sean detested these bureaucratic busy work tasks. All he wanted was to be in the field catching criminals.

"Yes, ma'am, I'll get on it," he said as he attempted to leave.

"Not so fast, Sean," Feldman called out. "What does DTTF stand for?"

The investigator had to restrain himself from rolling his eyes. "Domestic Terrorism Task Force."

She crossed her fingers on the desk and lowered her voice. "Does that sound like something you can just blow off?"

In reality, Sean thought it absolutely could be blown off. The DTTF reports consisted of scrubbing the crime stats of any "inequitable results" and compiling this information into a cookie-cutter slideshow for public release.

"No, ma'am, I recognize that it's very important." He was well-versed in the art of schmoozing. "I just needed to take a second look to make sure I got the numbers right."

Feldman seemed to know that this latter detail was false but continued anyway, "Just get it done, McDowell. I don't want excuses, and I don't want to have this conversation again. All of your DTTF reports need to be in to me no later than close of business today or I'm reassigning you off the Blaine case. I'll give it straight to Chen."

"I'll get that done right away," Sean kowtowed as he got up to leave.

As he exited the office, Jameila Agdal gave him a coy smile. She was his assigned partner for the Blaine case and his office crush. Sean, no slouch in reading people, knew she was interested in him. He restrained his carnal urges not out of respect for his wife but rather to protect his career from violations of FCIA in-office dating policies.

"Better get those DTTF reports done before we leave tonight," Jameila said as her olive complexion peaked above the wall of her cubicle.

Sean chuckled flirtatiously, "How about you do it for me and I just go?"

She stood up fully and put her hands on her hips in a playful scowl. "And let you get all the glory for catching Blaine? We both know I'm getting Feldman's job when she transfers, but I can't let you pad your resume too much."

Sean desperately wanted Feldman's job and still held on to the slight chance he could get it. Given Joe Blaine's high profile, the investigator who bagged him would be well-positioned for the promotion when Feldman transferred in six months, but even in all his denialism, he knew the demographic cards were stacked against him.

"Keep dreaming. And you know that Chen's in the running too. I practically had to trip him with my foot to nab this case." Sean shook his head and started walking back to his desk. "Some of us actually have work to do."

Jameila exited her cubicle to walk with him. "Hey, wait up! Did you finish reading the profile of this Joe Blaine guy?"

Sean nodded. "Yeah, he reminds me a lot of a case I had when I was at the Los Angeles office"—his memory reached back into his decorated career—"that Travis Maury guy from April 19th."

They arrived at his desk as she interjected, "He got denied his housing voucher too, right? Except this one seems a little more dangerous. He took down like three cops at once."

"I wouldn't be too worried." Investigator McDowell stretched his arms behind his head. "These guys have a way of getting caught up in their plans for payback. They always go back for revenge."

15

YOU MAY JUST GET THE CHANCE

The train pulled into a Utah railhead after a day and a half of travel. Each stop along the line brought another chance for capture, but Joe held out for the mountains after he saw a sign that read "Utah." He knew his uncle's place was about an hour or so from the border with Nevada by car. If he jumped too early, he could be dozens of miles from his destination. However, Joe had had enough of his bone-rattling transportation and decided to take his chances. His body was stiff as a board after weathering the frozen mountaintops and scorching deserts. Multiple times, he felt tempted to cast himself under the wheels of the train and end his suffering. Unable to follow through, he cruised at the intersection of agony and death without ever crossing over to a sweet release.

After the trek, his hands throbbed from both frostbite and sunburn. Toward the end of the excruciating ride, Joe managed to eke out some fitful rest pockmarked by disturbing visions. During one such dream, he jolted awake as the train's brakes locked on the track. He awoke from his slumber feeling numb from head to toe. He laid motionless, unable to move, until he gradually regained feeling in the same way a limb without circulation returns to one's control. Pins and needles cascaded down his body like a waterfall. After a period of adjustment, he was again in control of his body. He watched the serene mountain scenery pass by as the train grounded to a halt. A chill could be felt in the air as the elevation climbed. Joe's soul felt heavy in his chest after waking from the dream.

What puzzled him the most was that it did not seem like he had awoken at all. To his mind, either he was still dreaming or the nightmare was quite real. There was no break in consciousness between the end of the dream and re-entering his body. Uncomfortable with the implications of either possibility, Joe tried to stop thinking about his visions. After some screeching and scraping, the behemoth came to rest in the yard. Joe remembered the advice Wallace gave him to leave the rail yard as soon as possible. Soon, inspectors would come to check the cargo, and the train would change crews. Wallace told him that if he did not jump the train immediately, he stood a very high chance of being caught.

Having ignored this advice for the previous stops, holding out hope that he could get as close as possible to his uncle, Joe was somehow lucky enough to have chosen a car that remained empty for that leg of rail and so went undetected. Now, though, he heeded Wallace's admonition. When the train stopped its forward momentum, he leapt from the car and ran toward the fence, though he tripped as his malnourished legs buckled beneath him. Regaining his footing, he stumbled to the perimeter of the railyard. More mountains stood imposingly around his locale. Barely able to vault the chain link barrier, Joe knocked the wind out of himself with his graceless landing. Struggling onward, he noticed that this side of the rail hub was in the midst of a small town. Looking at his immediate surroundings, he spied a gas station, a small general store, and some mobile homes. His eyes fearfully flitted to and fro and failed to notice a young girl about twenty yards away next to a trailer home.

"Hi!" the little one called out.

Joe started and his heart raced. Any human contact put a deep fear of capture in him. He wheeled around to face the girl. She was about six years old with childish, blonde curls bouncing happily on her shoulders. Her big, blue eyes carried the unknowing burden of unpolluted innocence. Joe let his guard down momentarily and was able to crack a nearly undetectable smile.

"H—Hi," Joe mustered with a cautious wave.

She smiled and grabbed a few gummy bears from a plastic bag. "What's your name? My name's Felicity."

"My name's . . ."—Joe hesitated—"Jimmy."

"Hi, Jimmy, do you want some gummy bears? Your head looks like it hurts." Felicity extended her hand.

"No, thank you for offering." Joe's heart softened. "What town is this?"

She looked upward trying to remember. "I think it's called La—Lafayt . . . um Laf—" she stumbled with her words.

Joe felt his heart jump with vague realization. "Lafayette? Lafayette, Utah?"

Felicity's eyes brightened. "Yeah! My mommy keeps trying to get me to say it right."

A gruff voice from inside the trailer broke the conversation with a tirade of curses. "Who you talkin' to out there?!"

Joe scrambled and took off down the street. Looking back briefly, he noticed a dark, obese monstrosity stumble out of the screen door and grab Felicity by the hair. He dragged the screaming girl up the stairs of the trailer's porch and looked down the street at Joe. His eyes were blacker than night below a nappy and unkempt afro. Nothing but pure, animalistic malice lay behind the dark man's eyes. The last thing Joe saw before rounding a corner was a shrewish White woman coming out of the home and begging him to be gentler with the girl. Joe turned his head and kept running through the town in the mountain afternoon.

There were few people out and about in Lafayette, save for a few ranchers making their weekly town runs. A piano playing off-tune hymns in the church he passed revealed that it was Sunday, just before service would finish. Slowing to a walk to appear less suspicious, he thanked God that this town hadn't advanced much in the past several decades. It was doubtful to Joe that the surveillance state had much proliferation in this community other than a few cameras at the gas stations.

As he caught his breath, he repeated to himself, "Lafayette."

He combed his memory for a match. He walked by a small general store with a filthy sign that read, "Dylan's Food Store / Proudly Serving the communities of Wetumpka, Four-Sleep, Jefferson, and Lafayette since 1999."

"That's it!" Joe had to suppress his volume with the realization.

Wetumpka was a small mining community high in the Utah mountains serviced only by a singular gravel road. At the edge of Wetumpka, a small trail wound its way further to a modest ranch where a certain Karl Blaine homesteaded with his family. Joe's mind flooded with the memories of coming to that ranch as an eighteen-year-old kid on his way out to college, what felt like centuries ago. Lafayette occupied a miniscule portion of his recollection of the trip when Karl brought him along to buy supplies. Joe was stunned that he recalled the name of a town visited for provisions years ago. Nevertheless, he couldn't remember how to get up to Wetumpka's high plateau.

Even if I knew the way, I'd never find Uncle Karl's ranch, he lamented.

Walking further, Joe seemed to find Lafayette's main drag. The Victorian- and federal-style buildings harkened back to a simpler time. The cold moisture of the wind chilled him slightly, but he felt refreshed by the crisp mountain air. A grassy square opened up along the main street with a sign indicating the name "Carson Park." A crudely-cast bronze statue of a pioneer stood on a limestone platform near a stagnant fountain.

Joe walked swiftly to the fountain and sucked in the alkaline water in the basin. Normally he would've gagged at the taste, but repeated sorties just short of eternity removed any further inhibitions toward survival. He splashed the water over his head and watched brown streams of muck flow into the basin. A wizened, old man sitting on a park bench peered judgmentally at the wretched husk watering himself at the fountain.

"Just what do you think you're doin', son?" he croaked.

Joe looked up at him with stale water still dripping from his cracked lower lip. He spied a wrinkled geriatric with sunken, blue eyes. His calloused and marred hands rested on a cane with four legs at the bottom. An oxygen tank knelt beside him like a faithful metal dog, while clear, vinyl tubing lay delicately under his sagging nose. Joe feared being turned over to the law, but figured it was best to not run off and elicit further suspicion.

He tried to put on an innocent face. "Just getting a drink of water."

The old man leaned forward on the bench and put his hands on his knees. "You oughta have a little more shame than that." He wheezed for air. "When I grew up here, you'd be hauled off to jail for acting like a drunk! Ever since Ingersoll became governor, this whole state's gone down the toilet."

Joe replied, "Not drunk, just a little down on my luck."

The elder reclined once more and narrowed his eyes. "Are you from around here?"

"No, just passing through."

The interrogator creaked, "Where're you headed?"

Joe calculated his reply. "Wetumpka."

"Ain't no mines up there anymore if you're goin' up for work," the old man sullenly replied. "It was a ghost town last time I drove up there. I s'pose it was two years ago, before I had to lug this lousy thing around." He swatted the oxygen tank with a fragile hand.

The fugitive sat on the edge of the fountain. "Well, that's where I'm headed. Can you tell me how to get there?"

"Just look it up! You can't be that useless."

For a brief second, Joe instinctually reached for his absent phone. "I lost my phone on my way over here."

The old man swore. "You are useless! C'mon over here. I guess I feel sorry for ya."

Joe cautiously made his way over to the decrepit figure on the bench. His joints ached in the humidity, and he felt a humorous comradeship of infirmity with the old man. Slumping next to him, Joe braced for whatever chiding was next.

"Take one." A wrinkled hand extended a cigarette.

Figuring he would most likely be dead before the old man, Joe took it and placed it in his mouth. His new acquaintance offered a lighter. After taking a swift drag, Joe thanked him.

"Don't thank a man for something you could've easily taken from him." He drew a cigarette for himself. "The name's Ricky."

"Joe." He felt no compulsion to conceal himself from this lonely elder.

The two men sat and smoked for a few minutes in silence. Ricky's hands trembled terribly. Each pull sanded his life down ever so slightly, leaving ash in place of sawdust and perhaps the only trace that he ever existed.

"I grew up in this town," Ricky recounted. "Left for the Gulf War and then never left again."

"Yeah?" Joe looked out on the small town cloaked in a dewy haze.

The pair looked out on Main Street, letting out transient clouds and puffing again. A few townspeople made their way slowly to and fro without paying the men much attention. Joe felt astounded at how confidently they strode, not looking over their shoulder constantly as one had to do in the city. Their pace was untroubled and plodding without a worry on earth.

The old man wheeled toward Joe like a container ship making a lumbering turn in a narrow channel. "You've got the look, ya know."

"What look is that?" Joe felt found out.

"You're a killer," Ricky intimated without judgment, "but you look a little young to have been in the sandbox. You a veteran?"

"No, not a veteran." Joe struggled to formulate a response. "Had to kill a guy who killed my wife."

Ricky swore. "Killing—their faces stick with ya for the rest of your life."

Joe had barely been able to see the face of the police officer he killed. His memory called up writhing images of a fear-stricken man painted with red and blue flashes in the night. Joe remembered vividly the taste of hot blood dripping from his mouth and the sinewy flesh he tore from the man's neck. This was the first time he had truly taken time to reflect on his killing and felt like an utterly depraved savage.

"They sure do," Joe took another drag.

"You serve time for it?"

Joe rested his back on the bench. "No, saved from that by an act of God."

Ricky let out a wheeze that Joe presumed was supposed to be a laugh. "God! God, he says. You still believe in that?"

Joe questioned himself for a moment. "I'm not sure. But something up there wanted me to go free. Although maybe it was so I could be preserved for a worse torment."

"Life's hard, and then ya die." Ricky wheezed once more. "I've seen too much to believe in God."

Joe used to be able to contend such objections but could only doggedly ward off his own. He finished up his cigarette and snuffed out the butt on the ground next to the bench. "And you haven't even seen the big cities. Stuff you wouldn't believe if I told you."

Ricky leaned forward in curiosity. "Is it as bad for White guys as they say it is?"

"Worse. So much worse." Joe stared blankly. "I guarantee you haven't heard half of it."

"Well, there's none of that here," the old man swore righteously, "and I'd be the first to burn any Inclusion Banner they hang in my town."

Joe turned toward Ricky swiftly. His eyes widened slightly, and the apocalypse overtook his voice. In an eschatological whisper, Joe slipped, "You may just get the chance."

Both men felt a numinous chill as the wind picked up and swept down the mountainside into the little town of Lafayette.

"You better not bring that here." Ricky lowered his voice and tried to keep his fear at bay.

Joe let his eyes drift skyward. "I won't—but it seems to follow me wherever I go. Wherever I flee, there it rears its ugly head."

Ricky became visibly uncomfortable and feebly lit a second cigarette. His insulated, small-town life quivered like a linen garment on a clothesline. He felt a deep, existential need to get this traveler out of his town as fast as possible lest he bring the plague with him.

"Where did you say you were going? Wetumpka?" The old man shivered.

Joe stood up and brushed himself off. "Yeah, I suppose."

"I'll drive ya there," Ricky hastily spewed.

"Can you still drive?"

The wizened figure contorted himself upright off the bench and declared, "I drove an Abrams tank at Medina Ridge, I can hoof it to Wetumpka."

Joe offered his arm in support, but Ricky slapped it away viciously. The men hobbled slowly across the park with the only sounds being the rolling wheels of the oxygen tank and Ricky's labored breathing. It seemed like they were some of the only souls out in the town, as the previous activity seemingly vanished. Doors were bolted shut and windows shuttered. Joe felt the temperature drop slightly as the pair slumped their way through town.

Eventually, they arrived at a run-down, yellow house with an ancient pickup truck beside it. Joe surmised that Ricky had bought the truck brand new when he returned from the war. It was an early-nineties, domestic model with faded and chipping red paint. An equally faded sticker on the back bore the insignia of the 1st Armored Division and read, "Old Ironsides."

"Alright, get in," Ricky spit.

Joe complied and vaulted himself up into the cab. He was greeted by a torn, vinyl bench seat and the peculiar mixed smells of air freshener and stale cigarettes. A pair of dog tags hung on the rearview mirror. To Joe's surprise, Ricky steadily made his way onto the seat and wormed himself up from the ground. With titanic effort, he lifted the oxygen tank and placed it beside him.

The old tanker took a deep, gurgling breath and reached for his keys. "Alright, you son of a—"

He turned the ignition and the crusty engine turned over sluggishly in the same way the old man lifted himself into the cab. A small pop from under the hood indicated ignition and fuel. The engine continued to labor for several seconds until at last it fired up.

"Let's get you outta here." Ricky let on more fear than he intended.

Joe felt numb to his newfound untouchable status. He felt a dragging chain around his neck tethered to the ghastly beast that pursued him. As the old man shifted the truck into drive, he looked back at the little town of Lafayette and prayed that his visit had not marked it for destruction.

16

REFUGE IN THE MOUNTAINS

After a series of perilous near misses, losses of traction, botched turns, and divine interventions, Ricky hastily amputated Joe's presence from his beloved town. The drive up to Wetumpka took roughly an hour. Taking the main road out of the city, he headed north until diverging toward an unkempt gravel road. Sage grass was just beginning to push aside the small stones and would eventually obfuscate its existence entirely. After a few more nerve-racking switchbacks and a swift rise in elevation, the aching brakes let out a yelp. The settlement didn't even have a sign marking its presence. There was an abandoned gas station with the price numbers missing and a former bed and breakfast. Two more defunct buildings stood with the logo of Mountain State Mines.

"See? Nobody here," Ricky stated abrasively, "not even a sign saying it's Wetumpka anymore. I'm one of the few who even knows."

Joe's eyes frantically searched for the presence of the trail leading to his uncle's.

The truck grinded to a stop after a brief lockup of the brakes on the loose gravel.

The old man grunted, "Alright, git."

Joe slid down from the high seat and looked back at the man. "Thanks for the ride."

Ricky frowned. "What did I say about thanking me? And I don't want you anywhere near my town. There's a curse on you. I can feel it."

The old man slumped over and closed the creaky door himself.

Spinning the tires, he reversed the truck and shakily headed back down the mountain. Joe watched impassively as the taillights disappeared down the steep, gravel road. He wondered briefly if Ricky would make it safely.

"Yeah, yeah, Abrams at Medina Ridge," Joe could almost hear the aged veteran call out from the cab.

Taking a moment to absorb his surroundings, Joe shuffled along the gravel road. His stomach ached bitterly with hunger. Austere pine trees crowded in and surrounded the settlement of Wetumpka. Joe closed his eyes and tried to remember coming there all those years ago. He vaguely remembered filling up with gas at the now-abandoned station and scowling at the high price. Joe recalled having to park next to the mine headquarters and his uncle coming in on an ATV.

Retracing his steps, Joe broke the silence of the mountains with the crunching of his feet. Standing beside the defunct Mountain State Mines building, he peered inside a broken window. A dusty metal desk sat dented and mangled in the corner amid a pile of trash. Graffiti marred the inside of the building, and dozens of empty beer cans marked where some small-town burnouts had staged a party. A superfluous "No Trespassing" sign laid derelict on the floor.

Suddenly, a two-stroke engine barked to life. Joe whipped around to find the source. A young boy wearing a camouflage jacket and helmet sped away on a small dirt bike. Joe had no idea he was even there. Taking off running toward the bike, he called out for the boy to stop. The boy continued to ride away as the tinny sound of the engine echoed through the mountains. The dirt bike escaped Joe's sight as it wound its way down a nearly imperceptible trail.

He breathlessly stopped running and rested his hands on his knees. Upon closer inspection of the ground beneath him, the fugitive noticed a series of dirt bike and ATV tracks leading around a bend in the mountainous terrain.

"I don't know if it's the right one, but it's got to lead somewhere." Joe questioned whether this was sound reasoning but pressed on nonetheless.

The mountains fell silent as the sound of the dirt bike faded away completely. The Hate Criminal trudged along feeling protected from state observation by the high mountain walls. He was weak from hunger and had to stop to rest in the high elevation. The sun chafed his aching skin rapidly despite the temperature being a balmy 65 degrees. Joe knelt beneath the pine trees, and dizziness overtook him.

After steadying himself on a nearby rock, he rounded the bend in the trail. This leg stretched for perhaps 100 yards before making another bend. Joe gazed along the straight and could vaguely see the boy next to his dirt bike amid shrubby grass far along the trail. The engine again came to life, and the boy sped off like a rabbit.

"I'm not going to hurt you!" Joe yelled.

His strength ebbed rapidly, and he stumbled from dehydration, malnutrition, stress, fatigue, and altitude. Joe's head grew leaden and forced him into an awkward run as it leaned forward. Tripping over a small stone, Joe was dealt painful abrasions all over his body by the ground. He managed to put out a hand to brace the fall but only succeeded in getting a palmful of needles from a pear cactus. Rolling over miserably, Joe looked up into the radiant sky as darkness clouded his vision.

He regained a modicum of consciousness as he was uncomfortably jostled and lifted onto a cold, metal rack. A blurry figure tied him down with bungee cords. The unknown man shook Joe to make sure he was secure. Satisfied with his work, the dark silhouette started an engine, which rumbled beneath him. He understood in his foggy state that he was strapped to some kind of vehicle. The blurry figure sped away with the saggy lump in tow. Joe's vision again went dark.

◘

His eyelids slowly lifted in his new locale. He found himself in a quilted bed in a small, wood-paneled room. A cloudy window let in the last traces of daylight from a dying sunset next to a cross hung on the wall. Looking down at his chest, he saw that he was wearing fresh, albeit ill-fitting clothes. His head was bandaged, and his hand was free of cactus needles. There was a glass of water, covered in condensate, on the knobby, wooden nightstand beside him. Joe chugged the water greedily and slumped back in the bed. The mahogany-colored door at the opposite end of the room cracked open. A little girl peaked her blonde head inside and immediately retracted with a gasp.

A motherly voice called out, "Alexandria Blaine, get out of there and let him rest!"

"Mommy, he's awake!" the girl cried and ran off.

Joe heard some shuffling outside of the door and a chair creaking.

The feminine voice called to another, "He's awake."

Several sets of steps moved toward the door. The hinges sung softly as a man wearing a thick, flannel shirt entered the room. He stood roughly over six feet tall with skin made ruddy by hours of labor under the sun. His dark-blond hair stood atop deep furrows on his forehead. Grave eyes the color of the cloudy Atlantic punctuated the man's face and gave the sense he carried some inarticulable burden.

"Joseph Blaine!" he shouted with a jovial smile.

Joe sat back in a daze. "Uncle Karl?"

Karl clapped his hands and approached the bed.

He sat next to Joe on the bed with a concerned look. "Are you doing alright? My son George said some creep was trying to follow him home. I came out there with a shotgun and everything! You look pretty rough."

Joe's mind continued to swim under the shock of ending up at his intended destination, and the lack of nourishment. "I—I'm doing okay."

"Eva, can you bring the soup in here please?" Karl raised his voice.

A few seconds later, a graceful woman entered the room with a dutiful smile. She wore an apron and a bandana on her head of shining, brown hair. Her beautiful, blue eyes shimmered like a brimming cup of goodwill. Yet beneath the charity, the same fear that struck Ricky shot through her otherwise sunny disposition.

Placing a bowl of broth in Joe's hand, she warned, "Drink it slowly, now. When was the last time you had some food?"

Joe replied in truth, "I don't know."

The couple exchanged concerned looks as he took his first sips. Hunger overcame him, and he began to slurp down the hot liquid.

"Take it easy now, Joseph," his uncle admonished.

Joe relented and placed the bowl on the nightstand next to the empty cup of water. His aunt and uncle took on an otherworldly character to him. Their assuredness of their identity and place in the world blasted his rootlessness. He couldn't stop looking at their eyes. The vibrant life contained within them reminded Joe of another set of eyes, which hunted him in panes of glass and polished surfaces.

Karl noticed the empty vessel. "Get him some more water, honey."

Eva left the room and closed the door softly behind her.

The uncle crossed his arms and furrowed his brow. "I understand if you're too weak, but do your best and try to explain how you wound up like this. Don't you know all you had to do was send me an email and I would've picked you up in Salt Lake?"

Joe looked out the window just as it began to get dark. "It wouldn't have been so simple. Things have gotten pretty out of hand for me. It's not safe for me to be here with you. I really shouldn't be here. I'm so sorry. It's too dangerous for me to be here with you. I don't know why I thought this was a good idea!"

Before Joe could fully sit up, Karl gently pushed him back down. "Wait just a minute. What's going on?"

Eva reentered the room and placed a glass of water in Joe's hand.

He took it, drank swiftly, and sat back. "I'm a wanted man! Please, just take me out somewhere and leave me. It's too dangerous to have me here."

His aunt gave a look of anxiety to Karl, who motioned her to leave the room.

After the door closed, Karl lowered his voice. "Hold your horses. Now, just what kind of trouble are you in?"

Joe took a deep breath and began to recount his tale from the point of waiting in line for the OIHO. He conspicuously left out the details about his stalking companion in the mirror. Some of the concepts were familiar to Karl, while others shocked him and had to be explained.

"Interview sheets, seriously?" he exclaimed incredulously.

Joe continued his account and began to well up at the point of forging the signatures.

Karl comforted, "It's okay, I would've done the same thing. You were just looking out for your family."

His nephew shook his head with angry tears in his eyes. "Just wait and hear the rest."

The story lumbered onward to the search, interrupted by Joe needing to wipe his eyes or take a drink of water.

"You gave up the gun from my dad?" Karl inserted abrasively.

Joe lashed out, "What was I supposed to do? The Equity and Inclusion Act actually gets enforced if you don't live in the middle of nowhere."

The uncle inhaled as if to argue further, but held his tongue. As Joe neared the point of Jill's death in his tale, his heart gradually sank in step with the story into despair. His mind tumbled through the trauma, dashing through each memory as if they were fragile leaves barely impeding a rock falling from a cliffside. After the great plunge, his conscience settled once more into a monotonous and bleak desolation.

"And then they shot her while I was being held down. . . ." He sobbed uncontrollably.

Karl leaned forward, put his hand on Joe's shoulder, and bowed his head, seemingly in prayer. "Lord, have mercy!"

"I was overtaken by rage! I killed one of the police officers and escaped. I don't even know why I ran. I just want to die!" Joe cried out in turmoil.

His uncle placed the other hand on his shoulder and gripped him firmly. "Take it easy, take it easy! You're safe now."

Joe continued to weep for a minute, then settled into the rest of the story as he trembled. Recounting the horrors of Rosenblatt's motel, he skipped over as much detail as possible. He couldn't bear to relive it, even in memory. Finally, he explained his rescue at the hands of Wallace and their daring escape on the trains.

"And that's how I ended up here, a wanted Hate Criminal and murderer. Now, I really should be going. I'm very sorry for endangering you and your family." Joe again tried to sit up.

Karl refused a second time. "Don't be rude to your hosts. I'm very confident you made it here undetected. The ATF would've already shot my dog at this point, if they knew you were here"—he laughed—"but in all seriousness, you've been through a lot these past couple of days. At least stay here a few days to recoup your strength."

Joe slumped into the bed and placed his hand on his aching head. "Only for a couple of days, and then I'm out of your hair."

"Stay and rest as long as you need. Just holler if you need something. You should probably try to get some more sleep," Karl said softly as he rose from Joe's bedside and exited the room.

Joe could hear the soft mumbling of voices in the other room and could only wonder what was being discussed. He heard bits and pieces of his story being retold to Eva, who greeted each wave of bad news with grieving sighs.

He heard muffled snippets in the same way a child listens in on his parents discussing a matter of grave importance. "Oh, poor thing.... Can we really...? Is he...? What will...? Joseph.... Yeah, I know ... but also ... the sheriff."

Feeling too weak to stay awake, Joe once again drifted into fevered, nightmarish sleep.

17

THE FRYER

"So, you're telling me that this desk jockey tech worker single-handedly broke free from three officers, killed one, evaded detection, then overpowered a fourth cop?" Sean asked the MLK Jr. County Sheriff. "No way! This guy had help."

Sheriff Li Yu put his hands on his desk angrily. "That's what the facts say. These White supremacist terrorists are killers! You know, his uncle is on the DTTF watchlist."

Sean gave an incredulous look to his partner. "Let me level with you, Sheriff. You're starting to believe the propaganda a little too much. There's just no way he did this alone, and his uncle hasn't popped his head up in a decade. We quite frankly don't even know where he is." He paused in confusion. "Why did this Wallace guy even turn up to catch him?"

"Well," the city cop began, "he was facing disciplinary action. Maybe he just wanted to redeem himself."

"What kind of disciplinary action?" Jameila piped up.

Yu shifted uncomfortably. "He made some . . . inequitable choices."

"You can drop the media facade. What did he do?" Sean pressed.

The sheriff winced slightly at speaking forthrightly. "There was a White woman who . . . was being forced to give reparations . . . and Wallace stepped in."

Sean gave a look to Jameila and muttered, "White supremacist sympathetic tendencies." After thinking for a moment, he continued, "Was he supposed to be out patrolling the night of Blaine's escape?"

Yu thought for a second. "No, he was assigned to the station that night."

The investigator smelled a lead. "Where did he find Joe Blaine?"

Again, the sheriff grew visibly agitated. "At a motel."

"A motel?" Jameila's eyes narrowed.

"You know, a *motel*." Yu emphasized the last word with a raised eyebrow.

Sean took the Lord's name in vain. "How on earth did he get there?! He should have been handed over directly to the FCIA!"

"We didn't take him there!" the sheriff defended himself. "It's the motel closest to his house. When Blaine escaped, he must've thought he could hide out there. My other guys at the station said that they were listening in on the motel owner's phone and Wallace just got up and left."

McDowell crossed his arms and relented slightly. "We've got to find this Wallace guy. He'll point us in the right direction, I'm sure of it."

His partner nodded and began jotting things down in a small notebook.

Yu tried to interject, "He may not be alive anymore. His car had bullet holes and traces of his blood."

"Did you find the body? Did you find the gun?" Jameila asked rhetorically. "I saw the pictures. There's not enough blood for a gunshot wound, and the bullet holes are in the wrong places if Blaine was doing it. Again, this guy was an office drone. This is not his work alone. I think your guy went rogue."

Yu tried to interrupt to save his department's reputation but was cut off by their next demands.

Sean turned to the sheriff. "You need to start playing the media game. Make a statement to the media and pin all of that rioting on him. Get creative. That'll raise his threat level and get me some more money to track him down." The investigator put his hands on his hips with a nod. "This is a real dumpster fire you've handed us. As long as we catch him, you might just get to keep your little kingdom."

Yu clenched his jaw nervously and agreed.

"Don't worry, you're not in the fryer," Sean said on his way out, "for now. If I find that you've been sending federal Hate Criminals to Rosenblatt instead of us, you'll be strung up by your balls. Count on it."

18

WHITE PLIGHT

WHITE-SUPREMACIST TERROR ATTACK IN MLK JR. COUNTY,
ONE OFFICER DEAD, ONE MISSING
By Anessa Shapiro
New York Associated Post

A Hate Criminal by the name of Joseph Arthur Blaine killed one officer and wounded two others and possibly a third in a deadly white-supremacist terror attack this past Thursday in Martin Luther King Jr. County. Corporal Ahmed Omar passed away due to a neck injury sustained while attempting to subdue the terrorist. The suspect is still at large and is likely armed and dangerous according to the MLK Jr. County Sheriff's Office. Authorities initiated a 24-hour Public Safety Lockdown (PSL) starting Thursday night in the surrounding area in the hopes of catching Blaine. After initial searches proved fruitless, the city extended restrictions through the weekend.

Blaine is wanted for fraud, conspiracy to commit a Hate Crime, arson, vandalism, possession of a deadly weapon with intent to use, and felony Hate Crime murder. The city suffered a spate of fires near MLK Jr. University, which law enforcement attributes to Blaine. They theorize that he set the fires to cause confusion and drain emergency services in disadvantaged Communities of Color.

"It's disgusting," Aaron Cohen, president of MLK Jr. University's student body, told the New York AP. "If he were a Person of Color, he would have been lynched or railroaded through the courts. The sheriff's office needs to do more to combat hate in our city. This happened

only a few miles from campus."

An anonymous resident remarked, "This is yet another example of our country's greatest threat. White male rage continues to ravage Communities of Color and hold our society back. I really thought we were past this."

Peaceful protests erupted in the aftermath of the attack in support of social justice and to demand reform of the policies that allowed this deadly terrorist act to transpire. Chants of the fallen officer's name could be heard throughout the city.

"We mourn the loss of our slain comrade, Ahmed Omar. He laid down his life to protect our community and save the lives of countless underprivileged citizens. I am hereby resolving today that we will work with state and federal authorities to bring this Hate Criminal to justice. White supremacy will not have a home in MLK Jr. County," Sheriff Li Yu said in an official statement.

Sergeant Darius Binger, one of the officers wounded in the confrontation with Blaine, stood next to the sheriff during the press conference. A third officer remains in critical condition due to gunshot wounds received while stopping the attack. A search helicopter found the squad car of another responding officer riddled with bullet holes near the rural town of Catalina. Authorities suspect that Blaine may be holding the officer hostage and are engaged in frantic search efforts.

A number of businesses headquartered in MLK Jr. County announced donations to the non-profit organization Victims of White Supremacy (VWS).

Joel Boeckman, a spokesperson for VWS, condemned—

As Karl read the article, he felt disgust at the sheer amount of lies it contained. Teaming with warranted hatred of the media, he believed Joe's account without reservation. He closed the tab on his computer quickly when he heard the door to the guest bedroom open. Karl was an avid consumer of the esoteric and considered himself to be above the smoke and mirrors of society. He had paid dearly for his resistance to the system throughout his life.

A graduate of the Naval Academy in Annapolis, he was once on course for a promising career through the established power structure. He graduated near the top of his class and was published in a peer-reviewed journal. His classmates used to joke that he would be the first to make admiral from his class. In the civilian world, alumni of the Naval Academy seamlessly climbed their way through politics, appointments, and business at the highest levels. A vast network of connections stood by to vault young Karl to importance.

While at the academy, Karl suffered an awakening of sorts. A close friend introduced him to a series of uncomfortable truths, which shook his worldview. Nevertheless, he felt that his contractual obligation to the Navy prevented any action. Young Karl Blaine thought he could slip through the cracks and glide his way to prominence despite his newfound knowledge of the system's rot. He fooled himself into thinking that he could just hide his beliefs long enough to gain an influential position and change the system from within.

Shortly after commissioning, however, Ensign Blaine was forced to choose between principles and earthly success. The beast system made its move to purge the military of undesirable ideological elements. He was offered the world, if only he would disregard his conscience. Standing firm, the riches of this earth were torn away from him. His choice bore him through a rocky transition into the fringes of society.

"Hey, good morning," Karl greeted softly.

Joe crept from the bedroom and sat dejectedly at the kitchen table. The rest of the house was asleep in the early morning.

"So, what did they write about me?" Joe droned.

His uncle felt embarrassed. "I'm sorry, it just came up in my feed."

Joe repeated, "What did they write about me?"

"It's a pack of lies as usual. Filthy ki—" Karl stuttered, "elites!"

Joe made his way to the computer and took the mouse. He clicked on the article and viewed the report. As his eyes scanned through the accusations and libel, his eyes rested on the name of Ahmed Omar. A small official photograph of the deceased policeman featured at the top of the page. Joe's heart dropped as he realized he had seen this face weeks before that fateful night. Omar's dark eyes flashed in his memory.

"Omar. . . ." Joe muttered softly. "I didn't know I killed the same guy who trashed my house. . . . I know his face now." He stared off into space, then repeated, "I know his face now."

Karl shifted in his seat. "Well, there's some justice."

Joe closed the tab and floated like a piece of driftwood back to the table. He deeply regretted finding out the identity of his victim. In the darkness of that night, he only saw the uniform and the weapon. It was better in his mind for the man to be a faceless cog of the system, perhaps even inhuman. With the confirmation of his identity, Omar's face breached the surface of vague recollection into the realm of horrified understanding.

Joe turned to face the window and peered listlessly at the serene mountain vista, barely illuminated in the dawn. Several cows grazed in an enclosure next to a chicken coop. A small creek continued its lengthy journey down the mountainside, while orange clouds sifted above. The timeless design of the scene provided a small comfort, but reminded him of his own transience and irregularity in comparison.

Refocusing his eyes, he caught a glimpse of his reflection. Joe recoiled in dreadful terror, knocking over several chairs and falling to the floor.

"He's here! No, no, no! Not here! Get away! Get away!" Joe shook violently.

Karl sprang from his seat and placed his hands on the convulsing wretch. "Joe, what's wrong?! Who's here?"

The uncle pulled a pistol from a concealed holster and searched wide-eyed for a threat outside the window. After failing to spot the threat, he tended to his guest.

Joe managed to get the shaking under control but could barely speak. "I'm f—fine. It's . . . okay. No one . . . is here."

Karl brought his eyebrows together in confusion. "Who did you see?"

"Nobody . . . just going crazy. . . ." Joe laid his head on the hardwood floor and tightly closed his eyes with a grimace.

A young girl sleepily walked into the room. "Daddy, what's happening?"

"Everything's fine, Allie. C'mon, it's time to do your morning chores. Go collect some eggs for us," Karl said in the tone all parents use when concealing concern as he holstered the gun.

Alexandria rubbed her eyes and shuffled to the door. She donned a pair of small shoes and exited the house.

Karl lowered his voice in the vain hope that no one else was awakened. "Let's get you back in bed. You're just a little sleep deprived, that's all."

Joe grumbled as his nerves calmed, "I've had enough sleep. I just have nightmares anyway. I'm off my rocker." He sat up and brought his knees to his chest.

His uncle sat on the floor with him. "You've been through a lot. Don't judge your sanity just yet. Take some time to recover and detox this out."

Karl rose with some minor popping of joints and walked into the hallway. Joe overheard some whispers, then his host returned to his side. After a short time, Eva came out with a small bag.

"Here, take this and hold it under your nose." She gave him a small vial of liquid.

The soft, purple scent rose in clouds into his aching respiratory tract. The smell calmed him and brought back memories of Jill's favorite perfume. His wife's face seemed to float in an ethereal vision before him.

"It's lavender oil. Good for the nerves and trauma," Eva stated. "I'll make you some chamomile tea."

Joe clutched the vial with white knuckles as he breathed heavily. The more he inhaled the vapors, the more his breathing slowed. His muscles released tension that previously went unnoticed. He closed his eyes and thought of Jill. At the very least, he could replace terror and guilt with bittersweet memories of his beloved wife.

"Do you think you can handle everything?" Karl asked Eva. "I want to stay with Joe today."

Eva gave a curt smile. "That's okay, there's nothing too big to get done today."

She gathered up her bag and set a kettle on the stove. After setting a tea bag on the counter, she went outside.

"Let's get you up on the sofa, at least." Karl helped his shaking guest to the couch. "I'll get your tea for you."

Joe sank into the plush cushion and felt weightless. He sat across from a brick fireplace with a painted white mantle. On either side of the mantle were vast bookcases filled to the brim. Where most homes had a television, there were pictures of the family, mementos, and Uncle Karl's old officer commission. Set beside the commission was a framed letter in official naval format. Joe recalled vaguely that his uncle was kicked out for disobeying an order but couldn't place the specific offense.

Karl broke his contemplation by handing him a hot cup of tea and sitting in the rocking chair that flanked the couch.

"I imagine you're pretty hungry by now. Alexandria will be back in soon with some eggs." Karl tried to get Joe's mind refocused.

Joe held the cup in his still quivering hands. "Yeah, you could say that."

After a period of awkward silence, his uncle made small talk. "So, how's your pa? I haven't seen my brother in years."

"He's fine," the nephew curtly replied.

Another awkward pause ensued.

Karl again spoke up. "Yup, my daughter Allie is five and George is eleven. George was just a little boy last time you visited. He's the one you saw on the dirt bike. Alexandria is the youngest. She was certainly a surprise for us!"

Joe nodded along politely.

"Do you remember my oldest boy, Roger? He's sixteen now and taller than you and I put together." Karl laughed jovially.

All Joe could do was nod, smile, and sip his tea. The thought of children depressed him. *Never going to have those now*, he thought to himself in desolate sadness.

Reading the room, the uncle changed the topic. "Don't worry about someone coming knocking at our house. You're safe here. There's no record of us living here. I made sure of that. We don't even technically have an address. That's why I had you go to Wetumpka all those years ago. We make our own electricity and have our own well. I've got some lucrative passive income sources going. I'm good friends with the local sheriff, and we have an arrangement to keep to ourselves. Trust me, no one will come looking for you."

Joe's mind still ran ragged with tension, fearing a knock on the door at any moment. It was only now after being out of danger that the trauma of the past couple days could fully germinate in his mind. It made him an emotional wreck.

Alexandria burst into the house with the exuberance and lack of coordination commensurate with her age. The sudden opening of the door cranked Joe's adrenaline back into the stratosphere, and his hands trembled terribly. Closing his eyes briefly, he took a deep breath and tried to steady his hold on the mug. Noticing his guest's displeasure, Karl softly chastised the girl to be gentler with the door. Alexandria scurried over to the kitchen and placed a basket of eggs on the counter.

"Take some bread for you and your mama and go help her out in the barn," Karl instructed.

Alexandria complied and ran out the door. George and Roger slumped out of bed and made their way to the kitchen. Making brief, obligatory greetings to Joe, they too grabbed their breakfast. Karl informed them of the daily tasks and scolded them to remember their schoolwork today as they shuffled out the door.

"Look, I appreciate you having me here, but I don't need a babysitter," Joe remarked quietly.

"You're right, you don't. You've been to hell and back, and if I learned anything from your story, it's that you're one heck of a survivor." Karl grabbed a book from the table next to his chair.

Joe rolled his eyes slightly at the word "survivor." He peered listlessly into the steaming liquid in the cup for several minutes.

After an interim of labored silence, Joe babbled, "I miss Jill so much. I feel totally responsible for what happened. If we had just moved into the government housing, we'd both be okay right now."

Karl leaned forward and squinted imperceptibly. "Are you sure about that?"

"What do you mean? My forging the signatures directly caused her death. I hate myself for that!" Joe clenched his teeth.

"Perhaps, perhaps. . . ." His uncle rocked slowly. "But doesn't the blame rest more squarely on the state? It was their negligence that failed to save her."

"Look, I know what you're trying to do, but there's no getting around it. This was my fault." Joe looked down at his lap with deep self-loathing.

"Was it your fault for being born 'privileged'?" Karl made air quotes. "Was it your fault for being White? Was it your fault for not wanting to live in a crack den, where your wife would be sexually assaulted if she ever left the house?"

Looking up at the mantle, Joe struggled to reply, "Well, no. And it wasn't necessarily because I was White, I mean—"

"Stop it!" His host slapped the coffee table.

Joe jumped slightly at the sound and looked at Karl. His uncle's gray eyes peered with caustic acidity into his own. Joe had seen this look several times before.

Karl lowered his voice. "Stop it. You're blaming yourself. Don't do the state's dirty work for them. And if you don't believe this whole thing went down because you're White, boy do I have some work to do with you." Years of isolation in the mountains with his family made his filter quite thin.

Joe couldn't bear the gaze and looked at the dead embers in the fireplace instead. Taking a brief glance at his uncle, the terrible, familiar look remained.

"*You* didn't kill your wife. Those vagrants didn't really either. The system did! The system did this. The same system that drove me into solitude up here." Karl slapped the coffee table again and motioned aggressively with his pointer finger.

Chafed at the last comment, Joe faced him. "Yeah, it really sucks for you, doesn't it! You just have to live up here with your wife and children and your own farm!"

Karl cocked his head to the side, pursed his lips, and looked upward. Taking a brief pause, he replied quietly, "I'm not minimizing your loss. You've sacrificed more than most could ever bear." Karl ran his fingers through his dark blond hair. "I know I'm a little abrasive at times. It's just that this thing's going to kill you if you let it. Maybe I'm starting a little early, but I need to save you from that. I can see the self-hatred, Joseph. I know that look. Believe me, I've seen it in the mirror. I'm not going to let the system take you too. No more! I've seen too many suicides in my day. Too many. . . ."

Joe's demeanor softened, and tears welled in his eyes. "It's just . . . where can I go from here?"

"I'll make us some breakfast," Karl nodded affirmatively and declared with a righteous gesture, "then we start!"

19

ABSURDITY

After a swift and silent meal, the two men left the house. Joe drew in his beautiful surroundings with a deep breath. He saw Eva shepherding the children through their morning lessons under a shady tree. His head still ached, and his body felt the collective burden of exhaustion, fatigue, and emotional turmoil. A gentle mountain zephyr fell on his back like a guiding hand amid clear sunshine. The pair walked quickly to a large foothill approximately half a mile away. A few rocks were strewn about at the base. The foothill itself stood like an ancient ziggurat, rising several hundred feet above the high, grassy plain of Karl's ranch.

Joe watched as his uncle milled seemingly without a point. He walked about, inspecting the small boulders and turning them over. He took a brief look at Joe then returned his eyes to a particular stone

"What are we doing?" Joe asked.

Karl firmly grasped a jutting edge of one of the boulders. "This one."

Joe shook his head. "What?"

The rock stood at his feet, viewing him with the impartial harshness of nature. It rose to about his knees and was a spectrum of brown shades. It was shaped roughly like a human heart sacrificially torn from its victim by the vengeful priesthood of destiny.

"You're going to roll this stone to the top and await further instructions," Karl commanded.

Dumbfounded, his guest shrugged. "What's the point of that? I've barely recovered from these past few days!"

"Do it," Karl repeated forcefully.

Joe walked over to the rock. "This thing is huge! Why?"

His uncle put his hands on his hips. "There is no reason. You just have to do it."

"I really don't see how this is going to help—"

Karl grabbed Joe's hand and placed it on the rock. "Start rolling. All the way up."

Joe yanked away and put his hand to his head. "Is this about earning my keep? Look, I'm happy to pitch in—"

"No. There is no reason. It's pointless. But you must do it." Karl again drew Joe's hand to the boulder.

Adding confusion to his growing list of burdens, Joe sheepishly gave the massive stone a shove. The edge nearest to him budged an inch, then thudded to the earth as his strength gave out.

"I can't even roll this thing on *flat* ground!" Joe swore angrily.

"The top—then await further instructions." Karl turned his back and started walking back to the house.

Joe unleashed a tirade of curses, swearing, and oaths at his uncle's back. Karl continued to walk with his hands in his pockets, ignoring his nephew's scathing words. Eventually, Joe realized his newfound tormentor was out of earshot.

He glared at the rock. *This is so stupid. I ought to just go off into the wilderness and die. That'll show him he shouldn't have told me to do this.*

Joe sat bitterly on the rock. He viewed the pastoral scene before him. He could still faintly make out Eva and the kids doing their morning schoolwork. Karl had started his work repairing the fence of one of the enclosures. They seemed to go about their lives oblivious to the raging hellscape beyond the mountains. He turned around and looked at the foothill.

Why didn't I just get shot by the cops? Just a centimeter to the left and my brains would have painted the neighbor's house. He sat on the craggy surface of the boulder. *Why was I saved by Wallace? Why weren't we picked off by the helicopter? How did the train end up here of all places?*

His life consisted of a series of near misses and near accomplishments: he nearly graduated in the top half at college; nearly got that job with Ferron Tech; and nearly became a father. Joe remained always at the cusp in a perpetual period of waiting and striving for the next best thing, only to miss it by a hair.

Now, the 'nearlies' had grown far more dire: nearly arrested; dead; sold into slavery; caught, or worse. The limbo of outcomes didn't change, but the outcomes they promised became threats. Always approaching but never arriving, Joe's life drifted from one near miss to another, as if locked into a cosmic asymptote.

"It's all so meaningless," Joe lamented aloud. He looked up to heaven. "Why, God? Do you hate me this much? Why don't I ever get anywhere? What did I do to you to make me your personal punching bag?"

Karl briefly looked up from his work to subtly check on his nephew. Seeing Joe gesticulate with his arms angrily stretched to the sky elicited a grim look from the uncle. Eva caught his eyes with a look of unease. Karl reassured her with a nod and continued to mend the fence.

"Strike me down! Kill me! Why can't I just die?! You won't let me kill myself!" Joe screamed at the heavens.

In a fit of frustrated rage, he gave the rock a mighty shove. To his astonishment, he mustered the strength to tilt the boulder onto its side. It teetered at a balance point for a moment, then fell back toward Joe. He stood still for a second in surprise. Some of Joe's muscles were already spasming. He took a deep breath and briefly closed his eyes. Crouching down, he got his aching fingers under the bottom edge and heaved with his legs. Painfully, the boulder shifted upward and onto its side once more. With a summary grunt, Joe pushed it the rest of the way over. It thumped the ground a few feet or so from its original location. He felt a primal satisfaction at having forced his will on the rock. Joe took a glance back to the house, then to the foothill. Its imposing height presented a daunting challenge.

"And for what?" Joe shook his head. "Maybe I really can do it. But for what purpose?"

The earthen ziggurat remained in the stance it had maintained since the forming of the land. Erosion and wind whittled it down over the years, but it stood defiantly on the plain under the watchful eyes of the expectant mountains all around. Its ancient form challenged Joe to a duel of endurance.

He rested for a moment, leaning on the rock and breathlessly staring at the foothill. A few yards separated the stone's current location and the beginning of its imposing incline.

Joe rubbed his face and stated resignedly, "I've been doing mean-ingless things all my life, I guess. Why should this be the exception?"

Bending at the knees again, he made a titanic effort to overturn the boulder's inhospitable form. Straining and swearing, Joe managed another few feet. Repeating the process several times more, he finally stood sweating with the rock tickling the foothill's base. Joe's hamstring tightened severely, and he cried out in pain. The cramping muscle exacted a paralyzing agony and forced him to the ground. He lay there groaning until the hamstring finally loosened after a few throbs.

Joe grunted, "It's meaningless! This is how everything goes. It's absurd!"

As the last word crossed his lips, Joe felt a wave of realization crash over him and carry his mind out into the open ocean of surren-der.

"It is absurd," he whispered, "absurd as absurd can be."

Giving his leg a firm stretch, he grasped the underside of the rock and submitted himself for another heave. The stone relented and turned over much easier than before.

"It's stupid." Joe lifted again. "It's pointless." The rock climbed the hill. "It's absurd." He made another turn. "But that's everything, isn't it?"

Karl ceased his work completely at this point and stood in veiled amazement.

"Eva, look!" he said excitedly to his wife. "But don't make it too obvious."

Eva turned her head and looked expectantly at the wretched form on the foothill far away.

Karl crossed his arms. "He's doing it!"

"How did you know this would work?" she questioned.

Karl replied abruptly, "It hasn't worked yet. He still has a long way to go."

Eva's motherly heart ached for the tortured soul. "How long does he have to do this?"

"Some people have to do it all their lives. I'm still rolling my boul-der up the mountain. And so are you. Different sizes, different slopes, different outcomes—we all have to surrender to the climb," Karl said bleakly.

She shifted uncomfortably. "Awfully depressing, isn't it? How will that help him? It makes me feel a little sad too, if I'm honest. I just hope you're not being too hard on him"—a deeply mournful tone submerged her voice—"he just lost his wife after all."

Holding the fence in front of him like a captain grasping the railing of a warship's bridge, Karl stated confidently, "We'll get to that, but he has to realize everything he's held to is pointless first before he can find any kind of purpose. I know he lost his wife, but we'll lose him too if he doesn't do this. This is the unpleasant chemotherapy for the cancer that's overtaken him."

"I feel like we're just adding to a long list of hardships for him right now." Eva rocked uncomfortably.

Her husband approached her and took her in his arms. "You know those miscarriages you had in the beginning, how hard that was for both of us. We had to watch everyone else get what we wanted while we rolled our boulder up the mountain. If we had quit then, we never would've had Roger and George." He stopped to ponder. "Then that gap when you just couldn't get pregnant at all, if we stopped then, we never would've had Alexandria."

Eva nodded quietly and looked lovingly at her children.

"So, we keep on rolling." Karl rested his head on hers. "We all just have to keep going."

Joe's sweat poured heavily on the boulder. The thin mountain air parched his throat and restricted his exhausted breathing. The rock stood just a small way up the foothill. He turned to look at how much progress he had made. Dissatisfied with the ratio of effort to distance moved, he resolved to not look back again. The miniscule distance he accomplished depressed him immensely. Setting his eyes on the foothill's skyline, he continued onward in dogged desperation. He found that the more he pushed the boulder up the hill, the less he could think about his troubles.

Three hours passed under the beating mountain sunlight. The thinner atmosphere amplified the effects of the sun, so Joe's skin burned faster and he became dehydrated. He grew dizzy again with exhaustion, but nothing would slow his progress. He at last was able to vent his frustration and defiant energy into the rock. With each turn, his hatred turned away from himself and toward the boulder. Joe concocted a sort of crusade against the rock and made it symbolic of all his ills. When he lifted it to the tipping point, he took great pleasure in viciously shoving it down.

Joe spit venom onto the stone: "You're not going to beat me."

Karl walked across the plain with a gallon jug of water after completing his maintenance on the fence. Checking his watch, he looked up at the sun. He could see that Joe was nearly halfway up the foothill and making steady progress.

He's moving faster than I expected, Karl thought to himself. *Yup, he's still got some Blaine left in him.*

After a short walk, he made it to within earshot of the sweating lump on the slope.

"How's it going?" Karl called out.

Joe made no reply and refused to even look back. He straightened his back, inhaled deeply, then resumed the climb.

His uncle hiked his way up to Joe's level. "Here's some water for you."

Joe maintained a steely gaze toward the top of the hill and remained silent. He continued to flip the rock over.

"Joe, you're doing great, but you really should drink some water." Karl, egged on by Eva's feminine worry, was concerned that he was being too hard on his mourning nephew.

Joe's eyes drifted to the sloshing water. He desired it deeply, but slapped the jug away. It tumbled down the slope and settled next to another boulder at the base. Satisfied with his outburst, he continued rolling the boulder without a word.

Karl raised his eyebrows. "Well, suit yourself. You still have to make it to the top. I'll leave the water where it landed if you want it."

Joe paid him no mind as his uncle descended the hill. All he could focus on was the rock and his struggle to surmount the insurmountable. His initial fire and fury gave way to shaky and weakening discipline. One flip at a time, Joe rolled the stone up the foothill. His body felt heavy, and his balance began fading again.

"I hope this kills me," he thought aloud, "then at last I can die as pointlessly as I've lived."

Yet Joe's strained and aching heart beat on. He began working more frantically, hoping that increasing his effort would hasten a dehydrated demise. The only thing this accomplished was faster progress and the intensifying physical pain of burning muscles. Delirious, his emotions ran wild amid the unstoppable tide of the forces that bore him onward.

Though his spirit wished for death, his flesh gave out and commanded him to return to the base of the hill for water. Joe cursed his instinctual programming that would not allow for self-deprivation to the point of death. If he had been a stronger-souled man, he likely could have mustered the will to kill himself. The same factor of weak will prevented him from overcoming his basic fleshly instincts. The years of deadening his spirit in subjugation to earthly desires meant that he simply did as his body commanded, despite his best efforts.

After testing to make sure the boulder wouldn't roll back down, Joe retrieved the water from the base of the slope. He sat in a pool of accumulating sweat on a larger stone, looking up at his progress, and sipped the water with self-loathing. Acknowledging the absurdity of the task germinated in his soul and at last sprouted the beginnings of spiritual strength. He would get the rock to the top of the hill not because he was told to, but simply because it was there. The exercise in sum turned to one of defiance. Toward whom, Joe was not quite sure. He only knew that finishing the task would either kill him or lead to a loud expression of the repressed man within him. Joe would either perish or transcend the toils of his present troubles in an audacious metamorphosis. The task itself had no meaning to him. There was no point in rolling the stone up the hill. Nevertheless, Joe discovered a greater meaning, independent of the rock, his uncle, the government, or even Jill's death. He discovered struggle, effort, and the ecstatic joy of simple resistance.

20

MY PEOPLE

Sean McDowell washed the blood from his hands in a filthy bathroom sink. Jameila stood behind him with her arms crossed. Hard panting came from the other room intermittently broken by gut-wrenching sobs.

"They always break." He looked down at the sanguine stains on his forearms. "Always."

Jameila shifted on her feet. "I don't like seeing this side of you."

Sean looked up at the mirror. "At the end of the day, what's done is done, and the bad guy gets caught."

"Why did you show him a mirror after your interrogation?" She pulled her windbreaker closer.

The investigator continued washing away the blood and felt words fall automatically out of the recesses of his mind: "I've found that showing someone a reflection of their broken state keeps them broken. No matter how much they heal, they'll always see that scared, cowering, little man." He lingered on his own reflection for a moment. "If you actually read the FCIA interrogation manual—"

Jameila rolled her eyes and interrupted, "What are we going to do with him now? Rosenblatt is going to throw a fit if he doesn't get somebody out of this."

Wiping his hands with a towel, Sean turned off the water. "We don't answer to him. This guy's going to federal prison. If Rosenblatt wants him so bad, he can come and get him there."

Just then his cell phone rang. Walking over to the counter, Sean picked it up and answered.

"What did he tell you?" Feldman squawked impatiently.

"Not a lot, but I have a surprise for you," Sean said coyly.

His supervisor waited in silence.

"You know Karl Blaine? He's one of the guys on our watchlist that we haven't been able to find—Joe Blaine's uncle." The investigator began to smile.

"Yes?"

"You won't believe this. I know where Karl is." Sean eagerly revealed his lead: "Northwestern Utah somewhere along Rail Line 287. I'm certain that's where Joe Blaine headed after hopping a train. It looks like we're going to get two for one."

Feldman waited for a moment to reply. "That's it? That's your big reveal?"

The investigator shook his head incredulously.

His supervisor continued, "You might as well say he's on the Moon! Don't try to impress me with surface-level trash like that." She let out a disgusted sigh. "Have you handed him over to Rosenblatt yet?"

"Rosenblatt?"

Feldman grew vicious. "Don't play dumb! He already had a claim on this guy. Rules are rules. Get him to the Windview, right now, unless you'd like to go instead."

The call ended abruptly, and Sean drifted in a sea of dumbfounded silence.

"I told you." Jameila pursed her lips and shook her head.

Sean cursed his boss in a tirade of profanities.

"You know she objected to you being promoted to the DC office, right?" she said while packing up her things. "Her boss overruled her and got you the spot because of your record."

"I guess I figured as much." He clenched his fist.

Jameila turned her deep brown eyes to her partner with a quiver. "Can I ask you something?"

Sean nodded and put on his FCIA windbreaker.

"Why do you do this job?" She paused for a moment. "I mean as a White guy?"

"Where are you going with this?" he asked cautiously.

Jameila leaned on the counter next to him. "I told you why my family fled Morocco, right?"

Sean racked his brain. "Because of the political repression, yeah?"

"In a way. The government paid lip service to multiculturalism and such, but my people, the Amazighs, always got the short end of the stick. My dad was in the Shurta and couldn't take it anymore." Jameila's stare grew far off. "Arresting his own people, kicking them out of their homes, suppressing his own culture. . . . One day he got orders to evict an Amazigh in Rabat. When he showed up to the door, he found his own cousin. My dad couldn't even look him in the eye as he hauled him away." She looked upward in recollection and sighed. "We fled the shame and never returned. He really resisted when I told him I wanted to work for the FCIA but thanked God that I would never have to turn a gun on our own people."

McDowell lowered his brow. "You're not getting radicalized by the forums we monitor, are you? Don't pull a Rivera on me."

She shook her head. "Look, however you rationalize it is up to you. I just could never do what you're doing to my own people."

"There is no 'my people.' It's a social construct. Irish, Spanish, German, British, and whatever else all mixed together into one arbitrary label." Sean shook his head. "Whites would be better off if they just stopped getting hung up on this race thing and got with the times."

Jameila sighed resignedly. "Well, I guess you're more faithful to the FCIA than I am."

The investigator ribbed with a smile. "That's why I'm getting Feldman's job."

She rolled her eyes and reciprocated a chuckle. "Yeah, yeah, we'll see about that after a few more of those phone calls."

"C'mon, let's get this guy back to the Windview," Sean said with a frustrated sigh.

21

THE SISYPHEAN HERO

It was the hottest part of the day when Joe subjugated the rock to its final flip onto the crest of the foothill. He stopped briefly to see if this was truly the peak. Satisfied that it was indeed the top, Joe sat down. His shaking flesh relaxed and contorted in alternating fashion amid more cramps. His breathing was rapid, and his side burned in a stitch. For the final stretch of the climb, he placed the water at the top and denied himself a drink until he made it. Having reached this milestone, Joe chugged the remaining water and rested himself leaning on the stone. When he turned to face the plains below, he noticed Karl making his way over to the hill. He carried a small lunch pail and a satchel. For the first time, Joe noticed the sheer silence of his locale. Even the wind seemed to tread with padded slippers on this otherworldly place, cut off from the earth's spiraling decline. Knowing it would take a good bit of time for Karl to make it to him, he slumped flat on the ground and let his body relax. Joe's chest rose and fell in an increasingly slower tempo as he stared at the wispy cirrus clouds above him. His vision began spinning slightly, and he closed his eyes. The beating heart within him, at first trying to escape, gradually settled into a tame, sedentary throb.

Karl suppressed the excitement in his voice. "Good job, you made pretty good time."

Joe opened his eyes slightly but said nothing.

"I brought you a sandwich and some fruit if you want it." Karl grew worried that Joe wasn't speaking.

The supine figure before him croaked, "No."

Frustrated, his uncle looked at the empty jug of water. "I see you drank the water. That's good. I'll just leave this here for when you want it."

Joe rolled to his side. "No need, I'll come back inside in a minute."

The elder Blaine winced imperceptibly but steeled himself for the tough discipline he had to mete out to this wretched soul. "You're not done yet."

This statement snapped Joe fully awake. "What?"

"Roll it back down."

The nephew lay dazed for a moment, then sat up. The prospect of rolling the stone down the hill irked him, but he at least considered it to be a fairly easy task. He nearly asked, "Why?" but restrained the urge. With a groan, Joe rose to his feet and placed his hands on the boulder. This time, the rock was begrudging and immobile. It took him several attempts to budge the stone from its position. When momentum finally took its course, Joe fell to his knees after transferring his weight.

The rock rolled slowly at first but quickly built up speed as it tumbled down the hill. As it descended to the plain, Joe's heart sank with it as if the two were tethered by a rope. His accomplishment collapsed along the slope leaving nothing as proof of his struggle other than a small rut in the coarse prairie grass. In a few days, the resilient grass would return to its original form and erase all traces of his afternoon of resistance. This thought once again plunged Joe into a black despair.

Karl helped him to his feet. "C'mon, son, walk with me."

His nephew complied, and the pair walked slowly down the hill. Joe looked with contempt at the various spots on the hill where he considered giving up.

At last, Joe's urges got the better of him and he blurted, "What was the point of that?!"

The uncle desperately wanted to reveal everything to him but made no reply except, "There wasn't."

Severely miffed, Joe grabbed his tormentor's arm and swore viciously as they arrived at the base. "What was the point?!"

Karl shoved him roughly. "There wasn't a point." He braced himself to deliver the horrible news: "Now, do it again."

The sad sack before him grew furious. "No! No, no, no!" Joe punctuated each "no" with a pointed finger. "What is this, some kind of mind game? Did I die and I'm actually in hell?! Is this some sick power trip of yours?"

His uncle looked down then resumed stern eye contact. He gave Joe a firm look of conviction and replied in a low, fatherly tone, "There is no point. Now, do it again."

Joe cursed his uncle with obscene words, but Karl maintained a hardened and impassive gaze. The nephew's tantrum gradually lost steam as it deflected off of Karl's convicting, gray eyes. They remained in a silent standoff as the earth spun around them.

"Do it again," Karl pursed his lips and stated in a quiet, almost compassionate voice.

Joe's own eyes welled slightly, and he sat beside the rock as his uncle turned his back and returned to the farmstead.

After the long walk, his uncle met Eva in the house. She sat in the breakfast nook next to a window facing the foothill.

"Oh Karl, you're being too hard on him. My heart's breaking." Her eyes bore evidence of wiped away tears.

"I know I'm being hard. I know. But the boy's been raised weak and kept weak by society. My brother's a good guy, but he never had the heart to teach Joe lessons like this." Karl moved over to the window.

His wife pensively put her hand to her chest. "He doesn't need a lesson right now. He needs recovery. What lesson is this even supposed to teach him?"

Karl lovingly grabbed her shoulder. "He wasn't going to recover. He was going to kill himself. You know it. That's the unfortunate truth. Do you remember Payton after his daughter got arrested for a Hate Crime?"

"I know, I know. It's just. . . ."

"It's okay, sweetie. That's why you're the mama. You've got the soft and loving touch. This is the kind of tough love that only a man—a father—can give." Her husband leaned down and kissed her forehead, then peered out of the window once more.

Joe sat dejectedly at the foot of the hill for nearly an hour. His mind raced back and forth on the same three things: Jill, his plight, and the man he killed. The whirling of thoughts in his haggard mind exhausted him more than the climb ever could. He looked over at the boulder in a resigned irritation. Destroying his body on this pointless task was the only way his mind could be subdued into silence.

"What's the point of this?" he commented on a situation much broader than his immediate surroundings.

Joe ate the sandwich and the fruit then set about rolling the boulder up the foothill. It was late afternoon when he broached the incline for the second time. The cirrus clouds gave way to complete cloud cover. The billowing forms above him shifted to a dark gray. A quarter of the way up the hill, Joe felt the first droplets of an impending rainstorm. Thirty minutes later, the misting turned to a full downpour. The ground beneath him became muddy and treacherous. On several occasions, his feet slipped badly in the increasingly slimy muck. The rock itself was not particularly slick due to its rough texture, but the going overall became very tough. Bolts of lightning started rolling through the plain.

Soaked and angry, Joe once again called out into the heavens, "I'm here! Here I am. You've heard my cry to strike me down! Bring a bolt right here on my head—"

Just then, a bright flash blinded him and the ground shook from the explosive crack above him. The piercing sound reverberated in the mountains and echoed deep in Joe's chest. He realized that he felt fear rather than relief when he thought the end had come at last. A few more peals of thunder rumbled down around the homestead. The fear remained as long as it took for the thunder's noise to dissipate.

If I'm not ready for death, what am I ready for? Joe knelt in the mud as the rain soaked him to the bone.

Looking straight into the sky amid the rain gave the impression of traveling through the cosmos at lightspeed. His soul was similarly vaulting through space, untethered, unguided, and tumbling aimlessly in the infinite stretches of the frigid void.

He broke the trance by continuing his strive up the foothill. By now his shoes were fully caked in mud as each failed attempt to flip the stone uprooted more grass. The progress became exceptionally arduous for him. Each successful turn of the boulder was preceded by at least three failures. Worryingly, Joe discovered the rock itself was beginning to slide down the muddy slope if he did not chock it in place with his weight. Buffeted by the wind and the rain, his strength gave out. Several more unsuccessful lifts of the rock revealed the level of his fatigue. At last, all he could do to prevent his progress from sliding down the hill was to sit with his back against the stone and hold fast.

The cloudy sky stifled a large portion of the twilight hours and hastened darkness over the hill. The rain continued to beat torrentially on the man and his burden. Joe found it difficult even to hold the boulder in place after a while, yet his will hardened under the blacksmith's hammer of adversity. Resisting the inevitability of the rock's slide gave Joe a sense of cathartic satisfaction. All his years were marked by letting the rock slide down the slippery slope unabated.

He found the reservoir of ecstasy heretofore unknown to him. Underneath the weak, battered body grew the welling spring of revolt. Joe could only drink from this well when under strain and mired in travail. He never knew of the vast reserves beneath the surface because he had never truly struggled. The fire of resistance, first a few embers lit by the spark of loss, caught a crusading wind into the fields of dry grass surrounding his soul. On the hill, the fires licked the icy exterior that kept him small and compliant. The crucible of adversity weakened his soul's prison, and he escaped through an organic, last-ditch effort to exist.

Back at the house, the rain and darkness obscured Eva and Karl's view of the foothill.

"You're not going to just leave him out there? It's coming down like cats and dogs." Eva folded her hands in worry.

Karl concealed his own misgivings about his methods. "If he wanted to come in, he would've by now. I'm not stopping him."

Eva made sure the children were not around and whispered, "He's suicidal right now. Can we expect him to look after his health?"

Her husband let some frustration escape. "Eva, we talked about this. This is the only way to save him. Yes, it could kill him, but he's guaranteed to"—Karl lowered to a whisper—"to die if we just let him stew. Trust me on this, babe, I've seen it before." He wondered for a moment if Joe's death would be on his head if he were to perish out there. "He has to pull through."

On the hill, Joe's feet slipped repeatedly just to hold the stone in place. It became a matter of intense agony to keep the boulder from sliding back down. Over the course of several hours, Joe managed to slow the decline to a few inches per hour.

He reflected on those he entrusted to stop the decline for him in his life. They merely stood aside of the inexorable boulder and always relinquished to the excuse, "Well, you can't turn back time. It's pointless."

"Pointless!" Joe yelled aloud. "But that's why it must be done!"

He tore the shoes from his feet and cast them down the hill. Water came down in sheets over Joe's battleground. Wheeling around, he dug his bare feet deep in the mud and struggled against the rock. It seemed to push back against him in equal measure, but at last it halted.

"God, give me strength!" he cried as he flexed every muscle in his body.

The boulder faltered for a moment then began to slide upward under his superhuman effort. Several more flashes from above lit up the plain.

"I'm not going to let you crush me!" he scolded the rock.

Joe entered a berserk rage with repeated screams. Lightning crashed around the hill at an intensifying tempo. The thunder called out a marching cadence of cosmic spiritual struggle.

The stone gave way for several feet under Joe's onslaught. He felt injuries forming all over his body but pressed on without hesitation. His soul took the reins of power and subdued the flesh. First, his left arm gave out and the muscles twitched uselessly at his side. Next, his right pectoral refused to flex. Whether his vision was darkened by the storm or impending mortality, Joe couldn't tell. The rock slid onward, but its far side halted the advance by digging into the muddy ground. He did not know where he was on the slope yet struggled fiercely to overcome the mire.

"One more push," a voice called out.

"I can't!" Joe yelped.

"One more push, you can do it," the voice said again.

Shaking his head, Joe bent his aching back and got his fingers under the edge. In a final fiery explosion, he spent the remainder of his strength flipping the rock. Joe even lacked the ability to summarily shove it down as it fell.

The voice was not satisfied. "One more."

Joe cried out deliriously, "My body's spent!"

"What about your soul?" it questioned.

"My soul?" Joe repeated, "I can't lift this burden with my soul. I'm spent."

The voice made no reply. Its absence frightened Joe. It seemed that if he did not please the guiding voice, it would be lost to him forever. In an effort to gain its approval once more, he dug deeper than he ever thought possible. Drawing from the newly discovered wellspring within him, Joe managed one more flip of the boulder. As the stone fell forward, Joe stumbled in tandem. He collapsed face down in the mud, his chest suffering from a piercing pain. The flatness of the ground he lay on stood out conspicuously.

A voice came through the dark, "Joe, it's pouring like crazy out here. Let's get you inside."

Managing to roll over, Joe saw his uncle Karl and one of his sons making cautious progress up the treacherous hill. Cold shivers ran over him as he noticed he had made it to the top of the foothill a second time. The rock sat next to him, firmly in place on the reduced gradient of the summit.

Karl and Roger came up alongside the weakened wreck and lifted him by the underarms.

"Wait," Joe objected, "wait, I'm not done yet."

"You made it to the top, Joe, it's fine."

Joe's muddy form managed to slip free. Crawling over to the rock, he braced his shoulder and pushed. Roger started to walk over to help him, but Karl blocked him with his arm. With a shattering yell, Joe flipped the rock back toward the declining slope. The boulder complied and fell down the hill amid the sludge. In the intermittent lighting of the storm's sparks, Joe watched it tumble and slide in the same rut he carved earlier. This time, his mark on the hill was far more lasting. Grass would take several weeks to fully cover his tracks, and even still, the gash in the earth would remain. Lasting change could only be won through extraordinary effort. As he trembled on his hands and knees at the crest, he was greater than the rock and bigger than the climb. Joe relished in his victory if only for a moment before he would descend the hill and do it all again. Satisfied with his work, he allowed himself to be carried away.

"Why did he do that?" Roger asked his father.

Karl could at last speak freely. "Because it had to be done."

PART III

BUILDING ANEW

22

SERVILE OR SPIRITUAL

Joe spent the next several days alternating between sleeping and eating. He didn't have the physical stamina to do anything else. At last, his mind rested and allowed him to be free of nightmares. The boulder exfoliated the blemishes from his mind and returned him to a numb baseline. He felt nothing, which was at least preferable to intense self-hatred. Joe's body ached terribly, and Eva had to bandage and ice several of his joints.

Karl let him sleep, relieved that his gambit seemed to have worked. The hardest part of Joe's detox was over, but Karl estimated there was still much to do. The uncle brought him from the brink of a self-hating death spiral, but he was far from a full rejuvenation. Though the foundation of Joe's mind was clear of the burned-out debris, it was now barren and without structure.

Three days after Joe's victory on the hill, the uncle went out to the detached garage to change the oil on one of the small tractors while the children were with Eva. This particular tractor sat idle while its more modern siblings did all the heavy lifting. It's gleaming metal and curved forms hearkened to a simpler time. He failed to notice Joe enter the space amid his focus on finding the correctly sized socket.

"Hey, Uncle Karl," Joe greeted quietly.

His uncle jumped slightly. "Geez, you scared me. How are you doing? This is the first time I've seen you somewhere besides the bedroom and the kitchen," he ribbed.

Joe gave an obligatory smile. "Yeah, I've sure been laid up."

Karl found the correct socket, attached it to the ratchet, and gave it several clicking turns in his hand. "Maybe you should keep resting. Your body looked pretty beat up when we hauled you in."

The nephew made no reply and instead looked around the garage at the various vehicles and gadgets. Karl placed a plastic pan underneath the tractor and slid underneath.

"I think I know why you made me do that," Joe said quietly.

The uncle gave several strained grunts trying to loosen the stubborn bolt. "Don't you remember? There isn't a point."

Joe clarified, "Well, I suppose it was pointless. There's no practical reason for rolling it up and down. But something you said when I was just near the top of the hill struck me."

Karl paused his work. "What?"

"About the soul," Joe continued. "It's a matter of the soul."

Confusion overtook the uncle. He racked his brain to remember something he said about the soul. "Remind me, when did I say that?"

"Right when I was two flips from the top, when you encouraged me to draw from the soul, not the body," Joe recounted.

Karl slid back from underneath the tractor and sat up. "Joe, I didn't say anything to you until Roger and I got up there."

The nephew stumbled back and furrowed his brow. "I heard somebody calling out, telling me that. . . ." his voice trailed off.

Karl pursed his lips. "Well, you were pretty delirious when we found you." He slipped back under the vehicle.

Joe thought silently, *Who was it then? Maybe I really am going crazy.*

After giving the wrench a good shove, the bolt at last loosened. Placing the ratchet at his side, Karl used his fingers to take it the rest of the way. Removing the drain plug from its place, the hot oil flowed in an opaque stream into the pan.

Placing the plug on a paper towel, Karl got up and leaned against a workbench. "So, what did it say?"

The draining liquid made a soft droning in the large space as the two men spoke among a nest of machines. A few birds chirped cheerfully outside.

"I mean, not much besides that. It told me to flip it one more time, so I did. After that, it told me to do it again. I replied that I couldn't, that my body was spent. Then it asked me about my soul"—Joe sat down on a stool—"then it stopped. I was scared when it went away as if the only life raft in a storm suddenly vanished. I knew I had to get it to the top if I was going to survive."

Karl listened intently and without skepticism. "Interesting, very interesting." He scratched at his stubble.

Joe continued, "Something strange happened to me on that hill."

"You know, Joseph, I'm very glad to hear that. I know I was hard on you, but you do understand right?" Karl fumbled his words.

"Well, I think I probably would have killed myself otherwise"—the nephew shifted uncomfortably—"if I could muster the will to do it."

Curious about the new level of Joe's mental health, Karl prodded, "So what changed?"

Joe thought for a moment then said, "When I was struggling on the hill, I just poured all of my burdens into the rock. The rock became my enemy, and I had to move it or it would kill me."

Karl let a small, proud smile spread on his face and nodded.

His nephew continued, "But I feel like there's more to this. Why did you keep telling me it was pointless? You very much had a point in doing it."

Noticing the oil had completely drained out, Karl again returned under the tractor. "Well, I suppose I can reveal my hand." He replaced the drain plug with a strained look on his face. "I believe everything in the material is symbolic of something in the immaterial. Take for instance this tractor. Materially, it's an arbitrary arrangement of metal, rubber, plastic, and chemicals. What would you say it evokes in the higher, symbolic sense?"

Joe contorted his face in confusion. "I'm not sure I get it. It's just a tractor."

Karl sat up and shook his head. "You're thinking like a rotten materialist. Maybe I should put you back on the hill."

"Well, I don't know!" Joe was visibly frustrated. "Just explain it to me."

His uncle lowered his brow. "No, you're a man! What's more, you're a Blaine. We don't get things explained to us. Nobody's going to give you the answer. Didn't your dad ever tell you that?"

"No."

"Robby, c'mon!" Karl shook his head in disapproval of his brother. "Our dad drilled that one into the two of us hard when we grew up." Taking a breath, he continued, "Water under the bridge. Back to the question at hand."

Looking at the tractor, Joe saw that it was very old and painted forest green. "It's just a tractor," he said blankly.

"Try harder," Karl punched with his words.

He recognized the brand as one that used to be made near his hometown before the factories went to China. Given the age of the machine, it certainly was made in the heartland by his neighbors. Joe let his mind relax and his thoughts flow without inhibition.

"It's like a snapshot," the idea came to him.

His uncle snapped with excitement, "Good! Now keep going."

He let his words gush: "They don't make these in the US anymore. There used to be a factory half an hour from my house growing up, but they outsourced shortly before I went to high school. I think this tractor was one of the last brands to still be made there." Joe paused pensively, then continued, "You're keeping the memory of an old America alive, even though buying a newer Chinese tractor would make more material sense."

Karl smiled. "Look at that, you're getting somewhere. See what can happen when you just think a little bit?"

The nephew rolled his eyes. "Okay, so things can have symbolism sometimes, but I don't see what that has to do with anything. And isn't that symbolism subjective? Who's to say it doesn't represent decline or industry?"

"I'll help you cheat a little bit." The elder Blaine wiped his hands on a towel. "Everything is meaningless, yet everything has meaning. The world is in a constant state of conflict between the material and the spiritual man. The material man will look at the earth around him and correctly conclude that nothing matters. The spiritual man will survey his surroundings and correctly conclude that everything matters. They are both entirely right according to their ability. The material man is physically and spiritually incapable of interacting with the higher plane. A worm correctly assesses his world as dark, wet, and cold. This worm is incapable of comprehending anything else."

Joe struggled to follow along. "So, there's the material and the immaterial. Okay, got it, but so what?"

The uncle threw up his hands in frustration. "So what? So, everything! Everything hinges on this central truth. It all boils down to this: whether a given person, or group of people, acknowledges and reveres the spiritual or not. That will dictate everything else."

The nephew sat back for a moment and contemplated his uncle's words. He did his best to humor the idea. Reflecting on all his experiences the past several days, he thought out loud, "So for the rock, materially the task was pointless and absurd. That's easy to perceive by my senses."

"But what of your spiritual senses? I know you have the capacity to be more than just a simple materialist," Karl prompted.

"Well, the boulder became a sort of nemesis. It obviously meant more to me than just a rock"—the nephew continued to think—"and the climb itself, I almost took joy in it."

"And why did you take joy? It was just a pointless task, right?" his uncle prompted expectantly.

"Oh, I don't know." Joe placed his aching head in his hands. "My goodness, my head. I don't know if I'm up for deep discussions like this yet."

Karl repeated the question without regard for his complaint, "Why did you take joy?"

Massaging his throbbing temple, the younger Blaine replied, "I suppose it was . . . well, the struggle, quite frankly. I've never really struggled for something in the truest sense of the word. I've labored, but never struggled."

The uncle let Joe dwell on this thought as he searched for an oil filter on one of the many shelves. Looking out of the corner of his eye, he saw his nephew reeling in realization.

"In the ancient world, slavery was not so much a condition of birth or race," Karl waxed contemplative. "What spiritually marked you as a slave was whether you did something pointless, some process that simply needs to be repeated over and over for all of time. The modern world seeks to make all of us slaves." He found the requisite filter and removed it from the box. "And it's pretty good at it."

"Couldn't you argue that this oil change makes you a slave? You'll just have to do it again. Doesn't that make it pointless to a degree?" Joe challenged.

"Look at the brain on you, kid!" smirking, Karl fired back his reply. "You're right. If I did this merely for the sake of the oil change, I would be submitting myself as a slave, a mere stooge of consumerism. But that's not why I do this. Like you pointed out earlier, I keep this machine alive because it's a symbolic relic, not merely a collection of nuts and bolts. By finding a purpose and dedicating my-self to it, I can find a higher state above the abject slavery of meaningless repetition."

Joe rolled his eyes and crossed his arms. "Sounds like a cope to be quite honest."

Karl set about removing the old oil filter with a chuckle. "And the merely material man would agree with you. Midwit intellectual slaves in universities all across America set out to make their war on this very proposition as a rite of passage."

"So, I'm in league with the materialists and college students. That doesn't make me wrong," the nephew stated matter-of-factly.

"But I know you're really on my side. You were able to take the rock to the top of the hill because you assigned a purpose, because you drilled into the well of spiritual vigor," the uncle countered.

Joe squinted and clutched his increasingly painful head. "So, everybody can just make their own truth?"

"You have to stop thinking like a neoliberal hack. Don't worry, I'll detox that out of you." Karl shook his head, filled the new filter with oil, and tightened it on the threads. "I set you on that hill knowing that there were some objective truths and purposes you could find in the task. If I believed that you would just assign any given meaning, the task wouldn't work. Given a strong degree of spiritual acumen, most spiritually capable men will arrive at mostly the same conclusions most of the time." He smiled at this tenuous declaration. "To me, this indicates the presence of some kind of higher truth that is attainable by all spiritually virile men."

"I don't think there's a large pool of people ready to agree with you," the nephew questioned.

"And the higher, spiritual men are indeed a minority." Karl straightened up and returned to the shelf.

Joe uncrossed his arms and upturned a palm in interrogation. "Well, that's just—oh, what is it called?—the No True Scotsman fallacy, isn't it? You mark truly spiritual men by their beliefs, but if they disagree with you, they are not truly spiritual men."

"How dutifully you serve your schoolmasters." The uncle re-pressed a laugh and grabbed a jug of oil from the top shelf. "That label is one of the most overused tools of the pseudointellectual to browbeat over purity. Spiritual health," he emphasized, "spiritual health is both a necessary and sufficient condition for interacting with a higher purpose and morality. It is not enough to merely be spiritual. One must have spiritual health as well. You've lived your life with your spirit churning, smothered, and unhealthy within you. You couldn't access an immaterial purpose because you ignored the possibility of its existence. That's why your life felt so useless." Karl walked toward the engine and turned toward his nephew before opening the hood. "You can choose to either be spiritual or servile."

Joe watched his uncle pour the viscous liquid into the engine. He digested the elder Blaine's words like harsh medicine. Reluctant to admit he found truth in Karl's argument, the nephew sidestepped. "For the sake of argument, let's say you're right. I ask again, so what?"

Karl took a moment to gather his thoughts. "So now you know that you have this ability latent within you. Now you can access a higher purpose. I can't tell you what that purpose is, but you are obligated to struggle for it. You hear me?" He slapped the cowling on the engine. "Obligated!"

At the sound of Karl's hand hitting the reverberating metal, Joe flinched slightly.

His uncle continued, "I'd take a long look in the mirror and find that purpose"—Joe felt a cold chill—"lest somebody dictate another sort of slavery to you."

Replacing the cap on the engine, Karl moved to the driver's compartment and gave the tractor a crank. After a few rotations, the machine proudly proclaimed its continued existence in a cloud of dissipating smoke.

23

THE REAL MAN

The two men continued to chat about the concept of higher, spiritual man for some time. All the while, Joe became more and more convicted of his existence, but shuddered at the implication. Unsure if his uncle's words were literal, he set about giving himself a hard look in the mirror. Since his episode in the kitchen, Joe avoided looking into his reflection at all costs. He hadn't told anyone about the continued revelation of a terrible and otherworldly disposition. Joe remained in fear of what truly laid beyond the material, a barrier attenuated with the menacing approach of an assassin. After the harried events of the past week, Joe grew fearful of what seemed to be an increasingly independent agency pursuing him on the other side of the glass.

Brushing past George without a word, Joe entered the bathroom, grabbed the small mirror on the counter, and retreated to his room. He took special care to keep the reflective surface pressed against his chest. Once in his room, Joe locked the door behind him and sat on the bed. Closing his eyes, he extended the mirror in front of him. After taking a deep breath, his eyes opened.

A shiver wound its way from the top of Joe's head down his spine. The mirror trembled in his cut and bruised hands. The fear of what he saw increased to its zenith as he looked away and closed his eyes. Finding the resolve to continue, he steadied his hands and looked aggressively into the mirror with heavy breathing. The sun shined brightly in the reflection, giving him a fiery complexion. Joe managed to calm himself for a firm examination.

Deep shadows exaggerated his features and gave him the appearance of a burial mask. He had darker blond hair, marred by a significant gash on the side of the head. Set below thick eyebrows lay shining, green eyes, peerless and unmoving in their beam. His nose was ever so slightly crooked, which gave his face a permanently pensive tilt. His jaw muscles rippled in a tight grimace. Underneath the sunburn and bruising, his skin marked the manifestation of generations of European adaptation to the harsh environment.

An uncontrolled burst of disquiet came about from Joe, sensing another in the room. "Who are you?" He felt bizarre talking to his reflection.

Joe bargained with the glass. In the past, all he saw in the mirror was what others dictated to him. In the eyes of the FCIA and MLK Jr. County, he was racist, privileged, an oppressor, a perpetuator of supremacy; Joe never questioned these canards in his old life. The system spit him out of the whale's belly into the harsh light of the world outside of the caretakers' horrid visions. Struggling with his new appearance, Joe groped for identity. He reminded himself to not limit his thoughts to just the material. "You're a fugitive, a killer, a Hate Criminal." Joe paused. "Were you always this Hate Criminal even when I saw you in the window at the OIHO?"

There was abyssal hatred in his eyes, but the ill-will was only partially directed at himself.

"Have you always been like this?" he pleaded with the reflection. "Do you make me, or do I make you?!"

Joe grasped the mirror by both sides and brought it close to his face, as if he was wrestling it in a fight to the death. His reflection did the same in kind.

"You're so sure of yourself and your convictions, so tell me the answers! Tell me who you are!"

A sort of mundane perfection existed beyond the transient, fragile glass wall between the two. Joe grew enraged at the barrier he could not break without shattering his vision in tandem. A knock at the door interrupted his strange correspondence. Hurriedly, Joe put the mirror face down on the bed and beckoned the intruder inside. Roger, Karl's oldest boy, peaked his head around the door.

"Hey, uh, I just need to grab something from the closet," his cousin said flatly.

Roger's eyes drifted to the mirror and showed visible confusion.

Joe noticed this look and felt a slight embarrassment. Brushing it off, he decided to speak freely. "Hey, Roger, can I ask you a weird question?"

The teen put his hands in his pockets and shrugged imperceptibly. "Sure."

"What do you see when you look in the mirror?" Joe asked hesitantly.

Roger, a very thoughtful boy for his age, felt his confusion deepen. "Well, I see myself." His eyes narrowed with a slight smile. "You're not trying to trap me in an esoteric debate about the self, are you? My dad pulls stuff like that all the time."

His cousin laughed and shuffled on the bed. "Just trying to figure something out for myself. I've been trapped in a few of those with your dad already."

Roger smirked. "Yeah, he does that."

Joe lowered his voice. "Do you ever notice your reflection? I mean really see it? I don't just mean your appearance. Do you ever feel like your reflection is . . . noticing you?"

"I think I know what you're talking about." The young man gave the question some thought. "It's a sort of introspection."

Joe put his chin in his hand. "Huh, that makes sense. The mirror is kind of a projection of your inner thoughts?" Deep down this explanation failed to satisfy his fears.

"Yeah, I guess so. I imagine it's different for everybody, but when I look in the mirror, I don't just see my appearance." Roger showed wisdom beyond his years. "We have to face a sort of mundane judgment. I know things about myself that others don't."

Joe followed along inquisitively. "But it seems separate from me. Like something outside of myself is accusing me."

"Gosh, I don't know." The teen's attention span waned. "The Bible talks about things written on the tablet of your heart, like your conscience. But what do I know? I'm just a kid." He rolled his eyes.

Sensing that Roger was growing tired of his incessant questioning, Joe simply nodded and crossed his arms. The teen shrugged once more and retrieved a rifle and a drawstring bag from the closet.

"I'm going out to shoot some prairie dogs if you want to come," Roger said in a tone that Joe could not evaluate as genuine or not.

"I think I'm good. I've never shot a gun before," the older cousin replied.

This piqued Roger's interest. "Wait, seriously?"

"My dad never took me, and then they confiscated all the guns."

The teen shook his head in disbelief. "Oh, you've got to come now."

Joe shifted on the bed. "Oh, I don't know. I don't know if I'm up for it yet."

"C'mon, get off that bed and let's go. I'll start you off on some tin cans," Roger said as he left the room.

Joe sat dejectedly for a minute. The sound of the gunshot that killed Jill rang out in his memory. Her beautiful face floated before him, marred by the path of a marauding bullet. He picked up the mirror another time. His reflection concealed compassion for his plight and egged him onward to face his fears.

He exited the house and found Roger loading the magazine of a small rifle under the same tree where they did their studies.

"Glad to see you came to your senses. You're not a real man until you've shot a gun!" the youth declared boisterously.

Joe's pride ached slightly at this jab, but he couldn't think of a decent reply.

"This is a .22 caliber. It's a real small bullet, but it can still do a lot of damage. Here, load this one—like this." Roger took a cartridge from the box and slid it into the opening of a magazine.

The elder cousin took the box and began awkwardly loading the bullets. Even in this enclave of relative freedom, he still felt a twinge of guilt holding the contraband. He couldn't even remember the last time he saw a gun that wasn't in the hands of a policeman or a soldier.

"How do you guys get ammo? I mean, I thought it was illegal." Joe's curiosity got the better of him.

The youth closed up the last box and cinched the drawstring bag. "Let's just say that the current laws only made ammo a little bit more expensive," he said with a chuckle.

Roger beckoned him to follow along the grassy plain past the foot-hill he had struggled on.

"That was pretty rough on you," his younger cousin commented. "I don't get why he made you do that."

Joe looked at the hill stoically as they passed. "It had a purpose."

The pair walked for several hundred more yards to a small berm with a section of pockmarked wooden planks. Roger gleefully ran over and set up several of the riddled cans that laid strewn around. Taking the rifle off his shoulder, he handed it to Joe.

"Okay, you're not supposed to dry fire a gun like this. It's rimfire."

The jargon went completely over the older cousin's head. Roger proceeded to walk Joe through the meticulous steps of loading, chambering, shouldering, sighting, and firing the rifle. He removed two sets of eye and ear protection from the drawstring and instructed Joe to put them on as he did the same.

"Are you ready to start?" Roger asked expectantly.

In all reality, the prospect terrified Joe. The memory of the gunshot that killed his wife played over and over. Suddenly, he saw himself back as he was that night: pinned, helpless, and unable to save Jill. Joe held the rifle for several minutes, simply looking down the sights. The firearm began to shake in his hands as his shoulders fatigued and his nerves ran ragged. The world silenced around him, and his heartbeat echoed in his ear protection. Joe's pulse rose. He now saw himself with that rifle, aimed squarely at his wife's attackers and all who acted to destroy their life together. He gained the will to draw in the trigger until the gun slung its payload downrange.

The small recoil surprised him. An aluminum can laid on its side with a small hole. A subtle smell of gunpowder drifted to Joe's nostrils as he lowered the gun. The scent instantly brought him back to that traumatic night. Closing his eyes, he took a deep breath. Instead of avoiding the negative stimuli, he sought to bathe in it. The memories flowed harshly, but he wanted to ride the encroaching tide of grief in a raft of resolve. Joe opened his eyes and re-shouldered the rifle to squeeze off several more rounds.

"Great shots!" Roger proudly put his hands on his hips.

Joe nodded silently and lowered the rifle. Remembering to put it on safe, he returned it to his cousin.

The youth tried to give it back. "I think you're ready to do some pest control."

"I think I'm done for the day," Joe said resignedly. "You go on ahead."

Roger relented and slung the rifle. "Well, at least you're a real man now," he chuckled and walked off beyond the range.

"A real man. . . ." Joe said to himself as he sauntered back to the house.

24

THE FEDS ARE BACK IN TOWN

"I think we're wasting our time here. This is the fourth town we've checked out along this rail line. How can we be sure that he was even telling the truth? You sure did rough him up a bit." Jameila looked out the window with detached frustration

Sean hit the steering wheel angrily. "Just trust me on this one. The uncle being in Utah, the story about riding rail—it fits together a little too perfectly to be a concoction under duress."

"We don't even have a firm location on the uncle," she objected. "If Joe Blaine is still somehow back in MLK, Feldman is going to filet you alive."

"He's not there, I know it." The investigator nodded as they pulled into the next small town. "I've got some guys back in DC on it with our satellites. Patel in the intel department owes me a few favors. I know he's over here." He rolled down the tinted window to look around. "I can practically smell him."

Jameila rolled her eyes and monitored her tablet. Thanks to later additions to the Patriot Act, all communications using a cellular network were public information and did not require a warrant to intercept. The FCIA could collect correspondence from any medium. All of the town's chatter within a given radius was readily visible on her tablet. The mountain of information was easily digested with a few key word filters.

"Anything good?" Sean asked impassively as he drove past the central square. The town's humble appearance was a stark reminder that these federal agents were well out of their comfort zones. The rural emptiness of the place emphasized the crowdedness of places like DC and MLK Jr. County.

"No, not really." Jamelia hung her head.

Her partner's resolve began to waver. After all of the fruitless towns and days wasted, Sean knew Feldman grew impatient for results.

He pursed his lips. "Maybe we should turn back and re-evaluate some of the towns we already passed. I mean—"

Jameila gasped, "Wait!"

"What happened?"

Jameila tapped away at the tablet furiously.

Sean grew impatient and pulled over. "Spill! What'd you find?"

"A guy named Dylan Lemieux just mentioned a guy named Karl buying extra supplies this week to the local sheriff." She paused and looked at her colleague. "Seems like this Karl is an important customer that the sheriff would keep tabs on him."

The investigator swore in giddy anticipation. "It may not be the Karl we're looking for, but hey, it's a lead! Look at the map and double-check that Railway 287 crosses through here."

Jameila swapped applications on the device and verified the information. "Yup! And Mr. Lemieux owns a general store two miles from here."

"Let's check him out!" Sean said with gleeful relief.

After a short drive through the town, they arrived at Dylan's General Store. Taking off their FCIA windbreakers, the pair went plainclothes into the store after formulating a plan of attack. The owner nodded at the strange customers with thinly veiled suspicion.

"Howdy, sir. Howdy, ma'am," Dylan said politely. "Can I help you find something?"

Sean approached the counter and flashed his badge briefly, too quickly to read. "How are you doing, sir? As a matter of fact, you can help me," he said in a conciliatory tone.

At the sight of the badge, the store owner bristled slightly. "Alrighty."

"We're with the IRS. Don't worry, you're not in trouble here"—Sean winked—"but one of your friends had a mistake on his tax form. Nothing major, but he doesn't seem to have an address on file with us. I'm sure it's just an admin error"—he forced a laugh—"so of course now we have to come all the way out here to make sure."

"Pretty good customer service for the IRS," Dylan said wryly. "Who is he?"

Jameila got in on the ruse. "Karl Blaine."

The shop owner nodded with increased suspicion. "I don't think that rings a bell."

Sean looked around the store. The buzzing fluorescent lights punctuated a few water-damaged ceiling tiles. Rows of merchandise sat haphazardly on particleboard shelves. A few faded signs from a bygone era impelled visitors to "Visit Lafayette" and "Enjoy your stay!" Above the counter was a photo, presumably of the generations of Lemieuxs that had lived in the town. Sean's eyes settled on a frame on the wall with a dollar inside. "Is that the first dollar you earned at this place?"

Dylan began to sway nervously. "Yep, been in business since 1999."

"You know you're not supposed to have that right? Didn't anyone tell you that cash was phased out? How much cash do you have?" Jameila began drilling the questions.

Before the shop owner could answer, Sean piled on, "Good catch. I think we might have to do an audit."

She nodded enthusiastically and pulled out her tablet.

"Wait, hold on!" Dylan put out his hands to stop the disaster. "I think I might know a Karl. My memory isn't as strong as it used to be. . . ."

Sean gave Jameila a sly look. "And if you happened to know a Karl, where might he live?"

"He don't have a proper address, see." The shop owner stroked his beard. "I'm not even sure I could find him."

"Do you keep your books in the back or electronically?" Jameila tightened the screws. "I'm going to need to see all your receipts too."

Dylan sensed the increased threat. "Honest! I don't know how to find him. He keeps to himself and very rarely even comes to my store! I think he's out by Wetumpka!"

"Wetumpka? Where's that?" Sean interrogated.

"It's one of the old mining towns in the mountains. I'm sure it'll come up on your fancy government tablet." The elderly man cowered in fear.

"That's more like it. Keep talking." Jameila put the device by her side.

"It's on an old trail by there. I think he's got some kinda ranch. I really don't know any more than that!" Dylan waffled.

Sean relented and stood up straight after leaning on the counter. "Alright, we'll check it out. If you're jerking us around, we know where you're at."

As the pair began to leave, the investigator turned his head. "Oh, one more thing."

Sean walked over to the frame and shattered the front pane on the counter. Carefully removing the dollar, he quipped, "US government property."

Dylan stood in blank fear and nodded meekly.

Jameila followed her partner out of the building after a brief staredown with the shop owner. On their way out to the SUV, Sean crumpled up the outmoded currency and threw it in the trash.

"That last bit was unnecessary," Jameila chastised him once they got into the car.

"Just showing him who's boss," he replied with a smirk. "Let's go pay that sheriff a visit. For whatever reason, he's been keeping tabs on Karl, and we're going to find out why."

25

THE PARABLE OF THE GUESTS

"And we thank you for bringing Joe safely to us and this wonderful food you've given us. In your name, Lord Jesus, Amen," Karl prayed fervently.

After Joe and Roger went shooting, the Blaine household gathered around an acacia wood table for their nightly dinner. The concept of a family meal with all members present was a foreign concept to Joe. As an only child in a weak household, meals were served haphazardly and without fanfare. Large gatherings like this were reserved for holidays and reunions in Joe's mind. He recalled the many Thanksgivings and Christmases where Karl and his family were conspicuously disinvited. Karl could never contain himself on political subjects, much to Eva's chagrin. Joe always remembered him as the crazy uncle growing up, continuously spouting zany theories about how the government was going to take the guns and genocide White people. Joe supposed those theories may not have been so crazy after all. Robert, his father, would always dismiss his younger brother as a radical.

"Can you please pass the potatoes, Joe?" Eva asked politely.

"Oh yeah, sorry." Joe wondered how many times he had been asked while zoning out.

Karl piped up, "You seem pretty deep in thought. What's on your mind?"

"That's a trick question; he's going to debate you on something," Roger interfered humorously.

The table chuckled and agreed.

"Now hold your horses, everybody. I'm not so one-dimensional," Karl objected. "I'll only debate him if he fires the first shot," he laughed jovially.

Joe politely smiled along. "Well, I don't suppose you'll like what I'm going to ask then."

"Go on, Joe. This house is a no-holds-barred zone, one of the last places on earth you can really speak your mind," his uncle bellowed.

He took a moment to compose his thoughts. "I remember holiday gatherings growing up," Joe started cautiously, "when the dinner would usually derail into a shouting match between you and my dad."

Eva crossed her arms and gave her husband a disapproving look.

"And he used to say you gave conservatives a bad name. But quite frankly, you seem more conservative than he is." Joe finished his thought.

Karl erupted in amusement. "Conservative! He thinks I'm a conservative."

The rest of the table laughed along as Joe felt left out of an inside joke.

"Conservatives do a fine job of giving themselves a bad name without my help." The uncle settled down.

Joe leaned forward. "Well, if you're not a conservative, what are you?"

"Now he's done it," George commented to Roger.

Karl launched into a passionate speech: "What even is a conservative? What has conservatism conserved? I used to vote for conservative politicians who promised to stave the decline. All they ever accomplished was delaying the inevitable, the insatiable, and the insistent. These politicians never turned back the beast nor retook lost territory. The measure of their success was not victory but rather how well they herniated themselves struggling against the crushing weight of progressivism." He took a deep breath. "No, I am not a conservative. I reject the capital 'L' Liberal dichotomy."

Joe sat dumbfounded. "Well, there's not really anything besides that, is there? You're either liberal, conservative, or something in-between."

"I am fascinated that you exist," his uncle ribbed, "a true specimen of system propaganda."

"Karl!" Eva chided.

Her husband put up his hands apologetically and sat back in his chair. "Liberals and conservatives are two wings of the same bird. One just happens to be ahead of the other in the race to complete oblivion." He paused for effect. "Do you remember what label your dad uses for things the government does that he doesn't like?"

The nephew thought for a moment, "Fascism."

Karl shook his head, "Right, he called it fascism. What does that term mean to you?"

"Well, that's what the Nazis were. It means authoritarianism and genocide. They were socialists too," Joe guessed bravely.

"Oh boy, I have some reading for you to do." His uncle scratched his chest. "No, fascism is a third position. The third position is neither liberal nor conservative because it rejects the premises of Liberalism altogether."

The nephew prodded, "So are you a fascist then?"

"I can't quite put a firm label on my views, but I reject the so-called 'Enlightenment' and the spiritual bankruptcy of modernity. I want a strong, healthy, spiritually vital society that has pride in its own people. I suppose you could call me a third positionist," Karl espoused. "My point is that there's far more to the story than you've ever been told."

Joe countered, "So why not be a monarchist? Isn't that what the Enlightenment tore down?"

"You're right, that is what the Enlightenment tore down. That's when the cancer of materialism and individualism first started metastasizing into the general population"—the elder Blaine shifted in his chair—"but the cat's out of the bag with the industrial revolution. That genie isn't going back in the bottle despite all of Ol' Teddy's best intentions. Monarchy is no longer viable in the industrial and post-industrial world."

Joe contemplated asking who Ol' Teddy was, but decided against it.

"Society is spiritually bereft as a direct result of rampant consumerism, capitalism, and globalism. Suicides are at their highest in the most prosperous countries," Karl postulated. "This runs counter to the promises of liberalism. They say, 'If you only surrender your Church, your race, and your family, we will give you the riches of the world.' The only thing people found at the end of that rainbow was a noose made of foreign imported rope they bought from an international chain store for $1.99."

The nephew jumped in, "Well didn't communism provide an alternative? You seem pretty critical of capitalism, so why not go red?"

George blurted out, "Better dead than red!"

"Good boy!" the proud father chuckled. "But in all seriousness, I see where you're coming from. If we're throwing out liberalism, why not give Marx an audition? Well, you see, communism and capitalism are really two sides of the same coin." Karl leaned over to Roger. "A coin of a particular type."

Roger gave a slight nod as his father continued, "They both arrive at the end state of a churchless, raceless, and mongrelized population of proles. The only difference with Marxism is that you also end up starving to death. While economically different, liberal capitalism brings the same societal evils; they just wrap it in shiny foil and sell it to you as opposed to shoving it down your throat with a bayonet"—Karl paused to think—"although the bayonets seem a little more common now than shiny packages in our current situation."

Joe couldn't disagree with this last point. Forced from his home at gunpoint, it didn't make any difference whether the police uniforms bore the red star or the inclusion banner.

"I get how communism and capitalism destroy the spirit," the nephew asked, "but why do you keep mentioning race? I mean, it's just skin color. I think there's a lot of anti-White racism, but it's just simple prejudice like any other sort of racism." Joe didn't particularly agree with this latter assertion, but he felt compelled to say so nonetheless.

Karl resisted the impulse to insult his intelligence. "I don't suppose I can fault you for thinking that. Most of the system's propaganda is devoted to making you think that very point."

Then Roger chimed in, "Why did you want to live in the privileged area?"

Joe was put on his back heal. "Well, it was nicer."

"Why was it nicer?"

"Because of socioeconomic conditions," Joe replied.

Karl joined the tag-team: "Who lived in the 'not nice' areas? Didn't the 'nice' areas get worse when the 'not nice' people moved in? Isn't that why you sought the 'nice' areas?"

Joe reeled under the interrogation. "I think economic factors are to blame primarily."

"Then why did the powers that be decide that the only way to improve those economic conditions was to force integration?" His uncle began leading.

"Now hold on, what are we talking about? Are you talking about Martin Luther King? I don't agree with the Equity and Inclusion Act, but I think the civil rights movement was a generally positive force. Judging by character is better than just on skin color," the nephew opined.

Karl clapped his hands. "Spoken like a true conservative. You're falling into the trap of accepting yesterday's liberalism as today's conservative principles. If MLK was alive today, he'd be wearing an inclusion banner and denying OIHO waivers with the rest of them. You can't just set the clock back to an earlier stage of liberal decline. The winding and ticking of that same clock brought us to this very point, didn't it?"

Joe pondered these things deeply. He reflected on his experiences and remembered sitting in the police car with Wallace. He recalled how he recoiled in disgust at Wallace's milquetoast posturing about "Real America." Since then, his mind descended from those adrenaline-fueled revelations, but the burning embers remained. Joe couldn't articulate why he recoiled then but was at last gaining the missing pieces of the puzzle.

Roger continued, "And that clock will continue winding so long as the mint of the capitalism-communism coin keeps pumping out new currency."

"I can't say I have a counterpoint," Joe replied. "I suppose society got to this point on the legs of some kind of agenda. But how does that prove that race actually means anything?"

Karl stepped in with a fatherly tone. "Picture your whole extended family for a moment: aunts, crazy uncles, cousins, everybody. Are there certain unique markers or characteristics of this family? Behaviors, looks, quirks, et cetera?"

The nephew took a moment to think then gave a simple, "Yeah."

"And if a stranger came to your family and started demanding that you take in bums off the street and leaving your doors unlocked, you would resent that, right?"

"I suppose I would," Joe agreed.

His uncle continued, "A race is like a huge family. And like a family, it has its own story, culture, and traditions. Culture and race are inseparable and are expressions of the same core elements. You wouldn't expect a guest of a completely different background to understand or carry on these traditions, would you?"

Joe argued, "Well, are the traditions worth preserving? They're just traditions."

"Traditions feed directly into culture like a wellspring. Without tradition, the river of culture runs dry and the whole ecosystem collapses," Karl continued methodically, "but that's a whole separate argument. The behaviors make the family and the family makes the behaviors. Changing either of those factors has serious consequences."

The nephew acquiesced on this point, "Alright, I buy that. Each race has a separate culture. That doesn't make one better than the other."

The elder Blaine furrowed his brow. "When did I claim some kind of superiority? All I'm advocating is that each family gets its own space to practice its own traditions without interference. Moreover, a blood member of a particular family is best suited for being a cultural participant in that family versus a stranger."

Joe wondered where he got the notion that his uncle was advocating some kind of supremacy.

"I can get on board with that I suppose," the nephew conceded.

Karl continued to press him and made a small tent with his fingers. "Return for a moment to the stranger making demands. Due to your family's altruism, you take him in out of pity. But imagine that this guest starts claiming that your existence as a family unit is offensive to him, and so he re-keys the house. He lets the first bum in, who then steals some plates. The second bum touches your sister. More and more bums move in and really start stinking up the place. The guest starts demanding that your family assimilate to the bums, not even taking into consideration whether you wanted them there in the first place. Worse still, he starts teaching the children to hate the family and siphons money from you to mail it back to his own family," his uncle crafted the parable.

The nephew objected, "No, I wouldn't like that at all."

Karl made a conciliatory motion with his hands. "Just humor me for a second. What if I told you this guest had been kicked out of over a hundred houses before coming to stay with you?"

"Well why did we even take him in, in the first place?" Joe

questioned the realism of the scenario.

Roger concealed a giggle.

"Very good question. But regardless, wouldn't you want to kick him out on the street?" the elder Blaine prodded.

Joe crossed his arms. "Certainly."

Karl sewed the final row of the tapestry: "Now imagine this scenario, but you're not even allowed to mention the guest's existence. Wouldn't that be absurd?"

"There's no way the situation would get to that point," the nephew objected.

Karl spread his arms to grab both ends of the head of the table. He leaned forward and gave Joe a stern look. "That *is* the situation."

Joe felt a burning sense of curiosity and a slight twinge of fear. He did not quite understand the parable but couldn't disagree with any of its premises.

Eva spoke up: "Karl took me through that exact progression while we were dating." A sweet smile spread across her face. "You'll understand soon enough. I think you're closer than you think."

"That's how I knew she was the one," her husband joked. "She didn't run off when I started my schizoid ramblings!"

The family shared a collective chuckle and continued eating the meal. All the while, Joe stewed in silence while he digested the tale of the stranger. The meaning danced around his head elusively. Joe understood the symbolism of the family at least. Raking his memory, he agreed that there was a unique, defining character to his own people. Moreover, he felt convicted to defend it from erasure. After finishing his plate, he took a brief, terrified glance at the distorted form in the reflective surface of his spoon.

Joe put the utensil down with wide eyes and whispered quietly, "But who are the guests?"

26

SPILLED MILK

Joe awoke late the next morning after a spate of nightmares about being trapped at Rosenblatt's motel again. He heard a concerned, hushed conversation beyond the door. Sleepily, he made his way out of the bedroom. When he entered the common area, he saw Eva concealing tears and Karl holding her hands in reassurance.

"Good morning." Joe didn't know whether it was appropriate to pry.

Eva turned her head to look out the window while her husband squeezed her shoulder.

"Hey, Joe, we need to talk," Karl said in a low, shaken tone.

The nephew felt his heart sink in trepidation. He walked outside and braced for whatever was next.

"I went into Lafayette for a supply run this morning, and I saw Sheriff Perry," Karl began slowly.

Joe had a feeling of where this conversation was going.

His uncle continued, "He pulled me inside the diner and insisted I have breakfast with him. He said that some feds are poking around the town looking for a fellow named Karl Blaine."

"Did the sheriff tell them where you were?" Joe asked anxiously.

"No, he's solid. And public record backs him up. There's no record of me being here. I bought the property with a phony social security card and driver's license." The elder Blaine turned to face Joe and showed grave concern. "So, how did they know to come looking for me in this neck of the woods? Did you tell anyone that you were coming here? And I mean anyone."

The nephew racked his brain worriedly. With a sudden sinking realization, he remembered telling Wallace he was headed to Utah along the rail. Worse still, he mentioned that he had an uncle in the area.

Karl noticed the anxiety forming on Joe's face. He grabbed him by the shoulders and interrogated, "Did you tell anyone you were coming here?"

"Not exactly," Joe began with trembling.

"Not exactly?!"

"I mean, that cop who helped me escape, he told me where each train was going"—the nephew nervously placed his hand on the back of his head—"and I mentioned I had an uncle in Utah."

Karl widened his eyes slightly and turned around. He walked a few paces with his hands on his hips and exclaimed, "Gosh, Joe! Don't you remember when you visited before college when I told you that you should never mention that I live here?!"

Joe's heart sank with the memory. "I'm sorry, it just slipped out."

"Slipped out?!" His uncle faced him once again and rubbed his face, "Okay, okay, it happened. We're going to stay calm. We adapt and overcome. The feds still don't know jack. You're lucky Perry ran interference for us, but he doesn't have a clue how much risk he just incurred and I don't intend for him to find out."

The fugitive moved over to a stump and sat down with his head in his hands. "I'm so sorry. I knew I shouldn't have come here."

Karl stood for a moment, then approached the sullen soul.

He placed a firm hand on Joe's shoulder, "Spilled milk, buddy. For now, they still don't know we're here, praise the Lord. You're not trained for this and mistakes happen. For what it's worth, I'm glad you came here. I would rather this than let another member of my own kind, my own family, get ground up by the system." He gave a look of stern compassion. "They must've gotten to that Wallace guy, poor wretch. I can only imagine what's happening to him now."

His nephew shivered at the thought. Rosenblatt's grotesque smile flashed before Joe's eyes.

Karl continued, "But you're a little too hot now to stay here. While I may lose a little bit of independence if they find out where I live, all is not lost. But I don't think I can have you here anymore," he stated mournfully. "Sheriff Perry is probably going to swing by sometime to keep up appearances. He'll notice if we have another member here he doesn't know about. He's on my side with most things but would never stick his neck out for a fugitive Hate Criminal."

"But I'll be captured out on my own!" Joe protested selfishly.

"Hold your horses. I've thought of that. You're a strong soul, but nobody can stand up to some of their interrogation techniques. Think about it. It's in my best interest to keep you out of the feds' hands," his uncle intimated.

The fugitive nodded slowly and looked out over the mountain vista without a word.

"I'm going to stash you in a motel in Lafayette," Karl started. "I simply can't afford for you to be found here."

Joe's mind descended into fight or flight. "No! I won't go to a motel! No! Absolutely not! I'd rather just off myself now than give myself up to another Rosenblatt!"

At first confused, his uncle understood his hesitation. "Don't worry, it's not like the big-city motels. It's no Ritz Carlton, but it's a legitimate motel."

Calming down, Joe replied, "But that'll be expensive. I can't accept being a drain on you like that."

"Don't worry about money. I've made some pretty shrewd investments over the years. Let's just say that my grandchildren will live very comfortably. Your stay will be a drop in the bucket," Karl reassured his nephew.

"I don't know about this. How will—"

"You just let me mind the logistics," the uncle interrupted. "No one will know you're there. I have a driver's license for you that I was saving for Roger to use. It'll say you're twenty-one, but I think you can pass."

"But what about the feds in Lafayette? Wouldn't it make more sense to stash me somewhere else?" Joe contested.

Karl pursed his lips. "I thought about that. If I have to make frequent supply runs, I need to minimize my time out in the open and on the roads. As more feds swarm, the roads in and out of the surrounding towns could become check points. The only reason we can sneak into Lafayette from here is because we're coming in off a dirt road that leads nowhere on the map. The other towns are too far to rough it cross-country, and I can't risk driving on more roads that might have check points, though there still might be some in the town. . . ." He sighed. "It's not ideal, but it's what we have to do.

Besides, they're looking for you here and know I don't live in town. Sometimes it's best to hide in plain sight."

Joe's mind began swimming at the prospect. He had a thousand questions whirling in his head as he feared leaving the safety of the ranch.

Karl sighed and looked out over his land. "There's so much I wanted to teach you."

"Well, for what it's worth, you taught me more than I ever learned before," Joe said wistfully.

"I hope so, my friend. It's a big, bad world out there. You've got to be tough if you're going to survive it." His uncle stood him up and patted his back.

Joe thought for a moment about the sheer hostility toward him that pervaded the air like a raging fire outside of this little enclave. Its presence hung in the atmosphere like a vast fuel-air bomb, floating inert so long as no one challenged it with the spark of resistance.

"We'd better get going. I hate to rush you out like this, but time is of the essence. Sheriff Perry could swing by any minute." Karl broke his contemplation and brought him back inside.

His uncle frantically moved around the house grabbing various backpacks and duffle bags. Joe followed along, and his body felt limp.

"Okay, there's food, water, and a credit card in this one. Should be enough to get you through the end of the month. I'll swing by periodically to resupply. There's an old cell phone in this pocket. Only put the battery in if you have to text me in a dire emergency. Don't call. I hope it goes without saying, but don't go to the police for anything," Karl instructed quickly while handing over the bags, "and don't go wandering around town. You're too hot right now."

Joe peaked inside the pack and found an assortment of water bottles, military issue rations, and foodstuffs. He took out a mysterious looking electronic device and unfolded it.

"That's a pre-2010s flip phone, before big tech got its operating systems into every last little phone manufacturer. It has a number saved that is connected to a spoofed online phone. I won't be able to see the content of your text. Think of it more as an SOS message. If I get the notification, I'm going to assume you're in grave danger, so don't use it unless you absolutely have to."

His nephew marveled at the old-school tech and wondered what princely sum it demanded for its privacy granting qualities. Karl instructed him to wait in the kitchen while he gathered some last-minute provisions. He returned with a small, hardshell case.

Opening the box, his uncle lowered his voice and spoke sternly: "I'm giving you this pocket knife. It's a vintage piece, so no serial number. Technically it's legal and grandfathered in, but don't get caught with it. Most cops would give you a hard time and assume it's contraband."

Joe grasped the knife in his hand and opened the spring assisted blade. It was a menacing piece with a blackened, four-inch blade.

"This is too much. I can't take all these things from you," the nephew protested.

Karl ignored his objections. "C'mon, it's time we get going. I've got a feeling that things are going to move pretty quickly," he belied his increasingly frantic anxiety.

On their way out to the garage, they ran into Karl's youngest, Alexandria.

"Daddy, where is Joe going? Is he leaving?" the little girl questioned.

Her father knelt down and grasped her hand. "It's okay, Allie, he has a new place to stay."

Alexandria waxed sullen: "But he just got here. I'm still working on his present."

Karl gave a look that revealed he had forgotten. "That was supposed to be a surprise. I can bring it to him later; we have to go."

"Wait, I'll grab it!" she darted off before her father could reign her in.

Karl shook his head and beckoned Joe to follow him to the garage, where he took the tarp off of a 4x4 light pickup with knobby off-road tires. The truck was a faded orange and had resolute, rectangular headlights. Heavy gashes and scratches evidenced its status as a frequent rock crawler. Karl began tossing the luggage in the bed.

"Won't people just steal it out of the back?" Joe pointed out.

His uncle took a moment to laugh. "Oh boy, you really have no clue where you are." He placed a bungee net over the cargo.

Alexandria burst in with a little cardboard box haphazardly decorated with multi-colored construction paper. "Joe, Joe, Joe!"

The little one extended the package to her cousin.

Joe's heart melted slightly. "Aw, well thank you, Allie."

"Open it! I'm sorry the wrapping isn't done yet," she said

mournfully.

Taking the little box in hand, he pried open the top while attempting to preserve as much of the decoration as possible. Inside lay an oblong stone about two and a half inches long.

Karl spoke up: "I chiseled that off the boulder for you a few days ago. Allie was going to make you a necklace out of it."

"Do you like it?" Alexandria smiled with beaming, blue eyes.

Overwhelmed with emotion, Joe hugged the girl and shook his uncle's hand. "I love it," he said tearfully.

"Never lose touch with the higher purpose, Joe. You've got some hard times ahead, but never lose your spirit. I can't tell you why all this is happening, but I know there's a reason. Existence is resistance. And resistance, no matter how seemingly futile, is your victory." Karl put his hand on Joe's shoulder.

The nephew embraced his uncle and thanked him for all he had done.

"Run along and tell everyone we're about to leave so they can say goodbye," Karl instructed his daughter.

As Alexandria ran off, Joe clutched the small rock in his hands. His uncle opened the sliding garage door and backed out the truck. The smell of the exhaust gasses disquieted the fugitive as they signaled another flight from danger. By now, the rest of the family had gathered by the garage to give him a sendoff.

"I packed you a satchel of books and this old CD player. I'm sure Karl won't notice a few things are missing." Eva smiled and winked at her husband.

Joe gratefully accepted the gift and hugged each member of the family, thanking them all for their hospitality and courage.

"Shoot straight, Joe!" Roger called out as they loaded into the cab.

Joe gave a polite wave out of the window as the truck lumbered off, onward to an uncertain fate.

27

NEW IDENTITY

The long drive down the mountain gave Karl ample opportunity to give Joe last minute instructions.

"Now, don't leave your room under any circumstances for at least two weeks," he said in a hurried tone as he sawed away at the steering wheel along the treacherous gravel switchbacks.

Joe shook his head. "Two weeks? I'll go insane!"

"You'll get caught," his uncle scolded. "You've had a little too much good luck so far. I don't think you want to press that."

The pair sat in tense silence for a quarter of an hour as they jostled back and forth on the winding, mountain roads. Joe estimated they still had an hour or so left before they reached Lafayette. As they pulled in and out of Wetumpka, his mind brimmed with questions.

"Who are the guests?" the nephew blurted.

Karl shifted the truck out of four-wheel low as the ground smoothed out. "You know better than to ask for the answer."

Joe's patience thinned. "It'll drive me crazy while I'm cooped up."

"We were given pattern recognition for a reason: to recognize predators. I don't have to tell you who they are. They'll tell you by their behavior: communism, runaway capitalism, mass migration, sexual perversions, manipulation of the financial system, those motels, the mass media," his uncle spoke in more innuendoes.

"What do those things have to do with each other? That just sounds like a laundry list of things you don't like." The nephew crossed his arms and looked out the window at the imposing scenery.

Karl simply chuckled and nodded his head. "You'll get there. No free answers."

His replies were terse and short. In truth, the situation stressed Karl far more than he revealed. The insulated and comfortable life he cultivated for himself and his family was in danger of being upended. He would do anything to preserve his enclave.

"Can I ask you a question?" Joe piped up again, grating his uncle slightly.

"Alright," Karl said as he engaged in increasingly nervous checks of the windows and mirrors.

Joe released his question like a slinger launching a stone: "If you hate what's happening in the world so much, why don't you do anything about it?"

Taken aback, Karl frowned and extended an upturned palm. "What do you mean? I do a lot to resist the system."

His nephew continued to stare out the window as the world whizzed by. "Well, you've successfully separated yourself from the system. But what about changing or destroying it?"

Karl pursed his lips. "Did I ever tell you why I got kicked out of the Navy?"

"I think so. You disobeyed an order, right?" his passenger followed along.

"Not just any order." The uncle took a deep breath. "Do you remember the lead up to the Equity and Inclusion Act? You were fairly young."

"I think so." Joe tried to remember.

"Well, most of those policies started in the military. The powers that be knew that public trust in the military was high back then. They knew if they could push progressive policies there, they'd be more likely to be accepted in the general population. It was a clever ploy, and it worked. Then there was South Africa," Karl recalled painfully.

His nephew rarely kept up with world affairs in his past life. "I know there was a war over there and we sent troops. But remind me, what happened in South Africa?"

"I won't bore you with the specifics," Karl began, "but the White minority started some violent resistance to the multicultural anarchy around them. In the ensuing bedlam, the US organized a coalition to restore order. I heard stories of our troops engaging in frequent atrocities against those 'evil racists.' All manner of horrific acts went unreported and unpunished because these Whites committed the cardinal sin of being labeled racists. The pent-up racial hatred for Whites in America was taken out on hapless Afrikaners. They became proxies. Roving bands of American personnel took armored vehicles without orders as mobile rape and killing vans. If anyone tried to stop it, they'd get the book thrown at them for racism. I saw this country show its true colors. My classmates from the academy cheered when the leader of the White resistance was captured by a SEAL team and beaten to death in the street by a mob after they handed him over." The uncle stared out the windshield for a short time. "I had a civilian friend at the time who warned me about how anti-White the system really was. I didn't believe him until I started seeing how much my fellow service members foamed at the mouth with glee and elation to kill the racist Whites in South Africa."

Joe vaguely remembered the parade for the returning forces. "So, what did you do?"

"Shortly after graduation, I had orders to meet a destroyer deployed out to that area. This ship had already launched dozens of tomahawk missiles in support of the anti-Afrikaner forces." Karl gripped the steering wheel tightly. "So, I refused to go. I took a stand on my conscience, and they gave me the boot."

Joe nodded. "Were there any others?"

His uncle grew sullen. "There were enough to make the brass sweat, but I was the only one from a service academy to refuse. A small minority of my friends hated what was happening too, but they couldn't afford to lose their precious careers. Those friends are commanding ships or flying fighter jets right now. They found out who they really served and what they really believed. The flag officers had long ago been screened for strict ideological compliance."

His passenger admired Karl's strength of conscience. "Didn't they court martial you? I feel like they would've thrown you in the brig for that."

"They threatened it to be sure, but they realized that it would give me a public stage to spread the word about the atrocities being committed. So, they quietly dismissed me with an other-than-honorable discharge along with a handful of others from the various services who refused. They sought recoupment of my education costs, but some sympathetic alumni paid it off. I tried to reach out to various media outlets, but no one would touch me with a ten-foot pole," Karl recalled angrily. "So, I gave up on society. I decided the best thing to do was pull the ejection lever. I had already made those investments I mentioned, and I made a good killing. I married my high school sweetheart, bought the ranch, and never looked back."

Joe processed these things silently. The off-road tires of the truck made a steady whirring noise as they descended the mountains down to Lafayette. He caught a glimpse of himself in the side-view mirror and felt compelled to press his uncle.

"I'm not minimizing your stand. Definitely something I'd struggle to do," Joe started slowly, preparing for the crescendo of his cutting question, "but what have you done since, besides watch the world burn?"

Karl grew frustrated and offended. "I deprive the system of my talent. I refuse to be used by them. There's no saving the system now."

His nephew felt compelled to press him more, but resisted the urge. They both lost a good deal to the system; however, Karl's exile was voluntary.

"We're almost to Lafayette; move to the backseat and lie down. There's a couple of bags and blankets back there. Hide yourself underneath," the uncle instructed, abruptly cutting off the conversation.

Joe complied and wondered whether this was primarily to shut him up or hide him. Nestling in among the woolen blankets and duffels, he concealed his presence. Karl took a brief glance to the backseat to adjust the cover.

◘

"I know that sheriff is hiding Karl. That whole story about that farmer named Carlos is total BS," Sean lamented after getting up from the bed and getting dressed, "and the store owner claiming to not know how to get to Wetumpka is a lie. The name's on his store for heaven's sake."

He sat for a moment to fiddle with his wedding ring in deep contemplation.

Jameila resented the abrupt transition from pillow talk to shop talk. Still caught up in the intimacy of the previous night, she sat up and kept herself covered with a blanket. "Well, I suppose we should get back to it."

Her partner climbed back into bed and caressed her face. "Oh, they'll still be around in a few more minutes."

She pushed his hand away. "That was just a one-time thing. Don't get any ideas. Feldman would kill us if she found out."

Sean's phone buzzed. Taking it in his hand, his face drooped in frustration.

The text from his wife read, "You forgot to arrange the windshield appointment even though I specifically asked you to this weekend. Oh, and I'm going out with the girls tonight. Don't worry about it," followed by a passive-aggressive kissing emoji.

"Who's that?" Jameila peered over his shoulder.

"Nobody." Her partner closed his phone screen quickly. "C'mon, we're burning daylight."

She dissented briefly: "What's our next lead? We can't find that stupid mining town anywhere."

Sean put on his windbreaker and beckoned her to follow: "With all our tech, it's easy to forget that sometimes the best police work is done by just asking the locals. I'll stop the first native I see with the flashing lights—put the fear of God into him."

Jameila got dressed quickly and followed along, conspicuously noticing Sean's wedding ring lying unattended on the nightstand. The pair walked over to the SUV and started their patrol in the early afternoon of Lafayette.

"Look at that," Sean chuckled, "our first customer right out the gate."

◘

Karl came to an abrupt stop. He waited in silence for a minute as his breathing grew shallow. Joe could hear him drumming on the steering wheel anxiously.

"Keep it cool and don't say a word," the uncle whispered.

Joe couldn't see anything beneath the thick blankets, and his own anxiety rose sharply.

"Good afternoon," a gruff voice answered as Karl rolled down the window. "Can you tell us where Wetumpka is? It doesn't show up on GPS."

Karl took a short period to gather his thoughts, making sure to keep his head down and praying that he wouldn't be recognized. "Uh, sure, neighbor. Just take that road back there for an hour or so and then hang a left on the gravel road that leads up the mountain. Not much up there nowadays. What's this about?"

"Thanks." The voice said nothing more.

Joe heard a few footsteps over to another car, which promptly sped off.

His uncle let out a rare slew of curses. "Those were feds!"

"Why did you tell them where Wetumpka is?!" the nephew questioned in fear.

"I didn't. I sent them in the completely wrong direction." He swore again. "This is heating up a little too quickly. I need to get you to the motel and get out of here as fast as possible."

Karl punched the gas and sped through town. After five minutes of tense driving, he pulled up to the motel.

"Okay, you can come out. We've got to make this fast," the uncle spoke quickly. "Here, put this on."

Karl handed Joe a surgical mask, baseball cap, and sunglasses.

"Here's your ID. Memorize it as soon as possible. Your new name is William David McDowell. Your birthday is June 14th. You're from Springfield, Illinois, and you're here because your family kicked you out." He lowered his voice. "The real Will McDowell died of a heroin overdose a few months ago. The Springfield coroner makes a pretty penny selling these things instead of entering them into evidence. There are so many ODs, nobody even notices." The uncle shook his head grimly. "I wrote your new social security number on the slip of paper with the card. The rest is up to you; just keep it all straight. The credit card is in William's name, and I'll be paying it off with crypto. They'll add your name to the federal guest registry at the motel, but since the coroner never canceled the ID card, it shouldn't raise any flags."

Joe's head reeled from the flood of information and stressed about having to recall it on the fly. Looking at the driver's license, he questioned whether he bore enough of a resemblance to the picture.

"Alright, grab the stuff out of the back and then I'm out of here. Don't worry about telling me your room number. I'll figure it out later. I'd get out to help you, but you never know who's watching. I'm not driving my normal car." Karl pointed to the bed of the truck.

Joe put on the mask and the hat. "Well, Uncle Karl, thanks for everything. I really can't thank you enough."

His uncle silently nodded with a concerned gaze then blurted, "Stay in your room for at least two weeks! I'll swing by for supplies then," as Joe climbed down from the truck.

The fugitive agreed quietly and retrieved the substantial load of bags from the bed. After he had the last satchel in hand, Joe gave the truck a summary slap on the quarter panel. Karl waved and sped off, leaving him loaded down with luggage in the parking lot of the motel.

Joe looked up at the dilapidated sign that read, "Mountain Springs Inn," and his eyes drifted to the rickety structure before him. A small shack at the entrance showed where to make reservations. A sheriff's vehicle drove by without incident, but not without making Joe's pulse skyrocket.

He walked up to the reservations hut and introduced himself. "How's it going? I'd like a room please."

A swarthy man in an office chair wheeled around to face him and hurriedly closed the tab of adult material on his monitor. After opening the sliding window, he said in a thick, South Asian accent, "Uh yes, we have room available. How long you are needing it?"

"Can I pay for two weeks up front? I don't know how long." Joe tried to keep calm and collected.

"Yes, we have the room available. Show me ID and a credit card." The motel owner extended a grubby hand. "You will renew by phone, and we will charge the card."

Fumbling through his various bags, Joe presented the requisite items. He clasped his hands nervously behind his back as the owner took the fraudulent cards.

"Here is our rate plus tax." The man handed him a slip of paper while entering William McDowell's information into the computer. "And you know we must report all guests to the register?"

Joe reluctantly agreed and looked over his shoulder, half expecting a SWAT team to swoop in at any moment. The Equity and Inclusion Act mandated that every hotel upload a list of its guests to a federal database to track movement of citizens. The fugitive felt relief that his alter ego wouldn't raise eyebrows on the register like his own name.

"Here is your key, room 389."

"Thanks." Joe gratefully snatched the room key and started walking toward the main building.

"Mr. McDowell," the owner called out.

For a moment, Joe walked on without registering that this was his new name.

"Mr. McDowell!"

Snapping at the realization, the fugitive froze and turned around.

"Yes?" Joe replied with a small crack in his voice.

The owner stuck his hand out of the window. "You forgot your ID and credit card."

Breathing a sigh of relief, the fraudulent McDowell broke into an awkward jog to recover the items. After grabbing the cards and thanking the owner, Joe chastised himself for making the mistake of not recognizing his new name. Shaking off the near miss, he made his way to room 389.

He swiped the card to unlock the room, then dropped his bags as soon as he passed through the entryway. As the door shut behind him, the room darkened considerably. Groping for the switch, Joe at last turned on the lights. As he placed the knife his uncle gave him on the nightstand, a large mirror by the side of the bed greeted him with a flash. He was trapped for at least two weeks.

PART IV

THE BEAST SYSTEM

28

SAM WILSON

Joe spent a while in the worn, beige seat by the window, separating the blinds with his fingers to monitor the traffic that passed by the motel. He preferred this nerve-racking activity over having to look at his new prison. The room bore horrible resemblance to Rosenblatt's throne room and smelled much the same. Joe checked the clock on the nightstand. What had felt like several hours had only been twenty minutes in the room. Its small square footage seemed to shrink by the second, boxing him into a paranoid nightmare of claustrophobic anxiety. The thought of two weeks, possibly more, without leaving the room sent his flight response into overdrive.

Seeking some kind of small comfort, Joe decided to try taking a hot shower. After making his way to the bathroom, he was greeted by a puddle of unknown, yellowish liquid in the tub. Undeterred, he turned the lever for the shower head. The pipes screeched as a gush of cloudy water spilled from the tap. A few air bubbles caused the liquid to stop and flow intermittently. After a few minutes of waiting for the water to get warm, the flow stopped completely. Joe attempted to fiddle with the tap, but to no avail. Shortly afterwards, the room telephone rang.

"Yes, hello, this is front desk," the voice on the phone stated.

"Hello?" Joe replied suspiciously.

"You must not use the hot water. The heater floods in the basement. We will charge the repair to your card if you do this," the employee said in an angry tone, then hung up.

The fugitive slammed the phone down on the receiver several

times until the handset's plastic cracked. Resignedly, he slumped onto the bed. The comforter bore a reddish and faded floral pattern specifically designed to conceal stains. What Joe initially mistook for polka dots were actually cigarette burns. Resting his head on the stiff pillow, he looked around the room. Pale, gray daylight cast mournful rays on the coffee-colored plaster walls and navy-blue carpet. A small TV hung on the wall like a crucifix beside a scratched particle board table. Several pizza boxes were stacked in the corner from the previous tenant, with moldy food still inside.

"Better than prison," Joe remarked with a twinge of irony, "I guess."

After hanging a blanket on the mirror, he retrieved a can of sardines from the main pack and turned on the TV. After avoiding several adult content channels, he settled on the cable news station.

"Welcome to ACS news. I'm your host, Daryl King. Thank you for joining us on this beautiful day in August for our coverage of the New York City Pride Day parade." The sound seeped out of tinny speakers.

Joe rolled his eyes but kept watching out of morbid curiosity.

"This broadcast is brought to you by Bronstein Pharmaceuticals. With me as my co-host today is Avril the Ferocious."

The camera panned over to the individual called Avril. Decked out in obscene makeup, the being smiled devilishly beneath an outlandish wig that stretched a foot above its head. A well-groomed beard curled around scarlet lips like smoke rising from a burning inferno. Spiraling horns protruded from the wig's edifice, from which hung shining, crescent moon tassels. It wore a sparkling, red linen dress, revealing extensive artificial cleavage.

The hideous being placed a clawed pedipalp on the desk and leaned forward to say in a preposterously over feminized voice, "Thank you so much for having me, Daryl." It extended its other appendage to grab his arm.

"It's a pleasure." Daryl seemed to conceal deep discomfort. "Now Avril, what are you most excited for in this year's Pride Day parade?"

Joe had seen many of these broadcasts before, always viewing them from a detached sense of vague disgust. Now, the disgust reached the point of nausea.

Avril replied, "As an April 19th Survivor, I'm most excited for the broad participation of children this year. We've been seeing younger and younger little humans coming out in support—it just gives my heart joy!" It chuckled.

Joe wondered what the April 19th Incident had to do with any of this.

Daryl forced a laugh in reply. "That's right. A recent study by the New York Associated Post shows that the average age of LGBTQM involvement is dropping steadily. When did you first get involved?"

The grotesque creature put a hand to its thorax. "I started doing drag when I was eleven. I will never forget how much my sixth-grade teacher encouraged and supported me. And petty, suburban, White moms wanted to get them fired! I'm just so glad I was able to have such an inclusive environment. I grew up without a dad, and drag just provided a way for me to express myself." It smiled, then turned to the camera to blow a kiss. "So Mx. Goldman, if you're watching, I love you and thank you so much!"

The newscaster nodded in righteous agreement. "We should never forget the sacrifices some teachers made years ago to bring about a more inclusive environment in our schools."

The camera cut to a view of Times Square where debauchery and indulgent mayhem unfolded for the world to see. Joe could spot in the crowd two men in a suggestive position next to a child waving the inclusion banner and an implement of deviant activities.

Daryl continued solemnly after a brief pause, "A small group of individuals showed up to protest the march today. Many of them are members of hate groups like Pro-American Families. We have Sam Wilson, one of their spokesmen, here to comment."

A small insert faded into the screen showing a middle-aged White man wearing a cross necklace. Joe leaned forward in interest.

"How are you doing today?" Sam said cheerfully.

"I'm well, I'm well," Daryl replied quickly. "Now, what is your motive for being here today?"

Sam smiled slightly and started to speak: "Well, I'm here to up-hold conservative family values."

The newscaster began questioning: "In your ideal world, what does an American family look like?"

Shifting slightly, the spokesman replied, "Look, I'm not a bigot. This isn't about hate. There are a lot of gays in my congregation, and I love them. Some of them are the best parents I know. I'm not here to oppose gay marriage or any outdated policies like that. My daughter is transgender. In fact, I fly a pride flag outside my church."

Joe started to grip the remote tightly.

"The pride flag," Avril jumped in, "is a hate symbol! It was useful for its time, but we've moved past that as a movement. It's time for the Inclusion Banner! The pride flag leaves out so many marginalized groups."

Sam piped up angrily, "See? This is exactly what the left does. This is why I left the Southern Baptist Convention. What is today called? Pride Day. Have we forgotten that? I don't have a problem with gays or trans individuals. I already said that. I'm here to oppose things like the Minor Attracted Persons movement."

The being chided angrily, "You're on the wrong side of history. You're so far in the past with your oppressive and outdated views. Somebody call 2016, am I right?" It paused to demand a chuckle from Daryl. "I'm so proud of how open and inclusive this parade has become to MAPs like myself, and frankly, I couldn't care less about your views, sweetie." It flipped its hair with a smile.

The conservative backpedaled in noncommittal language: "I mean, the pride movement was genuinely a good thing, but I think this may be a bridge too far. All I'm asking for are sensible measures to ensure that childre—minors involved understand consent and are fully educated to make these decisions."

Joe turned off the television. He couldn't contain his rage anymore. His uncle was right about the conservatives and their insipid groveling before Liberalism's tide. Shameful displays from those who were supposed to be defending Christian values didn't bother Joe in the past. Now, it ignited a churning sense of hatred and anger directed toward both the conservative and the MAP advocate. These were the two choices offered to American people: total moral corruption or slower total moral corruption.

Joe resumed anxiously looking out the window. A black SUV rolled by the motel slowly, seemingly searching for something. He narrowed the opening in the blinds and peered intently. A knock came at the door.

Joe's heart leapt clear to his throat as the adrenaline made his limbs shaky. He dove for the knife and huddled behind the chair.

"Housekeeping!" a feminine voice called out.

Another set of knocks came to the door.

In the fear-induced stupor, Joe's mind scrambled for the words, "I'm good, thanks."

As the cleaning cart rolled away, the fugitive lowered his chin to his chest.

He tried to slow his breathing but said to himself, "I can't keep doing this."

Joe closed the curtains completely and turned on all the lights. The buzz from the fluorescent bulb above him caused him to wince slightly. The Hate Criminal began searching through the bag of books and CDs for something to do. He found some classical music, audiobooks, a few history texts, and lastly a Bible. Taking out the Bible, he held it in his hands contemplatively. It was a black, leather book with golden, gilded edges. Holding it gingerly in his hands, the Bible's heft felt weightier than its true mass. Joe rubbed his fingers softly on the spine.

"How can two people professing to be Christians hold such different viewpoints?" he said to himself in reference to the stark difference between Sam Wilson and his uncle. "Is there some kind of outside influence?"

While Joe nominally considered himself a Christian, he had never fully read the Bible. He was like many Christians of his day. He owned a stack of Bibles that only functioned as dust collectors and wouldn't even make it to church with him on the rare occasions he attended. Joe vaguely knew who Jesus was and that he died for his sins. He could recall details from his Sunday schools growing up and could name most of the "characters" from the stories, but that marked the extent of Joe's biblical knowledge.

"Well, God, you've got me trapped in here with a Bible." He chuckled as he pulled up a chair to the derelict table. "I guess I should give this a read."

Intimidated by the length and complication of the Old Testament, he skipped to Matthew. Joe resolved to find whether his uncle or Sam Wilson was closer to Jesus's teachings.

The reading was difficult at first. Joe found his mind wandering from topic to topic, and his fear of being captured drew his gaze to the door. He closed his eyes and took a deep breath. Joe prayed for focus and wisdom.

Matthew and Mark soon fell like dominoes. Luke took a considerable amount of time but gradually gave way to John. Reading furiously, he tore his way clear through the Gospels before fatigue set in. Checking the time, he realized it was very late at night and many hours had passed. Joe's eyes grew heavy as he contemplated Jesus's life.

I don't think Jesus would be marching in pride parades, he thought to himself. *I don't think he would be a so-called sensible conservative at all—or even a Republican.* Joe shook his head as he turned off the lights. *He'd be making whips!*

As he climbed into the foul-smelling bed, he continued to think, *If Jesus wouldn't be a Republican or a Democrat, what would he be?* He paused for a moment, then spoke into the darkness, "What am I?"

Joe's mind swirled in a mix of fragmentary scriptures and nervous expectation of arrest as he drifted into restless sleep.

29

THE SLIP

The days passed on slowly like autumn leaves. They were already dead and spent, but Joe had to wait patiently for them to slough off the tree in their own time. By day seven, the smell of the rotten pizza drove him mad. Trying everything to dampen the smell, he threw the putrid pie into the tub's murky water in desperation. This only accomplished making Joe gag at the sight and smell of the horrific concoction. His own trash began piling up steadily as well. Stricken with digestive issues from his unconventional diet, the already sparse toilet paper ran dangerously low. With fear, Joe realized that he would have to sortie from his room at least to put his garbage outside. The issue of toilet paper presented a more dangerous, if not comical, prospect.

"That'd just be my luck. Getting caught with my literal pants down." Joe laughed grimly.

A dozen phone calls to the front desk went unanswered. After dismissing a few ludicrous plans to steal toilet paper from the supply closet in the middle of the night, he settled on the far easier course of simply asking the maid for more. Joe figured the likelihood of her recognizing him under the mask and hat would be low.

Lying in wait for housekeeping to come to his door, he sat in the chair by the window with his concealing attire already donned. His trash was crammed crudely into the solitary bag from his room's trashcan and placed outside the door.

Joe rehearsed the plan in his head, "Okay, I just open the door when she knocks, ask for toilet paper, and shut the door without any further contact."

What should have been a mundane task turned into a nerve-racking operation due to Joe's heightened sense of paranoia and fear of being recognized. The clock ticked past eighty thirty in the morning, and he anticipated her arrival any minute.

Right on schedule, Joe heard the cleaning cart rolling down his floor's balcony. Unable to see the necessary angle, he monitored her progress by sound. Making her stops at each room, she paused when she came to Joe's door.

"Looks like somebody finally put the trash out," a muffled female voice droned quietly.

After a few audible gags, she placed the horrible smelling bags into the cart and reluctantly knocked.

"Housekeeping!"

Joe interrupted her by opening the door slowly. "Can you please give me some toilet paper?"

The cleaning lady froze in shock. Joe could see she was an older woman with tender blue eyes and gray hair. Her body was thin, hunched over, and weather worn. A nametag bore the name Cynthia on a filthy apron.

Joe repeated his question, barely opening the door: "Can I have some toilet paper and trash bags?"

"Um, sure." Cynthia reached over to the cart with a furrowed brow. "I'm surprised you peaked out of your cave. How long were you in there? A week?"

Joe wanted to stick to the plan of snatching the toilet paper and closing the door. However, the prospect of some much-craved human contact and conversation overcame him.

"Yeah, I just needed some things," he said cryptically.

"Well, don't let it go so long next time." She gave a stern, motherly grin. "This smells awful."

Joe replied quietly, "That's probably a good idea. It drove me nuts."

"What brings you to Lafayette?" Cynthia made light conversation. Evidently, she was starved of human contact as well.

The fugitive shifted uncomfortably. He contemplated shutting the door in her face, but she reminded him strongly of his late grandmother.

Joe gave in to the impulse to socialize and repeated his alibi: "I had some trouble with my family."

She nodded and leaned on her cart. "Family, huh? No one will love you or hate you quite like family does," Cynthia continued mournfully, "but make the most of the time you have with them. You never know when they'll be gone."

Joe nodded sympathetically. "Boy, I feel that."

"You ever lose somebody close to you?" she asked with a sad look.

"Yeah, my wife." Joe took down his mask and held back the grief.

Cynthia's motherly instincts ached for the drained soul in front of her.

"I'm sorry to hear that." She choked up and placed her hand on his arm.

The pair had a moment of shared sadness and loss.

"My son died a few years ago." The woman's wrinkles contorted in heartache. "I warned him not to go to the big city with his wife and daughter. They'll eat you up, I said."

Joe removed the mask completely and propped up the brim of his hat.

Some tears welled in his eyes as he recalled, "The city's sure no place for a family these days."

"Travis got caught up in that protest in LA years ago," she intimated.

"April 19th?" Joe clarified.

Cynthia nodded and shifted the cart. "Shot someone who was trying to burn his house down." She teared up. "He never stood a chance in prison. Didn't even make it a year into his life sentence."

Joe shook his head and clenched his fist.

"His wife ended up in prison too. I just hope my granddaughter Erica is living a good life. I'm not allowed to see her or even try." She grabbed some tissues from the cart and wept bitterly.

The fugitive stepped from his room and embraced the grieving woman. At the mention of the granddaughter's name, Joe's heart rent in two. The memory of the malnourished girl in Rosenblatt's camp reared its head. The stories were too similar to be a coincidence. Joe decided he would bear the burden of this information alone. He was among very few individuals who could understand her loss.

"What you are doing?!" the swarthy motel owner called out angrily from the parking lot. "Do not screw the guests, you whore!"

Cynthia snapped away and replied, "I'm sorry, Mr. Padresh, I was just talking to the customer."

"I've got my eyes on you, whore!" Padresh screamed.

Joe burned with anger at Cynthia's mistreatment. He had half a mind to leap from the balcony and strangle the motel owner in full view of whoever would watch.

Noticing Joe's hatred, she deflected. "Sorry, I've got to get going. It was nice talking to you."

I ought to pound him into the pavement. After a moment, he released his clenched jaw and relaxed his hands. Joe turned to his new friend. "Well, it was nice meeting you too. What was your name again?"

She replied as she rolled the cart to the next room, "Cynthia. You?"

"Joe," the fugitive replied. He froze in fearful realization of his slip.

"Good to meet you, Joe," Cynthia said quietly. "Garbage collection is at eight thirty in the morning. Don't let it pile up!"

He closed the door quickly and cursed himself. "Now you've done it!" Joe made fists and brought them to his forehead.

Not only had he strayed from the plan of a quick interaction, but he also showed his face. Worst of all, Joe used his real name and gave personally identifying details. Seven days of isolation made his discipline loose, and his tongue ran uncontrolled after being starved of conversation. He prayed desperately that nothing would come of his blunder.

Joe had no reason to distrust Cynthia, but he could not afford even the slightest mistake. The ears of the system were everywhere, and the little town of Lafayette was not exempt from the beastly eyes that swept over the land, hungrily searching for the last unconquered souls.

30

SIDELINED

Sean McDowell poured over printouts of the satellite imagery of the surrounding area after a disquieting phone call with Feldman. Both Sean and Jameila had been assigned an additional duty during their time in Lafayette: campaign security. The assignment was one of geographic expedience, but Feldman made it clear that it was to become their new priority. Ever the careerist, he accepted the collateral job with an enthusiastic voice. In private, Sean's frustration reached a boiling point.

"That yokel probably pointed us in the wrong direction on purpose!" He swore angrily. "If I see him driving around again, I'll slap him with obstruction."

Jameila poured him a cup of coffee. "We should get back on task."

Sean spilled the cup when he slammed his hands on the shoddy hotel desk. "Back on task? This is our task. This whole campaign thing is a sideshow of a sideshow!"

"That sideshow," she emphasized, "is our current tasking from Feldman. For whatever reason, making sure these events go off without a hitch is a higher priority. Now c'mon, we have a meeting with Barry in ten minutes; let's go." His partner grabbed her jacket and placed her gun in its holster.

Sean crumpled a few pieces of paper in frustration. "This isn't even our specialty. We're investigators, not the political staff."

"We're technically supposed to be jacks of all trades"—Jameila made her way to the door—"and orders are orders."

"You go ahead. I'm going to keep looking." Her partner leaned

175

back in the squeaking chair and crossed his arms.

She frowned and opened the door. "We've already visited half a dozen defunct mining towns within a twenty-mile radius. Even if we do find Wetumpka, what makes you think you'll find the trail? It's a needle in a needle stack."

"One of the locals is going to talk." He burned with a predatory bloodlust. "I know he's here."

"Blaine or his uncle?" Jameila asked impatiently. "You're getting a little too hyper-focused here."

"Either of them. Both of them! I know that's where he went!" Sean rifled through a few more satellite images.

"I'll update you when I get back." His partner put her hands in her pockets. "You know, catching the Blaines isn't going to get you any favors with Feldman."

"She's sidelining us with this stupid campaign stuff precisely because she doesn't want me bagging a high-profile Hate Criminal on my first big assignment with the DC office"—he pointed angrily—"and I'm not letting that happen."

The investigator tapped his fingers on the desk as he formulated a plan.

31

UNTIL THE COLLAPSE

By day eleven, Joe's nerves calmed slightly since his slip. He had a few more brief conversations with Cynthia, who brought him some much-appreciated cookies on day ten. Joe anxiously awaited his uncle Karl's return to resupply him. He spent most of his time reading and listening to CDs. He finished the New Testament, most of the Old, and became enamored with the other books in the bag about political thought and history. Joe's education flowed like a waterfall, eroding years of assumptions.

It was now day fourteen, and Karl was supposed to come back to check on the fugitive. Joe separated the blinds to look out over the parking lot again. It was a cloudy day, and the scene outside his window was much the same as it had been for the preceding days. It was the same road by the same run-down cinder block buildings with the same foreboding air. The monotony was only punctuated by the occasional drunk, prostitute, or drug dealer. Even in this little town, the social decay was advanced. Ambulances arrived at the motel several times during his stay for what Joe could only assume were overdoses. A drug dealer had solicited him on day nine, but the fugitive turned him away without opening the door. Joe almost wished he experienced some small temptation to simply numb himself to his troubles and escape into artificial bliss, but inexplicably he did not. After a breakfast of military rations, he continued his study. Opening the Bible once more, he discovered a note tucked away deep in Isaiah. In Karl's handwriting, he found several references and half a dozen other verses scrawled on a slip of yellow legal paper. The top line of the page posed a solitary question: "Who are the heirs of Abraham?"

As he turned to the verses, Joe grew worried. His father, an Evangelical, obsessed over who was the chosen, who wasn't, and the special privileges and prophecies for each. As a young child, he lived in fear that his status as a mere Christian would never be enough for God. After combing his memory, he realized that worship of a foreign country and its people seemed far more important to Robert Blaine than opposing the destruction of his own. Frantically looking over the slip of paper again, he turned to Matthew 27:24–26, the account of Pilate presenting Jesus before the mob.

"Look at that," he muttered to himself, "they're proud of it. They even want their descendants to receive credit for it!"

Flipping to the final verse on the sheet, he trembled as he read the words of a verse marked in Thessalonians. He repeated aloud, "They oppose all mankind. . . ." Joe set the Bible down and furrowed his brow. "But they're just a different religion, right?" He looked up from the table and stared at the wall. "Or they're a family . . . a people with culture, traditions, and behaviors." The words of Karl's parable coursed through his neural pathways.

Joe's mind hungered for more information and had a thousand questions for his uncle. The fugitive chuckled. "He'd probably insult me and tell me, 'No free answers!'"

As he surveyed the scene outside his window, a particular individual caught his eye. She was noticeably overweight and wore a baggy sweatshirt bearing the image of a superhero. Her hair was shaved on the sides and topped with a curly, blue mop. She dragged a cart loaded with yard signs behind her. Lumbering her way down the sidewalk, she stopped in front of the parking lot and started planting her crop. They were not fully facing Joe, so he could not make out exactly what they were. However, he could see the color scheme very clearly. The design was the Inclusion Banner. Having seen it thousands of times on the streets of MLK Jr. County, Joe only needed a small glimpse to recognize it.

The blue-haired sack placed the signs as if she were sowing the seeds of some invasive species, knowing that any efforts at spraying herbicides or weeding would be futile in the face of its inexorable advance. She passed out leaflets to passersby and engaged in some conversation with interested individuals. The woman would look right at home among the rootless, genetic waste material of MLK Jr.

County, but here she was more foreign than even the opiate addicts who inhabited the motel.

Her presence in Lafayette shocked Joe. While it was no shining city on a hill, it appeared that the beast system's worst features had yet to make it to the sleepy mountain town. To his surprise, here was the vanguard of some liberal cause right on his doorstep. Joe wondered if that's how it started in MLK Jr. County, just one blue-haired mongrel making the first determined steps of metastatic rot. As she passed out of view, the woman left a trail of signs and stickers on lampposts, marking the territory for conquest. Joe grew angry at the prospect.

"Doesn't she know what that kind of politics brings?" he hoarsely whispered to himself. "The death, the destruction, the PSLs!"

Peering again, he saw one of the signs turn to face his window as the wind moved the cardboard softly. He couldn't fully make it out, but he could see that it was a campaign sign. Joe's heart sank with the realization. Not only was she the proselytizing first wave of a hostile religion, but she was also an apocalyptic prophetess heralding the way for one more powerful than her.

"Maybe she knows exactly what this kind of politics will bring," Joe stated ominously.

He yearned to do something about this new development. Having experienced the hardships of a fully enforced Equity and Inclusion Act, Joe felt compelled to warn the people of Lafayette of their impending danger. Stewing over his inability to act, a 4x4 pickup pulled into the lot and broke his dour contemplation.

Joe's heart leapt at the realization that it was his uncle's truck. He could see a number of bags in the bed indicating a much-needed resupply. Running to the door, he peeked his head out slightly to signal Karl to the correct room. After making cursory eye contact, his uncle tersely waved him back into the room.

Returning inside, Joe prepared a battery of questions. He felt excited to update Karl on his newfound knowledge. When his uncle made his way up to the room, Joe opened the door and ushered him in.

"Hey uncle Karl! It's been—"

"What were you thinking?!" Karl cut his greeting short and set the bags down.

Joe stumbled back and wondered what he knew.

"Peeking your head out like that! Way too dangerous for someone in your situation," his uncle continued to chastise.

"Sorry, I just thought you would need to find the room," the fugitive scrambled.

Karl separated the blinds and looked out of the window. "I think you got away with it this time. It doesn't look like anyone's staking this place out. You haven't left the room or talked to anyone, right?"

"No," Joe lied.

"You can't take chances like that right now. You would not believe the amount of feds I've seen crawling around. Lafayette is starting to look like DC!" Karl closed the blinds and sat tiredly in the worn chair by the window. "Things have gotten way worse than I thought they would. I'm starting to think I should've tried to get you out to the next town over. Too late for that now."

After a period of awkward silence, Joe piped up, "So how have things been?"

His uncle shook his head. "Not so bad. Sheriff Perry came rooting around the ranch, which I didn't like. He's a good guy, but a sucker for authority when it comes down to it." He paused for a moment to take off his hat. "Word on the street is that you're causing trouble in Nevada."

"Nevada?" the nephew asked in confusion.

"Allegedly there have been some attacks on the electrical grid, and the media's pinning it on you! So, congrats on your successful guerilla campaign," Karl joked glibly.

Joe shook his head. "How on earth am I supposed to be connected to that, let alone have the know-how? They can't be that stupid to think it was me."

"Very astute. You're right, they're not that stupid." The elder Blaine crossed his arms. "I happen to know what actually happened. It's summer, and the electrical grid in Nevada is being taxed to the limit keeping the casinos and all the urchins who live nearby cool. The aging system hasn't been updated or maintained in years, and Lake Meade is practically a puddle at this point. They have rolling blackouts every summer, but this time they get to foist the blame on you, instead of having to placate an angry, sweaty populace."

"Incredible," Joe reeled. "Will this mean they'll step up efforts to find me?"

Karl began unpacking his bag. "Perhaps, but more likely they'll just use it as an excuse to pass a new tax to pay for 'repairs.' I'm sure most of that money won't end up anywhere near the electrical grid. Alternatively, this is some FCIA hack trying to raise your threat profile to pad his resume if he catches you."

He placed a large stack of canned goods, boxes, and military rations on the derelict particle board table. Joe looked over at the haul and retched internally at the prospect of living off of this diet indefinitely.

"Did you see those campaign signs out front?" the nephew asked expectantly.

Karl rolled his eyes. "I sure did. Maria Cabezudo," he waxed sarcastic, "the hometown hero returns to save the backward rural troglodytes!"

"Who is she?" Joe asked.

"She claims to be from Lafayette, but in reality, her family lived here for just over a year before they moved out to Salt Lake. She'll tell you sob stories about coming from a poor, immigrant family. The Cabezudos are actually very well-connected with the Sinaloa Cartel." His uncle gave a wry smile. "After going to Harvard and doing some time on the beltway making coffee for senators, she's trying to make her own start in politics. She bought a house here to qualify for residency, and this year she met the minimum amount of time to run for office."

"There's no way she has a chance here in the middle of nowhere, not with big-city policies," Joe reassured himself half-heartedly.

Karl shrugged and raised his eyebrows. "You'd be right maybe about ten years ago, but the rural areas of the country are so hollowed out now. What's worse is that she has some big money behind her. She's on the dole from Isaac Yakov."

"Who's that?" His nephew heard the name before.

"Oh geez, where to start. He's the billionaire head of an NGO called the Open World Forum. Every election cycle, he selects little towns like this one for conquest. It's almost a sport for him. He releases the list of locations targeted for 'comprehensive work to stabilize inclusion,' which is code for dumping money in the local elections to firmly capture a town for the system," Karl recounted with pursed lips. "It's a slow death, but they've been marching through rural America, toppling the dominoes one by one. I saw Lafayette on the list about a year ago."

Joe objected, "Well why don't people do something about it? Why doesn't somebody run for office to keep Yakov's candidates out?"

His uncle leaned back in the chair. "Well, even if you beat his candidate for mayor, his new district attorney will trump up charges of racism or corruption. That is, if his new sheriff doesn't get to you first. Yakov already has his hooks into the county board. They just passed a resolution affirming Equity and Inclusion and getting rid of voter ID. That's pretty much game over."

Joe upturned a palm in interrogation. "So, you just do nothing?"

"Think about it, Joe. Even if you can find a few solid guys to run for these positions, people just don't care enough or have the balls to oppose this stuff. Sure, a lot of people don't like what's happening, but the population is full of invertebrate weaklings. They won't lift a finger to save the society around them as long as their own life remains relatively comfortable. They don't understand risk. By the time it does become uncomfortable, it's too late. Just a bunch of boiling frogs." Karl put his hands frustratedly on the armrests.

"If they just knew how bad it could get, Lafayette would be up in arms!" The nephew furrowed his brow.

"Up in arms, he says!" Taking a pause after a sarcastic laugh, Karl leaned forward and narrowed his eyes. "Do you remember when they made private gun ownership virtually illegal unless you had the impossible to obtain permit?"

Joe nodded and listened intently.

"Do you remember how they passed that?" His uncle continued, "After twenty-eight Black Bloc shootings, you had every conservative in America calling for gun control. Can you believe it? After years of resisting Democrat attempts to take the guns, the Republicans put the final nail in the coffin. Conservative voters were quaking in their boots at the thought of left-wing terrorists with legally acquired guns rampaging through the streets. Instead of defending themselves with their own guns, they demanded that the government step in to protect them. That's why you gave your gun in, wasn't it?"

"I'm not sure I get the connection." The nephew crossed his arms and stifled anger over the jab.

"My point is that America is too far gone to save. Everyone knows how bad it's going to get. If you tell the guy on the street all that you went through in MLK, he'll give you the 'wow, just wow' speech and then forget everything you said. He might just vote for the opposing candidate, if you're lucky. But when the Yakovite gets into office anyway, that guy will lean back in his recliner and say, 'Man, the world's going to hell!' and then turn his TV on to watch football. As long as he's safe and comfortable, he'll never act." Karl lowered his voice. "The American people worship safety over all else. Get that through your head. There's that material versus spiritual dichotomy I told you about. When your conception of life is purely material, death and risk become terrifying propositions to be avoided at all costs." He sighed, then continued, "I get it, you're young and full of fire. But the best thing we can do is wait for the collapse and get outside of the blast radius."

This last statement launched Joe into a passionate objection: "Isn't that just nihilism of a different color? How are you any different than the guy sitting back and watching football? At least he'll be entertained while society collapses—you'll just be miserable."

"You're naive, Joe." Karl shook his head. "I fear I've made you into an idealist."

The younger Blaine refused to relent. "There's got to be something we can do. What's the point of identifying evil if you do nothing to stop it?"

"Even if there was something you could do, think about your situation. If you show your face outside of this room, you'll be whisked away to prison immediately." Karl injected realism into the conversation.

Joe stumbled over his words. "Well, I—maybe *I* can't do anything. But in a principled sense, people who think like us ought to do something."

His uncle smiled slightly. "So, somebody else should do something."

"Those who can, yes."

Karl pressed, "But not you, right?"

"Well, I can't, like you said," Joe backpedaled.

The elder Blaine chuckled with a grimace. "You see? You're being an armchair general. It's easy to talk about action when you know you're not on the hook. Don't judge me so quickly. By having children and raising them in a Godly way, I'm doing more to resist than any political action could do."

Joe replied bitterly, "Well, that's out of the question for me."

Karl relented and took a softer tone. "You're doing a good job for what you have. The fact that you're here and not being shivved in prison right now is a huge testament to your struggle already. I'm telling you, when being alive is illegal, existence is resistance."

"That may be," the nephew remained unsatisfied, "but if anything, I've just made things worse. Jill's dead, and I don't even know how many people were killed or maimed as a result of my Public Safety Lockdown. I've got to redeem myself for all of that."

His uncle nodded along. "I understand where you're coming from. We all want to change the world." He paused as the icy grip of memory took hold of his speech. "I said it before, and I'll say it again: existence is resistance. Just hold out while the system eats itself alive, and then we rebuild from the ashes."

The Hate Criminal grew frustrated. "But what if that collapse never comes? How old are you now? It sounds like you've been waiting quite a while."

"If I die before the collapse, my sons will take the reins," Karl replied calmly.

"And if *they* die before the collapse, it'll be *their* sons, right? It never ends. I've been doing a lot of reading lately. It doesn't seem like anything collapses on its own. Someone has to give it a push at the least," Joe contended.

"Ah, I see you've discovered accelerationism." His uncle crossed his arms.

Joe shook his head. "I don't even know what that means."

"Look, you're just getting started down this path. I think you'll eventually arrive at my position. It's better to just ride the tiger than hop off and try to fight it." Karl looked out the window at the campaign signs again. "Come what may."

His nephew wanted to challenge him further but decided it was not wise to bite the hand that fed him. After some awkward silence, the pair discussed Joe's Bible study. He recounted reading about Jesus's life and his continued confusion at Karl's parable of the guests. The elder Blaine's heart grew proud of his protégé's rapid growth.

"You're getting close, Joe. I can feel it. I'll give you a hint." The uncle smiled slightly. "What is the Star of Remphan?"

Joe had never heard the name before. "I have no clue."

"Yes, you do. You've seen it hundreds of times. It's hiding in plain sight under another name." Karl rubbed his nose. "Two triangles representing the following phrase: as above, so below."

"I'm getting real tired of these riddles," his nephew sighed.

The elder Blaine smirked. "Stephen might be able to lend a hand."

"Who's Stephen?" Joe's frustration grew.

"No free answers." Karl relished the reply.

The nephew rolled his eyes and shifted the conversation to logistics going forward. Karl decided that he would return at irregular intervals to prevent any kind of surveillance noticing a pattern.

"It'll be less than a month, but more than two weeks. Do you think you can manage that?" the elder Blaine asked gently.

"Yeah, I think so," Joe nodded.

Karl began gathering his things to leave.

His nephew continued, "But how long do we have to do this?"

On his way out the door, Karl turned and smiled. "Until the collapse, my friend!"

32

TOMORROW TOGETHER

During his first period of isolation, Joe at least had a set number of days to endure. The idea of indefinite waiting and loneliness crushed him. All the while, the fluttering campaign signs next to the parking lot taunted his inaction. The window became a bizarre horror show where he could watch the impending doom arrive with full foreknowledge of its dreadful conclusion. All of this was undergirded by his inability to prevent it. The incongruity between knowing the future and not being able to change it tortured him in ways he could not articulate.

Joe tried shutting the blinds and ignoring the decline outside. As he did so, the blanket fell from the mirror beside the bed. His gaze drifted to the reflection and saw the fire in his eyes rising. Joe approached the mirror slowly. He walked in the same way a buck approaches another before a duel. His appearance was notably different since he last looked in the mirror. Joe's hair had grown significantly, and a scraggly beard made him look quite disheveled. He knew his shortcomings and his faults. Worse, he knew *all* his qualities. Every quality or talent that laid dormant elicited a greater degree of judgment.

"What do you want? Just tell me who you are!" he accosted the reflection.

He received no reply except the tightening of fingers and a widening of eyes. The green hue of his piercing gaze seemed to grow more intense by the minute. Joe's vision darkened in a shroud until he saw nothing besides his face. To his horror, it seemed like his reflection was acting independently, without command. He opened his mouth as if to speak. Joe braced for the words like one turns a shoulder to a biting, icy wind.

"Housekeeping!"

Joe snapped around in surprise. Taking a brief glance at the mirror, he covered it once again and went to the door.

"Hi, Cynthia," he said stoically.

She greeted him sweetly but seemed to notice something odd about his appearance. Joe grew self-conscious, but continued on as normal.

"Who did you have over?" Cynthia wondered.

Joe felt concerned that she noticed Karl. "Oh, nobody. Just an old friend." He deflected, "Did you see those new campaign signs going up?"

"Oh, I don't pay attention to politics," the old lady muttered, "but I don't like the look of this Cabezudo. She reeks of big-city politics."

The pair exchanged pleasantries until Cynthia felt that she couldn't stay any longer without drawing Padresh's ire. Joe closed the door and sat on the bed. The knife lay folded on the nightstand next to the room key, alluding to its potential. He could almost feel the burning gaze through the blanket over the mirror. The Hate Criminal faced an unfortunate dilemma. He couldn't bear rotting in the room any longer. Between the caustic figure in his reflection and the war raging outside, the motel was as much a prison as any other. This prison, however, plucked at the strings of his mind like a vengeful harpist.

"I can't stay here any longer!" Joe cried.

Rushing to the window again, he pressed his face and hands against the glass as if desperate for air. Looking out over the lot, it seemed peaceful apart from the Inclusion Banner signs. The sun shone beautifully over the mountains, and a few wildflowers bloomed in the bed of grass next to the reservations hut. A silence enveloped Joe as the wind quietly plied the blades of grass next to the sign. The natural and effortless form of the grass mocked the loud and incessant artificiality of the campaign sign.

Joe lusted for the feel of that breeze and to sit outside in the sun. He sat dejectedly next to the door for several hours and tried to take his mind elsewhere. Reaching for the bag of books, he rifled through its contents, finding nothing that piqued his interest. Joe's eyes drifted to the window again. The temptation of warm, unhindered sunshine overcame him. The short taste of the outside air he got when talking with Cynthia compelled him to stand up.

Well, maybe I can do a quick trip outside, he rationalized, *just to the end of the parking lot and back.*

Every rational fiber of his being screamed at him that this was a bad idea. He knew he was in grave danger and that Yakov's money also brought national media to Lafayette. There were dozens, possibly hundreds of individuals foaming at the mouth to be the one to catch him. Turning once more to look back after a few more hours of resistance, the room's dreary and tormenting void seemed palpable. Joe at last broke.

Feverishly, he put on an oversized, long-sleeved shirt, ball cap, mask, and shoes. He moved quickly, hoping to get out of the room before he changed his mind. On his way to the door, he grabbed the room key on the nightstand. The knife that laid next to it lingered in his hands for a moment. Joe actuated the spring assisted blade. Contemplating if he should risk bringing it along or risk going without it, he ultimately decided to fold it away and put it in the drawer.

He placed a fatigued hand on the handle. Pausing for a few seconds, he closed his eyes and took a deep breath. On the exhale, he opened his eyes and said, "Okay, just to the end of the lot and back."

The wide expanse of the world opened up to the fugitive as he stepped out of the entryway. The breeze filled his nostrils with the rich smells of late summer under his mask. Closing the door softly behind him, he walked cautiously toward the stairs. Joe's legs felt atrophied and weak after the inactivity of his isolation. The corner of the building separated him from the reservation hut. Taking a short glance around the corner, he saw Padresh viewing more adult material on his computer. Frowning in disgust, Joe also felt relief that he was distracted. Making a concerted effort to not look suspicious, the fugitive started walking toward the edge of the parking lot.

If anyone asks, my name is . . . Joe shuddered and realized he couldn't remember his fake first name, *McDowell.*

This realization caused him to waiver in his confidence.

Maybe I should just stay in, he thought to himself about a stone's throw away from the edge of the lot.

As the fraudulent McDowell started to turn back to his room, his eyes caught the presence of what appeared to be a young man. He was short and sickly, wearing a flannel shirt and beanie hat. A patchy beard made no indication of his true age. A small paunch protruded over his jeans despite his otherwise thin composition. Having spent a lot of time on the coast, Joe recognized him as decidedly "big-city." The man checked his phone and brought a curled index finger to his mouth to chew on like a baby's pacifier. After receiving some kind of guidance, he nodded and began looking around. Once he noticed Joe, he started to approach him.

Joe froze and began to panic.

If I run, I look suspicious. But I don't know what he wants. He's clearly not from around here. His mind ran wild.

"Hey," a suspiciously feminine voice called out, "how are you doing?"

The fugitive clenched his hands in his pockets and contemplated sprinting away like a gazelle.

"Hey there," it called again while approaching. "My name is Regan, and I'm canvassing on behalf of the Maria Cabezudo campaign. How are you today?"

As the figure approached, Joe could see that this was no man at all. The wide hips, narrow shoulders, and feminine facial structure revealed her comically constructed facade. Gathering his thoughts, Joe assessed her to be harmless.

"I'm good," he replied tersely.

"Good, good," she continued. "So, who has your vote for mayor?"

Joe wanted to blurt out his views, but he managed to hold back and simply said, "Nobody."

She nodded and scratched at her facial hair. "Yeah, politicians can be really shifty. I used to never vote."

Growing more uncomfortable, Joe felt the need to break away and get back to the room.

"Yup. Anyways, I've got to get going." He turned and began strutting away.

"Wait!" she called out. "Here's a flier for MC's campaign rally. It's tomorrow at Carson Park, eight p.m." Regan handed the flier to Joe and lowered her voice. "She has a lot of great policies centered on the homeless."

Joe took the flier and started walking back to his room quickly. Using his key card on the door, he rushed inside and shut the door behind him.

He cursed his weakness for going outside and the risky interaction he undertook. Joe felt his overgrown hair and beard and realized he gave the impression of homelessness to the campaign staffer.

"Well, I suppose I really am homeless," he joked to himself grimly. "At least my appearance is different than when I fled the city."

Taking a look at the flier, he took notice of the expensive glossy paper and well-designed graphics. It was certainly the product of a large-scale advertising firm.

The front fold read, "Maria Cabezudo / Tomorrow Together," along with a picture of the candidate handing out water bottles to refugees. She had large, brown eyes, dark hair that reached her shoulders, and tawny skin. Joe thought she looked much too young, innocent, and feminine to be playing the game of politics. He wondered how much of her actions and choices were truly her own. On the inside fold, he found the colors of the Inclusion Banner bordering a wall of text concerning all the horrible injustices being inflicted on the population of Lafayette by its outdated city government. The final fold was a series of promises, which read more like threats to Joe.

"We will ensure that Lafayette is brought firmly into the twenty-first century. As mayor, I promise that this city will be for all people. This is a nation of immigrants, and as an immigrant, I want Lafayette to reflect the changing and progressing face of America. Join me in this noble fight, and I promise we can accomplish Tomorrow Together."

Disgusted, he threw the pamphlet in the trash and returned to his regularly scheduled programming of looking out the window. Regan continued to hand out tracts of her religion to passersby. To Joe's dismay, a decent number of individuals took the fliers and engaged in lengthy conversations. She preyed on the waste material of Lafayette: the druggies, the burnouts, and the acolytes of the state's faith who were already in the town. The seeping tendrils of propaganda had earlier seeded a crop of faithful to harvest once the time was right.

Joe heard the rumble of diesel engines coming from the right side of his window. Straining his gaze, he discovered a convoy of buses lumbering into town like a line of armored tanks. They were privately chartered buses of several companies, but all had "Cabezudo for Mayor" plastered on in varying levels of professionalism. The first bus honked at Regan, who cheered them on as they rolled into the city. Joe counted at least six of them and figured there would be more coming from other directions. The windows were tinted, and he couldn't make out exactly who was being bused in.

Curiosity and hatred stewed within him like a poisonous cocktail. He fled MLK Jr. County, but it seemed to follow him to his mountain refuge. Joe wondered if Lafayette was one of the last places on earth that wasn't fully defiled by the beast system, but this thought gave way to grim resignation that the town would soon be devoured and excreted into the sewers of multicultural rot.

"Someone has to do something!" Joe slapped the window. "Somebody's got to do something to stop it!"

Suddenly, he felt another presence in the room. Carefully, he checked the opposite wall with his peripheral vision. The blanket fell slightly and only half revealed the mirror.

Joe sat in the chair and looked pensively at the nightstand's drawer.

"Somebody has to stop it," he whispered quietly, as fear, anger, and frustration built up within him.

In a burst of courage, he strode up to the wall and tore the blanket from the mirror. Basking in the cruel shock of his conviction's light, Joseph Arthur Blaine resolved to act.

33

BIGGER FISH

Barry Kaplan, a veteran campaign manager of the Open World Forum, rudely fielded a series of questions from his staffers.

"Okay, are we all clear? I can't believe I have to clarify this, but keep the crowd contained until the speeches are over and the cameras are turned off! This is amateurish!"

The group, crowded into a small conference room, nodded. Sean and Jameila lurked at the outside rim of the crowd in bleak detachment. The investigator stewed with resentment that his Nevada trick barely made a ripple in Blaine's level of national attention.

"This is so stupid," Sean whispered to Jameila, who gave a disapproving frown.

One brave hand shot up to ask a question: "Mr. Kaplan, are we expecting any—"

"Hold on," Barry interrupted, "where's your task partner?"

"Uhm. . . ." She wavered in her resolve.

"Senator's son thinks he can do what he wants!" The campaign manager slammed a folder on the conference table with a series of curses. "Ask your stupid question!"

As the trembling staffer asked her question, Sean filed out of the room with his partner.

"What a waste!" He stormed angrily down the hallway. "All this chaos is going to let Blaine slip out! I guarantee it!"

"We don't even know if he's here, Sean. Let's face it, we're not going to find him right now, and we have bigger fish to fry." Jameila followed along.

"Bigger fish!" He continued, "I have better things to do than babysit a bunch of college students managing a protest!"

"Not according to Feldman," she quipped, "and frankly, I'm tired of your complaining."

"Taking her side now?" Sean turned toward her aggressively.

"We have a job to do!"

"Yeah, catching bad guys!" he burst out.

Jameila put her hands on her hips and squared up to her partner. "I don't want to have to tell Feldman my partner has gone rogue. I'm assigning you to Cabezudo's house."

"You can't assign me!" Sean pointed in her face. "I'm the lead on this investigation."

"What investigation?" Jameila shook her head. "We have a new assignment, and I'm taking the lead. You're too caught up in your own fantasies!"

He got close in to her face. "You're just trying to butt me out of Feldman's job!"

"Oh, like you've been doing with this obsession with catching Blaine?!" she fired back.

"Get the sheriff to protect that politician." Sean turned to leave. "I've got real police work to do!" He stormed out of the building to continue his desperate search for Wetumpka and his elusive prey.

34

THE SACK OF LAFAYETTE

Joe arrived at the square shortly before eight p.m. He donned his usual disguise of a mask and ball cap. He also wore a ragged, old, red sweatshirt he found in one of the bags with the hood pulled on top of his hat. Joe took the pocket knife in the center pocket. He hoped this tattered sweatshirt didn't have any sentimental value to Karl. Before leaving his room, he grabbed the piece of the boulder Alexandria gave him and put it in his jean pocket. Joe originally feared his attire would make him look too suspicious but soon found that he blended in quite well with the other rally goers.

The scene shook Joe to his core. The square was awash with a loud rabble dressed in all manner of streetwear and tattered clothing. Having spent some time observing the people of Lafayette, Joe knew that the vast majority of these people were certainly not from the area. If their clothing did not give them away, their behavior and appearance revealed their origin. There were men and women of every color, but mostly dark in complexion. As he approached the crowd, it opened up and swallowed him whole without him realizing it. Joe was soon shoulder to shoulder with the mob.

A few Whites were among the center group, but their appearance was heavily Africanized and they wore the tell-tale clothing of Black Bloc members. There was a troop of androgynous degenerates dancing in a circle while abrasive hip hop played on the loudspeaker on stage. Rootless, mystery-meat urbanites writhed and wriggled to the music as a trio of deviant males engaged in passionate, lewd acts. Some of the revelers climbed the pioneer statue in the square and graffitied its face in red. A group of dark men armed with billy clubs at the edge of the square eyed Joe suspiciously. He estimated there must have been nearly five hundred individuals at the event.

A swarthy, afroed imp scurried around the rally with a satchel, handing out something to the crowd. As he passed Joe, he handed him a small plastic bag with a pill inside. Looking around his immediate surroundings, everyone near him began popping the pill and cheering. Joe pretended to take it as well in an effort to avoid attention. In reality, he tossed it down the neck of his hoodie. A few media outlets were broadcasting the rally but conspicuously kept their cameras pointed at the stage.

Joe noticed a few White liberals awkwardly orbiting the outside of the group. Whether they were truly from Lafayette, it didn't matter. They all had submissive smiles on their faces, which belied a growing discomfort with the rowdiness of the rabble. Like wallflowers at a high school dance, the White liberals stayed in groups at the edge of the rally meekly waiving campaign signs. Joe felt a deep hatred for these traitors who would willingly vote their homes away and have their neighborhoods subjected to PSLs. However, his anger gave way to pity as his eyes drifted among the White liberals to a terrified child cowering next to her short-haired mother. His heart sank with the realization that it was Felicity, the little girl who greeted him off of the train.

The loud and visually explosive scene overstimulated Joe's senses. He came to the rally completely without a plan. Joe had vague, naive, and childish notions of heroically stopping the gathering, but he soon realized the group was beyond anyone's control. Regretting his decision to come, he started to elbow his way through the dense crowd to egress. As he made it to the edge, one of the armed men stopped him with his club.

"We ain't goin' yet," he said roughly.

"I'm just going to my car." Joe tried to push past him.

"It ain't time yet!" The dusky man shoved him back into the mosh pit behind him.

The music faded, and the crowd gave a raucous cheer. Joe turned to see a smiling woman take the stage with a wave.

The mob yelled various slogans while Cabezudo egged them on. "Ho ho, hey hey, no fascist USA / Kill the farmer, Kill the Boer / No justice, no peace!" they cried. Finally, they settled into, "Lafayette is next! Lafayette is next!"

A man of African descent wearing a suit with a military campaign ribbon joined the stage with the mayoral candidate. Finally, Cabezudo calmed the crowd enough to start her speech. Starting with thanks to her staff for organizing such a large "turn out," she launched into an imprecatory sermon against the injustices the incumbent mayor inflicted on them. The crowd clapped and hollered despite virtually none of them even knowing who the mayor was. All they knew was that he was White and a racist. After finishing her statement, she gave the microphone to the man next to her. He introduced himself as Tavius Crawford and he was running for sheriff. He proudly pointed to the ribbon on his suit and commented that he earned it while fighting racism in South Africa. Joe shuddered when Crawford promised to crush injustice in Lafayette in the same way.

Toward the end of Crawford's speech, the crowd was worked up into a frenzy. A fair portion of them took on a terrifying, wide-eyed, and drug fueled complexion as the pills took effect.

"Now listen up," Crawford cocked his head as he gripped the microphone, "this town is ours now, ya'll feel?"

The rabble stirred in giddy anticipation.

"Because it's ours," he continued, "we're gonna show them how things are now. Let's show the racists that their time is through."

A girl next to Joe began sobbing with ecstasy as she tore at her hair.

Crawford lowered his head and intimated, "Lafayette is next!"

At this signal, the media outlets shut off their cameras and the armed men at the edge broke formation. The crowd metastasized from their containment in a torrent of yells and yips. Joe was carried away by the tide and had to run along for fear of being trampled. He noticed a few pallets of bricks that were not there when he approached. Rally goers began grabbing from the pile and throwing them haphazardly at the businesses on Main Street, including Dylan's General Store. Joe saw that some of the shops had put up the Inclusion Banner in the vain hope that they would be spared. A group of vagrants tied a rope around the pioneer statue's neck and brought it down to the raucous cheers of the crowd.

The speed at which the violence erupted shocked Joe, and he deplored his half-baked plan to attend the rally. The only objective he could hope to accomplish at this point was survival. Joe kept his hands planted in the front pocket of his sweatshirt wrapped around the knife. He would only draw it if absolutely necessary.

The crowd thinned slightly as they fanned out over the town, but Joe was still caught up in the flow. He caught a glimpse of the White liberals who cowered away from the horror.

A voice called out, "Get da racists!"

The horde swarmed toward the liberals and began tearing them apart with vicious abandon. Joe's heart ached for Felicity who was now certainly dead. Nonetheless, he had no time to mourn the little girl. He deeply feared for his own safety given his pale complexion. The mask and hoodie at least provided a level of concealment as the darkness of night overtook Lafayette.

At the first opportunity, he broke into a sprint to get away from the mob. The sounds of violence and rioting echoed behind him and drove his steps. Joe stopped to catch his breath next to a truck parked along a residential street. As his heavy breathing subsided slightly, he heard a distinct wheezing on the porch of the house beside him.

"Who's there?!" the old man's voice called out after the distinct pumping sound of a contraband shotgun.

Startled, Joe whipped toward the house. Suddenly, his memory struck him. The aging yellow house was Ricky's.

"Ricky, is that you?" Joe asked.

The old man swore angrily. "Who are you?"

"Don't shoot! It's me, Joe. You drove me to Wetumpka," Joe replied breathlessly.

Ricky's wheezing stopped for a moment. "You!" he cried. "You brought this here!"

The young man scrambled for words as the rioting grew closer. "No, you've got to believe me. I had nothing to do with this!"

"You did this! Lafayette was just fine before you brought your band of troublemakers!" Ricky cursed him with every foul word he knew then fired a poorly aimed shot.

Joe ducked instinctually and felt a shower of glass from the truck's window. Scrambling away, he heard another shot ring out as a group of pellets landed several yards to his left.

"Get back here, you coward!" the old man yelled. "You mother—" Ricky's tirade gave way to a horrible cough.

Joe continued to run away and huddled next to a trash can at the end of the street. He peaked around it and saw the encroaching flood of rioters making their way toward Ricky's house. They flocked toward the noise like flies to a carcass.

The old man's haggard figure slumped down the steps of his porch. Casting away the tubes of his oxygen tank, he lit a cigarette while loading his remaining shells. Ricky stumbled but managed to maintain his balance. A large vanguard of looters made their way within throwing distance of their bricks. A few enterprising rioters began heaving their payload at the wizened, old veteran. In reply, Ricky unleashed a salvo of buckshot into the crowd.

"Dis cracka gotta gun!" Joe heard one of them cry out.

Joe could see one of the rioters running wildly around with his arm hanging off. Another laid clutching his entrails on the ground. Before Ricky could expend the full tube of shells, the horde was upon him.

Joe ducked fully behind the trash can. He couldn't bear to watch the old man get torn apart. Closing his eyes, he cursed his helplessness and naivete. The huddled fugitive felt a deep sense of shame and cowardice at having done nothing to save him. Joe continued to run after failing to get a hold of his nerves. The visceral soundtrack of the sack of Lafayette behind him impelled his speed. A sheriff's patrol car whizzed by with sirens ablaze followed by an ambulance and a firetruck.

Joe ducked behind a car to avoid being seen by the emergency vehicles. As he prepared to continue his flight, his gaze became locked onto his reflection in the car's side-view mirror.

You coward! Turn and fight. He pulled down his mask.

Joe shook his head and took off his ball cap. Taking the knife from his front pocket, he looked back to downtown. A deathly orange glow marred the sky as the town burned. A fireball indicated that the town gas station fell into the hands of the saboteurs. A few gunshots rang out, marking the presence of some more illegally owned firearms.

There's too many of them. What can I do? Joe lamented and slapped his thigh resignedly. *It's pointless!*

As he did this, his hand made contact with the rock in his pocket. The pain surprised him and stung sharply. Reaching into his pocket, he pulled the piece out.

Rolling the stone in his fingers amid the sickly light of the burning city, he sat in grim realization. The memory of toiling up and down the foothill gripped him like a constricting serpent. Joe watched the fires of the inferno dance on the jagged edges of the little rock in his hand. It was a small part to a whole just as he was one data point among millions. He knew there was almost nothing he could do, but he understood that doing nothing was a more ignoble fate. Joe wondered how many others that night were on the cusp of action but meekly idled because their actions would feel pointless. The lessons of the boulder commanded him to say, "But that's why it must be done."

Joe made a fist and placed the rock back in its place with a deep sigh. He stood straight up, unfolded the knife, and clutched it tightly. Joe marched stoically toward the chaos with the knife open and concealed in his sweatshirt pocket.

He cut across the neighborhood to flank the rioters on the street. Joe again had no plan except a burning desire to resist the destruction and decline. He knew he would likely suffer grievous bodily harm or possibly death if he tried to stop the mob. Joe felt the deep guilt of all the deaths he had caused and witnessed while he stood idly by. The only penance for his inaction would be a bloodletting. Of whom, Joe was not sure.

The Hate Criminal turned a corner and saw a throbbing mass of rioters torching a few mobile homes. If the citizens fought back, it meant being investigated; investigation meant conviction; conviction meant a torturous death in the prison system. Joe noticed two individuals, male and female, looking a little too clean-cut presiding over the swarm. They wore black hoodies but suspiciously pressed khaki pants while carrying backpacks and bullhorns. He saw one communicate on a radio then confer with his colleague. They pulled out a tablet and bickered while the mob destroyed their current target. The level of organization and intentionality of Lafayette's sack disturbed and horrified Joe.

The Hate Criminal approached the two individuals from behind. In the noise and chaos, it was easy to go undetected.

"No, no, no," the male on the left said, "they didn't say anything about the White Oaks neighborhood."

"You weren't even at the brief!" the female countered. "It clearly says right here on the update"—she pointed to the tablet—"Group Blue move to White Oaks if all other locations are complete."

Her colleague objected, "There's no way we're moving them now. It's like herding cats."

As Joe stalked closer, he could see that they were young college students. The boy appeared to be White but dripped with beltway snobbery. His counterpart looked to be of some Asiatic race. Joe wondered if this experience would wind up on their resumes listed as a prestigious summer internship with some benevolent NGO.

The male turned slightly and noticed Joe's shadowy figure approaching. It did not immediately alarm him, but he did a double take as he noticed the man's determined gaze. Making a gesture, he directed the female's attention to Joe. The college students froze in alarm as he marched steadily toward them with the fires of the burning city reflecting in his eyes.

"Uh, hey!" the male called out impotently. "What are you doing?"

Joe drew the knife from his front pocket. The college students, assured of their enemies' complete disarmament, could not comprehend that he was not on their side. In his choice of targets, Joe settled on the male. While a soft looking fellow, the boy posed a greater physical threat. Second, Joe felt a greater degree of hatred for a traitor than an enemy.

When he closed to a few feet, the Hate Criminal rushed in and grabbed the male by the back of the neck. After a swift upward motion of his right arm, Joe buried the knife four inches deep in his adversary's chest. The boy gasped in excruciating pain and clutched at his attacker's face. Turning his eyes to the female, Joe tried to remove the weapon from the first carcass to dispatch her, but the blade remained stuck between the boy's ribs. She shrieked in horror and tried to direct some rioters to her aid. Joe panicked as he struggled to remove the knife. By now the boy laid on the pavement, breathing rapidly and trying to scream. Placing a foot on his victim's chest, Joe heaved at the handle. In the struggle, his surgical mask fell from his face without him noticing. When the blade finally came loose, he stumbled back and fell down. The female already made her escape and continued trying to gather some of the rabble to her defense. The bloodthirsty mass ignored her hysterical screaming and continued the looting.

Joe returned to his feet but nearly lost his balance. He watched the college boy's life slip away in grim fascination. He writhed and wheezed, gasping for breath. The orange light of the fires made the boy's shadow dance on the ground in otherworldly forms. Snapping from the trance, Joe looked around. The female was nowhere to be found, and the rioters began moving like a cloud of locusts to the next neighborhood.

He managed the wherewithal to see if there were any useful supplies he could gather from the boy. Rifling through the pockets, Joe found a wallet, radio, and a set of keys. On the key chain dangled a shape he recognized. As he held it up against the burning backdrop of Lafayette's sack, its sharp edges and acute angles stirred a new reaction in Joe. It was a six-pointed star.

His spirit churned within him as he recognized the symbol. The two triangles pointing in opposite directions brought forth Karl's riddle. Stephen the Martyr's speech to the Sanhedrin echoed in Joe's adrenaline-fueled mind in tandem. The Star of Remphan—at last it clicked for him, at last he understood his uncle's parables. The boy lying there was not a White man at all. He was a guest. Joe widened his eyes as the revelation flooded his consciousness.

Tossing the kabbalistic hexagram aside, Joe picked up the dying boy's bullhorn. "Get this honky! Get this White boy!" he yelled in a metallic din.

Sprinting away, he looked back to see if his deception worked. After ducking behind a trash can, he saw the mob converge on the student and unleash their hatred. A number of other organizers began arriving on scene, presumably having been alerted by the escaped female. They rushed in to try to save the boy but met stiff resistance. Soon enough, a full-on brawl broke out between the rioters and organizers. Joe took no small pleasure in watching the infighting. He wondered why this boy was important enough to warrant a rescue effort. More and more of the organizers rolled up in vehicles along with what appeared to be some kind of law enforcement.

The loud bang of an exploding teargas canister made Joe jump and clear from the area. The acrid smoke began drifting throughout the neighborhood as the rioters disbursed. Seemingly out of nowhere, large armored vehicles swarmed the town and began demanding that the participants return to the buses and that the protest was over. It seemed that the golems had overstepped their bounds.

Avoiding these ambiguous authority figures, Joe egressed back to the motel. Passing more scenes of carnage and destruction, he at least felt satisfied that the armored vehicles were putting a stop to the sack. The area around the motel, being generally disadvantaged and rundown, was the target of only a few roving groups. Entering the parking lot, he found Padresh at the counter, drunk and generally unaware of the chaos going on around him. Joe made his way up to his room and entered softly, closing the door behind him to blot out the sounds of sirens, teargas canisters, and shouting. Taking a look in the mirror, Joe gave a smile of spiritual satisfaction.

35

THE BEAST'S MANY HEADS

The killer sat raggedly by the door after a sleepless night of washing his soiled clothes in the sink and rinsing his blood-soaked hands. By the early hours of the morning, the riot was completely cleared. He replayed the scene of killing the activist in his mind over and over out of amazement. Joe felt astounded that he had the capability to take life in such a manner. He had killed Omar, but it was under circumstances of extreme duress and mostly by accident. He felt unsure of who he was after this premeditated and intentional violence. The boy's face took its place alongside Omar's in Joe's indelible memory. The scene of Ricky's untimely demise haunted his recollections of the night alongside the others.

Having no appetite, Joe sat numbly by the window for several hours in the morning. After a while, he grew concerned that Cynthia was late. His anxiety built slowly as the minutes and hours ticked by.

Was she killed? Joe worried in his thoughts. *Did I fail to save another?*

At last, his suspense broke when he saw Cynthia making her way up the steps. Overcome with relief and happiness, Joe exited his room and ran to greet her. She took a step back in fear at his approach but lowered her guard when she recognized him. They embraced in mutual consolation.

"I'm so glad you made it! Was it bad where you were?" Joe asked eagerly.

Cynthia put her hand over her mouth and struggled to speak. The tears flowed as she embraced him again, as if he were her own son.

"It's been a hard night. They came pretty close but stopped a few houses short. I thought a lot about my son and the LA protest. I guess I was wrong when I said he'd be safer here!" She wept again.

Joe patted the old lady's back and said in a comforting tone, "I'm just glad you're safe. Why don't you rest at home today?"

Cynthia shook her head. "Padresh would fire me on the spot if I asked. I'm already on thin ice coming late today."

He cursed the motel owner and released the embrace. "Can I do anything for you?"

She gave a sweet smile from her wrinkled, tear-streaked face. "No, no, I'll be fine. Just don't let your trash pile up!"

Joe chuckled quietly and walked with her toward his room.

"How about around here?" Cynthia inquired. "It doesn't look like they touched the motel."

He surveyed his surroundings. "Yeah, I don't suppose they did."

They politely said goodbye and mutually expressed their relief at both being safe and sound. Just after Joe returned inside his room, he caught a glimpse of his uncle's pickup rolling into the lot. He was grateful that Karl likely did not see him out of the room. After a period of anxious waiting, his uncle came up to the door.

"Boy, am I glad to see you're okay! I wanted to make an early supply run to make sure you made it through," Karl said boisterously as he entered.

Joe nodded. "Yeah, they didn't really come this way. How did you hear about what happened?"

His uncle let down his load of supplies with a sigh. "It's all over the news, but not in the way you'd expect. Apparently, Chuck Cohen's son Aaron got killed last night by some guy with a knife!"

The killer concealed his discomfort. He recognized the name but couldn't place his politics. "Who's Chuck Cohen again?"

A look of glee spread on Karl's face. "Only the chief rabbi of the Synagogue of Satan himself! He authored the Equity and Inclusion Act." He smiled again. "You know, maybe you're right. Maybe there is hope for America if a guy had the chutzpah to shiv Cohen's son."

Joe let the smile of spiritual satisfaction return to his countenance with renewed intensity.

"I was watching some pirate streams of the riots last night. There's only some very grainy drone footage of the stabbing unfortunately. It was some guy in a red hoodie. It looked like one of my old sweatshirts actually," the uncle joked, "but the lying media is painting the son as some hero of racial justice. They're claiming he died defending an anti-racism protest from a White supremacist terrorist. The killer was probably just mad they were firebombing his house, but the media won't tell you that." He leaned over and chuckled. "I'm honestly surprised they didn't pin it on you!"

The nephew nodded stoically and stared out the window.

Karl continued, "In any event, I wouldn't want to stick around in Lafayette much longer if I were him. The feds will turn this whole city upside down looking for the killer." He shook his head. "He ought to skip town."

After a period of silence, Joe asked out of politeness if anything happened to the ranch the previous night.

Karl laughed a little. "No, we were pretty well out of the storm. Sheriff Perry kept me apprised of the developments."

"I didn't see him doing much last night," Joe fired from the hip.

His uncle objected, "I'm not sure how you'd know that. I mean, what could he do? The FCIA would haul him in on Hate Crime charges, then Lafayette would really be in a pickle after he's gone."

The fugitive rolled his eyes imperceptibly. "I think it's in fairly dire straits now," he said grimly, "but what I don't understand is how this little stunt last night will swing the election. Won't this just galvanize resistance to Cabezudo?"

Karl lamented, "Well again, you may have been right even a few years ago. Last night was just intimidation. But ever since Equity and Inclusion, and the abolition of voter ID, they'll just do the same antics on election day—except the rioters will vote too. And there's not a thing anyone can do to stop it. If you so much as ask if they're a resident, fed commissars will make sure you never see the outside of a prison cell again."

"How do they just get away with this?" Joe asked petulantly.

"Because rats at the top like Cohen are invincible and they know it. The media runs damage control, social media censors any coverage of their tactics, and the feds smack anyone bold enough to peek their head up with a Hate Crime charge," Karl replied with frustrated gestures.

"I bet he's not as invincible as he thinks," the killer said quietly.

His uncle smiled. "Who's going to run against him and win? It's all rigged."

Joe leaned forward and lowered his voice. "I wasn't talking about elections."

"I wouldn't be too upset if that snake met a grisly end like his son, but another would take his place. The beast has too many heads. It'd be pointless." As Karl uttered the last word, Joe's eyes noticeably took on a fiery character.

"Yeah, pointless." The killer subtly clutched at the rock in his pocket.

The elder Blaine cocked his head slightly as if he realized what implication Joe took from his words.

Brushing this off, he continued, "Cohen is making a rare appearance outside of Washington at his son's remembrance ceremony. They've already scheduled the vigil at MLK Jr. University," Karl intimated. "That's where his son went."

Joe knew the area well. MLK Jr. University was one of the so-called West Coast Ivies priced so far above what anyone could afford without financial aid, connections, or the correct melanin content. The campus sat piously just a few miles from his old house, mocking his status as a lowly cog. It was as much a seminary as a center of material knowledge. Acolytes of the state religion received their formal education in its esoteric teachings and doctrine at this institution. It was much like an officer training academy for the militant forces at work with a commission to "deconstruct Whiteness" granted to each graduate.

"I imagine he'd be vulnerable outside of his DC hideout," Joe commented.

"Not likely," his uncle countered. "I suppose the security measures in MLK are a lot looser, but a guy like that doesn't leave the house without a convoy of armed guards. Any attempt to get him would be a suicide mission"—he looked out the window—"but a guy can dream, right?"

The killer nodded and twisted the stone in his pocket with his hands. "Cohen's got to pay for his crimes. I guess somebody who's got nothing to lose could make a move."

"Yeah, but nobody exists in a vacuum like that. Everybody's got something to lose." Karl placed his hands on his knees and got ready to leave. "With the feds preoccupied with finding Aaron's killer, I doubt you're very high on their priority list. It's best for you to just stay put for now. I suppose I shouldn't stick around too long. I'm glad you made it through okay."

Joe thanked him for the supplies and saw him out the door. As he watched his uncle exit the motel, the flames of action continued to burn in his soul in tandem with the fear of capture. He could only attain meaning through struggle, and his war was not yet won.

36

SELF-PRESERVATION

The elder Blain couldn't help but make his way through the battered town slowly, taking time to view the destruction in the daylight. He drove past scenes of burnt-out businesses, smoldering homes, and bloodstained streets. Emergency vehicles from a few surrounding counties arrived to assist in casualty evacuation and handling the remaining fires. As Karl turned onto the road leading to Wetumpka, he came up on Cabezudo's residence at the old Iverson Mansion. To no one's surprise, the home and its surrounding area was left completely unscathed. A police car sat outside with Sheriff Perry leaning forlornly on the door.

"Howdy, Sheriff," Karl said grimly.

"Karl," Perry greeted with a nod.

"Heck of a night you must've had," he said to the sheriff.

The lawman put his hands on his web belt, hung his head, and sighed, "Not really, I had to stick right here. I got orders from the feds that if anything happened to Cabezudo's house, I'd hang for it. My deputies did their best to handle everything else."

"What a just system, right?" The elder Blaine shrugged.

"Honestly, I reckon it's time to retire anyways. I'm losing the election. I ain't got any pretentions." Perry stroked his mustache. "I don't suppose this next sheriff will be too kind to your situation."

Karl sat for a moment in recognition of this fact. "We'll manage. Only you and a few others even know I exist, much less where I live. I'll just have to tighten the belt a little and be more careful."

The pair remained silent for a while as they both contemplated whether this statement had any truth at all.

The sheriff put his hand on his cruiser, looked out over the town, and broke the silence: "Ya know, people used to retire to places like this to get away from the way it is now."

"It's everywhere man. There's nowhere to hide." Blaine put his hands on the steering wheel and gripped it tightly.

Perry interjected, "You seem to have found a pretty good hideout. That is until they find you."

Karl nodded slowly and brought his eyes to the deep-blue sky. Looking out in the direction of his ranch, fragments of ash and debris floated in front of the otherwise unobstructed sunshine.

He reassured himself: "They won't find me."

"This town has just been crawling with feds asking for you. What are you doing up there?" the sheriff asked, bracing for the reply.

Karl shook his head. "Just existing, which I suppose is illegal to these rats."

"You don't have to tell me"—Perry furrowed his brow—"but whatever it is you've been doing has really attracted their ire. They keep talking about some nephew of yours and how he's a terrorist. Is that true?"

"Not at all," he replied sharply, "not even in the slightest."

The sheriff adjusted his broad-brimmed hat. "I reckon it wasn't true. They're just trying to tighten the screws on me and tell me I'm abettin' a terrorist."

Karl shifted uncomfortably. He had no desire to get the old lawman caught up in this situation.

"Have you told them where Wetumpka is?" he asked expectantly.

"That was a tricky one. I just claimed ignorance and gave them a map. I marked it up with a few dummy locations of old minin' sites I know of. Should hold 'em off for a little while." Perry crossed his arms and eyed the street. "I suppose they could just comb the area with a satellite and find you that way."

Karl grew anxious. "I'm sure they're poking around."

The lawman rested his hand on his pistol. "I don't know what you're up to, but ain't this the same as going to prison? You can't get groceries without sneaking in; you can't leave your property without the feds lookin' for you. What kind of life is that?"

"It's the only thing we can do. Society's beyond saving, so we've got to save ourselves." The elder Blaine shifted his truck into drive.

"I better get back. Stay safe, Sheriff."

"Good luck," Perry called out.

His tone gave Karl shivers down his spine. The way he said it seemed to indicate foreknowledge of some looming cataclysm.

The drive back to the homestead grew increasingly nerve-racking. As he took his usual turn on the gravel road leading to Wetumpka, he noticed a set of tire tracks too small to be his own. Karl began rapping the steering wheel with his fingers as his anxiety rose. A sinking feeling leeched its way into every thought.

After an additional twenty minutes of driving, he came to the alternate trail that led directly to his ranch. The steep gradient could only be traversed by skill and the truck's knobby tires. After a lengthy period of slipping tires and tumbling rocks, Karl crested the last ridge. He stopped for a moment to get out of his vehicle and looked down on the idyllic scene of his ranch from above. George was tending to the cows, while Roger moved a wheelbarrow. Eva and Alexandria sat sewing beneath a tree as the warm, radiant sunshine enveloped the plateau. Karl shed a silent tear taking in the peaceful pastures below. He would give anything to just live out his days in grave appreciation of his good fortune. He would give anything to scoop up the entire scene and move it to another dimension for its preservation and protection. A chilly wind sullied his contemplation and compelled him to return to the truck. Warmth returned to him when he made the final descent to the ranch.

Alexandria ran to greet him when he exited the vehicle. He embraced her like he never had before. The cherishing fatherly love overwhelmed him, and the tears returned.

"Daddy, why are you crying?" she asked with glistening, blue eyes.

Eva arrived shortly after and noticed her husband's worried countenance.

"What's wrong, baby?" his wife inquired.

Karl made his way over and kissed her deeply as if for the last time.

"I'm just happy to see you." Karl hugged her tight and patted Alexandria's head.

They could not see his face, but it took on a wide-eyed and haggard expression, as if he were some wild animal pursued by an invincible predator. Karl sensed a coming storm and desired shelter.

The sinking feeling returned as incomprehensible dread overtook him.

He ushered his daughter away and took Eva to the bedroom. Though he maintained a grave look on his face, he did his best to conceal his true thoughts until they were alone.

"I think we're going to have to move," Karl broke the news in a mournful tone.

"What? Why?!" Eva began to tremble.

Her husband placed his hand on her leg. "The feds are poking around a lot. It's only a matter of time until they find us."

"But why do we have to move? We're not wanted for anything, and we can hide what we're not supposed to have"—her tone grew desperate as tears began to flow—"and there's no proof Joe was ever here!"

Karl ran his fingers through his hair and sighed, "They'll catch us for something. Even if we're one hundred percent clean, they'll find some reason to haul us in. We're a threat because we made a life for ourselves that doesn't depend on them. They'll never forgive us for that."

"But now we have to give that life up?" she leaned her head on his shoulder.

"We're not giving up this life. We just"—he groped for words—"we just have to move it somewhere else."

Eva shook her head and sobbed. "I can't start over again! It was so hard on us when you got kicked out and we had to start from scratch. It was just a sheer miracle we found this plot of land with a seller willing to work with our needs."

Karl continued to try to console his wife, but to no avail. Eva's hot tears fell on his shoulder and began to soak his shirt. He needed to pull something sentimental and sweet to salvage the situation. Karl remembered those tension filled days after he was kicked out of the Navy. He proposed to Eva at a park with a ring he could barely afford. There was no fanfare, no photographer, just a man asking the love of his life to come on an adventure.

Suddenly an idea popped into his head. He would put on the old, red sweatshirt he was wearing when he proposed to her years ago. Karl would ask her to come with him on another adventure. He felt satisfied that this gesture would calm her down and make her feel loved. Karl squeezed her shoulder and got up to get the surprise.

Moving into the storage room, he began rifling through various bags to find it. Karl knew exactly which bag to look for. With a growing sense of frustration at not finding it, he rechecked the room.

"Oh gosh, it's at the motel," Karl muttered to himself, disappointed he could not follow through with his loving gesture.

Making his way back to comfort Eva, he stopped dead in his tracks.

"No!" he whispered aloud and widened his eyes. "It's at the motel!"

Flying over to the computer, he furiously searched for the grainy footage of the previous night. Zooming in on the killer in the red hoodie, Karl's heart dropped to the floor as he recognized the outline of the knife. He was certain that it was the same sweatshirt.

"No, no, no!" The uncle slammed his hand on the desk. "Why'd you do it, Joe!"

A million thoughts screamed into his head like a locomotive pulling into the station with failed brakes. If this was the publicly available footage, he imagined that the feds had access to even better footage. Worse still, the perpetrator's mask fell off during the scuffle and would soon lead to his identification. Karl sat in horror staring at his screen.

"I take you in and save you, and this is how you repay me?!" He slammed his hand on the desk again, knocking over the computer monitor. "Why didn't you just stay put like you were supposed to!"

In frustration, he took the monitor and threw it across the room.

Eva came slinking out of the bedroom, her face awash with tears, "Karl, what's going on?!"

Her husband snapped around with a crazy-eyed look of abject terror.

"We have to go, now! Joe did something stupid, and now it's only a matter of time before they come up here and arrest all of us," Karl said in a rushed and horrified yelp.

Eva moaned and slumped to the ground with her head in her hands.

"There's no time, baby. Gather up the kids and have them grab their go-bags. Just like we practiced." Her husband embraced her tightly.

She began to rise, but her trembling legs impeded her movement. "Oh Karl! Why did you take him in? Why did you do this?! I knew this would happen! I can't do this!" Eva continued in utter fear, "Can't we hide him somewhere or something? What did he do?"

Karl hushed her and hugged her tightly. "Baby, I'm so sorry. We have to get out of here. Joe getting caught is an inevitability at this point," he remarked grimly. "If they find him, they find us. Then we're really screwed. They'll make him talk. The only way we can stay here is if they never catch and interrogate him."

Eva gripped his arms bitterly. "There has to be something we can do!"

As she uttered these words, a horrible plan formed in the dark, savage recesses of Karl's mind. The fear of pursuit and the irrationality of flight took the reins of his consciousness like they never had before. Karl's eyes drifted to the guest bedroom door. Clenching his teeth, the guilt of his proposed action already began to seep into his spirit. Karl smothered this feeling viciously in the name of self-preservation.

"Don't worry, sweetie, I'll take care of it," he whispered softly.

"What are you going to do?" Eva asked pleadingly.

Karl hushed her once more. "Don't worry, baby. We might not have to move after all. I'll take care of it."

She looked up at him with welling eyes. She wanted to know what he was planning but wanted the comfort and stability of their home more. Eva nodded silently and kissed her husband.

Karl rose from the floor and went to the closet in the guest bedroom where Joe slept all those weeks ago. Removing the false backing, he drew out a pistol and a loaded magazine. Concealing them in his coat, he strode fearfully out the door.

37

JUST A COINCIDENCE

Jameila swore in a storm of stress and pulled at her hair.

"Yes, ma'am," she agreed obsequiously on the phone. "Yes, ma'am, I will get on that. . . . No, ma'am. No, that is not my understanding."

Sean stood by with pleasure at seeing someone besides himself receiving a dressing down from Feldman for once.

"Yes, yes, okay, that will be my top priority." She sighed and proceeded to end the call.

"It sucks, right?" He gave a wry smile.

Jameila glared at her partner. "Shut up, you wouldn't have prevented this."

Sean declared gleefully, "While you were presiding over the death of a senator's son, I found Wetumpka!"

"Great," she replied sarcastically, "and then the trail went cold, right?"

"Nope, I found a trail, and I'm checking it out first thing tomorrow morning if you want to come." Sean put his hands proudly behind his head as he leaned back in the chair.

The investigator's phone rang. He gave a perplexed look at the unrecognized number and picked up the phone.

"Mr. McDowell, this is Ms. Sheila from admin," a rude voice greeted him. "You are not authorized to stay at 581 West Oak Street."

"What?" Sean remained incredulous.

"The Mountain Springs Inn? It's not on our list of approved motels. You need to move out and find other lodging," Ms. Sheila informed the investigator with a righteous fury.

He shot back in confusion, "I'm not staying there. We're at Pinecrest on Barrel Street. I got it straight from the list."

"You need to move out. According to my records, you're staying at the Mountain Springs Inn on 581 West Oak Street. You didn't report your reservations to us, so I had to search your name on the federal guest registry for Lafayette," she continued after some audible typing on her computer. "Let's see here. . . . Yup! William McDowell at 581 West Oak Street. You need to move out."

Sean furrowed his brow. "William? That's not my name. It was my brother's name."

"I'm not seeing any other McDowell on any Lafayette guest registry." Ms. Sheila grew more agitated.

"We checked in under my partner's name. Check Jameila Agdal."

Ms. Sheila clacked away on her keyboard for an interminable amount of time. After a period of brief silence she stated, "Oh, yes, Pinecrest Inn and Suites. That is authorized lodging, but you'll need to move out of Mountain Springs. That is not authorized."

Sean's frustration built up to a boil. "I'm not staying there! I'm with my partner at the other place."

"William David McDowell. That's what my records show." Ms. Sheila remained assured of her conviction. "I don't want to argue with you. Close out the reservation tonight. Also, your stay up to this point will be coming out of your travel allowance."

The investigator stumbled back in confusion as the admin lady hung up on him.

"What was that?" Jameila asked expectantly.

Sean remained dumbfounded. "That was admin saying I'm staying at the wrong hotel."

She chuckled slightly. "Classic admin being totally useless. We picked this hotel straight from the list."

"I know, but that's not the weird part. She didn't know my first name obviously—too incompetent to do that—but she said someone named William David McDowell on the registry was checked in to one of the motels in town." His eyes widened as his brow lowered.

"That's your brother's name, isn't it? Probably just a crazy coincidence." Jameila brushed it off and then groaned as she checked the time. "Ugh, the debrief with Barry is in twenty minutes. Let's go. I feel like walking tonight."

Sean sat with his phone trembling in his hand. "I'll meet you there. I just want to check on something."

"It's just a coincidence, Sean," she reassured him as she left the hotel room. "Don't wait up too long."

He nodded and waved her out the door. The investigator sat in silence for several minutes, his mind ablaze with confusion. The memories of receiving the call about his brother's overdose coursed through his memory like a raging torrent. Something beckoned him to check on this individual. Sean recalled seeing his brother's face on the coroner's table for identification. With his father deceased and his sister out of the country on vacation, he was the only one available to identify the body in the absence of a driver's license.

He shot up in sudden realization. "They said he didn't have any ID on him!"

Frantically, he scrolled through the contacts on his phone. After settling on Patel, he gave him a call.

"Hello?"

"Hey Patel, it's Sean. I need a quick favor."

Patel paused for a moment. "You've been cashing in a lot of those recently."

The investigator followed a hunch. He remembered a Dixon, Illinois coroner that the FCIA picked up a few months ago for selling IDs of overdose cases on the dark web. After some interrogation, the man admitted that he was one of many feeding a central supplier. The central hub hadn't yet been found and came to the attention of the DC office.

"Don't twist my balls right now. I need you to comb through the crypto transactions we've picked up for the coroner ID sales network investigation, specifically from the Springfield, Illinois area," Sean rattled off his request.

His intel counterpart sighed. "That's a lot of data. What are you looking for specifically? Any specific date?"

He relayed the date of his brother's death.

Patel scrolled for a moment. "Yes, actually. Exactly three months ago to a central Illinois IP address. We flagged it because it went to an IP address associated with a coroner. It looks like the buyer used one of those privacy coins, but I think we've cracked this one." He typed into a search bar and waited a few seconds. "Ha, easy. ChainTank finished their contract on this one about five weeks ago."

"That's some luck!" The investigator grew giddy with anticipation.

"We can't trace it to a specific buyer yet, but I can see what else they've bought. It looks like they've made several recurring deposits to a credit card," Patel read out methodically.

"Can you see where the card was used?" Sean interjected.

"Get with the times. That's child's play." His intel counterpart laughed. "Lafayette, Utah."

Sean nearly dropped the phone. "Lafayette?"

"Yup, you really owe me for this one. I'm one of the few guys that can see through the smoke and mirrors like this." Patel congratulated himself. "What's this concerning?"

"I want you to call me the second you see anything about an ID with the name William David McDowell!"

He hung up the phone and stared at the filthy carpeting of the hotel room in dead silence. It was not so much the crime that bothered him. He had no pretensions of restoring family honor or preventing the dishonor of his brother's memory. Sean always envied the family name, but now some vagrant purchased his birthright. The Blaine case faded away from his mind as anger fueled his desire to catch whoever was using the title of William David McDowell III. After shaking himself back to reality, he got up from the chair and grabbed his keys.

◘

It was late evening, and the sun dipped mournfully below the distant mountaintops overlooking Lafayette. Joe watched the town darken through his window in a tortured silence. Briefly, he opened the door and took a deep breath of cool, fresh air before closing it again. Turning to the interior, he viewed his pile of supplies on the bed. Joe had stripped the backpacks for everything essential and condensed his load into one backpack. Joe rehearsed the plan in his mind several times and prayed for courage. He couldn't stay in Lafayette, but he had to stop running from the fight.

Joe planned to wait for a few more hours until the sky was completely dark before making his move. He shut his eyes and did his best to recall the route to the train station. Confident in his ability to find it, he opened them again and let out a nervous sigh. The minutes passed like hours as he waited for the light to fully decline and give him optimal cover. He walked over to the door and placed his hand on the knob several times but restrained himself from executing the plan too early. Finally, as the last vestiges of light vanished from the little town of Lafayette, Joe took a deep breath and opened the door. A dark, silhouetted figure blocked his path.

PART V

FRUITION OF THE FIRE

38

TAKE A GOOD LOOK

"Karl?!"

His uncle pushed into the room and pulled him in before slamming the door shut.

"What's going on?" Joe asked in fear.

"What's going on?! Yeah, Joe, what *is* going on?!" Karl hissed angrily.

His nephew furrowed his brow. "What's this about?" he said as he realized the compromising backpack on his shoulder. "This isn't what you think."

"Oh, give it up, Joe. I know you've been leaving the motel." The uncle let his anger brim.

Joe silenced and backed up with his head low.

"And I know about you stabbing Cohen's son! How could you be so reckless? You've put my whole family in danger," Karl let out in a hoarse whisper.

"There's no way anybody can pin that on me," Joe backpedaled and trembled with adrenaline.

"Well, I figured it out! I bet I'm only a few steps ahead of the feds. Your mask slipped off, Joe. They'll be here as soon as they figure out where you've been staying," the uncle yelled and shoved his nephew onto the bed.

"It's not under my name!" he said with a panicked voice. With a flood of anxiety, he remembered his slip with Cynthia.

Karl pointed an accusatory finger at him. "They'll figure it out. You're done!"

"I was planning on skipping town tonight anyway, so it'll be okay!" Joe sensed his uncle's fierce wrath.

Karl put a hand inside his jacket. "I can see that." He lowered his voice and shook his head. "I'm sorry, Joe. I tried to help you. I really did. But you've put my family in grave danger. I'm so sorry for this."

His eyes began welling up as his hand remained planted and immobile in his coat.

"What are you doing?"

"I'm sorry, Joe. I'm so sorry"—Karl's hand trembled as it slowly moved—"but you've destroyed the only home my family has ever known. I can't let you fall into their hands. I can't afford to let you be interrogated. You'll give me up."

"Uncle Karl?" Joe's mind raced at the growing realization of what was happening. "Please! It doesn't have to be like this! I'm leaving town anyway!"

His uncle shook his head slowly while maintaining horrified eye contact with the trembling wretch before him. At last, his hand cleared the seam of his coat to reveal a slim, black pistol with a suppressor threaded on.

"No! Uncle Karl, please listen!" Joe pleaded.

"Why didn't you just follow my instructions?" The pistol shook tremendously in his hands as he raised it. "Gosh, Joe! All you had to do was just exist!"

The nephew closed his eyes and prayed. Mistake after mistake, death after death, collateral after collateral, Joe's course left a trail of havoc wherever he went. He couldn't bear the thought of dying with destruction being his only legacy. Joe had enough of pleading: pleading with the OIHO, pleading with Rosenblatt, pleading with Wallace, and now with his own family. With a resolved fire brewing in his soul, he stood up.

The two men stared at each other. As Joe's eyes grew more confident and stoic, Karl's slumped into anxious contemplation. The barrel remained pointed directly at his nephew's forehead.

"I want you to look in that mirror," Joe finally broke the silence with a placid imperative.

"What?" Karl inquired with a tremor in his voice.

"Look in the mirror!" Joe's tone crescendoed like the crack of a whip.

His uncle's gaze drifted to the reflective surface behind his captive.

"Do you see it? Do you see that man?"

"What man?!" Karl's frazzled brain sputtered.

"Take a good long look. You'll have to live with him for the rest of your life." Joe pointed authoritatively behind him again.

The uncle refocused his eyes on the mirror. He saw his haggard self, pointing the pistol at his own blood. He too felt another presence in the room.

"No matter what you tell anyone else, he'll know. He'll know, Karl." Joe gained the same look in his own eyes.

Karl averted eye contact with both of them for several seconds. "There's no other way!" he said with his gaze averted. "If you fall into their hands, my kids will get sold into sex slavery and my wife and I will go to prison. Or worse!"

"If you kill me, then what? You'll just keep running?" his nephew asked angrily.

"No, they won't find us. It'll—"

"Wrong!" Joe swore in fury. "They will never stop pursuing you. They'll never stop seeking until they have your very soul! You can pull stakes and run to the next Lafayette, but Yakov or someone else will find it too. From place to place, from hideout to hideout, these people will never stop!"

"I just wasn't careful enough this time. This never would've happened if you hadn't come to me!" Karl lashed out.

Joe pursed his lips. "You know that's not true. Even if I hadn't come, Lafayette was still on Yakov's list. It was only a matter of time before they ran Sheriff Perry out and then came down on you. It's fight or flight, and there's no place to fly anymore."

His uncle clenched his teeth tightly. Gripping the pistol with white knuckles, he attempted to steady the sights. Karl tried to focus his eyes on the front post, but his body refused. The spirit within him drew his gaze to the mirror and its terrible judgment. He tried to simply block out the truth reflected before him. All he wanted was for things to go back to the way they were.

"There's just no other way!" Karl whispered as much to himself as to his prisoner.

After a period of silence and staring down the barrel, Joe pointed aggressively. "Material and spiritual man!"

His uncle lowered the gun slightly at this interjection.

"You taught me this," the nephew continued, "the difference between material man and spiritual man." Joe paused to catch up to the boldness of his words. "The truth is that you're to the point of murdering a member of your own family all in the name of comfort!"

"You're wrong. I'm doing this *for* my family." Karl lowered the pistol to a more sustainable position directed at his nephew's chest.

"You're doing this for material comfort. Look! Look and tell me that's not what he says too!" Joe gestured behind him like an apocalyptic preacher.

Karl kept his eyes planted on his nephew. He knew exactly what his conscience would have to say about his intentions no matter how much he fooled himself. Making one last assault on his spirituality, Karl raised the pistol to Joe's head and gripped the trigger. The more he squeezed, the more his weapon shook in his hands. He reassured his grip with his other hand and breathed heavily. Joe could hear a series of tortured, grimacing yelps as Karl attempted to muster the nerve, his breathing growing increasingly rapid and shallow. In between grunts, his uncle chanted, "It's the only way," as if it were some kind of incantation. The fugitive closed his eyes and prayed.

Suddenly, the sound of the pistol clattering to the floor caused Joe to flinch violently. He opened his eyes and realized what happened. He saw his uncle crumpled on the floor with his head in his hands. A tsunami of relief washed over Joe. While he had no fear of death itself, he did fear not accomplishing his destiny.

Joe sat on the floor with him and placed his hand on his shoulder. "You don't have to worry about me being alive much longer."

"What do you mean?" Karl looked up with reddened eyes.

"I'm going to make the system pay for its crimes," the killer muttered softly with an ecstatic rush, "and I'm going to pay for mine."

His uncle lowered his brow. "What could you possibly do?"

"I'm going to kill Chuck Cohen," Joe cried righteously. "I'm going to finish what I unknowingly started last night. Cohen wrote the Equity and Inclusion Act. He made the OIHO," he hissed. "Chuck Cohen killed my wife!"

Karl leaned back in stunned surprise. "Now just how do you plan to do that?"

The shining fury dampened slightly. "Well, I'm going to ride rail back to MLK Jr. County, then figure it out from there. I know it's a suicide mission."

"I won't disagree with you there"—the uncle sat up slightly—"but I frankly don't think you'll make it within ten miles of him. It's more likely you'll be captured, and if that happens—"

"I won't let myself be captured," the Hate Criminal interrupted, growing in conviction. "Too many of our people died because I engaged in half measures. There are no more half measures." Joe lowered his tone. "This is a matter of redemption for me."

Karl replied slowly, "Joe, even if you get him, there are a thousand others waiting in the wings to take his spot!"

"But I will have struggled against the tide nonetheless!" The younger Blaine's countenance brightened to an eschatological flash. "Materially it's pointless. But spiritually," Joe cried, "this is my crusade! I'll kill him not just for my wife but for every one of us who got dragged from their beds in the middle of the night by the mob! For every little girl torn from her parents and sold into slavery! For the prisoners trapped in the motel system! For all of our people, I'll make this man pay for his crimes and let him know that a spiritually healthy White man still draws breath!"

Karl remained silent and in awe of the fruition of his nephew's transformation. He felt shame that this young man stood in judgment of his own materialistic failures. The depressed, useless lump that showed up on his doorstep was now a formidable warrior. Karl resignedly acknowledged he had been surpassed.

"And when I die, I'll die nobly. I will go to meet the Father knowing that I snuffed out one of Satan's most faithful servants. If I am in danger of capture, I will not give them the satisfaction. Whatever the outcome, I will have striven"—with each word Joe pounded his fist on his chest—"struggled, bled, and rolled my boulder up the mountain! Yes, it may seem pointless"—he stood up and looked back to the mirror—"but that's why it must be done."

His uncle laid his head low before the warrior. He looked back on his life and lamented how he had simply observed the decline and perdition of his people.

"Joe . . ." Karl began slowly, "you're right. I know you're right. But knowing what is right and doing it are very different things."

Joe observed the shivering wretch before him with impassivity. The uncle attempted to speak further, but words failed him. Instead, he extended the pistol to the warrior in sullen resignation. This time, the gun's handle faced Joe.

"Take it," Karl said softly, "and do right."

His nephew took the weapon in his hands and firmly grasped it.

"Maybe you're right about me running, but somebody has to be around when things collapse. After this is through, my children and my children's children will inherit the earth. Our people need guys of both our stock: the warrior and the builder. We can't have all of one or all of the other"—the elder Blaine took on a conciliatory tone—"but Providence has chosen you for the former. Who am I to stand in your way?"

Joe set the pistol aside and brought Karl up to his feet. "You were just protecting your family. They're the future I'm struggling for too."

"I'm sorry, Joe. You've really passed me up," his uncle said with a tearful, wry smile.

"I need to get to the railhead now. I'm behind schedule," the warrior stated.

Karl took a moment to run Joe through how to operate the pistol, and then handed him his pack. "I'll drive you there."

The younger Blaine nodded as they exited the motel room, making sure to remove everything that could be of evidentiary value. Walking to the truck, they threw the bags and clutter in the bed before driving off.

"Well, you skipping town will buy me some time," Karl said matter-of-factly. "I just hate to do this to Eva."

"I understand. Bringing home bad news is a big burden." Joe recalled driving home from the OIHO to break the news of homelessness to his wife. "But deep down I think you knew how impermanent your ranch really was. That's why it scared you so much when there was a credible threat of losing it."

The uncle made no comment. He raised his eyebrows in somber realization and continued driving to the rail yard. A dark SUV zoomed by them in the opposite direction. Karl commented that it was likely an FCIA vehicle. As they pulled up to the chain link fence, the elder Blaine pointed out the westbound train. The pair shared a somber goodbye, one of those mournful, bitter farewells one experiences only once or twice in a lifetime. Before heading off, Karl handed him an additional bag of gear and called out to the warrior, "God bless you, Joe! In truth, I envy you."

Joe looked over his shoulder at his uncle and nodded silently. In truth, a small part of him envied his uncle too.

After a short wave, he climbed the fence and found the appropriate train car. His uncle drove away to sweep up his life off the mountain. Though retreating, they would never surrender. Theirs was another kind of crusade. After the truck's taillights disappeared around a corner, the warrior took in the crisp night air. Like many great men of his people before him in time's immemorial scroll, Joe turned his eyes west.

39

DAY LATE, DOLLAR SHORT

"Yes, how can I be helping you?" Padresh quickly closed several tabs on his computer.

"I'm going to need to see your guest list," Sean instructed breathlessly, after flashing his badge.

It was late at night, and the investigator had to pound on the door of the reservations hut for several minutes. "I assure you, there is no problem here," the motel manager attempted to deflect. "We upload the guest list to the federal registry on time always."

Sean grew impatient. "I'm not trying to get you in trouble. I just need to see your guest list and verify something."

Padresh scrolled on his computer for a moment and printed a sheet. Grabbing it from the printer, he handed it to the investigator.

"William David McDowell. Room 389. What can you tell me about him?" Sean interrogated with a tremor. He could've just broken down the door and put an end to it, but he wanted to keep his unauthorized side investigation under wraps.

"Nothing really, I do not snoop my customers." The manager shifted. "My cleaning lady should have more informations."

Cynthia came through the door. She took on a look of fear and surprise when she saw Sean's FCIA jacket.

"Good evening," the investigator perked up, "what can you tell me about William McDowell, room 389?"

She stood back and looked pensively upward. "I don't remember anyone by that name."

"You've never cleaned room 389? Who's staying there?" Sean

230

pressed.

Cynthia grew uncomfortable with his tone and just wanted to be left alone. "I'm sorry, sir. I don't know anyone named William McDowell." She thought for a moment. "389. . . . There's just a guy named Joe there. I don't know about a last name."

Sean's eyes noticeably widened. His intuition begged him to follow this improbable lead. "Joe?! What's his last name?! Has he been visited by an older man named Karl Blaine?"

She became worried that her friend might be in trouble. "I don't know, officer. I don't know his last name. There has been a periodic visitor. He's not in danger, is he?"

The investigator tersely demanded the room key and sprinted toward the stairs. He panted raggedly as he felt that his prey was nearby. The fortuitous whiplash from seeking his brother's ID to finding Joe excited his deepest ambitions. Sean rounded the staircase toward room 389 with the prospect of humiliating Feldman nipping at his heels. Catching his breath for a second, he paused before whipping open the door so he could fully experience his triumph.

"FCIA! Nobody move!" Sean cried as he moved into the room with his pistol drawn. Frantically searching the room, he found that it was empty. Only a few bags and discarded clothing lay strewn around the dark room. Rifling through one of the bags, he tossed it across the room in a flurry of frustration.

Sean slumped into the chair by the window with his head in his hands, cursing and swearing. With a jolt, he realized the seat was still warm. Jumping up, he prepared to make a search of the immediate area, but he was interrupted by his phone ringing.

"Hey, where are you?" Jameila asked in an annoyed tone.

"Jameila! I think Joe Blaine is here! He's in Lafayette!"

"Wait, hold on, calm down. How do you know?" she asked in a repressed tone.

"I don't have anything firm yet, but I think he's been using my brother's ID. That slimy coroner sold it to the uncle. He gave it to Joe, and then Joe used it to stay at the motel. He could be in Lafayette right now!" Sean chattered away in impatient excitement.

After a period of extended silence, Jameila mournfully said, "I know."

"What?!"

She continued, "Our analysts just got back to us with their report on the drone footage of Aaron Cohen's stabbing. It's Joe Blaine. You were right." Jameila swore bitterly. "He's here, just like you said."

Sean interrupted impatiently, "What are you telling *me* for? Tell Feldman! We need to get the hunt for Blaine started ASAP! We need birds in the air!"

She breathed sharply. "She's not going to like being told she's wrong. I better do it."

He giggled with satisfaction. "If I didn't think it would torpedo my career, I'd demand to do it myself. What I'd give to see the look on her face when she hears this!" He paused to bask in the vicarious triumph. "I'm coming to pick you up right now. Let's catch this scumbag!"

"Not so fast, Sean." Jameila's voice sounded encumbered with a large weight. "I already called Feldman. I think she'll keep you on your current tasking."

"We already did that stupid rally," he gestured with his pistol. Thinking better than to keep waving around his gun, Sean holstered it with a touch of embarrassment.

His partner sighed in frustration. "I don't claim to understand it either, but you have to stick around for another rally. They're bringing in a different investigator from DC to handle Blaine."

Sean kicked over the seat. "He could be in Mexico by that time! We need to act now. Screw it, I'm calling her."

"Sean, get a hold of yourself. This is above your head. Feldman doesn't want you to catch Blaine and this next rally has some big money behind it." Jameila lowered her voice considerably. "There's going to be weapons. It's a big operation."

He paced back and forth in the room like a typewriter's carriage. "That scheming witch! Is she really that petty that she'll let Blaine escape to keep me out of her job?"

She took a deep breath before replying, "I'm not supposed to be the one to break this to you, but the rumors are already going around. You've been reassigned. You were right, but that doesn't mean jack now. I'll pass the new information about the motel and the ID along to Feldman, but you better save it for the debrief with the new team."

"Let me guess, they got Danny Chen to take the glory while we sit idly by." Sean sat on the bed and crossed his arm across his torso.

He glanced briefly at the large mirror by the bed while Jameila remained silent for a considerable amount of time. Sean slowly made the connection and understood why she kept on saying "you" as opposed to "we."

"You're still on the case, aren't you?" The betrayal made his voice crack slightly.

His former partner stayed quiet until she blurted, "The rally is still a good assignment. It's definitely a—"

Sean hung up the phone and hurled it across the room, shattering the mirror on the opposing wall.

40

DOUBT, REDOUBT

Morning broke suddenly in the Nevadan desert as the sun beat cruelly on the hot, metal surface of the train. Unlike his flight from MLK Jr. County, Joe sat in peaceful acknowledgment of his suffering. The sandy wind that bit at his skin glanced off like rain on a windshield. As the train wound its way toward the high mountains before him, Joe welcomed the pain of the icy cold too. He was better prepared this time: morally, mentally, and physically. He was on a journey of atonement, filled with a cool resolution.

Joe clutched at the stone in his pocket like a holy relic while praying for strength and skill. He made his first ride on the train under duress and fear. Now he harnessed its momentum and rode it like an iron horse westward to do battle with the system.

Joe gripped the railing of the train car tightly. A grain of doubt germinated.

What if I get captured? What if I can't get to Cohen? Am I up to this task?

These questions started as a small trickle in his mind but soon gave way to a flood.

"Who am I kidding?" Joe said aloud while the train chugged along beneath him. "I'm no warrior. I just stabbed some college kid."

The late summer Nevada sun once more demanded its toll of sweat from the traveler. The fire of resolve dimmed and became starved of air.

Maybe what they say about me is true. Maybe I really am just a violent troublemaker. Joe sat in dour contemplation on the train car ledge. He ceased his incessant fondling of the pistol's grip in the bag and zipped up its compartment. A black despair, kept at bay for weeks, returned to him and sapped his strength.

Karl was right. I'll never make it within ten miles of Cohen. I'm not a super soldier. I'm just some office drone dealt a bad hand. I've never even fired this gun. The fugitive slumped on the platform and pulled the pistol from the rucksack again. *Maybe it's better if I just end it all before I do something stupid and get captured. All I've done is bounce from mistake to mistake like a pinball leaving a lot of death in my wake.*

Joe reflected on the scenes of horror he ran away from on the night of his PSL. Worst of all, Jill's terrified face hung before him like a taunting talisman of his inability to shape the world around him.

"Jill. . . ." He hung his head and rested it on his knees.

Joe contemplated shortening his journey and reuniting with his wife. After all, there would be no danger of capture. However, his reawakened sense of spiritual honor prohibited such an exit, as did his rejuvenated faith. The hand of Providence hurtled him westward beyond his control. Joe was being carried as inevitably as a stream seeks the ocean.

The despair gave way to grim recognition of the titanic, unavoidable task before him. Failure was not an option, and capture was out of the question. He prayed that the task could be taken from him, but Joe knew the answer was no. The guilt of the trail of perdition behind him demanded a price to be paid. He wondered what would become of little Lafayette. He understood that his act of defiance drew the vindictive ire of the beast system against the town. They would not suffer such a blow to prestige without overwhelming retribution.

Nevertheless, their bloodthirst would give him the necessary cover to egress westward. Cohen's publicity stunt in MLK would be a sideshow of the broader holy war against Lafayette. The seething, burning eyes of the beast would be focused squarely on the little town for its impudent murder of one of its heirs.

He mourned the consequences for Lafayette, but the anticipated atrocities only hardened his resolve. He would strike at the beast's heart.

41

THE CHOICE

The train pulled into Catalina in the early afternoon of the next day. Counting the number of stops from Lafayette and peering at rusted signs, Joe decided to make his jump from the train while it was still decelerating toward the rail yard. Given his elevated profile and the shining noon sun, chances of detection were high if he waited to dismount inside the confines of the rail hub. Joe first tossed his bags, then took his own leap of faith while the locomotive chugged along at a brisk ten miles per hour. Tucking his legs, Joe winced at the rough grating of the sage grass and rocky earth as he tumbled. After catching his breath, he shakily made his way to his luggage several hundred feet away. The train whizzed by him with a terrible racket until the sound subsided with the final car.

Joe inspected the damage to himself and his bags. His pants were thoroughly torn, along with the skin underneath. His left arm caught part of a cactus, and his neck felt out of place. Joe felt increased regret when he inspected the bag of gear Karl gave him. The compass was thoroughly destroyed, along with one of the lenses of the binoculars. The medical kit, while smashed, was still mostly salvageable. The pistol appeared to be intact as it was rolled up in clothes and the remaining food. Shouldering his pack, Joe lifted the binoculars to his eyes and found they were still usable through the remaining lens. He saw the town's sign off in the distance oscillating and warping in the heatwaves of the beating sun. Below it, the fugitive recalled Highway 82.

Trudging his way across the soybean fields, he thought of Wallace. Joe wondered if he betrayed him. He thought it best if he didn't know. After half a mile of arduous trekking and rolled ankles, Joe stopped for water and to formulate his plan of approach to MLK Jr. County. His dry throat welcomed the gush of moisture as he entered yet another soybean field.

There won't be any Wallace on the other side of those mountains to drive me in, Joe thought to himself, *and I'll die of thirst before I ever get there with this pack.*

He shaded his eyes to glance up at the sun in the sky. The fugitive began to sweat heavily in the dry heat. A dozen plans cascaded through his mind, each more risky than the last.

"I could try stealing a car," he said aloud while continuing his walk to the highway. "I suppose it's either that or dying of thirst or getting lost in the mountains."

His risk of capture at this vulnerable juncture was extremely high. His steps increased in pace until he settled into an awkward jog with his heavy pack jostling to and fro. With a concerted sigh, the fugitive slowed back to walking.

"Take it easy, Joe," he reassured himself. "Just relax and keep plugging along."

Where he was going, Joe had no idea. For now, his direction was reaching Highway 82. All he could do was follow the current of destiny toward the sea. Surmounting a small ridge about a hundred yards before the highway, he laid prone to look through his binoculars. A sky-blue pickup truck made its way noisily along the road away from the town. Beyond it, he spied the imposing slope he traversed with Wallace. It seemed like decades ago. Joe again meditated briefly on his former companion.

The choice was unfortunately clear. Trying to hike the rest of the way was totally out of the question. The likelihood of either capture or death by dehydration presented an untenable course of action. Joe grasped a handful of finely ground rocks with his hand and threw them down in frustration.

He swore bitterly. "What am I doing? I can't steal a car!"

Joe also recalled that nearly all cars had remote kill switches as standard equipment with most older models being retrofitted. Moreover, the traffic cameras ran checks to see if the driver was the registered owner. Even if he successfully stole a vehicle, this radically increased his risk.

He dropped his binoculars and rested his head on the ground. The fugitive cringed in horror as he realized the solution. He would have to take a driver hostage.

"I can't do that." Joe again grasped the earth.

The alternate courses of action all culminated in either capture, death, or failure of his mission. While still dangerous, this was likely the only way to get anywhere near his target. Joe let out a series of resigned curses, then descended the ridge to a dip in the terrain before the road. The position provided reasonable concealment due to some bushes on either side. Settling in and trying to stay as close to the ground as possible, he waited for the sound of an oncoming car. Donning a mask from his pack, Joe tried to slow his heart as the heat rose.

After thirty minutes, the whirring of tires broke the serene desert quiet of Highway 82. Joe peaked his head up and looked through his binoculars. A sun damaged, turquoise, import sedan plodded toward Catalina with a loose, screeching belt. Joe pulled the pistol from his pack and prepared to make his move. His pulse pounded, and his breathing grew shallow. Closing his eyes, he got up on his elbows in anticipation. Just before springing the trap, Joe caught a glimpse of the driver. He was a solitary White teen bobbing his head to music.

He hesitated, causing the sedan to pass the killer unknowingly. Joe watched the tail of the escaping car shrink on its way down the road.

"I can't keep hurting my own," Joe grimaced. He felt a small relief at not having to take his hostage yet.

Before he could reinforce his nerve, a cherry-red, late model SUV came barreling suddenly away from the town. Joe scrambled to grab his binoculars, but realizing he didn't have enough time, looked up just in time to catch a glimpse of an inclusion banner hanging from the rearview mirror of the quickly approaching vehicle. Joe's muscles twitched instinctually.

He leapt up and stood in the road with his pistol drawn. The SUV slammed on its brakes in a panicked stop. Joe closed in quickly to point his weapon aggressively at the driver, who was of some swarthy, urban, mystery meat variety. If he were not so hopped up on adrenaline, Joe would've felt intense relief. The frightened driver put up his hands and sat bolt upright. He seemed particularly effeminate and festooned in gaudy clothing. Joe saw light blue nail polish glisten from the driver's petite hands. He was satisfied he picked a good target.

Making his way to the rear doors of the vehicle, Joe yanked at the handle. Unsuccessfully pulling at the door several times, he slapped the tinted window and demanded entry. The driver fumbled with the switch and eventually the door unlocked. Pulling the door open, Joe's heart dropped to the floor.

In the backseat lay a sleeping White baby in a car seat. The fugitive hesitated and stood scatterbrained.

"Please, don't hurt me!" a feminized voice squeaked from the driver's seat.

Joe saw that this baby could not possibly be biologically related to the dark driver. It also struck him as odd that the man pleaded to save his own skin rather than the baby's. Realizing it was far too late to back out and select a different victim, Joe reluctantly climbed in and slumped his bags carefully next to the child.

"Drive!" Joe commanded as he closed the door.

The driver sped away and continued to accelerate well past the speed limit.

"Drive like you normally would. I'll paint the windshield with your brains before you try to get a ticket," the Hate Criminal said roughly, although he doubted his resolve to do so.

The effeminate man wiped away tears as he nodded shakily. "Please, I'll give you what you want. Just leave me alone!" he said as he tossed his wallet to the rear seat.

It hit the side of the baby's car seat and stirred him slightly. Joe took the wallet and inspected its contents. The driver's name was Tevin Reed-Brotzman, and his address was in MLK Jr. County.

"Are you headed back to MLK Jr. County?" he asked quickly.

Tevin nodded tearfully.

"Keep driving there. If you try anything, you know what'll happen." Joe concealed the growing panic over what to do with the baby. Worse still, he had virtually no plan for when they got into the city.

"Please, just let me go. I won't report the car stolen," the driver sobbed quietly.

Joe took another look at the wallet. He found a card indicating he worked for Child Protective Services.

"If you want the kid, just take him. They don't pay me enough for these runs anyway!" Tevin pleaded with a whimper.

The Hate Criminal sat back in disbelief.

The effeminate driver continued his bleating, "If it's money you want, we can just split the profits! Just, please, don't hurt me! Do you work for Rosenblatt? Maybe my boss can cut a deal."

Joe felt a bubbling cauldron of hatred stew in his soul. He thought about greasing the government-sponsored trafficker on the spot. The killer gripped the pistol tightly, but cooler instincts prevailed. He couldn't afford to be in the driver's seat of the SUV with the more advanced facial recognition software on the freeway system. He could take back roads, but dealing with the body and driving a stolen vehicle presented considerable challenges.

Joe looked over at the child beside him. He lay peacefully in the car seat, lulled by the noise of the road. He wore a small, denim jumper with a knit cap. Waking up slightly, Joe saw that he had brilliant, blue eyes. The baby's parents were probably poor Whites who made politically incorrect social media posts or some other mundane offense. He shuddered at the thought of this mongrel tearing away the child from his parents under the guise of government oversight. The baby also posed a dilemma for his intended actions in MLK Jr. County. He couldn't leave the baby at a hospital or police station. Either he would be snatched up by traffickers or handed right back to CPS—the same outcome. This was one of his own people and someone he had the power to save.

"Where do his parents live?" he asked his captive.

Tevin shrugged. "How should I know? I just picked him up from the last guy!"

Joe pressed the barrel of the suppressor to the driver's head. "Where do his parents live?!"

"Look, they don't have any more kids. This was their only one." Tevin grossly misjudged his captor's intentions. "If you want more, I have connections, but you need me alive! I know lots of motel managers if you know what I mean. Congressmen, senators—everybody!"

The Hate Criminal perked up his ears. "Senators?"

Tevin nodded enthusiastically as he drove. "Oh yeah, I won't name names, but I can help you out. You just need to keep me alive!"

"Chuck Cohen?" Joe asked with a small tremor.

"Let's just say I was heading there." The captive raised his preened eyebrows. "You must be one of Rosenblatt's guys if you're asking about Cohen."

The conundrum deepened for Joe. He desired to get the poor child back to his parents, but that risked compromising his fortuitous opportunity to get Cohen. Moreover, the evident connection between Cohen and Rosenblatt offered the potential to settle two scores at once.

"Don't worry about who I work for," he stalled for a better answer.

Tevin continued to drive the lengthy journey around the mountains toward the freeway leading to MLK Jr. County. Joe figured there was just under three hours left in the drive, and the baby was getting farther away from home with each passing minute. The temptation to block out the precious cargo and get straight to Cohen lured Joe's warrior spirit.

Maybe it'll work out and he'll end up in a good home, Joe thought to himself and tried to focus on his ultimate target. He tried to ignore what likely would happen to the boy if he was not rescued. Joe gripped a piece of trim in frustration then resignedly formed a plan.

"My boss doesn't like kids like this. You've got to take him back," he haggled.

The driver furrowed his brow. "I don't work for your boss."

Joe drove the barrel deep into Tevin's neck. "Yeah, you're right, you don't work for my boss. You work for me now, got it?"

The social worker wiped away nervous sweat from his forehead and nodded.

"Now turn this car around and get this baby back to his parents." Joe knew this put his mission in serious jeopardy but refused to compromise on his newfound principles.

"When my boss hears that you held up his shipment, you're gonna pay!" Tevin snapped effeminately.

Joe rapped his captive's head with the pistol and instructed him again to turn around. Tevin finally complied and heaved the SUV about. The Hate Criminal looked over at the little boy and affirmed his decision. He refused to have any more of his people's deaths on his head. After roughly twenty minutes, Tevin finally admitted the parents were in Catalina. The captor breathed a sigh of relief that this delay would not be excessively lengthy, though Joe was prepared to hold Tevin hostage clear across the country if it meant this baby could be saved from destruction. He prayed subtly and thanked God for this break. Joe sat back and looked out the window at the arid mountain landscape. He knew that once the baby was dropped off, Tevin wouldn't be allowed anywhere near Cohen. While firm in conviction, Joe's resolve grew tainted with the knowledge that the perfect opportunity to get his target slipped through his fingers.

42

CULMINATED CONUNDRUMS

Despite the tinted windows, Joe felt compelled to keep his head low as they pulled into Catalina. He couldn't see much besides the tops of storefronts and a few ghastly Inclusion Banners. After an additional ten minutes of driving, Tevin brought him to a relatively isolated trailer home. Joe peaked his head up to survey his surroundings. To his horror, a car sat parked outside with a bumper sticker that read, "Catalina Police."

He cursed his captive viciously. "You set me up!"

Tevin began pleading, "No, no! I promise!"

"You're handing me over to the cops!" Joe flipped off the safety of the pistol.

The social worker began to weep. "This is the place, I swear! He's not a cop! I'm not giving you up!"

The Hate Criminal shook his head and kicked himself for being an idealist.

If only I had just kept going, I'd be shooting Cohen instead of this worm, Joe thought to himself and prepared to pull the trigger.

Suddenly, the door to the trailer opened and a tearful woman stumbled out.

"Please, give me my baby back!" she cried as she ran toward the car.

Her husband came out and restrained her. The man froze when he saw the vague outline of Joe's pistol beyond the tinted windows. The Hate Criminal saw him jump and tried to conceal the weapon in his jacket.

"I'm not going out there." Tevin shook his head. "I'd get beat!"

Feeling disgusted with his captive, Joe also wanted the honor of returning the lost child.

"If you run off, I'll kill you. You're still taking me to Cohen," Joe menaced the social worker roughly.

Opening the SUV door, Joe hoisted the car seat over his bag and disembarked. The parents stood with their mouths agape. The mother squirmed with the intense instinct to be reunited with her baby. Her husband kept her reined in, still suspicious of what was happening.

Joe approached the skittish couple and placed the baby at their feet. At last, the mother broke free and grabbed her child. Hugging him close, she sobbed intensely. The husband maintained a speechless countenance.

The SUV peeled away quickly with chirping tires. Joe whipped around and shouted after the social worker. His heart sank when he remembered that all of his supplies besides the pistol in his jacket were in the backseat. He took off after the car but knew his chase was futile. Joe considered drawing his weapon and firing, but the SUV had already rounded a corner behind a house. Joe grabbed his hair in frustration. The loss of his supplies and opportunity to see Cohen was devastating.

"Tell me what's going on!" the father demanded with trembling.

Joe stayed facing away and put his hands on his hips. He took a deep breath and took off his mask. The baby cooed quietly, while the mother sobbed in happy reunion.

"I'm a colossal screw up, that's what's going on," the fugitive said and turned around.

"Who are you?" the husband asked again.

Joe recalled asking himself the same question in the mirror at Karl's house. Taking a far more philosophical tack than the father intended, Joe simply replied, "I don't know."

"Do you work for those scumbags?" he pressed.

The Hate Criminal bowed his head. "Not at all. I want to kill every last one of them."

Taking a nervous look around, the father instructed him to come inside quickly. Joe apathetically complied. Following inside, he saw an old Catalina city flag framed on the wall next to a shadowbox with police ranks inside. The parents shared a long, tearful period of embracing with their baby, thankful for his safe return, and they thanked Joe profusely. He moved awkwardly to the kitchen table and sat down, brooding over Tevin getting away with his golden chance.

"Are you a cop?" he asked his new hosts.

The man shook his head and said, "Used to be," then turned to his wife and child again.

Joe continued to look around the room until his eyes rested on a picture frame sitting next to a vase of dead flowers.

"Wallace!" The fugitive walked over to the frame and picked it up.

The picture was of his host and Wallace in police uniforms.

The husband perked up. "Wait a minute, you know Jerry?!"

Joe hesitated to answer.

"He was my old partner before I got kicked off the force," the man said in surprise.

"Why'd they kick you off?" The fugitive wanted to gauge his host's loyalty to the system before revealing his hand.

"That mayor! She wanted to send me to LA." He pursed his lips and frowned. "Wallace stayed on and went to MLK Jr."

"Did you hear what happened to him?" Joe was genuinely curious if the man knew anything more than he did.

"Well, I heard he went missing because of some terrorist. I'm not sure I buy that though." The former cop scratched his head. "He was really a stand-up guy. I hope he's okay."

The mother took the baby away to nurse in the other room after thanking Joe again.

"The name's Matt." He extended his hand.

Joe shook it but withheld his name. This action heightened suspicion in Matt.

His host crossed his arms and narrowed his eyes. "Hold on, are you a fed or something? Why were you in the car with that social worker?"

Sensing that Matt's goodwill was waning, Joe came up with an alibi. "I saw him driving and knew that wasn't his kid. I stopped him and made him drive back to you guys."

The father shook his head slowly. "So, you just had the stones to stop a CPS agent and turn him around?"

"Are you upset that you got your child back?" Joe made a frustrated gesture with his hand.

"Well, no—"

The Hate Criminal interrupted, "Then don't ask too many questions."

Joe was still sour over losing his chance to grease Cohen and Rosenblatt in one go.

"I just want to know who's in my house, that's all." Matt shrugged. "I guess, if you know Wallace, you can't be that bad of a guy."

"He saved my life," the fugitive opened up. "I was hauled in on Hate Crime charges."

The former policeman crossed his arms. "Hate Crimes, what a joke. I'm so glad I got off the force."

After a period of silence, the fugitive asked, "How'd you get wrapped up with CPS?"

"Gosh, I don't even know. It could've been a number of things. The CPS guy just said it was due to inequitable parenting." He pursed his lips. "Maybe somebody informed on me. Maybe somebody spied on my house. Who knows. I'm fairly open about my political views to people." Matt shook his head. "Those rats will be back for my boy soon, I imagine. Even with response times getting slower and slower, I bet we don't have a lot of slack before law enforcement comes looking for you too."

"What are you going to do?" Joe looked at the picture of Wallace again.

"I haven't thought that far ahead." He laughed. "I'm just happy my son is back here with us. Thank you, from the bottom of my heart, for bringing him back to us."

Joe clenched his jaw. "It was an obligation. Don't thank me."

Matt grew very curious about his strange guest. "I don't mean to pry in your business or look a gift horse in the mouth, but I've got to know who you are. It's not every day some stranger saves your infant son."

The Hate Criminal stood up to look out the window. "I'm just a guy in over my head and on the wrong side of the law." He glanced back at his host. "And I'm sure you're in no mood to turn me in."

Matt shook his head enthusiastically. "Ever since I turned in my badge and saw what they did to my Catalina PD, I'd never help a cop again." He sat down at the table. "As far as I'm concerned, if you're on the wrong side of the law, you're on the right side of me."

Joe returned to the table with a curt nod. With this statement, he felt liberated to be more open with Matt. Reaching into his dusty jacket, he pulled out the pistol and placed it on the table. The sight of it made his host jump slightly, but he settled into interested curiosity.

Matt swore eagerly. "Where'd you get a thing like that?!"

"That's not important right now." Joe turned toward him slowly. "I made a big sacrifice when I chose to bring your son back here."

"What do you mean?" he inquired cautiously.

"I'm on a mission of sorts, and I was holding that CPS guy hostage to take me to my objective. I didn't see your son in the back when I jacked his car, and I couldn't bear to have him sold to . . . some very bad people." The fugitive laid out his situation slowly, as if plotting something on a graph. "Now he's gone, along with all my gear, but I still need to complete my task."

Matt crossed his arms after listening intently. "Look, I appreciate what you did and all, but I don't think there's much we can do. We need to make our preparations to get out of here."

"All I need is for you to drive me to MLK. You can drop me off, and then you can get your family out of here," Joe made his request.

The former cop put his hand on the table in consternation. "I can't do that! The cameras will see me and know I was involved in whatever it is you're doing!"

"You're already going to be marked for the slaughter when that social worker gets back to his office," the Hate Criminal laid out the situation with building frustration. "I only have the next day or two to get to my target before he goes back to a much harder to reach place. I had it all lined up until I listened to my stupid conscience and saved your son. At least let me use your car. You owe me this!"

Matt chafed at this pushy demand. "Look here, buddy, I'm not doing that. Just because you saved my son doesn't mean I owe you my life. If I help you, my whole family could end up dead. Why is this so important?!"

Joe slapped the table with his hand and raised his voice. "I'm going to kill the man that did this to you. I'm going to kill the man who killed my wife. I'm going to kill the man who kicked you off the force and sent Wallace to MLK! You not only owe it to me, you owe it to your people! You're the only one who can help me right now."

His host sat back in amazement at his conviction, but stood his ground. "I don't believe in that race stuff."

"I only saved your son because of that 'race stuff.'" Joe made aggressive air quotes. "I don't expect you to understand or even appreciate what I'm doing, but I'm doing it for you and every one of our people who has suffered because of this evil system."

Matt frowned and leaned forward. "What, are you some kind of Nazi?"

Joe grew angry at the man's obtuse understanding of the world. "Call me whatever you want, but I promise you that I'm a friend. I'm fighting for your side whether you're on mine or not."

His host continued to be obstinate. "I'm sorry for all the things that seemed to have happened to you, but all those are separate stories"—he sighed—"different causes."

The Hate Criminal shook his head in anxious disbelief.

How can't he see it? he thought to himself. *It's so obvious that it's all the same thing and attributable to very specific individuals.*

Joe's demeanor softened after a moment of this contemplation. It was easy to be harsh on this unawakened man for his lack of awareness, but he realized that Matt didn't know simply because nobody ever told him. He heard system propaganda all his life and never knew there were actual people responsible for the way the world was. Joe could not judge the man who never saw water for his ability to swim.

"We don't have much time, so I'll make this quick." The warrior put his hands on the table and leaned forward. "Picture your family. Are there certain unique markers or characteristics of this family? Behaviors, looks, quirks, et cetera?"

Matt agreed, caught off guard by the cryptic question.

Joe smiled slightly as he reproduced the parable: "And if someone came to your family and started demanding you change everything about it, you would resent that, right?"

43

BUCKET OF BOLTS

"So, you're telling me that they made the Equity and Inclusion Act too?" Matt asked in bleak amazement as they walked out to the garage after intensive conversation and debate.

"You'd be surprised what you'll find once you start noticing. If it hurts us, it's quite frankly easier to assume they are involved than to just prove yourself right later," the warrior quipped.

While time was short, Joe had to take him on a crash course of his own mental journey. He skipped to a few "free answers" to help Matt's expedited understanding. All of the reading and study Joe did in the motel flooded from his memory. Initially obstinate to his guest's assessment, the former police officer's resistance waned with example after example. The countless wrongs dealt to Matt by the system made him receptive to finding out who was behind the wheel. Once Joe explained the situation, the conversation shifted to his mission in MLK Jr. County.

His host conceded to lend him an old project car. The vehicle was too old for remote kill switches and had been out of the system for thirty-five years. Joe desperately needed transportation and hastily agreed. Originally intending to have Matt drive him, he settled for driving himself.

"Ain't she a beaut?" he said as he removed the tarp.

Joe's heart sank slightly at the sight of the rusty, sun damaged hulk of mid-century, Detroit iron. At one time it must have been a beautiful, seafoam green. Now its hue settled into the color of the first peeks of blue sky through a rainstorm. The roof bore the scars of a removed vinyl top.

Joe shook his head. "This thing runs?"

"It'll make it on a one-way trip. I've got her firing good, and she kicks into gear, but don't go over fifty. These tires are older than you, but they hold air." He kicked the dry rotted rubber with his foot.

The Hate Criminal turned his eyes to heaven and chuckled for a moment, then returned his gaze to the pitted chrome on the bumper. "It's a bit conspicuous, isn't it?"

"Look, you're lucky I'm even giving you this. I need to get my family out of here before CPS comes back, and this car isn't going to cut it," Matt leveled with his guest and rapped the top of the car.

"What about the plates and traffic cams?" Joe objected again.

"Believe me, the surveillance state is not as competent as you think. That's really more of an act to scare people into compliance," the former cop related his experience. "They'll always catch you eventually, but they have to sift through mountains of data before they can get you. They have to be actively looking for you in a specific location for a quick capture." He wiped some dust off the door handle. "Okay, yeah, you'll set off some traffic cams for out-of-date registration. Then what? They'll send a bill for the ticket a few days later to the guy I bought it from in Millington, Tennessee because his name's still on the title. He's probably dead by now."

Joe pushed down on the bumper to test the creaky suspension. "And what about facial recognition?"

Matt shrugged his shoulders. "Well highways are totally out; you'd blow out the tires going that fast anyway, but you can take the backroads and cover your face at intersections with your hand or some kind of mask. I want to help you, but this is really the best I can do. I need to get my family safe."

Joe got the door open after a few pulls at the rusty door handle. Peering inside, the interior greeted him with a torn bench seat.

The former cop handed over the keys. "And this Cohen guy, what does he have to do with it?"

Patiently, the warrior bore with him. "He wrote Equity and Inclusion. He's one of the worst of them."

"So, killing this guy will stop all of that?" Matt showed his naivete.

Joe placed his hand on the top of the car and prepared himself to enter the chariot of his impossible task. "No, people like him will be trying to destroy people like us as long as the other still exists." He stepped a foot into the cabin but hesitated to enter. "We're here on this earth to struggle, and it's God's Will that we do so righteously."

His host furrowed his brow and attempted to understand. "I mean, isn't it pointless? Even if you get this guy, it just keeps going."

The warrior put his hand in his pocket and rotated the rock in his fingers with a wry smile. "That's why it has to be done."

Swinging into the driver's seat, Joe settled in and looked at the dash. The archaic dials and widgets bewildered him, but he thanked God that it was an automatic transmission. Matt gave him an old atlas of regional roads and handed him the keys. Afterwards, he ran the Hate Criminal through the seemingly esoteric startup procedure.

"Don't take the choke off until the RPMs rise to about two grand. If you think it's dying, just pull the lever back out and let it warm up a little more," the shadetree mechanic instructed.

Joe put the keys in the ignition and gave it a crank with the choke engaged. Pumping the gas pedal, the engine kicked over and fired after significant coaxing. The backfiring exhaust caused him to jump tremendously. As the adrenaline subsided, the seeming impossibility of his success set in.

I'll never make it in this bucket of bolts, he thought as he reached for the seatbelt.

Fumbling for several seconds, he discovered it lacked a belt completely. Intense regret and trepidation seeped into his aching mind.

Even the kamikazes had harnesses, he joked to himself.

The resonating pulse of the wizened inline six rattled the car as well as his resolve.

"Pull it out of the garage and just let her warm up for a bit. I'll grab some extra gas, then you're out of here," Matt raised his voice over the clanking racket.

Joe nodded silently and awkwardly jostled the shift lever into drive. A horrible crack signaled the transmission was ready for battle. Letting his foot off the brake, the wheel bearings protested being awoken from their slumber with a screech as he pulled out of the enclosure.

Joe sat white knuckled with his hands draped over the enormous steering wheel. The vibrations foreshadowed the coming turbulence and trial. Slowly yet deliberately, he adjusted the rearview mirror until his eyes came into view. His mysterious pursuer greeted him subtly with a lowered brow. The same force he saw in the window at the OIHO and dozens of other inflection points started to become more clear. Unrecognizable, yet fearfully familiar, he felt the inevitability of their union. The world drifted away into a soundless whisper as Joe became enveloped with his destiny. His counterpart in turn clenched his jaw to conceal a hairline crack of fear in his impassive gaze. Joe nodded assuredly and adjusted the mirror to face the world behind him.

Letting the choke in, Joe felt the RPMs drop into a slow gurgle from the engine bay. Keeping the engine alive with intermittent pushing of the gas pedal, he kept an anxious eye on the temperature gauge. Climbing slowly, the needle waltzed to a stopping point just below halfway. He reached into his jacket, pulled out the pistol, and stuffed it into the glovebox.

Matt returned with two large gas cans. He dumped the contents of one into the tank and placed the other in the trunk, with the cap securely on.

Joe's stomach began to churn within him. The prospect of actually acting on his redemptive journey terrified him. As long as he could sit there idling, the world could spin on and forget him. However, Joe knew that the world would never just let him be. The beast system would never forgive him for his defiance. Worse still, he sat under conviction for the unknown number of deaths to his own people he caused. The only way for Joe's tormented conscience to be silenced would be through cold, calculated action and hot, flowing blood. There would be no allowance for doubt or fear when the rubber met the road at the end of the driveway. Once he crossed the threshold of Matt's property, Joe would be entering the colosseum with the beast.

Matt slapped the quarter panel and made him jolt.

"Alright, any questions?" he asked.

"No, I think I've got it," Joe said with a poorly concealed tremor.

The former policeman put his hands on his hips and nodded. "I just want to thank you again for saving my son. Really, from the bottom of my heart."

"Raise him right, now. He'll have to fight every battle you shirk." Joe gave a curt smile and paused. "Remember that."

He reflected on his own father and his father before him. If they had sacrificed and fought the conflicts they should have, he would never have to take such drastic action. It never mattered how much they conserved. It was far more critical what they conquered.

Matt smiled and said, "Don't worry about us. As long as we're together as a family."

Joe pursed his lips and nodded imperceptibly. Manually rolling up the window, he thanked his host one more time. He attempted to give the horn a quick honk as he pulled away, but the electronics failed.

As he began pulling through the town, Joe reflected on his decisions. He wondered if it would have been better to let Tevin take him directly to his target. Any longing for this outcome faded away when he remembered the look of heart-wrenching relief of the mother reunited with her baby. Joe saved the boy from certain torture and destruction at the hands of evil.

You can't put a price on that, he reflected as he came to a stop at an intersection.

He had to remind himself that he was not on a journey of revenge but rather of redemption.

Placing his mask back over his face, he peered at the traffic camera. A man about his age looked on with interest at the vintage automobile and its bizarre passenger. Noticing the observer, he drove away from the stop quickly after the light turned green.

Joe egressed from Catalina as fast as he could without attracting suspicion. The one cop car he passed stood idly by as he rumbled down the street. Out in the open plain, next to the soybean fields, Joe kept his bearings headed south and west to circumvent the mountains on the dusty backroads.

After about an hour, he noticed a peculiar smell leaching into the cabin. His head started to hurt terribly, and it became hard to think. Joe craned his neck to look around inside the car and found light gray gas seeping through the floor of the rear seat. Standing on the spongy drum brakes, he pulled off to the side of the road. He did not dare turn the engine off, lest it refuse to start again. Joe removed his mask as he made the rounds to each door and lowered the windows. Coming to the backseat, he lifted the rotted carpet. To his dismay, he found a rusted hole clear through the sheet metal. Worse still, the crumbling exhaust leaked fumes directly under the hole into the cabin.

Out of the corner of his eye, he noticed a car coming eastward toward him. The early evening sun shrouded the car and made it impossible to ascertain the nature of the vehicle. Joe could see that it was a lightly-colored sedan, but nothing more. Figuring it was worse to be seen outside of his rickety transportation, he hopped back into the cabin and nonchalantly got back on the road. As the vehicle came closer, Joe's heart jumped in fear and cursed how conspicuous his car was.

The opposing vehicle turned on its sirens and wheeled around after Joe passed.

44

UNDER THE HOOD

Joe sputtered a series of panicked exclamations as the squad car flew up in his rearview mirror. He reached into the glovebox and retrieved the pistol. Holding it in his left hand, he pinned it closely to the side trim of the door to conceal it at the ready. As he pulled off to the side of the road again, Joe's breathing grew shallow. The cop drove in behind him and turned the lights off. The fugitive closed his eyes for a second, clenched his teeth, and prayed fervently.

"Good afternoon," the cop stated tersely from a distance as he approached the driver's side.

Joe gripped the pistol and prepared to make his move once the officer was alongside.

"Don't worry, you're not in trouble," the approaching man chuckled.

The Hate Criminal hesitated and turned his head to see an older, Hispanic cop sauntering up to the door. He was short, perhaps five foot eight, and seemed to lack any hair on his head at all.

Joe kept the pistol low down on the door and greeted the man. The exhaust gasses began filling the cabin, and he was forced to shut off the engine.

"Nice wheels, man. That's a '68, right?" The officer stood back to admire the vehicle.

In reality, Joe had no clue about any of the details of the car. Worse still, he didn't even recognize the logo on the steering wheel.

"Yeah, that's right." Joe tried to seem knowledgeable.

"What sort of engine ya got in there? V8?" the cop asked

255

enthusiastically while eyeing the rusted hood.

The fugitive at least knew the answer to this one. "No, it's an in-line six."

The officer gave a playful grimace. "Man, I bet it'd be worth a million bucks if it had the V8. Where'd you get it?"

Joe grew visibly uncomfortable with the incessant questioning. "Uh, my uncle bought some property and it was in the barn."

The law enforcement officer raised his eyebrows. "What a find! I've got a '71 back home. It's got the inline six too. Missing a ton of parts though." He imperceptibly smiled. "Looks like yours has most of the ones I need."

The cop leaned on the door frame and craned his head to look around the interior. Joe's heart clawed at the confines of his chest to escape the rushing adrenaline while the officer's gaze passed just above the pistol.

"I'm going to have to put you under arrest." The policeman dead-ened his tone.

"What?" Joe widened his eyes and gripped the pistol with white knuckles.

"You've got the original dashboard compass! Do you have any idea how rare that is?!" He laughed jovially. "Man, you should've seen the look on your face!"

The fugitive shook his head in waves of anxiety and released his grip slightly.

"How much?" the officer asked expectantly.

"What do you mean?" Joe furrowed his brow.

The officer leaned in more into the cabin, directly over the pistol, to point at the dashboard compass. "How much for the compass? I want to buy it off of you."

"Oh, I don't have a card reader with me, sorry." the Hate Criminal stumbled over his words and did his best not to shiver in fear.

The cop leaned back out of the car. "Don't worry about that. I can just run your plates and wire the money to the card associated with the registration. Name your price."

Joe felt the jaws of incarceration closing in around him as the sit-uation spiraled out of control. "Actually, it's not for sale."

"No shot. Everything has a price." He relented slightly and placed a hand on his utility belt. "I get it if you don't want to part with the compass. Let me look around the car first and see if there are any other parts I could buy off ya."

The fugitive considered gunning the engine and making his escape. This plan sputtered in his mind in tandem with the car's expected performance. As the cop made it around to the back of the vehicle, Joe noticed his face droop into a frown.

"Wait a minute." He stormed up to the driver's side door. "I'm going to need you to step out of the vehicle and show me some papers."

His mind racing, Joe almost pulled his weapon. He figured that the cop must've spotted the well-out-of-date registration sticker. Just before twitching the necessary muscles, an idea popped into his head.

"Hold on, how about we make a deal?"

The cop narrowed his eyes and crossed his arms.

"I'll give you the compass, and you let me go," Joe negotiated his release with fear coursing through his veins.

"Thirty-five years out of the system!" The cop stepped back slightly and gave a look of amazement. "That's at least a couple grand fine, buddy."

"You don't think I know the value of that compass?" Joe gambled.

The officer shook his head. "Nah, man, it's worth a couple hundred max."

The Hate Criminal pressed his luck, "Okay, well I guess I'd rather pay the fine than lose out on it."

"Your funeral." The cop turned away and started walking back to his squad car.

Joe began panicking as it seemed his gamble went wrong.

His captor wheeled back around. "Fine, but I'm taking the side-view mirror too"—he stopped to look over the car again—"and the door trim."

The fugitive breathed a sigh of relief. "Alright, we've got a deal."

The cop returned with a tool box after Joe stashed the pistol underneath the seat. He heard the prying of a screwdriver on the outside of the door followed by a wrench on the side mirror.

"Alright, lemme get inside to get the compass," the cop instructed him to get out of the car.

Joe reluctantly complied and exited the vehicle.

"That's a gnarly gash on your head. How'd you get it?" he asked the Hate Criminal as he climbed inside. "Looks like a gunshot wound."

"Construction accident. Somebody dropped a tool from the scaffolding and I wasn't wearing my helmet."

The cop nodded disinterestedly and began removing the rare part. After some mild cursing in Spanish, he got the corroded base free.

He held it in his hands for a moment and marveled. "My '71's value just went through the roof!"

Joe waited politely until the cop left the cabin.

"Alright, you're good." He gave a wide smile followed by a wagging finger. "Get that tag in order. Keep this up and you won't have a car left to register."

The Hate Criminal nodded and thanked God as the cop returned to the squad car with his loot. The officer heaved his vehicle around and returned to his eastward heading. After waiting for a moment, Joe turned the keys to restart his ancient set of wheels. He felt his soul rend in two when the only sound from the engine bay was a stubbornly clicking solenoid.

Joe swore viciously and turned the key off. Tightening his fingers on its sticky handle, he aggressively gave it another crank. His show of force was met with a paltry whisper from the starter motor followed by complete silence. He surveyed his surroundings with a growing sense of anger and frustration. The evening sun still kept the temperature uncomfortably hot without the soothing airflow coming through the windows. Only an hour outside of Catalina, he was still in the arid wastes skirting around the mountains. Joe estimated that he still had at least four hours left of slow, backroads driving. Matt had given him only a few plastic bottles of water. He lacked the provisions for a long, drawn-out journey.

Joe gave the ignition a few more desperate cranks to no avail. Despite knowing virtually nothing about engines, he clutched at the hood release lever. Sliding off the torn bench seat, he felt his brow breaking out in sweat. Joe winced slightly at placing his hands on the scalding hot hood. Wrapping his hand in the bottom of his shirt, he opened the engine bay. Even with his lack of knowledge, he knew that the wet, black stains were signs of an oil leak. Joe ignored this as he could do nothing about it. He stood dumbfounded at the labyrinth of hoses, wires, and metal before him.

What am I doing? I've never even changed a battery. The fugitive wiped the perspiration from his face.

He noticed the insulated lining on the underside of the hood was sagging down. A small inscription written in black marker peaked out from under the crumbling liner. Joe moved the material to reveal the writing.

"Billy McDowell Sr. was here—1968"

Joe reached into his pocket and pulled out his fake ID. He wondered if this individual was related. Perhaps he was a grandson or distant relative. The lineage and expanse of heritage struck him suddenly as he looked at the ragged marker strokes under the hood.

Joe reached out a finger and touched the writing. Billy McDowell's world might as well have been a different planet. He probably owned a house in a safe neighborhood on a single factory worker's salary, supported a family, went to church, and stood for the pledge of allegiance. Joe felt a wellspring of envy surge in his heart for the life of Billy McDowell.

Teamed with his covetousness was a tide of what the Portuguese call Saudade and the Welsh Hiraeth, a deep longing and nostalgia for a place he'd never experienced. Billy McDowell, his world, and legacy were all dead. Nothing could be done to resurrect any of it. The doomed wasteland of Joe's present age crushed his spirit.

He could almost see that pristine suburban street with green grass, sprinklers going, and kids playing on the sidewalk. Joe saw Billy coming home from a long shift at the Pontiac factory to the warm embrace of his wife and children. The radio hummed softly about simple troubles and easy enemies. As the heat rose from the relic of Billy's time, Joe snapped from the illusion. He reached desperately for the arms of that ever-ticking clock. If only he could hang from the minute hand and pull it back just one notch. If only he could experience the blissful ignorance of Billy's world.

Joe repeated aloud to the inscription, "But the winding of that clock brought us here, didn't it, Billy?"

Billy McDowell's avatar of graffiti stood frozen before him, incapable of receiving judgment.

Taking the ID card in hand, he marveled at the picture. William's half-hearted smile and sunken eyes closely resembled Joe after Jill's death. The card was of little use to him now. He knew that the feds would find his motel room and connect the ID to him. Joe resignedly tucked it underneath the hood insulation next to the inscription. At last, Bill and his descendent could be reunited after all this time.

"I guess it's not your fault, Bill," Joe said resignedly. "No one took the time to tell you otherwise."

He let the hood fall to its latch with a crash resembling cymbals at the end of a mournful requiem. Joe shuffled back to the bench seat and sat with his head in his hands. Out of detached frustration, he reinserted the keys into the ignition. Accidentally turning it, he heard a lurch from the starter. The sound caused him to jump slightly in surprise. Shaking with anticipation, he gave the key another turn.

The past roared back to life under the ancient hood. The slamming of the latch had the unintended effect of jostling loose the corroded starter solenoid, freeing it again for operation. To Joe however, it appeared that the ghost of Billy McDowell and his world had come back to life to assist him in his mission. The car took on an avatar greater than its material form of twisted and rotting metal. Just like the aging tractor in his uncle's garage, this piece of 1968 came about directly because of the conditions of its time. It was vast, vulgar, and confident. Nothing like it could be built before or since. As much a snapshot of time as any photograph, the vehicle was a living, breathing embodiment of what used to be. Not willing to chance the engine restarting again, Joe reluctantly refilled the tank with the remaining gas from his trunk before hopping back in and shifting the transmission into drive with determination. Westward, the hulking symbol carried its fateful passenger to redeem its past.

45

CRIME OR PUNISHMENT

In the darkness of an early, moonless night, Joe strained his eyes to see the road. A solitary holdout among the four headlights still functioned. The final incandescent bulb provided paltry illumination on the dusty ring road around the mountain range. Joe passed through a few no-name, small towns and farming communities. Some older folk of these small towns eyed his unconventional transportation suspiciously, though these were overwhelmingly the exception. With all the emphasis on individuality and passivity, a man driving such a distinctive car elicited few questions or comments. Joe also passed a small number of local law enforcement vehicles but encountered no problems.

After a few more white-knuckle hours of driving with virtually no visibility, Joe's rickety vehicle was now perilously close to the outskirts of MLK Jr. County. The fumes from the exhaust caused his head to pound terribly, and his eyes drooped from fatigue. He drifted in and out of consciousness several times. Joe cursed and slapped his face, trying to coax his aching body back into operation.

"I can't stop to rest, no time," his voice croaked raggedly.

In desperation, he clawed at the radio only to find a gaping hole in the dash. Unable to keep himself awake, Joe succumbed to his fatigue and the vehicle began to swerve.

His car lumbered and careened out of control as he jolted awake to the sight of an oncoming road sign. Plowing through this marker, the windshield shattered and showered him with shards. Joe wrestled with the enormous steering wheel, but the lack of power steering made this a feat well beyond his available strength. He felt the rumble of a broken fence beneath the wheels and could see a large earthen berm directly in his path. Standing on the ancient drum brakes, the tires locked up. Joe could only put up his hands and brace for impact. The conspicuous lack of a seatbelt flashed in his mind.

The car at last made contact with the berm and the front suspension collapsed with a mighty crunch. He did not make a direct perpendicular hit, but the vehicle smashed in at a glancing angle and went up the slope slightly. As he regained awareness of the situation, he felt a terrible pain in his chest. Looking down, Joe saw that the steering column had punched him square in the sternum. He wheezed for breath as he slumped out of the cabin. Steam poured out of the engine bay as the ancient machine bled out.

Joe fell to the ground and rolled away from the car. He groaned loudly as he felt the continued pain in his chest. He also noticed several large cuts from the windshield glass. At this point, a radiator hose ruptured and started to spray scalding coolant on the fugitive. Scrambling to get away, Joe managed to rise and run for a few steps. He crumpled several feet away and laid down, propped up on his elbows. Joe removed his mask, which was now soaked with hot antifreeze. His heart sank as he realized that his odds just grew exceptionally long.

The Hate Criminal pulled at the neck of his shirt to look at his chest. There was no bleeding, but he could see a tremendous bruise beginning to form. Rubbing the area with his hands, the sternum appeared intact. Above him stood an impressive array of stars, the night blacker than deep space. Looking west, he could just make out the faint glow of a large city. Stumbling to check the road sign he destroyed, he could just faintly make out the inscription on the mangled metal: "Berrent Valley 6 / MLK Jr. County 9."

Joe muttered to himself as he winced in pain, "Nine miles. Just nine miles. I can make it." Freezing in realization, he went back to the car to retrieve his pistol.

He found the weapon under the seat and closed the door gently. The hissing of the escaping coolant echoed in the hot desert night. Joe took a moment to run his fingers along the quarter panel. It saddened him to see a piece of old America mangled and destroyed like that, but his sentimentality shattered in a more spectacular fashion under the weight of his current task.

Joe Blaine set out toward his destiny. The fugitive's legs quaked under the stress of the previous few minutes. Each breath brought on a stabbing pain from his injured chest. He looked back pensively at the smoldering wreckage. His wounded and dying comrade motioned him on, prepared to accept death. As Joe turned away, the steam wheezed from the vehicle like the terminal breathing of a felled warrior.

"Just nine more miles, and then I'm in MLK," he reassured himself.

The awkward length of the pistol with the suppressor jostled in his jacket and made walking with a normal gait impossible. He had to pin an arm at his side at all times to keep the concealed weapon from slipping out from his jacket. The hissing of the radiator faded away as Joe trudged along in the cool night air. Looking up at the sky once more, he took a deep breath through his nose and out his mouth. The array of celestial bodies above him gave him a fearful understanding of his smallness among the grand scale of cosmic events.

"Will I be remembered?" Joe asked no one in particular.

His legs steadied under him as he settled into a methodical pace.

Probably not. Then again, the alternative would be to work tirelessly at a job I hate for people I hate for a system that hates me, until I gracelessly expire in a nursing home while being neglected by foreigners, he mused in a dark contemplation.

After an hour of walking and ducking in the drainage ditch any time a car drove by, he passed a crossroads and another road sign: "Berrent Valley 3 / MLK Jr. County 6."

An arrow indicated that the road to the left led to Berrent Valley. Stopping to catch his breath, he continued onward toward his destination.

Just six more miles. He carried on breathlessly.

Joe froze in sudden realization that he left his ID under the hood of the car. "It's too late now, not that I could use it anyway."

As the outskirts of MLK approached, he started passing more and more gas stations, liquor stores, and residential areas. Finding a mask on the side of the road, he put aside his disgust and put it on out of expedience. A dumpster next to a convenience store yielded a dark green boonie hat. Looking thoroughly homeless, Joe seemed to blend in well among the late-night riffraff on the outskirts of the county.

The transition from country to abject ghetto came suddenly. Joe recognized it as the former suburb community of Rolling Elms. He also remembered its reputation for endemic violent crime and drug use. This was one of the first suburbs to go completely "equitable" and lose its desired status under the burgeoning weight of government housing and weekly murder tolls. Under any other circumstance, the fugitive would've avoided walking through such a dangerous area, especially at night. Unfortunately, he had no choice but to continue on.

"Hey, White boy!" a voice called out.

Joe refused to turn his head and kept walking west.

"Hey, cracka!"

He heard the voice follow behind him.

"I got some good, mang. Hit me up!"

The Hate Criminal continued to ignore the dealer.

Undeterred, the purveyor pursued his potential customer with a tirade of unintelligible curses. "I'll bust you up! Don't you walk away from me!"

Joe heard running steps approaching aggressively. Wheeling around, he drew his pistol.

Upon seeing the seriousness of the situation, the dealer relented. "Mang, I was just playin'. You don't gotta be so serious!"

Joe closed in with his would-be attacker and pointed his weapon at his head.

"Give me your credit cards," he demanded.

The dealer protested as he drew his wallet out of his pocket, "Why you doin' me like this? My homies'll mess you up when they find you! You Hate Criminal! You racist! There gonna be a real good PSL fo dis one."

"Give me all your inventory too," Joe ratcheted up the consequences as he menaced his pistol.

He didn't fear being seen or turned into the police, given this area's status as a "no-go zone." One armed robbery of a drug dealer would make no more of a splash than a common traffic accident. While there was a bounty of surveillance cameras, his hat, mask, and scraggly facial hair generally concealed his appearance. The dealer continued his colorful protestations but eventually forked over a few bags of what appeared to be heroin. After taking the items, Joe kicked the man in the groin and left him writhing on the pavement.

Satisfied with his work, he walked calmly away from the scene of his "crime" and continued his journey west. Joe smirked as he considered the fact that he did more to clean up the streets than the sheriff's department ever had. He disposed of the drugs in a dumpster, taking a brief moment to stick them deep into one of the trash bags inside. Looking in the wallet, he found two credit cards and dozens of crumpled receipts. Joe figured that he could use the cards once or twice in an emergency before eliciting the attention of the surveillance state. Walking confidently, he managed to avoid further harassment outside of a few territorial troglodytes making threatening remarks.

After another few miles, he noticed several women standing on the street corner a block ahead of him. Joe knew that they were unmistakably prostitutes. Not wanting to be solicited or seen, he crossed over to the other side of the street after an SUV with large rims and blaring music passed by. He continued walking next to an adult superstore when one of the women caught his eye.

"Courtney?" he whispered to himself.

Joe remembered her as his coworker, and he recalled her stoic reaction to the layoff list. While he couldn't discern the outcome based on her expression back then, her current employment revealed her status. He also knew that she had a disabled son who needed exorbitantly expensive medical care. Courtney's destitution and degradation tore at Joe's heart.

Without warning, she turned her gaze toward him. Even under his disguise, it seemed as though she recognized him. Joe averted his eyes and attempted to just keep walking. Her plight grieved him, but he had a job to do. After walking another block, he crossed back over to the right side. Checking his tail, he noticed with a start that she was following him at a distance.

"Joe? Is that you?" Courtney called out.

The fugitive stopped in his tracks and panicked. Weighing the options, his foremost concern was detection. Nevertheless, his desire to help her overcame his more cautious instincts.

"Joe!" she said as she walked up on him.

"Keep your voice down!" he cautioned her.

As she came closer, Joe could see her appearance more clearly. A once beautiful and dignified mother was reduced to a battered commodity. Her heavy makeup and gaudy clothing poorly concealed a myriad of bruises.

"It's so nice to see a familiar face!" She looked as though tears were only seconds away.

Joe revealed that seeing an old acquaintance in a world of hostile strangers was welcome to him as well. "It's good to see you too. Listen, I can't talk long. I'm in a lot of trouble."

"Come with me," Courtney instructed. "I know a place we can talk."

Leading him down a grubby side street, she ushered him into a small, ground level apartment. As they entered, Joe noticed large stains of black mold on the wall and a set of dripping pipes. In the corner lay a filthy bed where he presumed she plied her trade.

"Courtney," Joe began, "it's nice seeing you, but. . . ."

She frowned at him. "I was just hoping to catch up. I know you're a married man."

The fugitive shook his head glumly. "I'm a widower now."

Courtney directed him to sit at a small table near the door. "I'm so sorry to hear that."

"We've both ended up in dark places, it seems." Joe crossed his arms awkwardly over the concealed pistol in his jacket.

Joe's declaration seemed to reveal her plight for the first time. Courtney took a moment to look around her apartment as if she had never seen it before. She nodded as tears welled into her eyes. "I can't do this anymore!"

Joe got up to comfort her with a hand on her back.

"How did it get like this?" Courtney's tears flowed freely now. "It seems like it was just yesterday that we were complaining about Mr. Raab in the breakroom."

Thinking for a moment, he made his reply: "We're just refuse of the system." Joe stared off into space as the sounds of Courtney's weeping filled the room. "They killed my wife and made me a Hate Criminal just because I wanted to keep living in my house."

The prostitute nodded as she placed her head in her hands. "I wish I could go back to the day right before we got laid off and just live the ignorant bliss one more time."

Joe felt compelled to tell her that this would just lead her to the same fate but didn't have the heart.

"It's going to get better," he reassured her. "I'm going to set some things right."

"How could you possibly make any of this better? We're trapped in this hellish nightmare! It's all pointless," Courtney cried bitterly.

"Maybe"—Joe clutched at the stone in his pocket—"but I'm going to set some things right."

"Well, I hope you do. I know better than to ask what you're doing." The prostitute raised her eyebrows and managed a curt smile.

Joe returned to his seat. "How's your son?"

"He's doing okay," Courtney began. "He's in the other room. He has headphones on during the night," she intimated with a wince.

The fugitive nodded in understanding. "I'm so sorry it's come to this for you. Is there any way I can help you?"

She shook her head. "No, I've got bills to pay. This is just my life now."

"It's not every day you get a man with nothing to lose offering to help." Joe lowered his voice. "I can make some people go away for you."

"No, no." The prostitute smiled politely. "I couldn't trouble you like that."

He shrugged reluctantly as she offered him something to eat from the fridge. Joe felt bad about taking her food but could not resist.

The pair went on to reminisce about old acquaintances for a quarter of an hour. Joe had forgotten the names and places of most of the stories. The lives of their old friends invariably ended up either gut wrenchingly grim or mind numbingly pointless. Such were the two outcomes offered by the system to its citizens. The ones who regained employment continued spinning their hamster wheel for businesses that hated them. Those who couldn't find a job ended up like Courtney.

"You remember Tyler?" she asked.

Joe smiled slightly. "Yeah, he was a good guy. As soon as I saw him get laid off, I knew I was done for."

"He's working at Xinjia Processing over in China now," Courtney recalled. "I wonder how it is over there."

"There's no paradise on earth. But we all seem to have this notion that there ought to be, and we keep digging like rats to find it." Joe released his despairing take.

This visibly depressed his host.

"But it'll get better, just you wait," he attempted to inject some positivity.

Nevertheless, the conversation mostly died down. Courtney checked her phone then proceeded to swear in fear.

"I've been off too long!" She started to scramble to gather her things.

"Wait!" Joe reached into his pocket. "Let me pay for your time. It's the least I can do. I don't want you getting in trouble on my account."

"Oh, Joe, it doesn't matter," Courtney lamented. "They always find some reason to beat me. I couldn't ask you to do that."

"I insist." Joe pulled out one of his illicit credit cards. "Charge extra. It's under a fake name."

She smiled and took the card from him. "You're too kind."

The fugitive watched her swipe the card on her phone with a strong desire to help her more.

"I bought an hour," Courtney said with a smile.

"Good." Joe nodded then sighed as he rose from the chair. "Well, I suppose I have to get on with my journey. Enjoy your time off."

"Thank you so much, Joe." She got up with him and stood by the door. "I don't know how to thank you."

"Just hold on. Things will get better." The fugitive put his hand on the doorknob.

"If you want to . . . I mean, you already paid for it." Courtney put her hand on his.

"No," Joe replied emphatically while recoiling his hand. Seeing that this hurt his host, he softened his tone. "I'll be with my wife soon. I'm sure of it."

The prostitute nodded softly and smiled as Joe left the apartment, onward to his ultimate confrontation.

46

THE GAMBIT

"Sean?" Patel said apathetically on the phone.

"Hey, man, what do you have?" Sean replied eagerly.

"I really need to keep a tally of your favors. I heard you weren't even on the Blaine case anymore," he said with a sigh.

The investigator grew impatient. "C'mon, just spill."

"The things I do for you," he muttered. "That ID came up again."

Sean perked up. "William David McDowell?!"

"That's the one." Patel drafted an email. "I'm sending you the report now. Super weird. State troopers found an old 1960s Pontiac wrecked on the side of the road with that ID hanging out of the hood insulation of all places."

"Where?" he interjected.

His intel counterpart bristled, "About six miles from Berrent Valley near MLK Jr. County. You know, you really owe me big time. You really take me for grant—"

Sean hung up the phone as Barry Kaplan exited the conference room.

"Hey! Get back in here. We're in the middle of the protest brief and you step out to take phone calls? What could possibly be so important?!" Kaplan said with a mild sprinkling of curses.

The investigator gave him the middle finger and pushed past him with a return salvo of foul language. As Sean walked by the conference room door, he saw the awe-stricken expression of several of the organizers.

"And screw you all too!" he cried as he passed the entryway.

Sean's pulse slowed as he tore out of the building toward his SUV. Entering the vehicle, he took a deep breath wondering if news of this outburst would make its way to Feldman's ears. The "protest" was planned for tomorrow evening. Knives, grenades, Molotov cocktails, and a few guns were placed all around Lafayette in unmarked vans. Sean resented the assignment of overseeing the chaos. This was not out of principle but rather because it meant he couldn't be pursuing Blaine—and by extension the promotion. The investigator knew that whoever caught this high priority Hate Criminal would be showered with whatever they desired.

Sean thought about calling Jameila with the new information, but this notion was quickly dispatched in his mind as soon as he pictured Chen's smug face in Feldman's office. A plan started forming. Shifting his SUV into drive, he sped away from the campaign headquarters. Throwing caution to the wind, he started driving southeast toward Salt Lake City. Sean dismissed an incoming call from Kaplan with relish. He figured he had about twenty-four hours to execute his impulsive plan before all was lost. If he could capture Blaine all on his own, they may just forgive his insubordination. It was a tremendously risky plan, but Sean could not abide being passed over by his rivals.

As he sped toward Salt Lake, the investigator felt doubts creeping into his mind.

What if he traded the ID for something? It might not even be him, he wavered. *Why would he be going back to MLK Jr.?*

As Sean drove, his intuition overcame his doubts. As he racked his memory for the various cases he worked and Hate Criminals he put behind bars, he remembered a common thread.

"He's going back for revenge like they always do!" Sean slapped the steering wheel. *And I'm going to catch him in the act!*

Arriving at the airport after the lengthy drive, he blocked Kaplan's number after a few more missed calls. Sean also noticed a missed call from Jameila and a text from Danny Chen on his cracked phone screen. The clock was ticking on his gambit. Flashing his badge around, he managed to bluff his way onto a small charter flight from Salt Lake City to MLK Jr. that left in thirty minutes. As he waited for the flight to take off, he looked through the police report Patel sent him.

1968 Pontiac. . . . Where on earth did he get wheels like that?

Who's his network of support? He scrolled through the pages of the report on his phone.

"Sir?" The flight attendant broke his concentration. "Please put your cell phone away. It's time for takeoff."

Sean reluctantly complied just as another call came in. This time it was Feldman. With more trepidation than he cared to admit, he denied the call and shut off his phone. He was completely off the reservation now.

The small charter flight taxied on to the runway and made a swift ascent into the sky. The serene world above the clouds shone in a brilliant display of the providential paintbrush. Reflecting on the Blaine case, Sean was deeply troubled by his almost supernatural evasion of the FCIA. Never before had he so grossly underestimated his target and been consistently one step behind. The possibility that his quarry was being guided by an immaterial force welled up in his mind like a leak in a ship's hull. Nonetheless, Sean balked at the conception of the divine, living life as a rabid rationalist. If it could not be deduced through hard evidence, it could not be so.

They always go for revenge, Sean thought silently while looking down at the increasingly small civilization below. *Who is he going for? Or what?* A thousand questions continued to swirl in his harried mind. *Can I really pull this off?*

The flight finally landed after Sean batted away several attempts at small talk from his seat partner. As soon as he was cleared to do so, he turned on his phone and unbuckled. With a shudder, he saw three more missed calls and five text messages. Ignoring his better impulses, he opened the texts. There were a few from Chen warning of disciplinary action followed by a text from Feldman reading, "What are you doing in Salt Lake City??"

He sighed and thanked his lucky stars that his supervisor at least thought he was still in Utah, though he knew that this would only buy him a few hours of time. Running from the plane, Sean dialed the sheriff of MLK Jr. County.

"Hello?"

"Sheriff Yu, this is Sean McDowell," he began slowly while running through the airport toward the car rentals. "I've got a task for you straight from the Washington FCIA office, but you need to act in secrecy. I need all the resources you can throw at me. If you mess this up, I'll make sure you're put on meter maid duty for the rest of your career."

Yu sounded miffed at Sean's demanding request but felt inclined to not call his bluff. "What is this concerning?"

"Joe Blaine is back in MLK Jr. County."

47

THE HERO'S RETURN

Joe left MLK Jr. County a broken, listless, and dying man. Escaping for the unknown, he engaged in a fatal duel with the dark recesses of his mind. A trophy of that fateful battle against the crushing pressure of hopelessness jostled in his pocket, a constant reminder of his aim. Nevertheless, the battle's conclusion had given way to war's desolation.

He felt the numinous presence of a watchful force grow stronger than the sun behind him. Averting his gaze from every reflection, he still felt the piercing eyes shoot like arrows through his heart. The prospect of confronting it terrified him, as each step acted as a countdown to a final reciprocation. Wavering slightly, Joe could not resist his feet marching in lockstep with destiny.

When Joe passed the sign reading "MLK Jr. County / Equity is Our Value, Inclusion is Our Purpose," a cool sea breeze barreled down the avenue into his face. The sun had already risen to its late morning perch. Its warm rays caught his back like a solar sail and propelled him westward. Joe recognized various landmarks and locations. He was roughly ten minutes by car from his old house and MLK Jr. University. A banner memorializing Aaron Cohen hung over a crumbling overpass bridge. The standard slew of graffiti impelling onlookers to "say his name" covered storefronts and retaining walls alike. Joe had no idea whether Senator Cohen had already made his public appearance or if his son's remembrance ceremony was over.

Meanwhile, his unknown enemy, Sean McDowell, pursued him with reckless abandon. Compelled by career, fame, and accolade, the investigator brought the whole surveillance state to bear on the Hate Criminal. He coerced the sheriff into compliance, concealing the true nature of his visit. Sean knew he would be summarily defenestrated if he failed, perhaps even labeled a Hate Criminal himself. The small chance of glorious victory fueled his delirious hunt for Joe Blaine. If his family was a peripheral consideration before, now they were practically on Mars in the mind of the laser focused investigator. Sean demanded from fate a final confrontation with this threat to society. The ideological engine he served watched with dripping teeth for the coming slaughter. Its hunger demanded blood, and it mattered little whether it was the Hate Criminal or the investigator. For Sean McDowell, the only thing that mattered was the hunt, and the approval he so desperately craved.

The same amber finality that covered the days leading up to Jill's murder enveloped these two men as they careened toward each other in an uncontrolled freefall. An unignorable third party watched both of them, viciously trying to make contact at every opportunity.

Joe stood at the corner of Martin Avenue and 48th Street. Waiting for the traffic to pass along, he pressed the crosswalk button. He mused whether the urban legend that the button doesn't actually do anything was true.

A few individuals waited next to him at the crosswalk. Not a soul among them knew that they were in the presence of a very wanted man. Keeping his face shielded with the mask and boonie hat, Joe knew that likely every last one of them would fall over themselves to turn him in. Looking at their faces, he saw a veritable spectrum of diversity. The only community they shared was their Pavlovian hatred of people like Joe.

The sign chirped a cheerful tune and indicated it was safe to cross. Looking up across the street as he walked, the fugitive noticed a colorless, one-dimensional rendering of the inclusion banner on the sign where the white outline of a man used to be in days past. While all crosswalks had been like this since the implementation of Equity and Inclusion, it was the first time the replacement truly struck Joe. Such was the vindictive and petty nature of the cultural zeitgeist that even the vague notion of a White man had to be scrubbed from public life.

As he neared the ocean and the downtown skyscrapers loomed above him, the Hate Criminal groped for his destination. Cohen was his ultimate target, but he had only a foggy idea of where to find him. Cross referencing the signs advertising his son's remembrance ceremony with a bank's digital clock, he realized with dismay that the event started over forty minutes ago at the university. Joe chastised himself for arriving too late. Raking his mental map, he figured he was about a twenty-minute walk from the campus. He could break into a run, but this risked attracting unwanted attention given his disheveled appearance. Moreover, Joe didn't want to risk embarrassingly dropping the pistol concealed in his jacket. He settled on walking as fast as he could while keeping a hand in his jacket pocket to keep the weapon in place.

Turning his face, he walked past a loitering policeman standing next to a liquor store.

"Got somewhere to be?" the officer called out.

Joe's heart stopped. "Yes, sir," he managed to reply while scurrying away. He recognized him as Sergeant Darius Binger, one of the officers from the fateful night of his attempted arrest.

"I'm watching you, White boy!" Binger yelled after him, apparently failing to recognize Joe under the mask.

Passing camera after camera, the fugitive continued his walk unabated, albeit with considerable unease at being recorded at every step. His calves burned with the increased speed. Joe wondered if his speedwalking was attracting more attention than simply running. Slowing his pace, he regained his bearings. The road signs grew more and more familiar as he neared within a block of the OIHO building downtown. His route would pass directly by the fateful location of his old life's demise. Joe's heart tumbled in his chest as the office hoved in view like a square rig ship of the line, bristling with a broadside of painful memories. A mournful snake of inequitable individuals wrapped around the block. Given the fact that the housing certification process was long over, Joe surmised that this line was for some new draconian measure.

Maybe because of my actions, he wondered bitterly.

As he walked past the procession of compliant wretches, he recognized the pane of glass where he first felt a peculiar sense of dread at his reflection. It was different this time. He stopped dead in his tracks, eyes locked with the ethereal being. A woman waiting in line shifted uncomfortably when she noticed him staring intently. Joe at last slowed his walk to a crawl as he approached the line in a perpendicular path. The woman continued to fill with unease as the strange man seemingly approached her. The overweight man behind her also noticed Joe.

"Hey, you can't cut in line!" he said with mouth agape and pointed finger.

The Hate Criminal took no notice of these two figures and remained entranced by his reflection. Scales seemed to fall from Joe's eyes as the full knowledge of his pursuer came to the fore, though he still did not reveal himself. If he could, he would have done so long ago at the OIHO when Joe first sought his housing certification, in the haggard reflection of the rearview mirror, or a dozen other points. The Man had watched the sum total of Joe's life, attempting to punch through the veil of social acceptability, but met a stalwart wall of safety's seduction. At last, the repeated battering of the storm broke the dam free. The growing agency Joe observed in the mirror made sense now. It seemed so obvious yet so obscure that the Man had always been there: searching, reaching, immolating. The repressed identities, hopes, and fears of a generation made their stark appearance on the vibrant, shining surface of that fateful window.

"What are you doing?" the woman bleated.

Joe walked directly through the pair, pushing them aside with his shoulders until he was at last face to face with the pane of glass where his fate was first sealed. Joe extended a solitary hand while the Man responded in kind, and Joe saw who he could have always been, and who he could still be. Taking off his hat and mask, the world became utterly silent around him. The burning, green eyes across from him bound his spirit with lashing tendrils. The inexplicable dread he felt when waiting in line to kiss the feet of his oppressors vanished in the transformed current of new life. Nevertheless, Joe's new boldness did not satiate the Man. He still demanded more.

Suddenly, the glass shattered before him. The world's silence fell away in a horrific cymbal crash of noise. After jolting forward, Joe stood stunned for a moment. A deep, burning pain in his side formed into a rapidly intensifying crescendo. Looking down at his abdomen, he noticed a warm, red flow. Joe placed a hand on the wound then turned a bloody, trembling palm toward himself. He was bleeding profusely.

48

THE MAN IN THE MIRROR

Joe turned around in a heat of fear. Standing before him on the sidewalk was Sergeant Darius Binger. A wild hatred brimmed in his eyes as smoke poured from the barrel of his gun. The crowd of people at the OIHO scattered in every direction at the sound of their confrontation, causing Binger's second shot to strike the woman Joe had pushed past. The Hate Criminal quickly went for his own pistol, but just as he trained the sights on Binger, a third shot blew out Joe's left shoulder. With the Man guiding his hand, Joe managed to pull the trigger.

The policeman dropped immediately on the sidewalk. Stumbling forward, Joe saw that his bullet miraculously met its mark between Binger's eyes. Making such an improbable shot would have shocked the killer had it not been for the excruciating pain of his wounds.

Joe groaned and stumbled to his knees. "Not yet . . . not like this! I am not yet atoned!"

The blood poured freely from the gaping holes in his side and shoulder. The adrenaline barely masked the dual agony of his injuries and the possibility of failing his mission. Looking up for a moment, Joe noticed that the policeman's car was still running. By now, a considerable amount of commotion and screaming developed around the scene.

He mustered the strength to enter the driver's side of the vehicle. Slumping into the seat, he reached across his body to pull the door shut with his good hand.

The radio crackled on the dashboard: "Cruiser 148, do you have eyes on the suspect? Assume he is armed and dangerous."

Joe reached into his pocket and pulled out the rock. Placing it between his molars, he bore down to cope with the pain. After fumbling with the shifter, he managed to get the squad car into drive.

The transponder continued to chatter, "Cruiser 148, come in."

The various cars on the road made way for the still flashing lights of Joe's new ride as he sped toward the campus. He would reach his target at all costs.

"All units, 571. I repeat: all units, 571 on cruiser 148," the dispatcher called out after several minutes.

The sweat pooled on the Hero's brow as the blood from his wounds quickly soaked his shirt. The leather seat grew slippery as he attempted to stay upright. A police helicopter swirled above him, keeping an eye on his every move. Joe figured that his time to act was growing short. Given the heightened awareness of law enforcement and his rapidly deteriorating physical stamina, the prospect of making it to the remembrance ceremony faded.

"All units, 571 headed northbound on—" The police cut off his cruiser's radio.

Joe perceived the tightening net around him. A hard choice loomed like an oncoming train. There was not enough time nor energy to make it to the university campus. However, Rosenblatt's motel was just a block away. The police were likely to initialize a remote shut off for his car at any moment. He could settle for the lesser target or potentially lose out on his mission altogether.

Joe cocked his head slightly and took a hard look in the rearview mirror.

"Is this enough?"

The Man's eyes remained aflame like oil burning on the surface of the ocean.

Jolting the wheel, he made a hard right toward the Windview Motel. At the very least, he could settle the lesser score.

A drone marked with FCIA lettering zipped by the front of the car and paralleled his course, just as the dingy sign of the motel came into view. The miserable shantytown in the parking lot writhed and wriggled in the rising warmth of the day. As the engine cut off, he made a reckless cut across traffic. The squad car jostled over the curb, and Joe squeezed the rock between his teeth as his pain spiked. A few motel urchins watched impassively as the disheveled man dismounted the vehicle. As he limped toward the staircase, he noticed a black SUV with government plates parked next to a luxury sedan. Joe surmised that Rosenblatt had visitors at the moment. He could hear sirens approaching in the distance while the FCIA drone hovered over the parking lot. Joe's heart rate pounded incessantly as if trying to escape his chest.

◘

Sean McDowell sawed at the wheel of his car like a junkie in pursuit of his next high. Sheriff Yu sat in the passenger seat, nervously clutching a rifle.

"Is this guy really dangerous?" Yu asked with a tremor.

Sean's voice ran ragged. "Shut up, will you? Keep an eye on that drone. It should be right overhead of the stolen cop car. Where's he at? Did you cut his engine yet?"

Punching the brakes, the investigator swerved around a stopped vehicle in a turn lane with a considerable amount of cursing.

"Where's he at?!" he yelled.

Sean knew his fate hung in the balance as an FCIA disciplinary team was en route at that very moment to haul him in.

Sheriff Yu went pale.

The investigator slammed the steering wheel with his hand. "Get your head in the game!"

"He turned toward the Windview Motel! He stopped in the parking lot after we killed the car," Yu replied.

"Got it!" Sean swerved in traffic with an eye on the GPS.

The sheriff rocked in his seat. "No, you don't get it! That's Rosenblatt's motel."

His federal counterpart nodded coolly. "He's after revenge."

"No, no, no! Cohen is there right now!" Yu bounced his knees in abject fear.

"Senator Cohen?!" Sean asked with a sinking realization that a bad situation just got a whole lot worse. "Why is he there?"

"His security detail radioed in that he was going there after his son's ceremony for a. . . . Oh, this is bad! This is so bad! We are so screwed!" The sheriff began to babble incoherently as he considered the consequences of a sitting senator being put in danger on his watch.

Sean grasped the gravity of the situation as well. "But his detail is with him, right?!"

Deep down, he knew the answer. With the secretive nature of figures like Rosenblatt, they seldom allowed outside security details in their kingdoms, even for government officials. Given the consequences of interfering with the motel system, no one dared to make a move on these fortresses of depravity. Sheriff Yu remained silent as the pair clenched their teeth in fear.

"Then we've gotta get there now!" Sean yelled while swerving around a cyclist.

◻

Joe kneeled to catch his breath at the foot of the stairs up to Rosenblatt's office. He removed the rock from his mouth as his breathing grew labored. Out of the corner of his eye, he saw Erica once again. Her tortured eyes recognized him in a fit of fear. Joe let out a smile.

"Erica, your grandmother Cynthia loves you! She's in Lafayette, Utah! Go there now!" he sputtered the information as fast as he could while the blood poured. "Please, go!"

Erica lit up in the vague realization that she wasn't totally alone in the beast system's cold clutches. This knowledge cut through her drug-induced haze like a silver blade. He nodded with closed eyes and waved her on. Erica smiled imperceptibly while clutching her unrecognizable stuffed animal. Joe steadied himself on one of the motel balcony's support pillars as she scurried away. The pain and blood loss made even simple tasks difficult.

Gripping the rock in his hand, he breathed deeply at the foot of the stairs leading to Rosenblatt's office and began his crawl toward the summit. With each step, he felt weight being lifted from his soul. First, the guilt of Jill's death melted away. Following closely behind, the sack of Lafayette and Ricky's demise faded from his memory. Soon poor little Felicity and his PSL washed away too. All the retreats, concessions, and supine failures sloughed from his spirit as he climbed. Step after step, reach after reach, he carried his burdens up the mountain. His body was spent, but not his soul.

After the struggle, Joe surmounted the last step before the second level. His wounds forced him to extend a bloody hand to the railing as his balance teetered. The sirens drew near to him like flies to a fresh carcass. Stumbling forward, he found the door to Rosenblatt's office. He could just barely make out some muffled conversation.

"It's a terrible thing that happened, just terrible! I'm glad I could be of service, Chuck," Rosenblatt's distinctive accent echoed through the door.

"I thought we discussed a much younger boy," the customer scathed.

Three knocks interrupted their conversation.

"My apologies, it's probably my men. I thought I tasked them across town!" the motel owner's voice waxed vicious as he made his way to the entryway. "I told you two—"

Rosenblatt's beady eyes widened in the face of his judgment.

"You!" his voice croaked in a persecuted whisper.

Joe made no reply as he entered the room with his pistol drawn. The motel owner recoiled from him like a magnet of the same pole. Rosenblatt stumbled back and tripped over a chair. At this point, Joe noticed the customer sitting beside the desk. He was older, well-dressed, and wearing a tailored, navy-blue suit with an Inclusion Banner pin on the lapel. The guest surprised him, but changed little of his plan. Joe had no idea who this was, but he judged that the man deserved death for soliciting the motel's business. He recognized the feminized boy cowering next to the desk from his first encounter with Rosenblatt.

Directly behind the fearful, squirming group hung the Mirror: unity was close at hand.

"Wait, hold on," the manager pleaded. "Let's not get any—"

Brain matter sprayed the face of the panicked guest. The well-dressed man rose to flee, but Joe unloaded the rest of his magazine into his chest. He kept pulling the trigger long after the slide locked back. The feminized boy sat trembling on the floor with his hands outstretched.

"Get out of here," Joe commanded. "You're free."

The boy gratefully complied and fled the room, nearly tripping on the corpses as he closed the door behind him.

At last, he was alone with the reflection. In a swell of emotion, all barriers separating him from the Man evaporated like a morning mist. He was permitted to look him in the eye without the perennial dread that marked their other encounters. He knew him well. He had always been there, germinating in his soul and convicting Joe of his failures. The Man gave Joe the full look of satisfaction and fulfillment he so dearly and unknowingly pursued. He finally conquered the incongruity between what he was and what he ought to be. Approaching the Mirror slowly, Joe extended a bloody hand. His becoming was over. He simply was.

"Come out with your hands up!" a police megaphone called out.

The Man smiled and nodded. Joe's journey was at an end. He checked the desk drawer to see if his wife's picture was still there. Rifling through the items, tears came to his eyes when he reunited with the photo. Joe said a final prayer as he prepared to leave his fleshly bounds. Dropping the pistol on the ground and placing the picture next to his heart, the Hero stepped over the bodies toward the door. Before leaving the room, he took the rock and cherished it in his hand.

"The door's opening!" Sheriff Yu gripped his rifle as he leaned on the squad car's hood.

Sean's heart pounded in anticipation of laying eyes on his quarry. By now, all the urchins in the parking lot had scattered from the half dozen police cruisers on scene. A brief moment of silence overtook the city. As the door peeled back like a curtain on some ancient tragedy, the investigator saw him.

"Get your hands in the air!" Yu cried as several more police cars arrived on scene.

Joe peered down at his pursuers. He strode confidently to the top of the stairs and let the rock slip from his fingers. He watched it tumble down the steps with triumph. After a deep breath, Joe began his descent. He was happy.

"Get your hands up!" the sheriff commanded with a crack in his voice. "Should I shoot him?" he asked Sean.

The investigator froze. He knew that it was too late. This bloody figure descending the stairs had bested him. Sean could vaguely hear more approaching sirens apart from the county sheriff's vehicles. These undoubtedly signaled the impending arrival of the FCIA disciplinary team to arraign him for insubordination. The career he sacrificed so much for crumbled beneath his feet. He gripped his weapon in desperation. The front sight rested squarely on the Hate Criminal. Sean's finger drifted from its position on the slide toward the trigger. As his finger tightened, something shifted in the corner of his eye.

Taking a brief glance at the side window of the cruiser, he saw what he had been avoiding his whole life. It horrified him; immolating, churning, writhing, clawing—the Man made contact. Sean's eyes widened as the reflection's damning eyes searched his soul. He didn't see the proud, accomplished FCIA investigator of his most intimate aspirations. A coup occurred on the other side of the glass, and the world went silent. On a cloudless day in a motel parking lot, Sean McDowell remained transfixed with what he saw reflected. An accusatory finger raised. Those of his own people that he beat, tortured, and imprisoned rose in judgment to condemn him. Those he sacrificed on the altar of success cried out for justice. Sean made countless such blood sacrifices to the beast, hoping to receive accolades and prestige in return. Now, looking at his empire of dirt, he found that he had been promised everything and given nothing in return. Sean McDowell felt his soul contorting under the weight of his guilt.

The cacophonous noise of the sirens, Yu's panicked shouting, the Man's scalding judgment, and the beating of his own heart collapsed the investigator's resolve. His fingers grew weak, and his vision clouded. Stumbling for a moment, Sean attempted to raise the pistol at Joe once more in a final grasp at his idol. As his arm trembled, he dropped the weapon in a flood of spiritual fear. The pistol drifted from his hands and fell through space on a providential course. As it hit the ground, it fired a single bullet aimed nowhere at all.

The sound panicked Sheriff Yu and the other police officers, and the parking lot erupted in gunfire.

"No!" Sean reached out in terror.

As the shots rang out, Joe reached the bottom of the stairs and faced the crowd. Standing there as the curtain lifted and the lights turned on, he knew his lines well. The pain of the impacting rounds made little impression on him as he fell to his knees. He strained his arms upward—not in surrender, nor for the crystalline, radiant sky. Rather, he grasped fiercely at heaven for the rock. Joseph Arthur Blaine submitted himself for one more climb.